Thru The Eyes – of the Beholder

Troy, N.Y.

1913 - 1920

By

Alice Corbett Fiacco

Edited by Christopher Corbett-Fiacco
Copyright © 2016 Christopher Corbett-Fiacco
All rights reserved.

ISBN: 1497581656
ISBN-13: 978-1497581654

For more information, contact:

Christopher Corbett-Fiacco
CCFSDCA@gmail.com

Dear Readers,

Although this book falls under the literary category of the historical romance novel, it was inspired by the very real experiences of a great many people, some known and related to me, others unknown to me personally, but real people – people who lived and loved and celebrated life when life was to be celebrated, who suffered and grieved when life was difficult during the historical, cultural and personal transition from agrarian to industrial life in the early years of the twentieth century, people who mourned the loss of those who died from diseases long forgotten, and who died during warfare, which is, sadly, still with us – real people who passed on when their time came, and were mourned by others in turn.

My mother, Mary Duffy Corbett, was one such person. Her grandparents and her parents and siblings and aunts and uncles and cousins and friends and neighbors… they were such people as well – real people who lived their lives as genuinely and as honestly and with as much fortitude and dignity as necessary to muster during those years of hardship and uncertainty; long years before there was any such thing as a social safety net, a minimum wage, child labor laws, or even a full two-day weekend; a time when American women didn't even have the simple right to vote.

Because the characters – as well as certain elements of the storyline – were inspired by my mother's storytelling of the times and events during which she lived, they have become so real to me that sometimes it's difficult not to think of them as friends and family, too, as distinct from "mere" characters upon a page. They live and breathe on these pages. They laugh, they love, they lose loved ones for whom they weep. And that is life. I sincerely hope they'll become a part of your life as you read about theirs.

In the Spring of 1971, after a lifetime of listening to my mother's stories and realizing that another generation, my own sons and my nieces and nephews, and their friends, too, found those stories of interest and delight, as my father and my brother and sisters and I had all those years before, when first we heard them, I was inspired to begin researching the times and events of those days through old newspapers and magazines and encyclopedias at the Troy Public Library, and I began to write this novel by hand.

If it was not for all the help I received from my son, Chris (Christopher Corbett-Fiacco) – my "Man Friday" (fellow researcher, typist, editor, book cover designer and guide to the worldwide web) over the past twenty-eight years, this novel would never have been completed.

I also received quite a bit of assistance from my son, Michael Fiacco.

And my darling husband, Leo, who helped and encouraged me.

I thank you for your interest in my work and sincerely hope you'll enjoy reading this novel!

Alice Corbett Fiacco

Table of Contents

Chapter One	Page 1
Chapter Two	Page 19
Chapter Three	Page 34
Chapter Four	Page 48
Chapter Five	Page 56
Chapter Six	Page 60
Chapter Seven	Page 72
Chapter Eight	Page 79
Chapter Nine	Page 83
Chapter Ten	Page 98
Chapter Eleven	Page 101
Chapter Twelve	Page 116
Chapter Thirteen	Page 119
Chapter Fourteen	Page 124
Chapter Fifteen	Page 131
Chapter Sixteen	Page 137
Chapter Seventeen	Page 149
Chapter Eighteen	Page 161
Chapter Nineteen	Page 171
Chapter Twenty	Page 180
Chapter Twenty-One	Page 197

Chapter Twenty-Two	Page 211
Chapter Twenty-Three	Page 224
Chapter Twenty-Four	Page 227
Chapter Twenty-Five	Page 231
Chapter Twenty-Six	Page 240
Chapter Twenty-Seven	Page 243
Chapter Twenty-Eight	Page 258
Chapter Twenty-Nine	Page 267
Chapter Thirty	Page 271
Chapter Thirty-One	Page 276
Chapter Thirty-Two	Page 280
Chapter Thirty-Three	Page 289
Chapter Thirty-Four	Page 299
Chapter Thirty-Five	Page 303
Chapter Thirty-Six	Page 307
Chapter Thirty-Seven	Page 315
Chapter Thirty-Eight	Page 318
Chapter Thirty-Nine	Page 320
Chapter Forty	Page 322
Chapter Forty-One	Page 331
Chapter Forty-Two	Page 333
Chapter Forty-Three	Page 336

Chapter Forty-Four	Page 348
Chapter Forty-Five	Page 360
Chapter Forty-Six	Page 366
Chapter Forty-Seven	Page 369
Chapter Forty-Eight	Page 372
Chapter Forty-Nine	Page 381
Chapter Fifty	Page 388
Chapter Fifty-One	Page 417
Chapter Fifty-Two	Page 422
Chapter Fifty-Three	Page 428
Chapter Fifty-Four	Page 431
Chapter Fifty-Five	Page 437
Chapter Fifty-Six	Page 443
Chapter Fifty-Seven	Page 457
Chapter Fifty-Eight	Page 461
Chapter Fifty-Nine	Page 482
Chapter Sixty	Page 493
Chapter Sixty-One	Page 498
Chapter Sixty-Two	Page 506
Chapter Sixty-Three	Page 510
Chapter Sixty-Four	Page 511
Chapter Sixty-Five	Page 518

Chapter Sixty-Six	Page 523
Chapter Sixty-Seven	Page 525
Chapter Sixty-Eight	Page 527
Chapter Sixty-Nine	Page 531
Chapter Seventy	Page 535
Chapter Seventy-One	Page 538
Chapter Seventy-Two	Page 540
Chapter Seventy-Three	Page 544
Chapter Seventy-Four	Page 547
Chapter Seventy-Five	Page 565

BOOK ONE

March 25, 1917
Troy, New York

Alice Corbett Fiacco

CHAPTER ONE

She stood in the hallway in complete awe, unable to believe what her eyes envisioned. It was like a dream: the room was so big and bright, with a great big sparkling light on the ceiling and beautiful pictures on the walls. And everywhere she looked, and everything her eyes beheld, was shiny and beautiful.

Then she thought of the hallway in the house *she* lived in. It was dark and narrow, with paint peeling off the walls; and the outside railing on the stairs had some of the rungs broken or altogether missing. Even though her sister Kitty cleaned down the stairs every week, everything always looked dirty and worn.

Kitty said the hallway needed to be painted, but there was no money for extras like this. Their brother Mike called the landlord a skinflint who couldn't care less about the tenants in his house. All he ever cared about was the rent.

That morning, Mary's little brother Danny had died. Her Aunt Nan had brought her to this big beautiful place where she was getting permission from her employer to go back to help her sister, Mary's mother, who was in the family way. Aunt Nan had placed Mary inside the front door and told her to stay right there and not to wander off out of curiosity, the way she sometimes liked to. She said she would be back in just a minute. On the way over, Aunt Nan had told Mary they were going to her house, and now Mary stood amazed at the thought that her aunt could live in such a grand place. It was as if Aunt Nan had opened up a story book and Mary had wandered onto the page.

As Mary continued looking around, she noticed two doors to her right. In between them, hanging on the wall, was a big painting of a family. As she stared at the painting almost longingly, she felt suddenly drawn to it.

Seated in a chair in the center of the painting was a lady with brown hair and brown eyes in a blue lace dress, a beautiful string of pearls around her neck. She had a kind, relaxed smile on her pretty face. Mary's eyes drifted to the right, where she saw a little girl, slightly younger than herself, wearing a beautiful blue velvet dress with a matching bow in her long brown hair. Her eyes then moved up behind the girl, where she observed a boy about as old as her brother Mike, although nowhere near as good-looking or happy. This boy looked as if he didn't want to be in the picture at all.

As she looked to the left of that boy, Mary saw a nice-looking man in a dark gray suit. His beautiful blue eyes were gentle and kind, just like her Aunt Mary's. He was wearing a vest under his jacket, and a gleaming gold chain hung from one pocket to the other. As Mary's eyes descended from his gaze and moved slightly to the left, she was amazed as she stared into the face of a young boy just a couple of years older than she, with perfect features and exceptionally beautiful brown eyes. No boy could really be so handsome, she thought.

Suddenly she heard a noise from behind the farther door to her right, on the other side of the painting. The door opened slowly as a young girl came into the hallway, pushing a baby carriage.

Mary looked at the girl, bewildered. She looked up at the painting on the wall. She looked back at the girl again and her eyes grew wide. This was the girl in the painting, and she was wearing that same beautiful blue velvet dress which Mary loved so. Mary caught her breath at the sight of it, and at that moment, for the first time in her life, she was suddenly aware of her own clothes, ill-fitting, worn and patched. Slowly she backed into the shadows of the corner of the room so as not to be seen.

And then she saw him follow the girl into the hallway. He seemed more handsome than a mere picture could portray and his breathtakingly beautiful brown eyes stirred within her unfamiliar feelings. Even though by most standards Mary would be called a mature little girl, there are those who would say it's impossible for a girl seven weeks shy of her sixth birthday to understand the meaning of romantic love. But they never would have been able to convince Mary that it was anything less than that. For to her, it was love that caused the longing she felt to be close to him, the longing to be able to reach out and touch him, to see him smile and to have him look at her through loving eyes. She deeply desired that he would feel for her the same overwhelming love that she felt for him.

She heard the girl call out to him, "Jack!"

Jack! She whispered it to herself in the shadows. "Jack! I love you, Jack," she murmured.

And as if her eyes had taken a picture and developed it and filed it in her mind, she would never forget that special scene. Throughout her life it would be available to her for instant replay in all its minute detail.

And from that day forward, he dominated her daydreams. Those feelings of love that she first felt for him would intensify as the weeks and years marched on.

"For heaven's sake, Mary, please set the table. Your aunts will be here soon. Don't wait until the last minute."

Her mother's voice pierced her daydream and brought Mary back to reality. It was seven years to the day that poor little Danny had died. But thinking of Jack, and imagining the life that she knew she would enjoy with him one day; Mary was, as always, filled with an unbridled optimism that nothing could destroy.

She whispered to herself with a smile, "Mary O'Connell..."

"Mary O'Neill, are you listening to me?"

"What? Oh, I'm sorry, Mama," she stammered, rising from her

chair, "I'll do it right away."

It was Tuesday, and Tuesday was Mary's favorite day of the week. Every Tuesday her aunts came to the house for supper. It was Aunt Nan's day off, and she always brought some fancy dessert she had made the day before at the O'Connell house. Most times Aunt Kate would be there too except when she was feeling too poorly to come over. Aunt Kate had had rheumatic fever as a child and it had left her sickly for the rest of her life. But it was Aunt Mary who was Mary's favorite, and whom she always looked forward to seeing the most. Aunt Mary lived with Aunt Kate and was a supervisor at Cluett and Peabody's.

Mary loved to visit with her Aunt Mary, who was always so kind and helpful, and was always so happy to see her. Mary was delighted when people told her how much she looked like her Aunt Mary. While her mother, Aunt Nan and Aunt Kate were no taller than five foot four and had brown hair and brown eyes, Aunt Mary had the most beautiful red hair and deep blue eyes and she was even taller than quite a few of the men in the neighborhood. Her eyes seemed to sparkle in the light and dance when she laughed. Everybody said that she had taken after their Pa, who had died young.

Mary was just finishing the table when her mother handed her the eye glasses which she'd carelessly left on the arm of the living room sofa again.

"You've got to be more careful, Mary. Somebody could have sat on these, or knocked them to the floor and stepped on them. Kitty paid good money for those glasses. Do you think money grows on trees?"

"I'm sorry, Mama. I'll try to be more careful."

Mama sighed – tired but likewise keen for an evening with her sisters. "And what is it your Aunt Nan always says about trying?" she prompted with a smile. "Don't just try, but do."

"Yes, Mama," said Mary with a smile, "Don't just try, but do."

She was so looking forward to tonight that nothing at all could dampen her spirit, because tonight she would enjoy not only the visit with her aunts and news of the world and perhaps an old family story or two, but the Irish Stew that was growing only more and more tender and juicy as it continued to simmer on the stove, giving not only the kitchen but the whole flat that marvelous aroma that seemed to smell as much of food as of warmth and family and home and love. Later on, when she and her younger sister Annie were in bed before the adults would call it a night, she would pretend to be asleep, as she always did on such nights, and listen intently to Aunt Nan tell the others all the news of the O'Connells, of Mr. O'Connell, who owned the local brewery and seemed such a kind man, and Mrs. O'Connell, who was so lovely and sweet-tempered and had brought Aunt Nan with her as Housekeeper from her own parent's household when she and Mr. O'Connell had married. In fact, they were so close that Aunt Nan was the only one of the household staff who actually called them by their first names, John and Victoria – and their eldest son, Edgar, and Gail, their little girl, but only in passing; for it was really only news of Jack that she strained to hear, lying there in the soft darkness, imagining the day when she would stand beside him on that staircase, or perhaps another staircase even larger and more magnificent; that day she knew would come – the day she would become his wife and begin the life of splendor which she anticipated so greatly.

The city of Troy is located seven miles north of Albany, the capital of New York State, where the Hudson and Mohawk rivers meet and where the Erie Canal connects the east with the Great Lakes to the west.

It was here, in 1827, that Mrs. Hannah Lord Montague invented the detachable collar, thereby launching the city's collar industry, which was why Troy was known the world over as The Collar City.

Mills, factories and foundries were numerous – manufacturing stoves, bells, brushes, fire hydrants, valves and surveying equipment. This enabled some to make the claim that Troy was one of the birthplaces of the American Industrial Revolution.

During the War of 1812, Troy butcher Sam Wilson had stamped the barrels of his meat being sent to United States' troops with the initials "US." The barrels of meat were said to come from "Uncle Sam," giving rise to the now-legendary symbol of the United States.

In 1819, Emma Willard was granted a charter and a subsidy by the New York State Legislature in order to open a girl's school, which was the first in the country to offer college-level education to women.

RPI, the Rensselear Polytechnic Institute, was founded in 1824, making it the oldest engineering school in the country.

Troy's International Iron Moulders Union was one of the largest in the country, and Kitty was especially proud of the fact that Kate Mullaney, of Troy, had organized the collar workers into the first all-female union in 1865.

But the history of Troy, New York was not very important to a young girl like Mary. She was much more interested in current events and romantic notions of the future – most especially, her future with Jack O'Connell.

Finally, they were all gathered around her at the kitchen table: Mama and Pa, Kitty, Mike, Pat and Annie, and her aunts, Mama's sisters, all three of them tonight, Aunt Nan, Aunt Mary and Aunt Kate.

Supper with her aunts was a downright festive occasion: everyone on their best behavior, but not stuffy like some families Mary had seen. They were a talkative, energetic bunch, exchanging news, opinions and puns freely and good-naturedly. Mary still laughed to herself as she thought of Molly, her best friend, and an only child, sitting and staring almost in shock one night at the sight of them talking animatedly, sometimes two or even three conversations across the table at once. Everyone was engaged in one way or another, and nobody left out.

It was a magical time as Mary cleared the table after supper. Pa bid them good evening with a flourish as he set out happily to meet his cronies at the tavern. Mike followed close behind, assuring Aunt Nan that he'd be home in plenty of time to walk her home after hooking up with his best friend Frankie for a round of gin, "the card game," which he assured them with a wink and a smile. Pat excused himself to retreat to the parlor with an armful of books to finish his homework, as was his usual evening custom.

As the women settled back with their tea and coffee, Kitty mentioned how the day's newspaper had reported that the women suffragettes in London, who had been imprisoned and on a hunger strike, were now being force-fed by means of a tube down their throats.

Kitty belonged to the Troy suffragette group, and she was visibly upset. She reminded them how she'd met Sylvia Pankhurst when she had spoken at Redman's Hall in Schenectady the previous year. Now, after being in jail for a month, Sylvia had written to her mother describing the ordeal.

"And of course her mother, Emiline Pankhurst, is the leader of the militants in London," said Kitty. "Well, Sylvia wrote that twice a day, five or six of the people in charge, and two doctors, pry open her mouth with a steel gag and force a tube down her throat. She resists as best she can, but of course there are several of them against her and they're so much stronger than she is. Her gums are bleeding constantly now, and her shoulders are bruised from struggling while they do it." Kitty's eyes flashed with anger. "How can they possibly justify such inhuman treatment? And doctors, no less! We'll have to send our support right away."

"And we will!" Said Aunt Nan as the others voiced their concern and agreement. "But before I forget, and not to change the subject, but speaking of the paper, did you notice they published the current standings of the newspaper subscription contest? Although my name wasn't listed, I do think I still have a very good chance of winning in my district," she said, referring to the contest which the Troy Times had advertised on January 3rd.

The newspaper would send eleven women from Troy and the vicinity on a fifty-nine day tour of six countries in Europe in midsummer. The winners of the contest would include the women who had sold the greatest number of paid subscriptions to the newspaper from each of ten districts, along with a chaperone for the group, whom the first-place winner would get to choose. The districts included five individual sections in the city of Troy itself, as well as all of Rensselear, Albany, Washington, and Saratoga Counties, and the state of Vermont, and all places not included in the other districts.

Nan had taken the contest seriously from the start. Ever since she was a girl, she had always loved history books, and now she hoped to actually have the opportunity to see some of the places she had read so much about and had glimpsed only in sketches and photographs. For a woman in her position, such a trip was little more than a dream that would likely never come true. The possibility of finding herself sailing the Atlantic to Europe, standing in front of the palaces and the Eiffel Tower, all-expenses-paid, was a once-in-a-lifetime opportunity which she could not allow to let slip past her.

Her employer John not only encouraged her to enter the contest but suggested she call all of their neighbors and friends, even giving her a list of other people he knew.

"I've really been working hard at this," Aunt Nan exclaimed, "and I've been keeping my fingers crossed because the newspaper will be announcing the winners this Saturday!"

"Oh, Aunt Nan, I hope you win!" said Kitty, and the others joined in with their hopes and good wishes. "Imagine going to Europe!"

Mary smiled to herself. She did imagine going to Europe, although she wouldn't say so out loud at that moment, or give them an idea as to how she anticipated getting there. But she knew, and that was all that mattered.

"Oh, and speaking of London reminds me. 'The Old Lady' is back," said Aunt Nan, shaking her head with obvious dismay, "and already she'd up to her old tricks."

The Old Lady was Mrs. O'Connell's mother. Years ago, Mary's grandmother had gone to work for her when Mary's grandfather had died at a young age, leaving her grandmother to raise four little girls – Mary's mother and her three aunts.

"Honestly, that woman. I've known her for over twenty-five years now, and I still marvel that she could have produced a daughter as wonderful as Victoria. Of course, Victoria always did take after her father, and I can already see his disposition in Jack and Gail, although Edgar takes after The Old Lady more and more the older he gets. But, oh, she's just the most mean-spirited, self-centered, demanding person I've ever encountered in all my life. And if you can even believe it, I think she's getting worse with age!

"Remind me to tell you later about her newest victims," she whispered to Kitty and Aunt Mary, who were sitting to her right, and although Mary's ears perked up at the sound of such a promising story, she tried to hide her interest. She was planning to go to bed earlier than usual in order to give Aunt Nan the opportunity to talk more about Jack's grandmother and the rest of the O'Connell family.

"You know, when you were talking about the violence and injustices against the suffragettes, I just couldn't help thinking about what Mr. Goodman told me on Sunday," Aunt Mary said quietly.

"Mr. Goodman?"

"The man who brings over and picks up my piecework on Sunday mornings," said Aunt Kate, who did not have the stamina to work a regular job but had managed through the years to do piecework at home, grateful for the help of her sister Mary and neighbors who would sometimes help to finish it for her if she wasn't up to it herself.

"Oh, I just felt terrible for the poor man when he told me about what happened," Aunt Mary continued. "This past Friday, Good Friday, no less, three Catholic boys attacked his son on the way home from school. They told him they were doing it because the Jews killed Jesus. Can you imagine? Oh, the poor child.

"'He's only a young boy,' he said, 'not even old enough for his Bar Mitzvah, and now he's afraid to walk home from school. Afraid it will happen again.' Of course I sympathized with him, and I told him that I'd tell Father about it right away, so he could put a stop to it. He's such a nice man, Mr. Goodman. He comes all the way across town on Sunday mornings just to pick up Kate's work so that he won't disturb her through the week, just in case she isn't feeling well, or is sleeping. His name suits him, I think, because he really is a good man."

"He certainly is that," Kate nodded.

"I've asked him a number of questions about the Jewish faith and traditions," said Aunt Mary, "and as he answers, I feel I'm in the presence of a very holy man. And I feel as though I've learned so much from talking to him."

Soon it was eight-thirty, and Mary lay in bed clutching the copy of Charlotte Bronte's Jane Eyre, which Aunt Nan had loaned her from the O'Connell library. As anticipated, she heard Aunt Nan ask Kitty to check on the girls and make sure they were sleeping. Hearing that cue, Mary immediately got under the covers, pushed herself further down on the bed, closed her eyes, and laid the open book on her chest as if she'd fallen asleep while reading.

Kitty's footsteps drew near and stopped at the doorway of the bedroom. Mary lay perfectly still. She heard Kitty tiptoe to her bed and felt the book lifted off of her chest. She could see through her eyelids as the light went out, and heard her sister moving out of the room, assuring the women in the kitchen that both of the girls were sound asleep. She smiled to herself, satisfied at her own performance.

"Mary must love that book as much as I did, Aunt Nan," said Kitty, taking her seat at the table. "She fell asleep reading it again."

Thankful to have such good hearing, Mary lay quietly listening, her body stretched out so that her head was way over to the edge of the bed so that she would be able to pick up whatever was being said. She felt almost forced by her curious mind to listen to everything she could possibly hear. Mama said, "Curiosity killed the cat," but Mary didn't think so.

"Listen to this," Aunt Nan began with a chuckle. "Most people just bring back trinkets when they go to Europe year after year, but The Old Lady brought back a person!"

"What?"

"It's true! She actually brought a French chauffeur with her from England. John's business has been taking him out of town more and more lately, and of course Joseph drives the family car, which generally means driving John unless the whole family is going somewhere, which usually isn't an issue, when Joseph drives John out of town, that leaves Victoria and the children at home without a car. So Mrs. Richardson brought this Maurice over to drive her while she's here and she wants John to hire him to use her car to drive Victoria and the children after she leaves. Her automobile is usually in the garage, anyway, so it does make sense. And of course it's obvious why she's so impressed with him. He jumps at her every command. He smiles and bows to her as if she were the queen!"

"He bows to her?" Kitty exclaimed.

"Oh, my heavens, yes, you should see it! He butters her up and of course she just loves it. She's so conscious of the whole class system and firmly believes that everyone should know their place. Of course, that means that her place is at the top and ours is at the bottom," she sighed. "Oh, he appears to be nice but for some reason I can't put my finger on, I just don't trust him.

"But even that wasn't her biggest news. She was telling her

friend, Mrs. Van Alstyne, that she's convinced that Miss Jane next door, who moved in last year with her aunt, is having an affair with a married man. She's bound and determined to find out who the man is and call his wife and tell her! Now, according to The Old Lady, she suspected this was going on before she left for England last fall, but she couldn't prove it. She says that this Miss Jane isn't a Miss, she's a Missus, and she had a family in the mid-West, and when her husband put her out of their house, Mrs. Sullivan, being her aunt, took her in. Well, you know me, I don't like to spread rumors. She's nice enough to say good morning and good afternoon to and she minds her business, but the poor thing has no idea what she's in for with this old dragon spying on her. Well, The Old Lady's bedroom is on that side of the house, so every night, she watches the shades go up and down and the lights go on and off, and she expects very shortly to catch the man!

"But even that isn't the worst thing that's rolled off her poisonous tongue since she got back. Now remember, what's said here never leaves this room. When I'm talking to all of you, I feel it's like talking to myself."

Now Mary held her breath, her eyes wide with anticipation.

"Well, she wasn't back more than two days when that Mrs. Van Alstyne came to visit, and there's no doubt in my mind that she purposely waited until I was within earshot, and she loudly proclaimed that she knows for a fact that our new priest's mother and grandmother were whores. Now isn't that just terrible? And what could I do about it? If I spoke up and defended him, she would have accused me of eavesdropping. Oh, it bothered me so much to let it go and pretend I didn't hear her."

"Oh, that's just a terrible thing to say," Aunt Mary sighed. "Father is so very kind."

"And he's so good about visiting the sick," said Aunt Kate.

"Yes, he is," said Aunt Nan, "and a gifted priest. We're lucky to have him. Of course, I shouldn't be surprised at anything that comes out of her mouth anymore. I've never met anyone who is even remotely close to being as self-centered and outright mean-spirited as she is. But like they say, you have to consider the source. You know, I still remember the day Mama first took me up there. I was only ten years old, and oh, I was just terrified of The Old Lady from the very start, the way she towered over me with that severe look of hers and that superior, commanding voice. Why, she scared the daylights out of me! In those days, I referred to her to Mama as The Mean Old Lady, because she was downright mean to me and the others. But Mama taught me to curtsy and say, 'Yes, Mrs. Richardson,' and, 'No, Mrs. Richardson,' and to just do whatever I was told to do and everything would be all right. And as long as I did that, it usually was all right. But still, I was petrified that I'd do something to make her angry and that she'd give me a whipping. Even at that age, she had me hopping all the time and all she did was complain that nothing was done right.

"Of course, she came from a rich banking family in London and from the time she was young, she always had people waiting on her. So when she calls, she expects you to drop everything and run to satisfy her every whim. To her, you're not a person who breathes or has any feelings; you're a machine that she controls and you'd better follow her orders or else. Many a tear I saw in our Mama's eyes, trying to please that selfish, demanding, complaining old woman. Poor Mama. She worked so hard for that old lady, sometimes in pain, and never once did she hear a kind word from her.

"Right from the beginning, The Old Lady tried to get Victoria to look down on me and treat me as badly as she treated Mama and the rest of us. Oh, I can still remember her telling Victoria, 'Now remember, dear, this girl is your servant now, so if you need anything brought to you or you want her to do something for you, you just tell her so. And if you drop anything or spill something, she'll clean it up. Don't you get your hands dirty. That's what she's here for.' But thank God it's not in Victoria's nature to be like that.

She has a sweet disposition, just like her father did, so when her mother left the room, Victoria smiled at me and said, 'I'm glad you're here. You can be my new friend.' She's just a gem, that one, always saying kind things to offset her mother's stinging words.

"And it's always amused me to no end the way Victoria will patiently listen and listen to her mother, and never interrupt or disagree with her. Then she just goes right ahead and does what she herself thinks she should do, and the funniest part about it is that her mother rarely scolds her. If she scolds her at all, it's very softly. Oh, sometimes I've had all I could do to control myself where The Old Lady is concerned. One of my greatest temptations has always been to give that old bitty a piece of my mind. Or even better, a good swift kick in the rear! I've always believed that both would do her a world of good. That's why I firmly believe I do all of my Lenten penance in one week when she's around," Aunt Nan chuckled at last. "And if there is any justice, she'll come back as an Irish scrubwoman!"

Aunt Mary quickly retorted, "Don't tell me you still believe in reincarnation."

"More than ever!" Aunt Nan beamed. "Between what I've seen, what I've heard, what I've read, and what I have personally experienced, I can't help but believe in reincarnation. It's an unsolicited conclusion that I reached years ago and I haven't read anything since that has changed my mind. Why, if I were to sit here and tell you that I didn't believe in reincarnation, I'd be lying."

"Well, I wish I could understand how someone like you, especially a Catholic, could possibly believe in such an unusual idea," Aunt Mary replied.

"Well, I'll tell you. The main reason I believe in reincarnation is because I believe that God is all just. It's hard to balance such a belief against the obvious injustices of life. Also because of people like Constantine, Joan of Arc, and Nostradamus, to name a few. Then there are also interesting subjects like clairvoyance, precognition, telepathy, transcendentalism and hypnosis to ponder. Consider the three dimensional person with a body, a mind and a spirit. Also there is psychology and the sub-conscious mind to analyze. But like I always say, only God has all the answers. If you'd really like to understand my reasons for believing as I do, I'll jot them down and bring them with me next week. I have my own theory about what life is all about. When you read my ideas and opinions on why I believe in reincarnation, then you can give me your opinion on why you don't believe in it."

Without taking time to catch her breath, Nan continued talking about Jack's grandmother. "The Old Lady used to go to London every few months for a visit, but ever since Mr. Richardson's been gone, she spends the spring and summers here, and the whole fall and winter back in London. Now every year, like clockwork, she arrives here the week before Easter and leaves in September, right after Labor Day. And Easter being so early this year, she came earlier than ever. It'll be too long a visit for me and the servants, I can tell you. But thank God she'll spend part of the time in New York City and Boston, and the summer at Lake George. And of course she'll spend August in Saratoga for the horse racing season."

"I for one was so glad to see the end of Lent," said Aunt Mary. "I always observe all the church's rules for Lent, and I don't mind one bit voluntarily giving up beer every year, but I'm always so glad when Lent is over and I can get back to my nightly treat."

"Well, you know how I feel about alcohol," said Aunt Nan. "I believe it's the ruination of the family. I'd really like to join the Women's Temperance Group at St. Joseph's Church, but since John owns a brewery, and he is my employer, after all, I'd somehow feel a sense of disloyalty."

"Well, it was old Doc O'Brien who first recommended beer as a tonic for Kate," Aunt Mary replied. "He said that a glass of beer at night might help her sleep better, and what's the harm in one glass of beer at night?"

"None that I can see," Aunt Kate smiled, and they laughed along with her.

Kitty spoke up, "I noticed, Aunt Nan, that you said 'ever since Mr. Richardson's been gone.' They never did find out what happened to him, did they?"

"No," she sighed sadly, "they never did. They hired all kinds of detectives, but it was as if he'd disappeared into thin air. But Victoria has never given up hope. She is completely convinced that he has amnesia and will return one day."

"Wasn't he carrying a large sum of money? Did they rule out that he could have been robbed?" Kitty questioned.

"Well, they never actually ruled out anything. They know for sure that he arrived at the hotel that Friday. That evening he had food brought to his room but after that, it's a mystery."

Kitty said, "Maybe somebody from the bank, knowing that he was carrying all that money, told somebody else, who tried to rob him. Or maybe some stranger heard about it, took the money, and maybe even killed him. Do you think that there could have been any truth to that rumor that he ran off with that widowed woman who left town at around the same time?"

"Heaven's, no! That I'm sure of. He just wasn't gaited that way. In fact, I'll never forget the day he left. It's still very vivid in my memory. I didn't think that much about it at the time, but when I first heard that he was missing, it came right into my mind because he had never done this before. That morning, right after he said goodbye to Victoria and the children, he put his hand on my shoulder and looked right into my eyes and he said, 'Nan, take good care of my little girl and the children.' Well, the children were just getting over colds, so it didn't seem that strange. But he seemed to hold onto Victoria longer than usual as he kissed her goodbye. I can still remember as the automobile drove off, he looked back at the house with a sorrowful look on his face, as if he were looking at it for the last time. That's why, of course, I wouldn't say this to anyone but you, that I've always believed that, considering the choices that he had at the time, that he purposely chose to leave."

"What do you mean? What choices?" Kitty asked.

"Well, let me explain it to you like this. When Mr. Richardson and The Old Lady moved over here from London, the only thing he really insisted upon was bringing all his books with him. So there are some fantastic books in that library, and through the years, he kept adding to his collection. One day shortly after I'd been there, when I had been dusting in the library, I noticed the great selection of books and wished I had the opportunity to read them.

"Well, a couple of years later they had me stay over at night to help Victoria, when she got a bad headache. Some nights when I couldn't sleep very well, and was first tossing and turning, I got in the habit of sneaking down at night and borrowing a book to read. I would cuddle up in front of the fireplace in my room and read, many times falling asleep reading. Since I was the first one up in the morning, I never did require a lot of sleep, I would hurriedly sneak down and put the book back before anyone would notice that it was missing. This particular night The Old Lady was in New York City visiting her sister, and Victoria had gone with her. When I got to the library, the door was open, but I was startled to see that Mr. Richardson was sitting there in the dark in front of the fireplace. Before I could even think to make up an excuse, he said to me, 'Come in, Nan, and turn the light on so that you can find the book that you want to read.'"

"Well, I nearly fainted," she chuckled, adrift in the memory. "'Oh, Mr. Richardson, Sir, I'm sorry,' I said, and right away he said to me, 'No need to be sorry, Nan. I don't mind sharing my books with someone who appreciates them as much as I do, and who wants to learn. Of course, my wife would never understand, so we'll just keep this as our little secret.' Apparently, he'd known all along what I was doing and never said a word to anyone about it. He was just like that! Then he said, 'You know, Nan, I really would love to have a cup of tea right now. How about joining me?'

"I could sense that he wanted to talk to somebody, so I did make the tea, and sat there in the library listening to him. Now by this time Victoria had already told me that her father had grown up in a small town, but because he was so smart, he had skipped a number of grades and was brought to London to meet her grandfather, a bank president. In fact, Victoria had said that someone at the bank had said her father was a mathematical genius. I'll never forget some of the things he talked about that night."

Aunt Nan stopped speaking and turned her ear to the window. "Oh, there's Frankie's dog barking," she said to Mary's chagrin. "He and Mike must be home. I'll have to finish telling you about Mr. Richardson some other time."

Mike appeared in the doorway. "Ready when you are, Aunt Nan."

Aunt Nan stood up and went around the table, exchanging hugs. "Hopefully, I'll see you all next Tuesday. Have a good week!"

"You, too!"

"I'll be back as soon as I walk Aunt Nan home, Mama." Mike's voice faded as he followed Aunt Nan down the steps.

Mary lay in her bed wide awake. Although disappointed that Aunt Nan didn't mention anything new about Jack, and had cut short her story about Jack's Grandpa Richardson, she pondered some of the interesting things she'd heard that night, anxious to tell Molly in the morning on the way to school.

CHAPTER TWO

It was Friday morning when Mary awoke to the sound of Kitty's voice from the kitchen. Still half asleep, she could not quite make out what Kitty was saying, but from the tone of her voice, it was obvious that she was angry at someone, and giving them a piece of her mind. Mary jumped out of bed and hurried into the kitchen, not at all surprised to find that it was Pa on the receiving end of Kitty's admonitions. Then Kitty turned to Mama and her voice was soft and kind as she tenderly kissed her mother on the cheek, instructing her not to work too hard. As Kitty turned to leave for work, she spotted her younger sister in the doorway.

"Mary," she said seriously, "make sure you help Mama before *and* after school today. She's looking tired lately and I want her to slow down and get some rest."

Mary smiled. "I will, Kitty," she said softly.

As Maggie turned to get Annie up for school, Mary asked, "Is there anything I can do for you before I go to school, Mama?"

"No, Mary," Mama smiled quietly, touching her cheek with a warm hand, "but thank you. You're a good girl."

Mary looked at Pa now. He was sitting at the kitchen table with his chin in his hand, sipping his tea. She glanced at the clock and realized he would be leaving for work soon. Whatever Kitty had said to him must have made him feel bad. He didn't look up to meet her gaze and smile as he usually did when she entered the room. His eyes were downcast and sad.

Mary moved swiftly to him. "Good morning, Pa," she chirped as if there was nothing wrong in the least, smiling sweetly, kissing his unshaven cheek. "Oh, that tea looks cold. Here, let me get you a hot cup."

"No, Mary, thank you, anyway," said Pa, avoiding her eyes. "I have to be getting to work now."

She put her arms around his neck and kissed him again. "I love you, Pa!"

"Oh, my sweet little darlin'," he said, mustering half a smile as he rose from the table. "I love you, too. Now," he said in a half-whisper, "you make sure you help your Mama extra today. Kitty is right. She does look tired, and we all have to do our best not to add to her work or worry." He pecked her on the cheek at last, grabbed his lunch pail and his hat and scurried out the door.

It was Friday, and Mary always looked forward to Friday, not only because school was out for two whole days, but mainly because, most Friday nights, she slept over at Aunt Mary's and Aunt Kate's house. She enjoyed that so much, especially spending time with Aunt Mary.

Every Friday afternoon she hurried home from school and did her chores and tried to get her homework done so that it wouldn't be hanging over her head all weekend. But as she ate her breakfast and got ready for school that morning, she just couldn't stop thinking of Kitty and Pa.

Kitty was the oldest, followed by Mike, Pat, Mary, Danny, who had died, and Annie. Kitty was always so good to everybody. And yet she didn't seem to have any patience at all with Pa.

As Mary walked to Molly's house to pick her up on the way to school, she started thinking about how good her Pa had always been to her. If he ever had any extra pocket money, he'd always buy her a candy stick. She remembered when she was just a little girl; she'd wait for him to come home from work, and he always left something for her in his lunch pail, a little caraway cake or a cookie or apple.

And she would tell him, "Pa, you left something in here again." And he would say, "I did? Oh, my goodness, what was I thinking? I guess I just couldn't eat everything Mama packed for me today. Be a darlin' and finish it off for me, will you? We don't want Mama to think I didn't like it." And she would stare longingly at the tidbit, amazed at her good fortune. But before biting into it, she would hesitate. "Are you sure you don't want it, Pa?" she would say, hardly imagining that anyone would pass up a cookie or a piece of fresh fruit. And he would say, "Well, if you don't want it yourself, maybe Annie would like it." And she would say, "Oh, no, Pa, I think Annie gets plenty as it is. I'll finish it for you. If you're sure." And he would assure her that he was certain he wanted for her to have it, and they'd exchange the happiest of smiles in those moments. Looking back now, she was almost embarrassed at how long it had taken her to realize it wasn't true that he couldn't finish his lunch, that he'd intentionally saved something for her so that she'd have a little treat at the end of the day. But she was just a kid then. And she was almost thirteen now.

Then she thought about all the times he'd be late coming home from work, and she feared he was sick again. She'd go up the alley and squat down to look through the windows of the saloons, trying to see if she could find him. Oh, she'd never forget that day about three years earlier when she'd spotted him in one of his favorite haunts and watched in horror as the bartender pulled him off the barstool and hustled him roughly to the door, shoving him out so hard that he hit the ground with a thud and a groan. "And don't come back again!" he yelled.

Mary had felt her jaw tightening and her teeth grinding. She was angry. Her eyes flared as she spotted a round white stone about the size of a half dollar. She snatched it up and flung it at the bartender as hard as she could. He'd just turned his back and was going through the swinging doors when it hit him right in the middle of the back. He pivoted instantly, rage dominating his squinting eyes. He stood for a few seconds, staring hard, his fists clenched.

Still bursting with anger at the way he had so roughly manhandled her Pa, she stood defiantly and shouted at him, "This is a dump. We've been thrown out of better places than this!"

He looked at her in disbelief. Then he burst into laughter. "Kid," he said, "I admire your spunk!" And he returned to the bar, laughing all the way in.

But there was no humor in it for Mary. She'd rushed over to Pa. "Never you mind, Pa. Who needs him, anyway? He's nothing but a bum," she assured him, helping him to his feet, pulling his arm up over her shoulder, her little frame shakily supporting his weight as they went staggering down the alley.

Mary remembered, too, the Sunday mornings when Pa wasn't sick. She'd arrive home from Mass and as she opened the kitchen door, she could smell the flapjacks that Pa had been making, and they smelled so good.

She'd sneak in, and when he wasn't looking, she'd take one or two and hide in the pantry and eat them. And she'd watch from behind the door as he came back to his plate and look, and look again, and scratch his head and say, "Let me see, now, I could swear I had more flapjacks than this!" And she'd laugh and he'd say, "Oh, my goodness, what's that noise? Could it be a mouse?" And she'd giggle while he hunted through the kitchen until he found her, and he'd tickle her, and they'd both fall down on the floor, laughing. Then he'd make more flapjacks and they'd sit together and eat them until they were full. Remembering it brought a smile to her face.

And Pa was the one who always helped her when she woke up with her eyes stuck together from sties. While Mama was getting everybody's breakfast, it was Pa who walked her out to the sink and put the boric acid solution in the eye cup, and he always stayed with her until her eyes were open enough to see again.

And how could she ever forget the way Pa had sat by her bed with tears in his eyes when she had that appendicitis attack? He'd looked as if he was the one in pain, and he'd smiled only when she'd patted his hand and reassured him.

"Don't worry, Pa," she'd told him, "I'll be okay." And with him by her side, she soon was.

And what about the time she and her friends had met Pa at Prospect Park, and she'd said, "Hey, Pa, how about treating us?" And he'd smiled that happy-go-lucky smile she loved to see on his face, and said, "OK."

And she'd whispered to him, "How many can you treat, Pa?"

"Well, now, how many are there?"

"Me and four friends."

"Well, we'll treat them all," he'd said grandly, and she could still remember the little group in their Sunday best, waiting for his verdict, and how their faces had lit up at his generosity.

All of Mary's friends just loved her Pa because he was always so kind to them. And even when he didn't have money to treat them, they always knew that he would have treated them if he could have. She smiled as she thought about how Pa was always so happy to see her, and that made her feel so special. "Pa is a good, kind man, and he can't help it if he gets sick sometimes," she told herself as she reached Molly's house.

Molly was already waiting on her porch and she smiled that good-natured smile of hers and said, "Good morning, Mary. What's new?"

The girls had been best friends since first grade, when Molly O'Connor had been seated directly in front of Mary O'Neill. Molly was a pretty young girl with dark brown hair and eyes and was just a few inches shorter than Mary.

"Oh, Molly, I'm just so upset about Kitty and my Pa," she explained.

"Why, what happened?" Molly asked, concern in her voice, as always.

Mary explained the situation and said, "Molly, you know my

Pa's a good man. He's good-natured and he's generous. He can't help it if he gets sick sometimes."

"I know, Mary," Molly reassured her. "Maybe if you pray on it, something will come to you."

As she made her way through the day, thoughts of Pa and Kitty came into Mary's mind. Kitty's attitude toward Pa had always bothered her.

That evening, at Aunt Mary and Aunt Kate's, as she was helping set the table for supper, she thought about it again, and it prompted her to ask, "Aunt Mary, why doesn't Kitty love Pa like I do?"

Aunt Mary thought for a moment. What could she possibly say to this child who loved her Pa so much? Clearly she was old enough that she could see the situation, but was she still too young to fully understand it? "Why don't we have a nice supper with your Aunt Kate, and later on, you and I can talk. How's that?" said Aunt Mary with a comforting smile and a hug.

Afterward, when the last dish had been washed, dried and put away, Aunt Mary called to her sister, "Can I get anything for you, Kate?"

"No, thank you, Mary," came the fragile voice from the bedroom. "I'm just going to rest for a while."

Aunt Mary beckoned to her niece to sit next to her on the sofa in the parlor, and with a quiet concern in her voice, she said, "Now, what is it that you want to talk about, Mary?"

"Well," Mary began, looking for just the right words to express her concern without seeming to be blaming her older sister, or to be angry at her, which she wasn't, really. "Kitty is always so good to everybody... everybody except Pa. I hate to say this, Aunt Mary, but sometimes she seems almost *mean* to him. And I just don't understand why."

Knowing that she would never be able to tell her niece the whole truth as she knew it, Aunt Mary wondered how she could possibly even tell her of the evening she'd stopped in for a short visit after work, only to find Kitty scrubbing other people's dirty clothes. In truth, it had all begun even before that, but that scene in particular, and the anguish it brought up still, she would never forget as long as she lived. She could see the whole thing in her mind as vividly as if it had happened just the week before.

It was a time when things were especially hard for Maggie's family. Nan was on vacation with the O'Connell family and Maggie had resorted to taking in washings to make ends meet. Aunt Mary could still remember how powerless she'd felt being unable to help Maggie and the children more. But with her own wages just enough to get by on, and with Kate's poor health, she'd had all she could do to keep up with their own rent, food, and Kate's medical bills.

"I made Mama go to bed," Kitty had replied to Aunt Mary's astonished questions at the sight of her niece bent over the wash basin in the kitchen. "Her being in the family way again, I could tell she was just exhausted. Her hands were so red and raw they were actually bleeding. Bleeding from scrubbing other people's laundry! I swear some people mop up the floor with their clothes when somebody else is going to do the dirty work for them," she sighed. "And I'm just furious at Pa." And then the story had poured out.

The week before, Mr. Hess, who owned the grocery store down the block, had warned Maggie that they wouldn't get any more credit until the bill was paid on. Pa had gotten paid that day and had promised Maggie on his way out the door that he'd pay down the bill before he did anything else.

Shortly afterward, Kitty and Maggie had gone to the store to pick up a number of items for a late supper, but when they got to the counter, Mr. Hess reiterated how he'd warned them about the bill, and said he was sorry, but he couldn't give them any more credit.

"But my Pa came in earlier and paid on our bill," Kitty protested. And then her heart was in her throat. "Didn't he?"

Mr. Hess stood with his arms crossed, shaking his head more in pity than anger.

"No, he did not. Last time I saw your Papa, he met up with one of his drinking buddies and they stood out front of my store talking and off they went laughing down to the corner saloon." He shook his head sadly. "Really, I am sorry, Mrs. O'Neill. I feel so sorry for you and your little ones, but what can I do? I cannot afford to feed another man's family."

Aunt Mary had been aghast at the thought of it. "Oh, Kitty, you mean to tell me you haven't had anything to eat today? Oh, for Heaven's sake, I'll run over right this minute and get you something."

"No, Aunt Mary, we have food," Kitty sighed, "but only because Mrs. Hess is so nice. She was standing behind Mr. Hess and when he turned away our order, she motioned for me to meet her at the back door. She handed me a bag of groceries and told me not to say anything. 'My husband is a good man,' she said, 'but we've known hard times too and he vowed before we left Germany that he'd never let his family suffer again. He just can't understand a man like your Pa, hanging out, squandering his money at the saloon when his family needs food.'" Kitty went on, "And I said to her, "Well, I agree with your husband. I don't understand men like my Pa, either. But my Mama and I appreciate your kindness! And I promise to pay back every penny we owe.' She smiled at me and said, 'I'm sure you will, Kitty. You're a good girl.'" Kitty shook her head disconsolately, too angry for tears.

"Oh, Aunt Mary, I'm so mad at Pa that I'm beside myself. How can he do such a thing to his own family? And Mama expecting another baby! God forgive me, but I honestly think I hate him."

"Oh, Kitty, don't say such a thing. He's your father!"

All of the pain and the hurt, and discouragement in her eyes pleaded with her Aunt Mary to understand. She was still hunched over the wash basin and the dark circles under her lusterless brown eyes showed how cruelly fate had aged her beyond her years.

"Then why doesn't he act like a father?" she said simply. "He doesn't care about us. Why, he cares more about his drinking buddies than he does about his own family."

"Oh, that's not true, Kitty. Deep down, you know that's not true!"

"I don't know whether it is or not, and to tell you the truth, I don't think I care anymore. Not for myself, anyway. All I care about now is making sure Mama and the children have enough to eat. Somebody has to face reality, Aunt Mary. And the reality is, he's never going to change. I've warned Mama that after this baby is born, she better not go with him anymore. Six children and four miscarriages are more than any woman should have to bear. And I told her, 'Mark my words: If you don't heed my warning, you won't be around to see this child grow up.' I said to her, "You have to choose, Mama, between this no account, drunken husband of yours or your innocent little children who need their Mother!"

"But, Kitty, he's sick. He needs our sympathy," Aunt Mary pleaded.

"Sympathy?" said Kitty, almost shocked at the suggestion. "We need your sympathy. What he needs is a good swift kick!"

"Well, of course I sympathize with everyone, I just meant that..."

"I know what you meant, Aunt Mary. You're a good Christian and you feel sorry for everybody. But I don't feel sorry for people like him. Maybe I should, but I don't. I know I'm supposed to respect him. 'Honor thy Father and thy Mother,' I've been taught. But instead, I resent him for all the extra heartaches he's caused Mama and me and the children. It's one thing to do without because you don't have enough, but to see my hard-working mother just a couple of months away from having a baby, scrubbing other people's dirty clothes until her hands bleed, is just too much, especially when it doesn't have to be this way."

She stopped speaking so that her anger would not get the better of her, then swallowed hard, took a deep breath, and said, "I met Pa's boss Mr. Finney on his way home from work one day and he said to me, 'Your Pa wasn't at work today. I really could have used him.' My heart was in my throat, I was so scared. I thought, don't tell me he's going to fire Pa! We'll be thrown out into the street! But he said, 'You know, Kitty, your Pa's the fastest blacksmith I ever saw in my life. Twice as fast as some. When he's sober. I told him if he'd only straighten himself out, I could get him plenty of work.' *Plenty* of work! If he'd only straighten himself out. And Mr. Finney *told* him so! And here we are taking in washing and we wouldn't have food on the table if not for Mrs. Hess' generosity! Oh, Aunt Mary, how can I possibly have sympathy for him?

"And then to see other men, who aren't any better off than we are to start with, get further ahead! Because they care about their families.

"Why, look at Mr. Corbett down the street. Mrs. Corbett told me that the first thing he takes out of his pay envelope every week is his donation money for Sunday Mass. Then every night after supper, he takes the children to the park so she can finish her housework. And *then* he even reads the Bible to his elderly father! It'd be easy to admire and respect a father like that. But I'm tired of lying awake at night in fear of us being thrown out onto the street."

Aunt Mary said, "Oh, Kitty, you never need to worry about that. Why, if worse came to worse, you could always come stay with us."

"It's wonderful of you to say so, Aunt Mary, but you don't have room for all of us. And I know that you have all you can do to get along yourself, with Aunt Kate the way she is. No, I've made up my mind that I just can't wait to finish school this year. I need to go out and get myself a job *now*. Mrs. Scully told me that there's an opening at the telephone company and she'll put in a good word for me, and I'm going after that job. We need that money! Besides," she sighed, "even if I did want to finish, there's no money for a white dress for graduation."

"Oh, Kitty, don't leave school. Graduation is so close, and you're so smart. You deserve that diploma, and it's always best to have a diploma, no matter what kind of job you end up with. I'll talk to your Aunt Nan. I'm sure she'll be able to help out a little more until graduation comes, and I'll get some nice white material and a pattern at the store and make you the most beautiful graduation dress you've ever seen! Just hang on a little longer; it won't be so bad," she said, reaching down and hugging her niece, then raising her from her knees and leading her to the table. "Now, you sit right here and rest up. I'll put on the kettle for a nice cup of tea and you'll relax and have a good night's sleep so you're nice and fresh for school tomorrow morning. I'll finish those clothes," she said, rolling up her sleeves.

"But you're still wearing your nice dress from work," Kitty protested.

"Oh, a few soap bubbles aren't going to hurt this old thing," Aunt Mary smiled as she knelt on the floor and started washing the shirt in the tub.

When Aunt Nan had gotten home and heard from her sister Mary that Maggie was taking in washing and what had happened at the store, she too was very upset with her brother-in-law. She cancelled a coat she'd put on layaway and, with the refund, paid off their grocery bill. She spoke with Mr. Hess and told him never to refuse her sister groceries again; that she would make sure their bill was paid, as need be. Up to that point, Mr. Hess hadn't known that Nan and Maggie were sisters. Nan and Kitty finally convinced Maggie not to take in laundry anymore, and Kitty did graduate from the eighth grade, wearing the loveliest dress she'd ever owned in her life.

Mr. Nelson at the phone company, impressed by Kitty's high grades and Mrs. Scully's outstanding recommendation, had helped to convince her that she should finish school, telling her that he would keep the job open for her. And the Monday morning after graduation, she happily started learning the switchboard.

But now, as Aunt Mary recalled this incident, and others which had taken place as well, as well as conversations with her sisters which she'd sworn never to betray, she knew that she could never tell such things to this child who loved her Pa so dearly.

"Well, now, Mary," she began carefully, "I think the main reason that Kitty doesn't love your Pa as much as you do is because of the different ways in which each person views the same situation. Like, for instance, your Mama and your Aunt Kate and I think that when your Pa drinks too much and gets sick, it's like a curse, like something beyond his control. Seeing the situation that way, while we feel awfully sorry for your Mama and the rest of the family, we also feel sorry for your Pa, too, because we don't believe it's the way that a kind, loving man like your Pa would choose to be. But your Aunt Nan and Kitty believe that he could stop any time he wanted to. Therefore, they think that when he spends his time and money in the saloons, he's just being selfish."

"Oh, but Aunt Mary, Pa's not selfish! He's one of the most generous people I know."

"Yes, Mary, I agree with you. Your Pa has always been a very generous and kind man. But sometimes different people have different opinions about people, even people they love, and under the circumstances, all that you and I can do is pray that the drink won't get the best of him, and that, someday, he and Kitty will have a better relationship."

Later, as she had every night of her life since childhood, Mary Fogarty knelt at the side of her bed, made the sign of the cross and bowed her head deeply, pressing her folded hands against her forehead. "Our Father, who art in Heaven," she whispered, "hallowed be thy name. Thy kingdom come, thy will be done on Earth, as it is in Heaven. Give us this day our daily bread, and forgive us our trespasses as we forgive those who trespass against us. And lead us not into temptation, but deliver us from evil. Amen."

She paused as she glanced over at her statue of the Blessed Virgin Mary on her dresser. She smiled a moment and it seemed as if the statue was smiling back at her. She continued, carefully considering her words as she spoke them under her breath.

"Hail Mary, full of grace, the Lord is with thee. Blessed art thou among women, and blessed is the fruit of thy womb, Jesus." At the mention of His name, she bowed her head more deeply. "Holy Mary, mother of God, pray for us sinners, now, and at the hour of our death. Amen."

She drew in a deep breath and exhaled slowly. She had read about many of the lives of the saints and their insights into prayer and meditation. For her, prayer was deeply relaxing. It consoled her. It was a safe, quiet place in her life, a place to which she could take refuge at any time of the day or night, where she would feel her mental, spiritual and physical strength rebuild, or quiet down, as need be.

"God help me to be better than I am," she continued, and paused again. "Jesus, meek and humble of heart, make my heart like unto thine." And, finally, "Sweetest Jesus, I implore that I may ever love thee more and more."

Finally, "God bless Papa and Mama, and Aunt Anna and Uncle Jim, and Danny. May they rest in Heavenly peace. God bless Kate, Nan, Maggie, Daniel, and Kitty, Mike, Pat, Mary, and Annie. God bless Aunt Elizabeth and Uncle Robert, and Uncle Joe and Aunt Frances, the O'Connells, the Kendalls, the Malones. God Bless the pope and all the bishops and all the priests and the sisters of The Church, and all the missionaries everywhere, and all my aunts, uncles and cousins, and all my friends and neighbors and co-workers and their families. And God bless President Wilson and his family, and all the officials, that they may govern with wisdom and goodness. Open our hearts to your love and forgiveness. Amen." She smiled and began to rise, "Oh, and God," she said, "please help to heal the relationship between Daniel and Kitty. He's a good man deep down, Lord, I know you know that, please help him to get well. And thank you for helping me to realize and appreciate all of the blessings you've bestowed on me. Amen."

Now, as she climbed into bed next to Mary, who was already asleep, she found herself thanking God too for this young girl sleeping peacefully beside her, whom she loved so dearly, and felt so lucky to be loved by her. And she smiled to herself as she said a last "Thank you, God" for the warm comfortable bed into which she now settled. She recalled the old second-hand bed frame that had to be pushed up against the wall so that it wouldn't lean too far to the other side. She also remembered that lumpy old mattress she'd made do with for years before Nan had been given the O'Connell's bedroom set when they'd bought a new one. Nan had turned around and given Mary her set and Mary was more than thankful and always wished that everyone could have as much as she did.

Now she became aware of two soft, lovely sounds. It had started raining and she could hear it falling gently on the roof. She had always loved the sound of falling rain, especially when she was warm and cozy inside. And the sound of Mary's heavy, rhythmic breathing was like a gentle surf rising and falling in the distance.

She felt for her rosary beads and began to pray to herself, feeling the roundness of the beads between her fingers. She tried to say her rosary every day, but sometimes, between work and helping Kate and other relatives, and friends and neighbors, it seemed that her extra time was often taken up. So she offered all her good deeds up to God and considered that a form of prayer.

If she had a really busy day, she would start her rosary as she lay in bed at night. Many times she would drift off to sleep before she was done. And she smiled at remembering how her own Mama had reminded her of the old saying, "If you fall asleep without finishing your prayers, the angels will finish them for you."

It had started raining harder now and she could hear the rain pounding overhead. Then, suddenly, to her horror, she could feel the rain falling into her face.

"Oh, no," she sighed under her breath, "the roof is leaking."

She hopped out of bed to get some pans to catch the water, and Mary awoke when the rain started falling on her, too. Together, they pulled the mattress down off the bed onto the floor and put pans on the springs to catch the rain. Aunt Mary checked in on Aunt Kate. "Thank heaven it isn't raining in there," she whispered upon her return, crawling onto the mattress on the floor. She lost her balance and tipped over onto Mary, and the two of them laughed despite themselves. They were also trying hard to be quiet so as not to waken Aunt Kate as they settled in as comfortably as possible.

As she finally sighed with relief, Aunt Mary whispered, "Even on the floor, this mattress is more comfortable than my old one. Thank you, God, for a comfy mattress and the fact that the roof isn't leaking on this part of the house, too."

"Amen," Mary whispered, settling in, sighing deeply and peacefully, contentedly drifting into sleep – safe and warm beside her Aunt Mary. She thanked God, too, for all of her own blessings, and, most especially, for her Ma and Pa, her brothers and sisters, and her aunts, without whom, life just wouldn't be the same.

CHAPTER THREE

It was Sunday morning and Mary and Molly arrived at church for the nine o'clock Mass. They slid into a pew toward the back of the church and knelt to pray, making the sign of the cross and silently murmuring the Our Father and the Hail Mary.

Mary liked to go to the nine o'clock Mass because the O'Connells attended that Mass, too. She and Molly would always get there early and sit in back so they could watch as Jack and Gail and Mr. O'Connell arrived and took their pew down front. Mary also liked to see what people were wearing, especially Gail, who wore such beautiful clothes.

Mary never envied Gail or wished her any less than what she had. She just wished that she too had beautiful clothes.

What really annoyed Mary was that Gail's clothes were always passed on to Annie, since Aunt Nan was in charge of Gail's wardrobe. Because Gail was always neat, and her outfits fit Annie within a few years, they looked as if they'd just come from an expensive store. Annie was already so spoiled and selfish that Mary didn't think it fair that Annie often had such beautiful clothes to wear to church and school while she herself had to make due with Kitty's less flattering hand-me-downs, some of which she really didn't like at all. But in the meantime, reading and thinking of Jack always brought her special joy. There was something deep within Mary that made her believe that some day she would meet Jack at just the right moment in time, and that he would fall in love with her and ask her to marry him. And they would live happily ever after. It was a constant daydream, rerun in her mind with only slight variations. These thoughts brought a smile to Mary's face as she silently sighed and closed her eyes momentarily.

She glanced back again to the middle aisle, and there they were, Jack and Gail and Mr. O'Connell. And as always, her heart started pounding faster as a longing to be close to Jack swept over her.

Her eyes were transfixed upon him until Father came out onto the altar to begin Mass and everybody stood up and blocked her view.

The sound of the choir echoed fully throughout the church as Mary glanced at the book that Aunt Mary had given her for her First Communion. It was one of her very favorite possessions and Mary stared at it a moment, thinking how beautiful it was. In the center of the cover, surrounded by sheaves of wheat, green leaves and red grapes, stood a gold chalice, with a Eucharist, a cross and a star above it. In each corner, a small, child-like angel hovered.

Mary opened the book and followed along with Father Duffy as he began. At the top of the first page of her prayer book, she read, "The Priest goes to the Altar." The picture showed the priest and the altar boy at the altar. Inset into the picture was another picture, of Jesus and three of his apostles, and at the bottom of the page were the words, "Jesus entering Gethsemane." On the opposite page there were prayers to recite.

Mary turned another page and it showed the priest and altar boy with their backs to the congregation. As she looked at this picture, the choir began to sing the Kyrie Eleison in Latin. The next picture showed Jesus with his hands bound, standing before Pilate, surrounded by soldiers. As she turned the pages, she could still see and hear Father reading from the big prayer book on the altar, and it was just as the priest appeared with the altar boy in her prayer book. Now the inset picture showed Jesus, a guard on each side of Him, standing before Herod. Mary would as usual follow along through the Mass, as the inset pictures showed Jesus stripped of His garments, and scourged, and condemned to death. Then He was carrying His cross along the Via Dolorosa. Then a picture showed Jesus being crucified, and Mary always felt so pained at the thought of it. She loved Him so much because she knew that Jesus was the savior who loved her and loved everybody who had ever lived. Jesus had come to lead everyone to God.

Now it was time for the Gospel. Father Duffy approached the podium and cleared his throat. "Our reading today is from the Gospel of St. John, Chapter 20, Verses 19 through 31.

"Now when it was late that same day, being the first day of the week, and the doors were shut, where the disciples were gathered together for fear of the Jews, Jesus came and stood in their midst, and said to them: 'Peace be to you. As the Father hath sent me, I also send you.'

"And when he said this, he showed them his hands and his side. The disciples therefore were glad, when they saw the Lord.

"And he said to them again: Peace be to you. As the Father hath sent me, I also send you.

"When he had said this, he breathed on them; And he said to them: Receive ye the Holy Ghost.

"Whose sins you shall forgive, they are forgiven them; and whose sins you shall retain, they are retained.

"Now Thomas, one of the twelve, called the twin, was not with them when Jesus came.

"The other disciples therefore said to him: We have seen the Lord. But he said to them: 'Unless I shall see in his hands the print of the nails, and put my finger into the place of the nails, and put my hand into his side, I will not believe.'

"And after eight days his disciples were again within, and Thomas with them, Jesus cometh, the doors being shut, and stood in their midst, and said: 'Peace be to you.'

"Then he said to Thomas: 'Put in thy finger hither, and see my hands, and bring hither thy hand, and put it into my side; and be not incredulous, but faithful.'

"Thomas answered, and said to him: 'My Lord and my God.'

"Jesus saith to him: 'Because thou hast seen me, Thomas, thou hast believed. Blessed are they who have not seen, and yet have believed.'

"Many other signs also did Jesus do in the sight of his disciples, which are not written in this book. But these are written that you may believe that Jesus is the Christ, the Son of God, and that believing, you may have life in his name."

Now Father Duffy looked out upon the congregation. He was a quiet and gentle man, known for his intellect and his sense of humor. Although he'd been at the parish only a short time, everyone had taken a liking to him right away. Mary always enjoyed listening to Father Duffy because he often wove history into his sermons, and made learning about the Gospels so interesting. While some other priests just seemed to drone on and on, Father Duffy usually spoke for no more than ten or fifteen minutes; and his sermons were always so uplifting that the parishioners would sometimes be talking about his words well into the week ahead.

"My dear people," he began quietly, "something has been brought to my attention which I believe is my duty and my obligation as a priest to speak to you about. As I stand here today, I'm sure I feel like some of you parents must feel when you wish your children would behave so that you didn't have to correct them. But sometimes, if we are to serve the Lord, we must do and say things that we would rather not have to do and say.

"As I look upon you, I see many people whom I know perform many good and kindly acts of charity every day of their lives. I'm sorry that you have to listen to the sermon I'm about to give, because it is not meant for you who in humility serve the Lord to the best of your ability, with goodness, love, and forgiveness in your hearts."

He paused, took a deep breath, and continued.

"On Good Friday afternoon, after the Stations of the Cross, three boys from this Parish, chased, pushed and threatened a young Jewish boy on his way home from school, accusing him of killing Jesus. I want you to think for a moment. How would you feel if it was your child that this happened to?

"I spoke to the boys involved and they shamefacedly admitted to me what they'd done. I asked them, 'Why did the three of you attack one boy?' Do you think that is fair? How would you like it if it happened to you?' And of course they admitted that they wouldn't like it at all.

"They told me the main reason they did this was because, as they put it, 'The Jews killed Jesus and they're no good.' Well, they were rather surprised when I explained to them that not only Jesus, his mother Mary, and foster father Joseph were Jewish, but all Jesus' apostles and all of His followers were Jews. And that it was not the entire Jewish people, but only some of the Jewish and Roman leaders, who lived back in Jesus' time, who were responsible for His death.

Father paused again, his eyes serious and sad.

"The boys promised me that they are sorry and will never do such a thing again. They said they were willing to apologize to the boy. I met with the boy's father and offered our apologies, and inquired how the boy is and what the boys could do, besides apologizing, to make up for this unacceptable behavior.

"He very graciously accepted our apology and assured me that his boy was all right. He was happy and relieved to hear that it wouldn't happen again." He sighed as he paused a little longer.

"I think that there is an underlying issue involved here. It is prejudice, and a great lack of compassion for one's fellow man.

"Prejudice is prejudice," he said simply. "It doesn't matter what person or group of people it is against. It always causes unnecessary heartache. From my chat with the boys, it was sad to me, but obvious, that some of you, and you and God know who you are, practice, and teach your children, prejudice. I feel that I must make you aware of the fact that one lie or one assumption, deliberately or carelessly spoken, can ruin other people's lives. Hate breeds hate. From a tiny seed of hate can grow a web of violence. It is like a poison that warps the mind, destroying every good, decent thought until finally there aren't any.

"The next time, before you start spreading gossip, lies and half truths, ask yourself this question. How would you like it if someone did this to you or yours?

"We all must realize that there is only one God and that we are all His children, regardless of color, race, or religion. We must truly understand that only God can judge. Only God can look into our hearts and read our thoughts.

"Unless we actually tear down all the barriers of prejudice, we will never be able to call ourselves true Christians. For what is a Christian, but a person who lives according to the example and teachings of Jesus?

"I would like to leave you with something my Gramma taught me when I was a young boy. My Gramma was one of the truest Christians that I ever knew. She was so kind and gentle and so loving and forgiving.

"She said, 'Don't allow other people's mean, hateful behavior keep you from doing what you know, deep in your heart, is the right thing to do. You be the person that you would like other people to be.'"

He blessed them as he said, "May God bless you always. Now let us all sing that beautiful hymn, 'Faith of Our Fathers':

"Faith of our Fathers, living still,
In spite of dungeon, fire - and sword;
Oh how our hearts beat high with joy,
when e'er we hear that glorious word;

Faith of our Fathers, holy faith!
We will be true to thee til death.
Our fathers chained in prisons dark,
Were still in heart and conscience free;
And truly blest would be our faith,
If we like them should die for thee.
Faith of our Fathers, holy faith!
We will be true to thee til death.
Our Mothers too oppressed and wronged,
Still lived their faith with dignity,
Their brave example gives us strength
To work for justice ceaselessly.
Faith of our Fathers, holy faith!
We will be true to thee til death."

After Mass, Father Duffy, as usual, pleasantly greeted the people who for one reason or another came back to the sanctuary to speak with him. He glanced out into the Church to see if there was anyone else waiting to see him. He noticed a few people as usual had stayed after Mass to say extra prayers, some kneeling in front of the statues of Jesus and Mary and other Saints.

The Altar boys had finished putting the candle lights out and asked Father if there was anything else that they could do before removing their altar boy outfits. Father smiled and thanked them.

The sun streaming through the window brightened up the room. It was so quiet and peaceful and as he started removing his priestly vestments, he thought with a mournful smile on his face, "Well, I guess we told them, didn't we, Gramma?" as all of a sudden his mind wandered back in time across the sea to the little village in Ireland.

Vividly he could see another young boy being called terrible names while being pulled and pushed by a group of ruffians. And that young boy was himself. As far back as he could remember, he was shunned by the other children. When he was young, he used to play all by himself in his back yard. One day he wandered out farther than usual and met a little boy about his age and they started playing together and having a lot of fun. When they parted, they agreed with each other to meet there the next day.

But the next day, before he had a chance to say anything, the little boy said, "I can't play with you anymore."

"Why?"

"Because your Gramma's no good."

"What do you mean?"

"My Gramma said she's not a nice lady, so I can't play with you anymore."

"My Gramma is too a nice lady."

"She is not." And then the little boy started pushing him.

A lady came along and shook him and accused him of starting the fight. She said, "Go home to that no good Gramma of yours and don't come back. We don't want your kind around here."

How vividly he could still remember how sad it made him feel, as he cried all the way home. He didn't tell his Gramma because he didn't want her to cry, too. And that was only the beginning of all the sticks and stones that were to be thrown at him, many stinging his head and face and arms and legs and other parts of his frail body. It seemed what hurt even more was the downgrading, hurtful, mean names that they called him and the Gramma he loved and the mother he never knew. "Your Mama and your Gramma were whores," they would shout whenever they saw him, so he learned to run fast and to try to avoid them as much as he could.

When he was young, his Gramma had simply explained to him that a man had lied about her and some people believed him.

She explained to him that the little boy's Gramma and she had been good childhood friends, but they had both loved his Grandfather. When his Grandfather asked her to marry him, her former friend, instead of wishing her well, accused her of tricking him and wouldn't speak to her anymore.

"But, Danny, don't allow other people's hatred to seep into your mind and cause you to become like they are. God wants us to rise above that selfish pettiness."

He could still see in his mind, his Gramma standing in the doorway of that little thatched roof farm house in the country. Even as she aged, the traces of beauty were still visible. But she worked so hard that most often her hands were roughened and calloused. What he would always remember the most about her was the light he could see in her eyes as she smilingly looked at him, and her soft voice that was always full of encouragement. He always knew how much she loved him.

He took a moment to reminisce about what a good time he and that little boy had together. They had laughed and played tag and smiled and talked and played in the sand. They might have become best friends, but for prejudice, and that same sadness momentarily swept over him. But he would not dwell in self-pity. He had learned long ago to get over it and get on with his life.

Then came the day when his Gramma said, "Danny, I must explain something to you, and I pray that you will be able to understand it." Her face showed great concern for him as she began her sad story. "Many years ago, when your Mama was just a little girl, there wasn't any food anywhere, and everybody was so, so hungry. Your Grandpa was a young man then, and he went off one morning with a small amount of money, believing that there must be food in one of the villages farther away. That was the last time I ever saw him. I never found out what happened to him. He was a good man and I know he would have tried to come back to us, if he possibly could.

"I could only imagine that maybe he went on and on from village to village and not being able to find any food, may have gotten sick and died. The only other thing I could think of is that maybe he was robbed and beaten for the little money he had. When people are hungry and desperate, sometimes they do terrible things.

"Word came back that the only people who had any food in Ireland were the English Landlords. Our landlord was in London and his son was in charge of his property. I had seen him a number of times before with his Father, and somehow I had the feeling that he was not only more tolerant, but he had a shyness about him and his eyes projected sympathy.

"The crying of the hungry little children prompted me to go to his house and beg him for food for the children. When the servant opened the door, I could see that he had guests. The table was set for a banquet feast.

"I told the servant I had to see him. When the servant came back from speaking with him, he beckoned me toward a rear room. I could hear laughter and gaiety. I waited and waited a long time. Finally, I could hear some of the guests leaving.

"When he came into the room, I explained to him about the situation and I begged him for food for the children. He told me that he had to see his guests and that he would let me know. As he left the room, I could hear men's voices in the other room.

"To make a long story short, I ended up spending the whole night on my knees in prayer. The next morning he gave me food and I took it back to the people. They were so happy and everyone had their fill, but soon a rumor started circulating that I had gone to bed with him.

"It seems his friends assumed that under the circumstances, he had traded food for my affections, and for the sake of his so-called pride, he let everybody go on believing the lie.

"As the lie spread, the townspeople turned on me. They said my carrying on with this English Gentleman tainted the food and that I'd made them a part of my sin. Even worse was when my father heard about it, he believed it. He wouldn't even listen to me pleading with him that it wasn't true.

"He slapped me across the face and called me bad names and then he forcefully cut off my hair and told me that he never wanted to see me again, that I had brought shame upon the family, and all the good Irish people who had so courageously fought for the cause, and given their lives fighting against the injustices forced upon them by England. He said that I was a disgrace to my ancestors in the worst possible way. With hatred in his eyes he said, you might as well have spit on their graves. He said he and the others would sooner have starved to death than to have me sleeping with the enemy, being a laughing stock, the butt of amusement to the English Landlords at their next and future get-togethers.

"And then he forbid the rest of the family to speak to me or have anything to do with me. The only solace I had at the time was that my saintly Mother had gone on to her Heavenly reward and did not have to endure his bitterness.

"Only my one younger sister Kathleen believed me and has always tried to help me secretly, or she too would have been disowned. God knows I didn't do anything wrong. You believe me, don't you, Danny?"

"Yes, Gramma, I believe you, and I love you and I'll always take care of you."

"You know, Danny, I was so sad and hurt that they wouldn't believe me. I started praying that God would make them understand. But as time went on, I realized that they were never going to change, so I asked God to help me to accept it, and not become bitter, like they were.

"Over the years Father has helped me as much as he possibly could. He tried to talk to people on my behalf, but they wouldn't listen because of the hatred they felt toward the English. Father gave me the Bible which has been a great comfort to me.

"What always hurt the very most was watching your Mama and you suffer for a good deed that I did. So many times I wished so much that I could have protected you both. And even now I would give anything if I could only spare you from knowing these things. But I feel as if now that you are old enough that I must tell you the whole truth.

"Remember, Danny, years ago I told you that your Mama had gotten sick and died. It really was a form of sickness that killed her. A mental sickness that had built up from years of loneliness and disappointments.

"Your Mama was a sweet little girl, so good and kind, but she also was subjected to the cruelty of some of the people. She had been a lonely little girl who had grown up scared inwardly and outwardly by the stones and hateful words heaped upon her, by her so-called Godly neighbors. She was shy and sensitive and their hatefulness really hurt her deeply. You know your favorite place overlooking the sea? That was her favorite place, too. She was only seventeen when a neighboring farmer's nephew came for the summer to help him on the farm. They met there one day on the cliffs overlooking the sea and started talking to each other and became friends. Then over that summer they started meeting every evening. I had never seen her so happy. I thought at last she had found someone to love her, and take her out of here. Then it was time for him to go back home. He told her he loved her and as soon as he could, he would come and get her and they would get married.

"Then, as she would explain to me months later, one thing led to another and he kept pleading with her that if she really loved him she would let him lay with her, because after all they were going to be married. And they went too far. Even as she told me, she reassured me that everything would be all right because they loved each other, and at that time she really believed that he would come for her and marry her.

"He had raised her hopes so high with his promises of marriage. No letter came from him and the time went by and you were born. In a matter of months I saw her go from hopeful to desperate. You were a beautiful baby and she loved you. She really did. It was as if not hearing from him took its toll on her.

"It was pitiful watching your Mama become so nervous and so sad and depressed. We found out that his uncle and his family had told the young man that we were no good whores and that he deserved better. He got back home and started courting another girl. Then one day came the news that he had married this other girl. That was the final blow. She had lost all hope in the future.

"The next morning when I got up, I searched the house for her and couldn't find her anywhere. I went outside calling and calling her name. Finally, I went into the barn." At this point, she took his hand as tears welled up in her eyes. A deep sadness spread over her face. "She had hung herself."

"Of course, I've always missed her. I felt sad for what happened to her. But, Danny, I want you to know that you have always been such a joy to me.

"I made up my mind long ago not to look back and allow other people's hatred to make me bitter.

"With faith in God, I started looking forward and praying and believing in the dream that someday you would be able to go to America. It's a dream that has always kept me going. Now, because of all your hard work, we have saved enough for your passage, and I want you to go now, before anything else happens. Father has a friend in America who said you can stay with him."

"No, Gramma, I couldn't leave you. I'll keep working and we'll save enough so that we can both go together."

"No, Danny, no. Please listen to me. If you stay here, it will take you so much longer. I want you to go and begin a new life. In the meantime, Kathleen and her family, and Father, will help me."

After much protesting, he finally agreed, under one condition. "Gramma, do you promise me that if I go first, that as soon as I save the money, that you will come?"

With a smile on her wrinkled face, she said, "Yes, Danny, I promise that I will come when you send for me."

But it was a sincere promise that she would be unable to keep. A few months after he left, with her Bible on the stand beside her bed, clutching her prayer beads in one hand and his letter in the other, Margaret Duffy died.

Father Dunn assured Danny that his Aunt Kathleen, her daughter Bridget and he were there. He would tell him that she died peacefully in her bed, with a smile on her face and a thankful prayer on her lips. Her last words were, "Father, please send this Bible to Danny and tell him I always had such fond memories of us reading it together. Tell him he made me so happy, by making my dream come true."

Even in death, Father Duffy always felt very close to her and experienced great comfort thinking of her. The things that she taught him had become a part of him. He had always admired Father Dunn and appreciated how much he had helped him and his Gramma.

On the day he became a priest, he made a vow to spend his life doing as much good as he possibly could in his lifetime. The Bible phrase, "Be not overcome by evil, but overcome evil with good," became his motto.

CHAPTER FOUR

As they gathered together as usual on Tuesday evening, the main topic of conversation was, of course, the terrible flood that had swept through Troy and surrounding areas on Thursday. Martial law had been declared in Troy, when several fires broke out from gas line breaks. Record flooding of the Mohawk and Hudson Rivers had washed out bridges in Amsterdam and Glens Falls and cut off Schenectady from surrounding towns.

As always when disaster strikes, each had a story to relate about how the flood had disrupted their lives and the lives of family and friends, neighbors and co-workers. There were many stories about so many people helping. Mike and Frankie had helped lay sand bags around the city. Pat had spent much of the weekend helping Father Duffy and Father Kennedy put together relief boxes at St. Mary's.

"They're collecting a fund for the victims of the flood," said Aunt Mary with concern in her voice. "Some poor folks have lost everything!"

"I read where the Relief Committee is working with the Salvation Army and the Nurses Association to help provide clothing," said Kitty.

"And I read that the Union Furniture Company on River Street is giving free mattresses to victims of the flood," said Aunt Nan, "That's awfully good of them, especially when you think of how much merchandise that is. And did you see the picture in the paper of the flood in Dayton, Ohio? Some people escaped the flood only by riding freight trains loaded with rocks to keep the cars on the tracks! Now that sounded scary."

"We've been awfully busy at the phone company with all the extra calls," said Kitty. "Did you see our ad? I'm so glad they put it in the paper. I just hope it makes people stop and think twice before making unnecessary calls."

"What kind of an ad was that?" Aunt Kate asked. "We don't generally get the newspaper through the week."

"It was about unnecessary phone calls during emergencies," said Kitty, flipping through the newspaper on the table and holding up the page for them to see. "'Just suppose every man, woman and child in this locality were to suddenly crowd into the railroad station all at once to take a certain train,'" she read aloud. "'Then suppose a poor woman had to take this same train to visit her dying husband. How much chance would she have of getting there on time, or at all? That poor woman is like the person making a really necessary call when the fire bell has just rung. She can't do it. Why? Because her curious and thoughtless fellow humans all want to ask where the fire is, and the operators can't answer them all.'"

"Isn't that clever?" said Mama.

"And it's true, too," Kitty said, shaking her head as if in disbelief. "Why, I actually had a man call and ask if I knew when the buses would be running again."

"Did you hear that the subscription contest has been extended another week because of the flood?" Aunt Nan said more seriously. "Now the paper will announce the winners this coming Saturday. Just keep praying that I win in my district. I'm sure it's going to be awfully close."

"Speaking of the paper, did you see the story about the American Suffragettes?" Kitty asked excitedly.

"I haven't had a chance to read a newspaper since Sunday," said Aunt Mary. "What was it about?"

"I'll read it to you," Kitty offered. "I put it in my scrapbook. I'll go get it."

"We need more like her," said Aunt Nan with a smile.

"Here it is," said Kitty, settling back into her chair. "'American Suffragettes Start Campaign. Forcible Feeding. American women are collecting various instruments used in the forcible feeding of obstinate Suffragette prisoners now in English jails. Screws and pliers used to force the jaws apart. Feeding tubes and other implements. It will be exhibited first in New York, and then in other American cities, and then offered as a gift to the Smithsonian Institute.'"

"Screws and pliers?" Said Aunt Kate, as if sickened at the thought of it.

"On a happier note, I heard that labor bill passed that prohibits working children from operating dangerous machinery," said Aunt Mary. "I still just feel awful about that poor little boy in Cohoes who lost his hand in that machine he was working."

"Ten years old," said Aunt Kate, shaking her head sadly, "in one of the carpet mills, I think."

"Oh, wasn't that terrible," said Mama. "His whole life will be that much harder, the poor thing."

"Suffer the little children," said Aunt Kate sadly.

"Speaking of the working class," said Aunt Nan, "by which I mean, us, today's paper said that five hundred textile workers are out on strike."

"Oh, I read that," Kitty said excitedly. "They want a fifty-four hour work week for sixty hours pay. I for one hope they get it. For Heaven's sake, fifty-four hours a week is plenty for anybody to have to work. Why, I'll bet the big wigs don't work like that."

"You're right," said Nan, "they don't."

"Oh, and talking about money," Kitty went on, "did you notice in today's paper that J.P. Morgan's will was read? It must be nice to have that kind of money and not have to worry about working and living from hand to mouth all your life. It just doesn't seem right to me how some people have so much while others struggle every day just to make ends meet."

"Well, now, you know I don't believe in judging anyone," said Aunt Mary, "but I can't for the life of me understand how somebody could accumulate so much money while knowing that other people are enduring even more suffering because of a lack of money."

"Well, J.P. Morgan helped a lot of people with his money, and many causes," said Nan. "I personally believe that some people were meant to have money."

"Oh, Nan, I can't in my wildest dreams imagine how you could justify a statement like that," said Aunt Mary. "What on earth do you mean, some people are meant to be rich?"

"I didn't say rich," said Nan, "I said that I, personally, believe that some people were meant to have money. I believe... Well it's much too involved to get into right now. Some day when I have time on my hands, I'll write down what I'm talking about, and then, as always, I'll welcome your comments. Which reminds me," she said, digging into her bag and retrieving a few sheets of paper in a binder, which she handed across the table to her sister Mary. "Here are those ideas about why I believe in reincarnation. I put in some blank sheets of paper, too, so as you read along, you can give your opinion on why you don't believe it. You know my philosophy always is, the more ideas the better."

Nan Fogerty was the youngest and the shortest of the four sisters. She was barely five feet tall and weighed just under one hundred pounds. Although she was 35 years old, she had a natural youthful appearance. Everyone knew she was a highly intelligent woman. In addition to the probable hundreds of books she had read over the course of her lifetime, she had read an entire set of the Encyclopedia Britannica and she had a truly amazing capacity to remember in detail what she had read.

The evening flew by as usual, and as Mary lay in bed pretending to be reading a book, but listening intently, she heard Aunt Nan whisper to Kitty, "Go check to see if Mary and Annie are asleep yet. I want to tell you about what that new French chauffeur did to me this week."

With that, Mary quickly set her book beside her, pulled the covers up around her neck and started her snoring routine. She had done it so many times by now that she snored just loudly enough to be believed. As usual, she heard Kitty's footsteps advance to the doorway, pause, and tiptoe off again.

"They're both sound asleep," she heard Kitty say. "Now, what happened?"

Aunt Nan quietly began to relate what she considered to be her tale of woe. "Well, you remember last week I told you about that French chauffeur the Old Lady brought back with her? Well, I was just trying to be friendly and helpful, considering he's a stranger in America and maybe he's a little homesick and he doesn't know the country. But apparently he completely misunderstood my intentions. Each day it seemed to me that when no one was around he was getting a little pushier. At first, I told myself, this has got to be my imagination, or maybe that's just his way or the way things are done in his country. I tried to shake off my suspicions and avoid him without being too obvious. Then, Saturday morning, Victoria gave me a list of the wines she wanted me to bring up from the wine cellar for the menu she'd planned over the weekend, and she asked him to go down with me and help carry up the bottles. Well, he was standing behind me, and I got out the four bottles that were on the list, and I put them on the table for us to bring upstairs, when the first thing you know, he put his arm around me and he said, 'There, now doesn't that feel nice?'"

"What?"

"Yes! Why, I was shocked! I just couldn't believe it. I felt embarrassed and angry at the same time. My first impulse was to slap him right across the face, but the old lady was lingering at the top of the stairs and she doesn't miss a trick, that one. She not only has eagle eyes but supersensitive hearing, and I just knew she'd blame me for something like that. So I gave him a good elbow right in the ribs and a kick in the shins and I told him, 'Don't you dare put your hands on me!' I got free of him and I ran up the stairs, and I left him to carry the wine bottles, and I promised myself not to let him catch me in such a vulnerable position again!"

"What a terrible nerve," said Maggie.

"You're right, though. It sounds like you'd better watch out for him," said Kitty, and the others shook their heads at the thought of it and nodded in agreement.

Aunt Mary glanced at the clock and said, "Oh, my goodness, how time flies! Kate and I were saying on the way over how tired we are today. So, if you're ready, Kate, let's get going, shall we? Meanwhile, Maggie, Kitty, we'll see you girls at Mass and for dinner on Sunday, and we'll see you next Tuesday, Nan."

"You know, when you mentioned The Old lady," Kitty said to Nan, "I couldn't help wondering if she caught that married man she believes is carrying on with the woman next door."

"No," said Nan, "but according to what I overheard her telling that friend of hers the other day, she's hot on his trail and expects to catch him very soon."

Suddenly the kitchen door swung open and in came Pa. He was in a good mood, still laughing to himself at the jokes he'd heard at the saloon. His eyes met Nan's and he exclaimed, "Well, if it isn't my favorite sister-in-law!" He leaned over as if to give her a big hug and she pulled away with a disgusted face.

"Get away from me, you! Why, your breath would bowl over a skunk!" She protested. "And don't give me any of your blarney. I am not loaning you any money!"

Pa stood erect, acting the offended gentleman. "And did I ask for money? Well, now I guess you just can't be nice to some people, they're so suspicious," he laughed. "Why, you ought to be ashamed of yourself, Nan Fogarty, at your lack of trust in your fellow man.

You'd just better say extra prayers tonight to become more trusting. And after me trying so hard to fix you up with an eligible man. Now, now, don't thank me," he waved off her imminent protest, "I've seen homelier women than you catch a man. But of course I couldn't tell him how skinny you are," he winked at Maggie.

"Don't you dare try fixing me up with any of your chums," Nan sighed in disbelief. "Why, just the thought sends a shiver down my spine," she said with a shudder. "The man hasn't been born yet who could make me change what I have for the likes of your kind. Why, I have a modern bathroom right next to my bedroom and they don't even turn the heat down at night. In fact, every night I get on my knees and thank God I'm where I am. And looking at you right now makes me realize just how lucky I am. Well, you can thank your lucky stars that you're married to my sister and not me, because I'd never put up with your shenanigans. I'd meet you at the door with a frying pan in my hand!"

"Oh, why it hurts just to think of it," he laughed again. "Being married to you, I mean." And he winked again at Maggie, who smiled despite herself.

"Our dear mother was always such a good judge of character, I still can't understand how you got past her."

"Well, I know I'll be sorry for asking, but I'm curious," said Kitty. "Who are you trying to fix Aunt Nan up with? Anybody we know?"

"Oh, he's just a grand fellow. Every bit the gentleman. Been a widower going on a year now."

"Mr. Thompkins!"

"Well, yes."

"God have mercy on me!" Nan roared. "I knew Mrs. Thompkins. Such a nice lady. Such a shame to have died so young. And I suspect the likes of him staggering in three sheets to the wind every week is what put her in an early grave. But I should thank you. For the warning. If I ever see you two coming along, I assure you, I'll run the other way as if you were the black plague! As far as I'm concerned, that couldn't be any worse."

Maggie finally spoke up and said, "Oh, Nan, he's only teasing you because it's April Fool's Day." And they all laughed at the realization.

"No, no, really," Pa went on, "I really have been trying to fix her up. But you might as well forget about it, because I just couldn't talk him into meeting you. I have a suspicion he's seen you on the street and just didn't want to admit it to me. So I'll do you a favor and tell you a little joke I heard. It couldn't help but sweeten even a sour disposition like yours."

Nan rolled her eyes at Maggie and shook her head with an indulgent smile. "Go ahead."

"Well," he began, "A little girl goes to market for her mother, and the butcher says, 'Well, little girl, what can I do for you?'

"The little girl says, 'How much are chops this morning, Mister?'

"Butcher: 'Chops, twenty cents a pound, little girl.'"

"Oh, twenty cents a pound for chops. That's awful expensive. How much is steak?"

"Steak is twenty-two cents a pound.'"

"Little girl says, 'That's too much. How much is chicken?'"

"Butcher, getting impatient, 'Chicken is twenty-five cents a pound.'"

"Little girl: 'Oh, twenty-five cents for chicken? Well, my Ma don't want any of them.'"

"Butcher: 'Well, little girl, what do you want?'"

"Little girl: 'Oh, I want a pony, but my Ma wants five cents worth of liver.'"

"Cute," said Nan. "And it puts me in mind of a poem entitled, 'Nothing Suited Him.' 'He sat at the dinner table there with a discontented frown. The potatoes and steak were underdone, and the bread was baked too brown. The pie too sour, the pudding too sweet, and the mincemeat much too fat. The soup was greasy, too, and salty 'twas hardly fit for a cat.' 'I wish you could taste the bread and pies I have seen my mother make. They were something to like and 'twould do you good just to look at a slice of her cake.' Said the smiling wife, 'I'll improve with age, just now I'm a beginner. Your mother called to see me today and I got her to cook the dinner!'" She smiled, and they all broke into laughter at the punch line as Mike walked in the door.

"And on that happy note," she said, rising from the table, "I'm off."

"Oh, so you finally admit it then, do you?" said Pa, and they laughed again as the evening came to a close.

CHAPTER FIVE

It had been a long day at school, and Mary had just finished telling Molly and Catherine that since she didn't have to visit the girls' room, she'd meet them outside when they were finished. But as she watched them walking slowly toward the staircase at the rear of the building, she decided instead to give them a good scare. She knew she was faster than they were, and could easily run down the hallway to the staircase at the front of the school and beat them down to the bathroom, where she'd hide in a stall and jump out and scare them as they entered.

She rushed down the hallway and jumped down the stairs two at a time, panting excitedly as she closed the door behind herself and stepped up onto the toilet seat in the stall closest to the door, crouching so as not to be seen.

She could hear their voices coming closer and she was still giggling to herself as she got ready to pounce on them and yell, "Boo!" as soon as they entered. But when she heard her name mentioned as they came through the door, curiosity got the best of her, and it forced her to remain quiet and listen.

"Well, I can't help it, can I?" Catherine said. "It's not my fault my parents won't let me invite Mary to my birthday party because of her father. But if you don't say anything, she won't even know I'm having a party. And if she finds out later on, I'll just say that I thought she said something about going someplace with her sister Kitty that day."

"Well, I wouldn't even want to have a party if Mary couldn't be there," said Molly, her voice aggravated. "And I can't believe you'd outright lie to her just to protect yourself."

"Well, what am I supposed to do, tell her the truth? 'Gee, I'm awful sorry, Mary, but my parents won't let me invite you to my birthday party on account of your Pa gets drunk all the time.' That would only make her feel worse. And you know I'd invite her if I could. She's been one of my best friends since first grade."

"Well, I don't see how that could be. Best friends don't treat each other like that," said Molly. "In fact, under the circumstances, I won't be at your party, either. And you don't have to worry about me telling Mary, because I wouldn't want to hurt her feelings like that."

"Oh, come on now, Molly, that's not fair," Catherine protested. "Why should I have to suffer because her Pa's a drunk?"

Mary was stunned. It was as if her lifelong friend had slapped her across the face with those words, and it stung worse than any physical assault ever could have. Who on earth did Catherine and her parents think they were, making judgments and comments like that about her Pa? Her face flushed hot and red as she defiantly pushed open the door to confront her.

"Don't you worry about me ruining your party, Catherine. Why, I wouldn't even want to go to your dumb old party, anyway. And just because you and your family live in a nice big house and buy yourselves new clothes whenever you want, well that doesn't make you any better than anybody else!" she declared. "You're always putting on airs and looking down on other people. But when it comes to being kind and having good manners, your family is far beneath mine!" she shouted, a lump in her throat as she ran out of the bathroom and up the stairs and out of the school, not stopping until she reached home. Anger made her refuse the temptation to cry as she pulled in the clothes from the line and folded them into the basket.

Now, as she did her homework, she found it was hard to concentrate. Every now and again, she'd catch herself staring off into space and she'd hear a voice inside of her saying, "Who do they think they are, anyway?" Although she'd always considered Catherine her next best friend after Molly, she'd never really felt comfortable stopping to call on her. Catherine's parents always acted uppity, and they never invited her into the house. She'd always assumed they were like that to everybody, but now she had to wonder. And although she would love to have had Catherine's beautiful clothes and toys and live in a big house like theirs, Mary really didn't envy her one bit. Even with her Pa's drinking problem, Mary was grateful to have him for her father rather than Catherine's. He always seemed so cold and distant, and he was busy all the time. He and Catherine's mother often went on long business trips to New York City and Chicago and other places and left Catherine at home alone with the housekeeper.

"My Pa may drink," Mary told herself, "but when he's sober, he always listens to me and encourages me. And I always know he loves me."

"Mary," Mama's voice interrupted her thoughts, "I want you to take this soup over to your aunts while it's still hot. And mind you, be nice and quiet in case your Aunt Kate is sleeping. I was over there this afternoon and I told her I'd send some soup and homemade bread for their supper. And I added enough for you, too, so you can eat with them and help out a little tonight. I already left them an apple pie I made this morning."

"Okay, Mama. I'll leave in just a minute. I'm almost finished with my homework."

On the way to Aunt Mary and Aunt Kate's house, Mary continued to think about the situation. Even the promise of Mama's spiced apple pie couldn't turn away the disappointment that continued to nag at her. It was bad enough not being invited to a party, but the fact that Catherine would actually try to deceive her and talk about her family behind her back like that, made her feel even worse.

She had a hard time setting it all aside and listening as Aunt Mary and Aunt Kate talked during supper. Afterwards, Aunt Kate went into her room to lie down as usual, and as she and Aunt Mary stood at the sink doing the dishes, Aunt Mary asked if there was something bothering her.

"Well," Mary sniffed, "something happened at school today," and Aunt Mary listened intently as she related the story, and when Mary got to the part about Catherine deceiving her, the tears that she'd been keeping from herself began rolling down her cheeks.

Aunt Mary hugged her close and said, "Oh, never mind about them, anyway. It seems to me your birthday is just a few weeks away, and I've been thinking about it, and I've decided that on the Sunday before your birthday, I'm going to take you on the train to Albany. We'll go to Mass at the Cathedral and then out to dinner and to the picture show. How does that sound?"

Mary was stunned. Such a thing had never occurred to her before. "Oh, but Aunt Mary," she said, her eyes wide with wonder, "can you afford that?"

Aunt Mary laughed lightly, her eyes dancing. "Yes, Mary, I've been saving up for something special, and I can't think of anything more special than to splurge on your thirteenth birthday. You can invite Molly, too, if you'd like."

"Can I?"

"Of course you can!"

"Oh, Aunt Mary, you're so good to me!" Mary exclaimed, hugging her tightly, thoughts of her own birthday celebration now jumping excitedly in her head.

CHAPTER SIX

The whole family had gathered at the door and as it swung open to the sight of Nan arriving for their weekly Tuesday supper date, excited greetings and hooting and hollering could be heard out on the street.

"Nan!" Maggie beamed, throwing her arms around her sister and enveloping her in a strong embrace, "You made it! You did it! Oh, I'm so happy for you!"

"Oh, Aunt Nan," Kitty exclaimed, "You're going to Europe!"

"Congratulations, Aunt Nan!" Mary and Annie chirped in, almost simultaneously, hugging her around the waist while Pa, Mike and Pat started a round of, "For she's a jolly good fellow" and Aunt Mary and Aunt Kate stood laughing, contentedly awaiting their turn for a hug and a kiss.

"Why, my goodness, a royal welcome!" Nan laughed openly, clearly elated at having been one of the winners of the newspaper subscription contest, as well as at her family's obvious and sincere delight at her good fortune.

As excited as a little girl at Christmas, she dominated the conversation throughout the evening, but they didn't mind. They were as excited for her as she was for herself, and wanted only to help her enjoy the moment and revel in her success.

"Of course, the contest had officially closed at ten o'clock Saturday night," she related, "and we'd been invited to the newspaper office for the final count. Well, can you imagine our surprise and delight when, just before the judges started their work, luncheon from the Windsor Hotel was served! Oh, it was delicious!

"So, at ten o'clock, they locked the door, and as they expected, there was a flood of votes to be turned in by the candidates just before the door was locked, and the contest manager and his assistant were kept busy at it until midnight taking the money and subscriptions from the candidates.

"Then, at midnight, the ballot box was turned over to the judges, who included the Mayor and four cashiers from local banks. The judges had to separate the votes into each district, and then credit them to the contestants for which they were cast. The five judges kept at their work steadily and finished about 3:15AM.

"Then, as the Mayor made the announcement, each winner was applauded. Oh, it was so exciting, but nerve-racking at the same time! And when Mayor Burns called out my name, why I nearly jumped out of my chair. Europe, here I come!"

"And you deserve it," said Mike to the agreement of the others. "We all know how hard you worked on that contest. It's just a shame it was discriminatory..."

"What?" said Kitty, as if she hadn't heard quite right.

"Sure," he said, getting up from the table and putting his plate and utensils into the sink. "Discriminatory. Men weren't allowed to participate."

"Oh, go on you," said Aunt Mary. "He's only fooling with you, Nan!"

"Gosh, Auntie, I wish I was," he said, and they couldn't tell whether he was joking around or not, "but I don't see anything funny about having to point out to the Suffragettes at the table that while they're always talking about equality, this contest was only open to women. I mean, that is what discrimination is, isn't it? Shutting people out of an opportunity because of their color, religions, nationality, or – sex?"

"Oh, honestly," Kitty said, perturbed at the intrusion of his sentiment, whether serious or not. "First of all, most men have regular jobs and probably couldn't get the time off, anyway. And rich men can afford to pay their own way."

"I notice you didn't deny it's discriminatory, you just came up with a reason for it being okay," Mike continued, leaning against the sink. "But speaking of women's rights, I certainly hope you don't think those London suffragettes are justified pulling off some of those escapades that have been on the front pages all week."

"Oh, Mike, this is a happy night," said Maggie, "let's not argue all this stuff now."

"No, no," said Kitty, "if he has a point to make, let him make it."

"Yes," said Aunt Mary, "I've been so busy this week with other concerns. I'm curious about what escapades he's referring to."

"Well, for instance, listen to this," he said, reading from a newspaper clipping he'd fished out of his pocket. " 'Ever since their leader was sentenced to three years in prison, the suffragettes carry on an arson campaign. They threaten to burn the railroad stations in various parts of the United Kingdom. A group of suffragettes attacked the glass covers of thirteen pictures in an art gallery which they smashed with decorated hammers. A considerable number of window breaking and telegraph and telephone wire cutting outrages were committed during the night by militant suffragettes in various parts of the country.' Then there was the destruction of mail in the mailboxes. They actually put, quote, 'corrosive fluids, ink and burning rags saturated with oils' into mailboxes, and a lot of mail was destroyed," he continued with concern, "Why, people have the right to get their mail. Heck, there might have been checks in those boxes that people needed for their families. And not just men, but women, too. Hey, I understand anybody seeking more rights. I just don't believe that any group of people seeking to increase their rights have the right to trample on the rights of others."

"Well, I for one agree with you completely, Mike," said Aunt Nan. "Certainly there has to be law and order or a society is in complete chaos, and when that happens, a lot of innocent people get hurt, like that poor little boy they mention in today's paper who got killed in the riot of the Buffalo street car strike. Then in Auburn, in the twine-workers' strike, there's riots and disorder. According to the newspaper, howling mobs stormed manufacturing plants, but the National Guard is in control now, thank God. Violence just leads to more violence and nothing gets accomplished and there's so much heartache to so many innocent people, especially children, in many cases ruining lives."

Kitty piped up. "And of course you should know I'm fair-minded, and I agree completely with everything Aunt Nan said."

Aunt Nan continued as she glanced over at Mike. "The fact that some hot-headed women go too far has nothing to do with the fact that American women deserve the right to vote. No matter what else you think about any other aspect of the movement, your mother and your sisters and your dear old aunties deserve the simple right to cast a vote for the leaders in the country whose decisions impact our lives every bit as much as yours. And the simple right to work if we need work and we're qualified to do it."

"Bravo!" said Kitty, standing and applauding, and in a moment, all of the women and both girls were clapping as well.

"Okay, okay," said Mike, chagrined, "I've got to see Frankie before it gets too late." He walked toward the door and turned and said, "I'll be back to walk you home, Aunt Nan."

"Thank you, Mike," Aunt Nan smiled. "You're a good boy."

He smiled on his way out the door and Pa and Pat saw that as their cue to excuse themselves from the table, Pa to hook up with friends at the pub and Pat to hit the books before bedtime.

"Well now, one thing I'm sure we can all agree on is how nice it is that things are getting back to normal after the flood," said Maggie. "Have you seen the flood sales all over town? You really ought to check them out, girls!"

"Oh, speaking of the girls reminds me," said Kitty. "There's a free sewing class being sponsored by the Protestant Church on Thursdays at seven in the hall across from Proctor's Theatre, and it's open to the public. Mrs. Holbrook, who works with me, told me her sister is teaching the classes, and she's really a great seamstress. I've already signed up Mary, Molly and me. It's a great opportunity for anyone who would like to learn more about sewing, so spread the word. Now before we get on to any other subjects, Aunt Nan, you were telling us all about the contest. What more were you going to say?"

"Oh, just how happy I was about being one of the winners," she continued. "But you know, I couldn't help feeling sorry for the women who lost. Believe you me, I know how much time and effort it took to participate, and I can only imagine the great disappointment at not winning. But what surprised me the most was how many of the women who were in the lead last week were *not* the final contest winners in the long run. And of course they extended the contest that extra week because of the flood, because it would have been impossible for many of the candidates to send or bring their subscriptions and money into the Times office, I couldn't help wondering if some of the women held back subscriptions, or if having that extra week enabled them to get more subscriptions? You have to wonder, if the flood hadn't pushed everything back a week, would there have been different winners? I guess we'll never know. But I thank God that I'm going to Europe!" she declared with great enthusiasm.

"When exactly are you going?" Kitty inquired.

"And where exactly will you be going?" Mary questioned.

"Well," Nan said, reaching into her bag, "I have the itinerary with me.

"Let's see now, today is April 8th, so it's just about ten weeks away," Aunt Nan smiled excitedly. "We leave on the afternoon or evening of June 25th for New York City. The next day, we sail from Hoboken, New Jersey on the Hamburg American Line – that's one of the best cruise lines in the world – and we arrive in Hamburg, Germany, on July 8th. The next day, we travel by train to Berlin. But instead of telling you now about the details of the trip, I'll just tell you about the countries we're going to. I've already decided to leave a copy of the trip with Kitty. From Germany, we are going to the Netherlands, then on to Belgium, France, England and Ireland.

"The Emerald Isle," said Aunt Mary with an obvious reverence in her voice.

"Oh, when Irrrish Eyes are sssmilin'!..."

"'Tis like a morn in spring!" Mary chimed in.

Annie was sitting in between Kitty and Mary and she thought a second and sang out, "In the lilt of Irish laughter..."

They looked from one to another and smiled and joined in singing together, "You can hear the angels sing. When Irish hearts are happy, all the world seems bright and gay. And when Irish eyes are smiling, sure they'd steal your heart away."

There were peals of laughter such as had not been heard in the house in ages.

"When you're in Ireland, will you be going to Limerick?" Aunt Mary asked. "I remember our dear mother saying that at one time her father owned a shoe factory in Limerick."

"I don't believe so, but let me double-check the schedule," said Aunt Nan, reading aloud, "On Friday, August first, a 'jaunting car ride' through Dublin -- "

"Oh, how jaunty!" Kitty tittered.

"You don't know how right you are, Kitty. I looked it up in the dictionary and a 'jaunting car' is also called a jaunty car. So I *will* have a jaunty car ride!" She laughed.

"What is a 'jaunty car'?" Mary asked.

"It's a two-wheeled cart, pulled by a single horse, with seats placed lengthwise, back to back, instead of facing forward."

"Oh, doesn't that just sound lovely?" said Aunt Kate. "A ride through the Irish countryside..."

Aunt Nan returned to the schedule and announced, "Saturday to Killarney for a couple of days, and Tuesday to Blarney Castle."

Annie exclaimed excitedly, "Aunt Nan, will you be able to kiss the Blarney Stone?"

"Well, I don't know about that, but it really would be something special, wouldn't it?"

She turned her eyes once more to the schedule she was holding in her hand. "Let's see now, Wednesday we will be in Cork. Thursday, August 14th we will continue to Queenstown and embark for Philadelphia, where we are scheduled to arrive Saturday, August 23rd, then home to Troy on Sunday the 24th."

Kitty exclaimed, "No wonder you're so happy. That sounds like a fantastic trip."

Aunt Nan looked at her sister Mary as she said excitedly, "I just realized that I'm going to be in Ireland on your birthday, August 14th."

"I couldn't be happier that you're going to be in Ireland on my birthday. You can celebrate for all of us, in the beautiful land of Mama and Papa's birth."

"It's wonderful," Aunt Kate added.

"Amen!" said Maggie. "Thank God!"

Then Kitty said, with concern in her voice, "I'm always well aware of the fact that while some people are so happy as we all are now, other people at the same time have good reason to be sad. When you mentioned London, I couldn't help feeling sorry for Mrs. Pankhurst. Did you see the paper?"

"I didn't," said Aunt Mary. "What happened?"

"Well," Kitty began as she searched through the newspaper, "Mrs. Pankhurst defended herself well, but they gave her three years in prison!"

"Oh, my goodness!" said Maggie as Aunt Kate and Aunt Mary shook their heads in disbelief and sadness.

"What was she charged with?" Nan questioned.

"Here it is," said Kitty, "She was charged with having 'counseled certain persons whose names are unknown to place feloniously and maliciously certain gunpowder and other explosive substances with intent thereby to damage David Lloyd Sturges' country house at Walton Heath.' But of course she was innocent. Mrs. Pankhurst would never counsel anyone to do any such thing, and they know it! She pleaded not guilty," Kitty went on, reading directly from the newspaper again, " 'As the sentence of three years fell from the judge's lips, the women in the courtroom broke out in a chorus of shame and outrage. The women suffragette sympathizers went wild.' Well, you can imagine why! 'Standing on the seats, they shrieked at the court, the room resounding with such cries as, 'Keep the flag flying' and 'We will arrive.' The police were powerless to quell the tumult. The judge's warning that he would commit the entire party of women to prison for contempt of court fell on deaf ears, and they left the court singing, 'March on, March on.' It goes on to say that before she was sentenced, 'she informed the court that she did not wish to testify or to call any witnesses. Her only desire was to address the judge and jury and she spoke for fifty minutes! Mrs. Pankhurst denied any malicious incitement. She said that neither she nor the other militant suffragette were wicked or malicious. She complained that women were not tried by their peers, and she fiercely criticized the man-made laws and said that the divorce law alone was sufficient to justify a revolution by the women. She declared that whatever might be her sentence, she would not submit.' Then she said that from the moment she left the courtroom, she would start a hunger strike. She would, she said, quote, 'come out of prison dead or alive at the earliest possible moment,' and then they sentenced her. Three years!" Kitty exclaimed.

"How unjust!" Aunt Mary sighed indignantly.

"Why, it's an outrage," said Aunt Nan. "How can they hold her responsible for what other people do? She can't control other people."

"But on a more positive note," Kitty continued, "there's another article here just under that one. 'American Suffragettes descended upon Congress yesterday with petitions for a Constitutional Amendment for Women's Suffrage. After a mass meeting in a downtown theater, the petition bearers, more than five hundred in number, marched to the Capitol in a body. At the foot of the Capitol steps, the marchers divided, one party going to the Senate side, and the other to the House. Both eventually joined in the Rotunda, where members of both branches were bombarded with petitions. The bearers represented every Congressional District in the country. While galleries in the Senate were especially reserved for the marchers and their adherents, no bands or banner were admitted to the Capitol.'" As Kitty set the paper onto the table, she exclaimed, "So, little by little, our cause is progressing."

"It certainly sounds so," said Aunt Mary.

And so the evening went from topic to topic, and soon it was time for Mary and Annie to go to bed, from where, later, Mary listened intently. Finally, her ears perked up when she heard Aunt Nan whisper, "Go and check on the girls. If you're sure they're asleep, I'll tell you the latest about that over-aggressive chauffeur."

As usual, Mary played her part well, and in a moment she heard Aunt Nan continue.

"Actually," said Nan, "before I tell you about that, let me tell you the latest about the neighbor and the cheating husband. Well, The Old Lady called somebody to let the woman know that her Irish Catholic husband was cheating on her. I know she was delighted as she told her friend very loudly while I was passing the room. This way she had a double whammy. He was Irish and Catholic. I made believe that I didn't hear her as I walked by the room.

"Now, with regard to Maurice, just wait until you hear this one! On Sunday afternoon, Victoria and John and the whole family, including The Old Lady, had gone to dinner at the Harrisons, and of course Joseph had driven them. John had given Maurice the day off and he even said he was going to Albany to visit a cousin of his, and Victoria had told Nellie that she could have the afternoon off, too, since there was no one at home. Now, even though I should have been tired after staying up half the night and going to early Mass, I've been busy with the contest these past few weeks that I'd gotten behind on a few things, including my ironing, and so I thought, perfect, I'll have the whole house to myself and I'll catch up on everything undisturbed. Well, I set up my ironing board in the library so that I could listen to some relaxing music on the Victrola.

"So there I was, ironing away and singing along to this beautiful music and I had just set the iron down on the holder when all of a sudden someone grabbed me from behind. I was so startled and frightened that it took a second to think straight. I struggled but it was obvious whoever it was, he was stronger than me, and he wasn't letting go. When I heard his voice, I realized it was Maurice --"

"Oh, Aunt Nan!" Kitty exclaimed as her voice acknowledged disbelief.

"He said to me, 'I'm not going to hurt you. I just want you to listen to me. Then I promise I'll let you go.' 'You take your hands off me right this minute!' I said sternly, but he completely ignored my protest and started telling me some story about a cousin of his in New York and some Irish barmaid, I finally figured out that from that experience, somehow his cousin had convinced him that Irish women are overly affectionate, and even passionate!"

"Oh, my Heavens!" said Aunt Kate.

"Well, I said to him, 'Let me set you straight. In the first place, contrary to what your cousin may have told you, most of the Irish girls I know are proper young ladies and very good Catholics and wouldn't dare do what you seem to suggest.'"

"Good for you, Nan!" said Aunt Mary.

"Then he said, 'So you're Catholic. I'm Catholic, too. You just want to play hard to get. But that's okay, I like that kind of a woman.'"

"Oh, the nerve!" Kitty exclaimed.

"I said, 'You take your hands off of me right this minute or I'll scream.' And he said, 'Go ahead and scream if you want to. Everybody's gone.' And then I realized it was true, everybody was gone!

"Then he said, 'But there's no reason for you to scream, anyway. I wouldn't hurt you, I just want you to listen to me.' I thought, 'I'm sure he thinks I'm just another servant. Who would have told him I've been with Victoria and John for so many years? Nobody.'"

Kitty spoke up, "That's what I don't understand, Aunt Nan, Why don't you just tell John or Victoria? Why, they'd get rid of him and he wouldn't be able to bother you anymore." The others agreed.

"Well, I've thought of that, but I don't want to cause any trouble for Victoria or John with The Old Lady. She'd never believe that he would do anything wrong. She sees him as a perfect servant. He appears to be very polite and kind and very accommodating. The way he bows all the time, he certainly knows his place, and of course that's the most important thing to the Old Lady. I think he's figured out that I'd be too embarrassed to say anything, and if I did say something, I think he's prepared to just start apologizing all over the place that he was so sorry that he had innocently done something that caused me to misunderstand his intentions, making me look stupid. But anyway, I really feel as if I should be able to handle it myself by staying a step ahead of him. From now on, I'll make sure that I find out where he is and when he'll be back.

"As I stood there with him still holding onto me from behind, I thought to myself, talking to him is not going to do any good. I realized that he is so egotistical that he has a mental block. He really has convinced himself that I'm playing hard to get and that if I listen to him, I'll give in and he'll win me over. So I thought to myself, what can I possibly do right this minute to get out of this situation? So with a plan in mind, I said, 'Go ahead and talk, I'm listening.' And since I had stopped struggling, he loosened his grip a little, but his hands were still clasped together in front of me. So all of a sudden, very fast, I lunged forward and pushed his hand onto the hot iron and as he gave out a loud howl, his hands flung away from me and I pushed him sidewards so that he wouldn't knock over the hot iron and I turned and I ran up those stairs two at a time, and into my room, and locked the door fast. My heart was pounding so fast I thought it would never get back to normal, but at least I was safe from him. And even though a few minutes later I heard the door slam, I still was not convinced that he'd left the house. I wouldn't have put it past him to double-back, so I didn't leave my room until I heard the sweet-sounding voices of the family. So don't worry, I'll by on my guard and maybe in the course of time he'll finally get the hint and stop bothering me."

CHAPTER SEVEN

Since her children had grown older, Maggie had gotten into the habit of going to morning Mass. Father Duffy had just completed the Mass and changed his vestments and was now hurriedly rushing out with Communion to give a dying man the last rites of the Catholic Church.

Maggie was kneeling in front of the Statue of the Blessed Virgin Mary saying her Novena. She had hardly started when she heard heartbreaking sobs a short distance behind her. She turned around and saw Mrs. Powell, a woman who lived on the next block. Mrs. Powell was kneeling on the kneeling bench two pews behind Maggie. She had her face in her hands and was leaning on the pew sobbing with such force that her whole body was shaking.

Maggie's first thought was that something must have happened to her husband or one of her children to cause her this heart-rending grief. Warm, sympathetic Maggie rushed to her side to console her. She put her arm around her shoulder and with a voice filled with concern, said, "Oh Mrs. Powell, did something happen to one of your children? Or your husband?"

But Mrs. Powell was too distraught to answer immediately. She kept on crying, trying to catch her breath. Finally, she stammered, "No, my children and my husband are all right."

"Oh, thank God," Maggie answered. She said a silent prayer, asking God to help her help Mrs. Powell. Then she patted her on the shoulder as she said, "Mrs. Powell, it grieves me to see you so sad.

Couldn't I help in some way?"

"Nobody can help me," she replied sadly, as more tears rolled down her tear-stained cheeks. "I feel as if I'm bleeding inside, it hurts so much."

"What is it, Mrs. Powell, what is it that's making you feel that way?"

"Oh, Mrs. O'Neill," she said, blowing into her handkerchief and wiping her eyes, "I think if I don't tell somebody, I'm going to explode or go crazy and have a nervous breakdown. I just found out my husband has been cheating on me." She started sobbing again as she choppily said, "Ever since this woman called me several nights ago, I haven't been able to sleep and my stomach is tied up in knots and I feel so low and discouraged, and yet at the same time, I feel hurt and angry."

"Oh, Mrs. Powell, I'm so sorry," Maggie said with compassion on her face and in her voice.

And then realizing what she had blurted out, Mrs. Powell looked worried. "Oh, I shouldn't have told you. I don't want anybody to find out. I don't want my children to know that their father has committed adultery. It could hurt and embarrass them."

"Oh, Mrs. Powell, don't worry about that. I promise you that I will never, ever tell anyone. Now you come home with me and I'll make you a nice cup of hot tea. There's no one home right now and maybe we could think of some way that I could help you."

Mrs. Powell hesitated, but Maggie's warm, concerned eyes and caring manner comforted her. She blew her nose again and mopped up her tear-stained face and caught her breath and she managed a weak smile.

As Maggie poured the tea, Mrs. Powell seemed a little more calm, as if she had momentarily accepted the painful news. Mrs. Powell looked at Maggie pouring the tea, and she couldn't help thinking of her mother and all the times as a child and as an adult, she had shared not only a cup of tea but so many hopes and dreams and disappointments with her mother. Maybe it was the love and concern in Maggie's voice and in her actions that reminded Mrs. Powell that even after three years, she still missed her mother so very much.

Mrs. Powell felt a need to bring up and get out of her system the hurt and the anger and frustration that she was feeling. She looked at Maggie and felt as if she could trust her, but she still needed to be reassured one more time.

"Mrs. O'Neill, I really appreciate your friendship and kindness at this time. If I were to confide in you, could you give me your word that you would never, ever tell anybody, not even your husband or your children or your sisters or anybody what I tell you?"

"Of course, Mrs. Powell," Maggie said. "If it would help you in any way, I make that promise to you to never tell anyone what you choose to tell me."

And with this assurance, Mrs. Powell seemed a little more calm as she sipped her tea and sadly began her pathetic story.

"When we talked everything over, my husband said it had all started quite innocently. As you know, my husband is an insurance man, and he used to collect this woman's and her aunt's insurance during the day at her aunt's house. Then a little over three years ago, her aunt died. The woman was working during the day, so he had to go there in the evening to settle the claim on the insurance policy and keep collecting her insurance. He said when he first saw her, she reminded him of me. She had the same color hair and eyes and was about the same height and weight and around the same age, and she was very nice and friendly, but there was a sort of sadness about her.

"Then as he went every month to collect her insurance, she always seemed very glad to see him, and started offering him tea and crackers. He said she told him that she was very lonely since her aunt died, and that she had no other relatives or close friends nearby. He said he felt very sorry for her. This went on for a few months, and then came the evening when he went there as usual to collect her insurance money, and she started crying on his shoulder and telling him the story of her life.

"From what she told him, she had a husband and two very young children, and lived in a little town in another state. There was a traveling salesman who used to go through the town every couple of weeks, and he'd stop in. To make a long story short, it ended up that she and the traveling salesman decided to run away together. So she left a note for her husband, and went with the salesman the next time he came to town.

"They were together for a week when he decided to go back to his family. He had never written a note to his wife, and being a traveling salesman, she never found out. So when this woman went back to her husband, he wouldn't take her back. He was really angry. He accused her of making a laughing stock out of him. He said he didn't want to stay married to a woman he couldn't trust, and since it happened once, she'd probably do it again. She said she begged and pleaded with him to give her another chance, but he wouldn't. And then he said he thought the children were better off losing her while they were still too young to understand. He said his mother would take better care of the children. So her maiden aunt in Troy took her in. So my husband said he just felt sorry for her and tried to console her.

"He said after that he just innocently started stopping in every couple of weeks to see how she was doing and she was always so glad to see him. Then before long she started laying her head on his shoulder and kissing him. He said he knew inside that it was wrong, but he told himself she needed comforting, and what harm was there in that?

"Now at the time all this was happening, things were just so bad at our house. The bill collectors kept calling. I even suggested to my husband that we have the phone taken out, because it was just an extra expense and nobody was buying insurance. But he thought things would pick up and people would call soon. Jobs were scarce and our two older boys couldn't find work. They were running wild, staying out late night after night and sleeping late in the morning. And through the day they were always arguing and fighting with each other. They made me so nervous that sometimes I had pains in my chest and I'd find it hard to even swallow liquids. It was as if there were a hard lump in my throat. Sometimes my hands actually shook. I was always so afraid one of them would hurt the other.

"I wanted my husband to sit them down and talk to them, and warn them about staying on the right path, so that they wouldn't ruin their lives. All I could think of was those Shaughnessy brothers. Remember those two brothers who got into a fight, and the one pushed the other, and he hit his head on a sharp object and died? They sent the other boy to reform school. I could never get that poor mother out of my mind, and I was so afraid that something like that would happen to my sons. I kept begging and pleading with my husband to talk to them, because they wouldn't listen at all to me. But all of my words just seemed to fall on deaf ears.

"You know, Mrs. O'Neill, I have three older brothers myself and they were always arguing and fighting. They were all so opinionated and had quite the tempers, and first thing you know they'd get to pushing and punching, but when my mother got nervous and upset over it, my father would sit them down and talk to them. I was quite a bit younger than them, but I still remember him saying, 'You've got a good mother and you're making her nervous,' and they'd realize it and stop. And they had a great love and respect for him and my mother. My father treated my mother like a queen, and they had such a wonderful marriage.

"When my husband first told me he felt sorry for this woman, I couldn't help remembering a woman that my father met years ago and felt sorry for. My father was a mailman, and this woman he used to deliver mail to was from another state, too, and she didn't know anybody, either. And when she told my father she was lonely, he told my mother about her, and she used to come to the house with her little girl, to visit, while my father was at work. Sometimes she and my mother would take us children out walking together. Her name was Mrs. Hogan. She was such a very nice lady. I was only five or six years old at the time, but I can still remember her fixing my hair.

"And when I was a child, we had hard times, too, but my parents sat down together every pay day with a pencil in their hand, and together talked about the bills and who they could pay, and my father would take care of things. That's the kind of marriage I saw and that's the kind of marriage I wanted. When I married my husband, I thought that was the kind of marriage we would have, too.

"When my husband was courting me, he was so attentive and so thoughtful and respectful, and one time when we were at a restaurant, there were some men at the bar speaking quite loudly, using vulgar language, and he even went in and asked the bartender to speak to them, because he was with his girlfriend. I remember at the time, it reminded me of how caring my father was of my mother, and I guess I thought it would always be like that," she said wistfully.

"You know, Mrs. O'Neill, I've always envied you because you have sisters. My brothers are very good to me, but it's not the same. I see you and your sisters talking outside the church and sometimes I see them pass by my house on the way to visit you and I think to myself, I wish I had a sister. And if I did have a sister, I'd like her to be just like you."

"That's so nice of you to say," Maggie smiled. "But as Christians, we really are all sisters and brothers under God."

"Oh, I know, but I mean really, really a sister like your sisters are to you."

Maggie thought for a few moments of just how much her sisters did mean to her, and she realized she didn't know what she would have done sometimes, if it wasn't for her sisters. Then it dawned upon her. "Why, it's very easy to make that wish come true."

"What do you mean?" Mrs. Powell asked in a curious tone.

"What's your first name, Mrs. Powell?"

"Genevieve."

Maggie took her hand into her own as she said, "From this day forward, I, Maggie O'Neill, adopt you, Genevieve Powell, as my sister. I promise to give you the same love and respect as I give to my other three sisters. So help me God." And then Maggie got up and went over and embraced Genevieve and kissed her warmly on the cheek.

Genevieve was noticeably pleased and gave Maggie the best smile she could muster, considering the sadness she was feeling, just below the surface. "Thank you so much, Mrs. O'Neill. You don't know how much this means to me. And I promise in return to think of you as my sister. I only hope that one day I can help you as much as you've helped me today."

"Mrs. is far too formal for sisters, so from now on just call me Maggie, Genevieve."

Genevieve faintly smiled. "Thank you, Maggie. You've already helped me more than you'll ever know. But I don't want to keep you from your work."

"Don't you worry about the work. Work will always be here. Helping a sister in need is much more important."

And thus began a close friendship. Genevieve started visiting Maggie most afternoons after lunch, and the closer they became, the more she opened up and poured out, and shared with Maggie her deepest thoughts and heartache.

CHAPTER EIGHT

Kitty was barely inside the door when Mary rushed to her side. "Oh, Kitty, thank goodness you're home!" She exclaimed in a panic. "I've been a wreck all day!"

"What is it, Mary? What's happened?" Kitty insisted, her heart skipping a beat.

"Molly and I can't go to the sewing class anymore," Mary answered with great concern in her voice.

"What? The sewing class?" said Kitty. "Oh, for Heaven's sake, Mary, you scared me half to death. I thought something terrible had happened."

"It is terrible!" Mary insisted. "The Head Sister said we can't go."

"I know the Sister you mean," Kitty sighed with a sense of relief at the non-emergency which mixed with concern at how upset her younger sister was. "She's the stocky one who looks mad most of the time. Now calm down and tell me what happened."

"Well," said Mary, catching her breath, "The Head Sister came into the classroom today. She found out that some of us were going to those sewing classes sponsored by Protestants, and she said she came into the classroom to put a stop to it. Sister said that a good Catholic must never go to Protestant Churches or gatherings. She looked mad. I sit over to the side of the room in front of the door, so I could see she had a big stick behind her back the other kids couldn't see. She asked who had gone to the Protestant Sewing class. Some of the girls, including Molly, raised their hands, and then Sister had them go up to the front of the room and put their hands out and then she hit them hard on the hands with the stick, saying it was for their own good."

"Didn't you raise your hand?" Kitty asked.

"Well, to tell you the truth, I was just too scared to. I've always been afraid of that Sister. She's the meanest nun in the whole school! I tried not to look at her, so she wouldn't call me by name and actually ask me. I wouldn't be able to lie about it but I figured if she didn't ask me personally, then I really wasn't lying. But then she got really mad at Sister Mary Bernard, because when she saw Sister take the stick from behind her back and realized she was going to hit the girls with it, she said, 'Oh, Sister, couldn't they just say that they're sorry and promise not to go again?' In response, the Head Sister turned toward her as she angrily said, 'Sister Mary Bernard, remember your vows and leave this room immediately.'"

The Head Sister had strong beliefs. She actually believed that punishing these young girls would steer them from going to Protestant Church services and other Protestant gatherings, thus keeping them from being tempted to turn from the Catholic Church, which she believed is the one true church begun by Jesus Himself. She had been taught this by her parents and the good Sisters and the Church itself and she fully believed it.

"Sister Mary Bernard had taken the vow of obedience when she became a nun. She had to obey her superior. She would sooner have had the Head Sister hit her with the stick than have to stand by while she hit these young girls whom she loved. Tears came into her eyes as she waited in the hall, feeling sad and helpless, being fully aware that to say more could make the situation worse. "Oh, Kitty, Molly's hands were so red! And she said they were still stinging all the way home from school."

Kitty had listened intently and shook her head disapprovingly. "As far as I'm concerned, I think we're lucky the Protestants allowed us Catholics to participate in the first place."

Mary continued. "Anyway, Molly and I aren't going to the sewing classes anymore."

"Oh, Mary, don't do that. It's important to learn as much as you can about everything in life. It'll make you more independent, and less likely to have to rely on other people for your keep. Maybe I should talk to that Sister and explain."

"Oh, no, Kitty, no!" Mary exclaimed nervously. "Please! Promise me you won't say anything! In fact, right before she left, she said that if she finds out that any of us went to the class but didn't come forward and get what they deserved, then she'll give them twice as many whacks!"

Kitty sighed, "She must have taken that sour disposition into the convent with her. Thank God most of the Sisters aren't like her. I honestly have to wonder how somebody like her ever went into the convent in the first place. She certainly doesn't know what the words love and mercy mean. Too bad they can't all be like Sister Mary Bernard, or Sister Philomena, or Sister Amelda. And everybody says that Sister Pauline is like a walking saint."

Mary pleaded. "So, please Kitty, promise me that you won't go near any of the Sisters so that the head sister won't find out."

Realizing how important it was to her, Kitty said, "All right, Mary, I won't say anything. Now calm down, take a deep breath, everything's going to be just fine."

Mary had always loved school, but now she dreaded even getting up to get ready. When the alarm went off, she just wanted to pull the covers up over her head and hide from the world. The first thing she thought of when she woke up in the morning was that this could be the day Sister found out, and punished her, not only for attending the classes, but also for deceiving her. One night, she dreamed that Sister had found out about her attending the class and told her to come to the front of the room, where she held a stick that was three times as long and much thicker, and she just kept hitting Mary on the hands until they turned bright red. These thoughts made her feel nervous and sad. Even though she thought she had been right, she started feeling sorry that she hadn't just admitted it in the first place and gotten her whacks over with instead of silently suffering all the extra worry and apprehension. But, in time, she realized that her little secret was safe, and it moved to the back of her mind, as such things always seem to with the passage of time, and she began to look forward to school again, and to enjoy it as much as she ever had before.

CHAPTER NINE

As Mary rinsed and handed the very last dish in the sink to Annie, who dried it and put it in its place in the cupboard, there was obvious concern in Aunt Nan's voice as she continued to speak about the strikes and riots around the country and events throughout the world that had filled the week's newspapers and brought them all a growing sense of unease.

"It's hard to believe just how chaotic things have been this week," Nan said. "Did you read that in Buffalo, the armories were filled with soldiers because of the trolley strike? Apparently, they'd been patrolling the streets to protect the strike-breakers, and the trolleys were attacked! Windows were smashed with stones and strike-breakers were actually pulled off the trolley cars and beaten. According to the paper, the troops had practically turned the city into an armed camp. At one point, three thousand national guardsmen were called out to subdue an angry mob and the troops actually fired on the rioters!"

"Oh, that's just terrible," said Aunt Kate.

"Yes, and much worse than we'd heard," Aunt Mary agreed.

"And it all seemed to happen so quickly," said Kitty, "as if all that anger was just building up and then, suddenly, it just exploded."

"My heart went out to those poor people," Maggie sighed with concern in her voice, "especially when I saw that picture of a wounded soldier being lifted into a car. I always say a prayer and think to myself, 'He's somebody's son or husband. Or father.'"

"Yes, it is sad," Aunt Nan continued. "Thank God the Mayor mediated. Both sides made concessions, the strike is over, and according to Saturday's paper, the state militia was withdrawn."

"Wasn't there trouble in New York, too?" Kitty asked.

"Yes, and it's still pretty bad down there," Aunt Nan continued. "The track laborers on the railroad are demanding more pay and less work. Rioters have used stones and clubs and actually rushed the police right off their feet! One man was killed and several have been wounded. Then there's the strike at International Harvester in Auburn, where they're looking for time-and-a-half for Sunday work. The rope company strikers are working with state mediators. The Teamsters are demanding an increase of pay. They certainly have some valid points and I'm sure most of them deserve an increase, especially if you're forced to work on Sundays. Why, it's your only day off!"

"I certainly can't help feeling glad we don't live in those areas," Aunt Mary added.

"You don't think that sort of unrest could spread to us, do you?" Kitty asked, concerned.

"Well, I don't know, but I certainly hope not," said Aunt Nan.

"Those poor people," said Aunt Mary. "Of course I believe that everyone should get an honest day's pay for an honest day's work, but some of those tactics! Why, it's such a disruption of so many lives. I've been praying extra for everybody, but I have to admit I haven't had much time this week to keep up with the latest about the strikes because of our own problems in Troy. While those other workers are looking for more money, fewer hours and better conditions, they're saying that if the Underwood Tariff goes through, the way it is now, wages here would drop by half because Cluett's makes ninety percent of the shirt collars sold in the United States, and they say that we wouldn't be able to compete in the world market."

"I try to keep up on things as best I can, but I read and re-read everything about that tariff bill and I still don't understand it. It's so confusing."

"Well, I can certainly understand why," said Nan. "Apparently, it's a very complicated piece of legislation, and it seems that different states and sections of the country have different problems with the bill. For instance, I've read about a fight in the House of Representatives over the sugar tariff. And then the other day, the Democrats met behind closed doors to take the iron and steel tariff under consideration. Then there's the 'Anti-Free Wool Democrats' from nearly twenty states who say that if they're outvoted in the caucus, they'll exempt themselves from the binding caucus pledge and continue the fight in the House. And don't feel bad if you don't understand the bill itself, because you're in good company. It mentioned the other day that on the Senate side, study of the tariff bill continued, and that Democrats on the Finance Committee have called in experts to help them analyze the House bill."

Aunt Mary commented, "People at work are already starting to worry they may lose their jobs or have their pay cut in half. They're already living hand to mouth and payday to payday. Some, or I should say most, are barely surviving, with families to support. I went to that meeting last night to see what I could do to help the situation."

Aunt Nan looked at her sister Mary. "I can certainly understand why they're concerned at Cluett's, but thank God, I don't think we in Troy have to worry about some of the chaotic conditions they've got in other parts of the country. But I don't want you ladies to worry about money. We're blessed to have a guardian angel on our side. John has said to me more than once, 'You're family, Nan. If you or yours need help, you just come to me.' He's such a generous man. He's so good to us all."

From the stairwell outside the kitchen door they heard someone whistling, "Take Me Out to the Ball Game," and in bounded Mike with a wide grin.

"My, but it's nice to hear somebody whistle a happy tune to break up all this talk of doom and gloom," Aunt Mary smiled as he made his way around the table, kissing each of his aunts in turn as he greeted them.

"Well, I've got a darned good reason to whistle," said Mike. "The baseball season just opened, and you know how I love my baseball."

"We sure do," said Kitty, "and you're right, Aunt Mary, it is a nice break from the doom and gloom. Of course, I'm a baseball fan, too, so I don't mind hearing about it if the rest of you are game. So to speak."

"Your supper's covered on the stove, Mike," said Maggie. "Let me heat it up for you."

"No, Mama, stay where you are. It'll be hot enough. Your cooking is so good everything tastes delicious hot or cold.

"Well," said Mike as he picked up his dish and sat down at the table, "I heard they were expecting a great turnout for Johnie Evers' Day next month, and I wanted to be sure to get my ticket early. So a couple of us guys went right after work, and," he waved two tickets in the air, beaming, "we got 'em! I got Pat's ticket, too. Is he home yet?"

"No," Maggie answered. "I have his supper covered on the stove, too. He said he would be late because of some special school work."

Mike answered, "That's one of the very few things Pat and I have in common. That we both love baseball."

"Johnie Evers, the hometown boy who made good," said Aunt Nan.

"From Tinkers to Evers to Chance," said Kitty, "who could forget that slogan?"

"The famous double-play," added Mike.

"And now isn't he the manager of the Chicago Cubs?" asked Aunt Nan.

"Sure is!" Mike answered proudly.

"Well, I'm happy for you and 'the guys' that you got your tickets," said Kitty, a tad peeved. "But what gets me mad is, I know his sister and I would love to go and be a part of that great day, but, because I'm a woman, it wouldn't be considered proper."

"That's never stopped you before," Mike teased as he gobbled his dinner. "Besides, I saw in Saturday's paper where President Wilson threw out the first ball of the season in Washington, and his daughter was with him. So you see, you could go, if you really wanted to."

"Oh, sure, I can go to a ball game," Kitty replied, "But I'm talking about Johnie Evers' Day. Going down on the train to New York with a group of friends, getting out into the sunshine for the day with the fans, honoring the hometown boy, cheering on the team, having a cup of tea in the dining car on the way back. But of course it wouldn't be proper, because I'm a woman. Oh, well," she sighed, "I guess I really wouldn't want to spend that much money, anyway. I'd have to take it out of my piano fund."

"Well, then, it's all for the best," Mike grinned.

"You know," Aunt Nan said, "When we were talking about conditions in this country, I couldn't help thinking about Europe, especially as I plan for my trip. I wanted to see the castles in Spain, but frankly, considering the fact that someone tried to kill the King of Spain yesterday morning in Madrid, I wouldn't mind skipping Spain at all on this trip. Just think, three months from now, if all goes as planned, I'll be in Brussels, Belgium.

"According to the paper, the latest there is that the vast political strike for manhood suffrage in Belgium began at dawn yesterday when the night shifts came out of many of the mines and mills throughout the country, leaving them empty except for a few caretakers, told by the Socialist leaders to keep the property from deteriorating. At least a quarter of a million men laid down their tools. Troops occupied many of the great industrial centers of

Belgium, but over there, in contrast to our country, there are placards printed in large type that point out to the working men, 'This is a strike of folded arms, and not of raised fists. Respect the liberty of those who wish to work and the authorities will also respect in like manner the freedom of those who wish to cease work.' Complete passiveness is urged upon the strikers by the Socialist Union, which tells them that, 'Injury done to our opponents is injury done to our cause.'"

"Too bad more of the strikers here don't think that way," said Aunt Kate.

"Yes," Aunt Mary agreed. "It just never ceases to amaze me how some people looking for their rights don't seem to mind, or realize, that they're trampling on the rights of others with their protests and strikes. And when it degenerates into violence, you lose people's sympathy for your plight. It starts to look like it's just a bunch of hooligans making demands instead of what it usually is, which is decent, law-abiding, hard-working people asking for a more manageable work week and a living wage."

"I do believe most people are respectful and law-abiding," said Aunt Nan, "but there are always those hotheads with tunnel-vision who talk themselves and others into believing that, at least in their particular case, the end justifies the means. Then their thinking is so warped that they blame their violence on the people in charge for not giving in to their demands."

Mike felt obligated to put in his two cents' worth. "Like those suffragist fanatics in London. I mean, okay, so they're looking for their rights, fair enough. But apparently they don't care who gets hurt, or even killed, as a result of their actions. It's worse than selfish, it's downright dangerous. Did you see the headlines in last Friday's paper? It read, 'Lady Incendiaries on the Warpath Fired Grandstand.' It didn't sound very ladylike. Apparently that morning they had set fire to the grandstand of the Great Cricket Grounds at Turnbridge, Wales. If I lived over there, I think I'd be afraid to give people like that the right to vote. I'd be afraid they'd vote for radical people like themselves and ruin the country."

"First of all, Mike, please remember what you yourself just said. Some of them. It's not all of them," said Kitty. "But secondly, and more important, you can't deny people the right to vote in a democracy just because you might not like who they'll vote for. Well, I suppose you can, you already are doing that, but how is that democracy?"

"That's right," said Aunt Nan. "And let's not forget that when America gained its independence, men like you weren't allowed to vote because you didn't own property and the landowners didn't trust how you would vote. So where's the difference?"

"And colored men didn't get the right to vote until after slavery was abolished, so there's another group of Americans who weren't initially granted the right to vote, but now have it."

"Just like we will, one day," said Kitty.

"That's right!" they agreed, and cheered in unison.

"All right, all right," Mike smiled uncomfortably, "I was just talking about the radicals."

"And I agree with you, Mike," said Aunt Nan, "about the radicals. Apparently they left behind a photograph of Emmeline Pankhurst, to protest against her imprisonment. But that's just not a constructive way to protest such things. That building was extensively damaged and the loss caused by the fire amounted to several thousand dollars. Then there was an alleged attempt to burn the dirigible balloon sheds and aeroplane parks of the Army Flying Corps at Farnborough. Two lighted candles were discovered and extinguished before any damage could be done."

"Nobody is more in favor of the rights of women than I am," said Kitty. "But I really do think that those few fanatics in London, and there are only a few among thousands, are making a big mistake and hurting the cause of the majority."

"Oh, I agree," said Aunt Mary. "How can they possibly think

they can convince people that they're responsible enough to be trusted with the rights they're seeking, when they act that way? And let's face it, in a situation such as ours, we have to convince the people who have the power that we not only deserve the rights we're seeking, but that we're capable of utilizing those rights in an intelligent and responsible manner."

"Exactly," said Aunt Nan, "and when our group gets to London, I hope I get the opportunity to hear and observe first-hand exactly what's going on over there in the movement. But as for Mrs. Pankhurst, they finally let her out of jail on Friday."

"Oh, thank God," said Aunt Kate.

"Yes, and the article went on to say that she'd stayed on her hunger strike the whole nine days since her sentencing, just as she'd said she would," said Aunt Nan. "Under the terms of her release, she has to report to the police on a frequent basis, and her condition was described by the papers as 'very grave.' She was taken to a nursing home and placed under the care of her doctor."

Kitty said, "I think it's a downright shame things have gotten to that extreme. And the headlines in today's paper aren't going to help, either. Look at this," she said, holding up the front page for all to see. "'The militants display hatred of all things, use torch and bomb. British women persist in making of themselves dangerous and undesirable citizens – Campaign of Destruction, Hastings, England. Militant suffragettes today destroyed the handsome seaside mansion of a Unionist member of Parliament. The women not only set fire to the house, but placed explosives in many of the rooms.' It goes on to report that when the fire brigade was extinguishing the flames, there were explosions in different parts of the house, and a fireman was hit on the head by a piece of metal."

"Oh, isn't that terrible," said Aunt Kate.

"Yes, it is," Mike agreed, shaking his head.

"I can only imagine how concerned mothers must be for the safety of their families over there," said Maggie. "I just pray that no children get hurt from that kind of extreme behavior."

"Well, since we can't physically do anything about it, I guess all we really ever can do in a situation like this is pray, pray, pray," said Aunt Mary.

"Amen to that," said Aunt Kate.

"And speaking of the cause," Aunt Mary continued, "someone told me there were stories and pictures in last week's paper about our own suffragists in Washington, D.C. I was sorry I missed it, but I was so busy."

"Oh, that was in Wednesday's paper," said Kitty, jumping excitedly from her chair. "I've got it in my scrapbook. I'll go get it!"

"And that's my cue to duck out," said Mike good-naturedly, "before Kitty gets started on her favorite subject."

"Don't you want to stay and hear all about the women suffragists?" Mary teased him.

"Why don't you and Annie take notes for me," he winked. "I'll be back in time to walk you home, Auntie," he smiled on his way out the door.

"Thank you, Nephew," said Aunt Nan playfully.

"Here it is," Kitty beamed, "Imagine, there were women from every state in the country! I admired how organized they were," she said as she held open the picture for Aunt Mary to see. "Do you want me to read what it says?"

"Yes, please do, Kitty. You have such a lovely reading voice," said Aunt Mary to the agreement of everyone around the table.

Kitty cleared her throat and began in a full, resonant voice.

"'Votes for Women. Advocates Hope Congress will Heed Recent Visits of Delegates from Every State. Washington, April 9th. Women suffragists the country over hope something definite will come out of the recent visit of delegates from every state of the union to the members of congress at the opening day of the special session of the 63rd Congress. Following their presentation of petitions, formal resolutions proposing the constitutional amendment giving women the right to vote, were introduced in both houses, together with scores of petitions and memorials from various societies and individuals. Senator Chamberlain of Oregon and Representative Mondel of Wyoming introduced their resolutions in their respective houses. The largest delegation of women suffragists that ever presented the cause of 'Votes for Women' to Congress marched to the Capitol and left for every Senator and every Representative a personal plea for his support of an amendment to the federal constitution establishing women suffrage throughout the country. There were five hundred and thirty-one women in the delegation, two from every state and one from every congressional district, and each woman bore in a small envelope a copy of the petition destined for a particular Congressman. Though far less elaborate than the spectacular parade of the women suffragists on the eve of the Inauguration Day, the march through the streets from the Columbia Theater was in some respects more impressive. There was no attempt at allegorical costumes and floats, and dances were omitted. Instead, the delegates, after a mass-meeting at the theater, where several women made speeches, marched in a compact group down to Pennsylvania Avenue and along that thoroughfare to Capitol Hill. Most of the delegates wore white and the uniformity of costume and the carrying of the yellow flags of 'The Cause' and individual state flags at the head of the sections representing each state, were the only attempts at display. The simpler uniform seemed to produce a good effect upon the spectators, who lined the streets. There was no repetition of the horse-play that largely broke up the parade on March 3rd. And the police stationed at intervals along the line of march and the escort that accompanied the closely massed battalion of women had no difficulty in keeping an open passage."

"We don't have the vote in New York yet, do we?" Mary asked.

"No, we don't," Kitty frowned. "How many states so far have given women the vote, Aunt Nan?"

"Nine so far. Wyoming, Colorado, Utah, and Idaho gave women the vote before the turn of the century. Then Washington in 1910, California in 1911 and last year, Kansas, Oregon and Arizona. Although Michigan rejected woman suffrage, they opened the door on it, because they may have the suffrage question put up again to the people. And if it fails, they can try again, and again. That, at least, is encouraging."

"What really annoys me is those ridiculous anti-suffragist women in Washington," Kitty frowned. "I just hope they don't throw a monkey wrench into our chances. Listen to today's paper. 'Opposing Sisters.' Washington, April 15th. Anti-suffragists started today on what their leaders declared would be the greatest demonstration against women suffrage that the country yet has seen... Congress will be assailed and there'll be two public meetings, one on Friday night and the other, the following evening. Their program for the week includes a hearing before the Senate Women Suffrage Committee on Saturday. The suffragists on the same day will present their pleas after the opposing sisters have had their inning.'"

Kitty went on, "I honestly can't understand how any woman could be against other women having the fundamental right to vote for the leaders who make the decisions that affect the lives of every man, woman and child in this country. So don't vote if you don't want to, but sister, don't stand in my way just because you don't want to move forward."

Aunt Nan shook her head and sighed. "I think a lot of times it's a great lack of understanding. Some of those women who oppose the cause very likely come from privileged backgrounds and have no idea just how hard the majority of us have it, how greatly public policies impact our everyday lives and the lives of our children. Maybe if they did, they'd think differently. Now, Elizabeth Cady Stanton's father was a judge in Johnstown, so even though she was financially and socially better off, she saw first-hand just how terribly unjust the laws were for women and children, which is why she's worked so tirelessly to change them. She wrote that when she was young, she heard a woman crying and pleading with her father to help her. The woman's husband had died, and since married women could not own or inherit property at that time, their house and farm had been passed down to their son and he was treating her badly. Judge Cady told her that he was sorry, but there was nothing he could do because of the laws. In fact, years later, when Elizabeth and her husband had moved from Boston to Seneca Falls with their children, her father bought them a house, but it had to be in her husband's name because a woman was still denied the right to simply own a piece of property. Lucky for her, she had a good husband, the abolitionist Henry Stanton. And in 1848, they helped secure passage of a law in New York State giving property rights to married women. But notice I said, married women," she said, "They still hadn't given the right of property ownership to single women. That only came later, and thank goodness, or out of the four of us, only Maggie would be legally allowed to own a piece of property. In fact, 1848 was the same year as the first women's rights convention, but that's a whole other story for another time, and there are other things I wanted to talk about tonight. But before I forget it," she said, digging into her pocket book, "Kitty, I want you to take this two dollars and this coupon and go Friday or Saturday and purchase this five volume set of cyclopedias for the family. It's too great a resource and too good a price to let it slip by. Especially when I saw they'd been marked down from twelve dollars to a dollar ninety-eight! And I know the whole family will make good use of it, especially Pat and the girls.

"It couldn't have come at a better time. When I read the advertisement, I thought to myself, this is perfect. You will all be able to follow my trip, seeing pictures and reading about all the backgrounds of these famous historical places in the cyclopedias."

"Oh, Nan, you're too generous to this family!" said Maggie.

"Nonsense," Nan replied. "It's no more than you'd do for me if the shoe was on the other foot. Besides, these children are as dear to me as if they were my own. And sitting right here we have the next generation of Fogarty women. We've got to do right by them, don't we, sisters?"

To which Aunt Mary and Aunt Kate raised their tea cups in salute and smilingly proclaimed, "Here, here!"

"Oh, Aunt Nan, that is really something to look forward to," Mary exclaimed excitedly. "I will read your schedule every morning to Annie before we go to school. We really appreciate your thoughtfulness, don't we, Annie?"

"Oh, yes," Annie answered happily.

"Speaking of traveling on a boat reminds me that today is the one year anniversary of the sinking of the Titanic."

"Is it, really?" said Maggie. "Why, it doesn't seem possible."

"Those poor people," Said Aunt Kate, while making the sign of the cross and saying in reverence, "Jesus, Mary and Joseph."

"And there, again, the difference between rich and poor," said Aunt Mary, "which in that case was literally a matter of life and death, not only because of the lack of lifeboats but because the poorer passengers were kept down in the bottom of the boat, so even though there were a number of wealthy men who lost their lives, there were whole families of the poor who went down with that ship. I don't think there were any in third class that were saved, were there?"

"I don't believe so," said Nan quietly. "And you know, I have to say that was the only time in my life that I've ever felt sorry for The Old Lady. Her youngest sister was on board that ship, you know, with her husband and children, coming to America. Oh, it seemed as if she cried every day for a month. From what I understand, she hadn't spoken to her sister in years, and she intended to go to New York City to make up with her. There was quite an age difference between the older two and that youngest one.

When the mother died, the father put The Old Lady in charge of the household.

"As time went on, the younger sister got married to a wealthy business man and they moved to New York City.

"I've always thought The Old Lady considered Mr. Richardson far beneath her, but she was twenty-five when they got married and apparently there were no other available men seeking her hand in marriage.

"So when the Richardsons came to America, the youngest sister was left in the care of a governess.

"Well, as fate would have it, there were no young children on their estate for her to play with and unbeknown to them, she started playing with the son of the man in charge of the stables. And even though she was pretty, and as she grew up, went to many parties and social events, and associated with many upper-class young people, it seems her eyes always turned back to him with love.

"She realized that neither of their families would be able to understand, so she eloped with him.

"She left her father a letter which said something to the effect that by the time he read the letter, they would be married and that it was her idea to elope. She told him that she loved Sean and couldn't ever marry anyone else and that she wouldn't be happy living in that beautiful house without him. She asked her father to forgive her and that she would write soon and signed the letter, 'Your Loving Daughter, Elizabeth.'

"Unfortunately, within a few months, the father died of a heart attack. Of course The Old Lady is such a controlling person, she was really angry at her sister and considered that she had embarrassed the whole family. So she just disowned her. Then when her father died, she actually believed it was because of what her sister had done.

"Recently, her sister Elizabeth had written to her New York sister Dorothy to inform her that she and her family were coming to

America and that she would love to see her and The Old Lady again, before she and her family proceeded on to Virginia. She said she loved them and hoped they could find it in their hearts to forgive her.

"So they talked it over and decided they would meet with her at some secluded place in New York City. But they definitely would not meet her family!

"After the tragedy she still blamed her sister for making such a foolish choice marrying someone so far beneath her.

"It never would have dawned upon her, like it dawned upon me, that her sister very likely would have been saved if she had been in first or second class passages. The Old Lady had the money to make that possible."

CHAPTER TEN

"I wonder what's keeping Mike so long," said Aunt Nan, thinking aloud as she checked her watch against the clock on the kitchen wall. "He's usually home by now."

"Oh, my goodness, he is late, isn't he?" said Maggie. "I hope nothing's happened."

"Oh, I'm sure he's fine, Mama," said Kitty, hoping to change her mother's tendency toward worry. "He probably just got to talking with somebody. He'll be along. But meanwhile, Aunt Nan, when you mentioned the Titanic earlier, didn't I read somewhere that it originated in Ireland?"

Aunt Nan replied, "Although it was an English ship, it was built in Belfast, Ireland."

"I remember I was just astonished at the size of it," said Aunt Mary.

"Eight hundred fifty feet long. That's almost three football fields, end-to-end," said Aunt Nan. "And it took three thousand men three years to build it. When it was launched, it was the largest moving object in the world! 'The Unsinkable,' they called it. Of course they never imagined anything could possibly go wrong, and on its maiden voyage, no less!"

"Really?" said Maggie, drawn back into the conversation despite her concern for Mike. "I didn't realize that."

"Was it on its way from England?" asked Kitty.

"Not directly," said Aunt Nan. "It had sailed from Belfast to

Southampton, England, and on to Cherbourg, France. It left Cherbourg on the 10th and arrived at Queenstown, Ireland, on the 11th to pick up the last of its passengers before sailing on to New York. First Class tickets cost from one thousand five hundred dollars to four thousand three hundred and fifty dollars!"

"Oh, can you imagine?" Aunt Kate gasped.

"How on earth could immigrants have afforded such a thing?" asked Aunt Mary.

"Well," said Aunt Nan, "Second Class tickets cost sixty-five dollars, and Third Class Steerage, which an immigrant would have paid for, was thirty-six dollars."

"That much of a difference?"

"What's steerage?" asked Mary, who had gone to bed along with Annie at their usual time but reappeared at the mention of Mike's lateness coming home. She knew it wasn't like him, and although she hid her concern, Mama had picked up on it and patted her hand with a warm smile as she returned to her place at the kitchen table to rejoin the conversation.

"Steerage," said Aunt Nan, "actually refers to the fact that the boat is steered from below decks, by use of the rudder. So 'steerage' always referred to the bottom of the boat, which is where the poorer people, in Third Class on a ship, would be housed."

"Isn't that interesting," said Kitty. "I never knew that."

"I just find word origins so interesting," said Aunt Nan. "And as for the difference in price, First Class was really deluxe accommodations with dinners and dancing."

"And Third Class was 'bring your own lunch and we'll lock you in the hold,'" Kitty said with a note of sarcasm in her voice.

"You're pretty much right, there," said Aunt Nan, "but never mind dinner and dancing, the ship had a wood-paneled library, a swimming pool, Turkish Bath, a squash court and a gymnasium! Yet with all of that, there were only twenty lifeboats for *over* two thousand two hundred people! And at the time, they had more lifeboats than was even required by law! Another thing that's really sad to realize is that they had several warnings about icebergs from other ships. Oh, it really must have been horrible, though. Not only the panic and loss of life, but those in the lifeboats could hear the cries for help from people in the water, which was freezing cold, but they couldn't do anything to help for fear of being capsized by people trying to climb into the boats from the water. And there was fear that when the ship finally went down, the lifeboats would be sucked down into the ocean with it."

"Oh, isn't that terrible," said Aunt Kate with a shiver as she blessed herself and bowed her head and said, "Jesus, Mary and Joseph," an instant prayer.

"And then to find out later on, that some of those lifeboats weren't even filled," said Aunt Nan, "and so many more could have been saved than the seven hundred survivors, that just makes it even sadder. Oh, but listen to this! Not long ago, I read that a man named Morgan Robinson had published a novel in 1898 called 'Futility,' about an Ocean liner called 'The Titan.' In the novel, the Titan is the biggest ship afloat when it strikes an iceberg and sinks in the North Atlantic! Most of the Titans' 3,000 passengers die because there aren't enough lifeboats!"

"When I heard about the Titanic sinking, my first thought was too bad somebody in charge didn't read that novel and put more lifeboats on the Titanic. When you think of all that extra luxury, the cost of more lifeboats would have been nothing in comparison."

CHAPTER ELEVEN

By now Aunt Nan had looked at the clock at least a half dozen times, and with each glance, she grew more impatient. What could possibly be keeping Mike? Here it was going on nine-thirty and was supposed to have been home at nine. A hint of worry mixed with exasperation made her sigh deeply as Mary asked again about the Titanic. The story about "The Millionaires' Special," the unsinkable luxury liner that had gone down on its maiden voyage, had seemed to fascinate her niece tonight, and since Nan hadn't wanted to alert the others to her growing concern and impatience, she had kept the conversation going as a distraction not only for them but for herself as well. Somehow, though, she had a sense that something just wasn't quite right. Mike was always so reliable, and so punctual you could set your clock by him.

Although it had been many years since she'd had to get up early to start the fires in the kitchen, dining room and living quarters' and prepare for the others to awaken and begin their day in the O'Connell household, she had never seemed able to sleep beyond five-thirty in the morning. As Housekeeper, she was responsible for the household, and it was a responsibility she took to heart. These people were not merely her employers and co-workers, as they might have been in a store or factory. They lived together. She had helped raise the children. While the O'Connells took their meals in the formal dining room, the staff ate together in the side room off the kitchen. Housekeeper, Butler, Cook, Chauffeur and maids would sit two or three at a time, or all together at odd moments over a cup of tea and conversation. She honestly felt as if they were members of her extended family, and she knew they felt the same about her. She had a sense of pride in ensuring that everything was in place for a good start to the day. And although the children were adults now and had outgrown "bedtime," by eight or nine o'clock, Nan herself was about ready to nod off. Settling into her double bed with two pillows and a good book while the fireplace glowed warmly during that last forty minutes or hour before sleep took her away from the cares of life, was her own little slice of luxury. And there were still a few things she wanted to do tonight, before enjoying her bedtime ritual.

Those who knew Nan Fogarty would find it hard to believe that a woman of such force and self-assurance would feel the need to have her nephew walk her all the way home at night. But ever since she was attacked by that dog on the way home a few years before, she was deathly afraid of dogs. It was her only real fear, but a powerful one, and understandable, under the circumstances.

That night had been just like so many other nights. It was a clear and crisp spring evening. She'd visited as usual, and enjoyed dinner and conversation with the family. She'd left without a worry in mind, and was enjoying the fresh air and exercise, when she turned the corner and a huge German Shepherd stood squarely in front of her on the sidewalk, growling and snarling, displaying its yellowed fangs. He crouched low to the ground and she feared that he would lunge at her at any second. She was too frightened to move, and she felt her heart pounding wildly against her chest, and her whole body began to shake as she closed her eyes and screamed at the top of her lungs. She heard a rush of movement and opened her eyes to see a big man twice her size swat the dog hard across the hindquarters with a broom, and watched breathless as the dog spun around and advanced toward him, still snarling wildly. Then the man gave the dog one full swat across the face, and the animal turned and ran off through the alley with a yelp.

Even now, just the thought of it sent a cold sweat sweeping over her, and her heart pounded almost as hard as it had that night. She was truly convinced that if that man hadn't been there, that dog would have attacked her, and who knows how badly she might have been bitten. The thought of it made her shudder.

The man with the broom had helped her to calm down and was kind enough to see her home safely. As he walked alongside her, he told her that the same dog had tried to attack him twice already, and that if he hadn't had something in his hand each time, the dog would have succeeded.

He said that he'd confronted the wife of the owner, but she just didn't want to hear the truth about their precious dog. He told Nan that she didn't even believe their dog had snarled and bared his teeth.

"She said, 'I'll tell my husband what you said, but he won't believe you, either.'"

"I told her, 'I know dogs. I have a dog. And I know when a dog is growling and baring his fangs.'"

Nan had agreed that the animal was clearly bad-tempered, and suggested that maybe the owners had never seen that side of the dog, that maybe, to her and her husband, the animal was friendly and even-tempered.

"Even so," said the man, "this is the third day in a row that dog has broken free. The owner got the dog when he was a puppy and he was always tied to the big tree in their yard. Now apparently he has grown strong enough to get loose and he gets out of their yard by digging a hole under the fence.

"My next door neighbors were quite upset because the dog scared their children half to death. He said even though he has a fenced-in yard, he's concerned it's only a matter of time that the dog may leap over it. And he's not going to take any chance of that vicious dog biting his children.

"The first chance he gets, he said he is going to tell those people that his rifle is loaded, and if that dog comes anywhere near his children, he's going to shoot it. And even when he's at work, he said his wife will be home. She's from the country, and she's a better shot than he is! I pointed out that if they aren't concerned about the neighborhood children, maybe they'll be more careful for the sake of their precious dog."

By then, they were at the house, and Nan thanked him and he tipped his hat goodnight and cautioned her to be careful walking alone at night, and it wasn't until long after he'd left and she was settled safely into bed that she realized she'd never gotten his name, and couldn't drop off a proper thank you note with a cake or a pie to show her appreciation. She'd hoped to run into him again one night as Mike walked her home, but never had. Although she knew it wasn't really the case, she thought of him now as a guardian angel who'd appeared just when she needed him, and had vanished as quickly as he'd come to her rescue that night.

Nan was sure Pat would have been glad to walk her home, too, but he was a few inches shorter than Mike and slightly built, while Mike was taller than all of his friends, broad-shouldered and muscular from his years of manual labor. And Mike was not afraid of anything. In fact, should they meet up with that animal one night, she honestly thought the dog would be afraid of Mike instead of the other way around.

"What was that story, Aunt Nan?" Mary asked.

"Hmm?" said Aunt Nan, brought back from her thoughts to the conversation at hand.

"Kitty said there was some story about a family that thought their kids died on the Titanic, but they weren't on the ship?"

"Oh, yes," said Aunt Nan. "I'm always amazed at that element of fate. It's interesting how many people who were supposed to be on the Titanic, for one reason or another, weren't aboard when she went down. I heard about that family story a short time later. It was in Fonda, about thirty miles west of us, past Amsterdam. It seemed the father couldn't afford to bring the whole family from Ireland all at once. So he came over to work, and after some time, he sent for his wife and youngest children. Then he kept on working, and saving, and in a while, he'd saved enough to send for his oldest daughter and two of the other young children. It's a common thing, you know."

"And not just among the Irish," said Kitty. "I went to school with an Italian girl whose father did the same thing."

"Well, they can earn so much more money over here than they could if they stayed over there and tried to save up enough for the whole family," said Aunt Nan. "Anyhow, that girl and her younger brother and sister were scheduled to sail on the Titanic, and when the ship went down, and their names didn't appear on the list of survivors, naturally it was assumed that they had perished, so they had a funeral mass for them. But, thank God, it turned out well, at least for them. Apparently, someone had offered her a bit of a profit on her tickets on the Titanic if she'd sell them, so she did, and pocketed the difference, and she and the younger ones came over on the next ship out of England, the Olympic, which sailed several days after the Titanic.

"Well, can you imagine the shock and delight when the three of them showed up on the family doorstep in Fonda almost two weeks later?"

"Oh, my, it's like something out of a picture show!" said Aunt Kate.

"You know what they say, 'Truth is stranger than fiction,'" said Aunt Mary. "And the truth at this point is that time has gotten away from us tonight. Do you realize it's nine-forty?"

"Oh, my goodness, it can't be!" Kitty exclaimed.

"It is! But I really do think Mike is okay and just got delayed and will be here soon. Kate and I will say extra prayers." She glanced over at Mary as she said, "Mary, you stop at the house on your way to school in the morning and tell your Aunt Kate why Mike was late. Maggie, girls, thank you so much for another wonderful evening!"

"Good night, Aunt Mary! Good night, Aunt Kate!" Mary and Kitty said in unison.

"And I will stop at your house on my way to school tomorrow," Mary added.

"Good night, girls. God bless you and sweet dreams!" Aunt Mary replied.

"And I second that," Aunt Kate smiled, blowing a kiss across the room as Maggie walked with them to the front door.

"Kitty," said Aunt Nan as her sisters left the room, "did Mike say anything in particular about where he was going tonight that might account for his lateness?"

"Not that I know of."

"Oh, this isn't like him at all," Maggie said nervously as she re-entered the room. "He should have been home ages ago. Oh, I hope nothing's happened."

"Now, Maggie, don't get upset," said Aunt Nan. "I'm sure he's just lost track of the time."

Kitty added, "Or maybe he had to help one of his friends do something at the last minute."

Aunt Nan said, "Why don't you see Mary off to bed and check on Annie, and Kitty and I will take a run over to Frankie's. He's probably over there, and just forgot it's Tuesday."

Mike and Frankie had been inseparable since they were little boys, being less than two weeks apart in age and growing up only two doors apart from each other. Even so, Mike always seemed so much older than Frankie, not only because he was quite a bit bigger, but Frankie seemed to defer to him and to let Mike take the lead in their endeavors. They were best friends, and the families used to say that if you were looking for one, you might as well check to see where the other was, because that's where you'd find them both.

Aunt Nan and Kitty arrived at the Kurowski house and Aunt Nan tapped on the front window rather than knocking on the door, hoping to catch someone's attention without awakening the children or anyone else who might already be sleeping.

Frankie's face popped into view and she motioned for him to come out onto the porch, which he did in a minute, nodding good evening to them both.

"Frankie," said Aunt Nan in a low voice, "is Mike here?"

"No, Miss Fogarty," he said quietly.

"He isn't home yet. Wasn't he with you tonight?"

"Well, I..." Frankie stammered, not knowing what to say in answer to the question.

"Well, where is he?" Aunt Nan impatiently asked.

Frankie looked perplexed. He just didn't know how to answer her probing questions and still keep Mike's secret.

Aunt Nan had known Frankie and his family from the time he was a young boy.

"Frankie," she said, "let's get one thing straight. It's late, I'm tired, and I want to go home. But in order for me to go home, I have to know where Mike is and that he's all right. I don't want his mother worrying unnecessarily. Now if you know where he is, you'd just better tell me right now because I am running out of patience with you."

"Gosh, Miss Fogarty, I'm sorry," said Frankie, "but I promised Mike I wouldn't tell where he was going."

"Going?" she said, astonished at the word even as she repeated it.

"What are you talking about, Frankie?" Kitty demanded.

"I promised Mike I wouldn't say."

"Frankie, I don't care what you promised Mike," said Aunt Nan, her voice rising. "But you better tell me where he is right this minute or else."

Frankie's eyes opened wide and he stepped back a little, then sighed. They could see that he was conflicted and concerned.

Frankie looked down at Aunt Nan. He was much taller than she, but there was always a quality in her voice and in her manner that had always told him that when she said 'or else,' she meant business.

Then he glanced over at Kitty. From the time he was young, he was always a little afraid of Kitty. She had always been bossy with Mike and him and all their friends. Kitty was the most dominating, fearless girl Frankie had ever known.

Frankie looked back and forth from Aunt Nan to Kitty. Finally, he motioned for them to follow him down off the porch onto the sidewalk, a little further from the house.

"Well, I guess you're going to find out, anyway," he sighed, speaking just a speck above a whisper.

"Find out what?" Kitty asked.

"Well," said Frankie, "let me explain what happened. Then maybe you'll understand and you won't be so mad at him. Or me."

"Fine," said Aunt Nan. "Explain."

"Well, when Mike got to my house tonight, he was really happy. He was whistling, 'Take Me Out to the Ballgame.' He gave me my ticket for Johnie Evers Day and I paid him for it. I distinctly remember he put it in his right hand pocket on our way over to Mr. Stewart's house to pick up his pay from last week. Mr. Stewart's main customer pays him on Tuesday. Mr. Stewart has always paid Mike on Tuesday in that same big white envelope he collected from his customer. As you know, Mr. Steward is a very honest man, so he always has Mike double-check the amount in the envelope. As usual, Mike left the money in the envelope, doubled it over a couple of times and put the envelope deep down into his left pocket, so he wouldn't lose it. As you know, Kitty, he just takes a couple of dollars for himself for spending money through the week and hands you the envelope to help pay the bills with."

"Yes, Frankie, I know that," said Kitty. "Since the time we were young, Mike's always done his best to help provide for the family, and he's always been so reliable. That's why this is so out of character, and why I wish you'd just get to the point."

"Well," said Frankie, "after Mike put the envelope in his pocket, Mr. Stewart said, 'I'm afraid I have some bad news for you, Mike. I'm going to have to let you go.'"

"Oh, no," Kitty sighed.

"Mr. Stewart explained how with six children at home and Mrs. Steward in the family way, he just couldn't afford to keep him on. He said he always intended for his oldest two, Albert and Freddie, to come work with him after they'd graduated eighth grade, but he's got to have them start right away, even though Albert isn't even all the way through the seventh grade yet and Freddie isn't even going to be able to finish sixth grade. He said between the two of them, they should be able to handle what Mike's been doing by himself. He said he'd be sure to let Mike know if he heard of anybody who needed help, and told Mike to make sure he gave out his name and number at the store so he could vouch for him."

"Mike has worked for Mr. Stewart for five or six years now, ever since he quit school," Kitty said, shaking her head.

"So where is he now?" Aunt Nan asked Frankie. "He certainly couldn't be looking for work at this hour."

"Well," Frankie continued without looking directly at either woman, choosing his words carefully so as to soften the blow and portray Mike in the most sympathetic light possible, "Mike was feeling pretty low, so we went over to Ned's."

"Ned's Saloon?" Aunt Nan exclaimed.

"Uh huh."

"Oh, that's all we need," Kitty sighed, "for Mike to follow after Pa."

"Oh, no," Frankie assured them, "it was nothing like that. Mike thought maybe some of our friends would be there and somebody might know of a job. But nobody did. So we just had a beer and was shootin' the breeze, and then these four fellas we knew from school said they were going to a friendly little poker game, and they asked us if we wanted to go with them – "

Impatient for him to get to the point, Aunt Nan and Kitty exchanged irritated glances and took a deep breath. The only thing that kept them from interrupting was their fear that it'd take Frankie even longer to finish.

"Well," Frankie continued, "we've never played for more than pennies, and that's how the game started out. And Mike actually won a few pots. I whispered to him, 'Mike, why don't we just go home?' But he said he'd look like a poor sport if he left when he was winning. Besides, he said, he had this overwhelming feeling he could win. And he did win a few more pots. But then, even though Mike was against it, the rest of the fellas agreed to up the ante to five, and then ten cents, 'cause most of the players come from better homes and weren't hurting for money at all. So to make a long story short, Mike started losing. And even after he'd lost his spending money, he felt so confident he could win it back, well, he dipped into his pay envelope." Frankie looked at the ground and sighed dejectedly. "Within an hour, it was all gone, and he had to leave the game. By that time he was feeling terrible and trying to figure out what to do next. Then he remembered one of the men said his cousin worked on the docks in New York City and made good money. He looked at Mike and said, 'You're big and strong, I'll bet you could easily get a job there.' I'd left the game when they were still playing for pennies, so I had some money left, and when Mike asked to borrow it for food to hold him over, of course I loaned it to him. I tried to talk him out of it, but you know Mike, once he makes up his mind. He said he'd call you all tomorrow morning from New York and explain it all to you. He made me promise not to tell, so you can see why I... I didn't really want to say..."

"Do you mean to tell me that Mike is on a train right now going to New York City?" Aunt Nan exclaimed.

"Yes, Ma'am," Frankie answered.

"Frankie Kurowski, I could ring your neck!" Kitty glared angrily. "You should have told us right away instead of wasting all this precious time."

Aunt Nan touched Frankie's shoulder as she looked him in the eyes. "Think carefully, Frankie," she said, "how long ago did Mike leave?"

"Less than an hour ago," he told her.

"Come quickly, Kitty," she said, linking her right arm with Kitty's left arm as they hurried back to the O'Neill house. On the way, Aunt Nan told Kitty to explain everything to Maggie in such a way as to minimize the situation, while she called John to let him know she'd be late.

As they walked through the kitchen door, Aunt Nan went immediately to the telephone in the living room. Kitty went to kiss her mother and reassure her that everything would be fine.

Nan called John and explained what had happened and why she would be late getting home. John immediately began asking questions. What train is he on? Where was he going? What time did he leave? As soon as Nan gave him this information, John, who always had a train schedule on his desk, informed her that the next train to New York City would be leaving in forty-five minutes, and that if she wanted him to, he could send Joseph to pick her up and take her to the train station and get her a ticket on the train.

In the meantime, he would call the Kingston police and have them take Mike off of the train on suspicion of theft. John was from Kingston and knew several policemen there.

"The main thing is to get him to come home. New York City is no place for a young man like Mike. Try to talk him into coming home, but as a last resort, if he won't come freely, tell him I will press charges. We can drop them once he gets home safely and you've had the chance to convince him to stay home."

Joseph, John's chauffeur, picked her up, drove her to the station, purchased her a ticket and handed her a white envelope containing money and telling her that Mr. O'Connell said to use as much money as she needed.

When Nan arrived in Kingston, there was a policeman waiting to take her to the police station, where she found Mike both very surprised and at the same time notably happy to see her. He looked a little worried as he told her the police were holding him for theft. He said, "I didn't steal anything from anybody, there must be some mistake."

Nan explained to him what John had done so that she could bring him home. Right away she scolded him for making his Mother worry so.

"Don't you think it's already hard enough for your Mama putting up with your Pa, without you adding to her burden? Having her worrying about you being all right? I'm so disappointed in you. For Heaven's sake, what were you possibly thinking of? I really thought you were too smart to do such a foolish thing."

"I'm sorry, Aunt Nan, but you wouldn't understand. I lost my job tonight and I didn't know when I'd find another one."

"Oh, so you think that's smart? You lost your job, so you start gambling?"

"I know it's hard to understand, but I'm good at playing poker and I had this overwhelming feeling that I was going to win. It was such a strong feeling that I had to try. I even envisioned winning a whole week's pay."

"And did you win?" she asked with a bit of sarcasm in her voice.

He looked sheepishly as he replied, "No."

"Then listen to me very carefully. The next time you have that overwhelming urge to gamble, just remember this day and all the extra worry you caused your Mama and a lot of other people."

"I'm really sorry, Aunt Nan, and I promise you, it will never happen again. I've learned my lesson. In fact, I feel like a heel, knowing I let everybody down."

Officer O'Grady, who had picked Mike up at the train station, was a childhood friend of John's. He was sitting close by listening to the conversation between Aunt Nan and her nephew Mike. As he walked over to them he said, "That's the most important thing, Mike, that you've learned a lesson and promise that it will never happen again. Miss Fogarty, you look as if you could use a nice hot cup of tea or coffee, and perhaps something to eat, to hold you over 'til you get back to Troy. There's a nice little restaurant close by and I've checked the train schedule, so we have plenty of time. Then I'll drive you to the train station and you'll be all set."

On the train, on the way to Troy, Mike fell asleep, but Nan was too keyed up to sleep, and was very concerned that if she went to sleep, she might miss getting off the train in Troy. She said some prayers and tried to think of happier times.

A couple of hours later the train pulled into the Troy station. The light of the new day was just beginning to brighten up the city.

Thank God we're home, she thought, as she shook Mike to awaken him.

As Aunt Nan stepped off the train, she was surprised but glad to see John standing on the platform.

"Glad to see you got back safe and sound, Nan," he said to her with a smile on his face.

She turned slightly to the left as Mike stepped off right behind her. "John, you remember my nephew, Mike O'Neill, don't you?" she said with a tired smile upon her face.

"Of course," he smiled, as he looked at Mike and put his right hand out to shake hands with him. "It's nice to see you again, Mike. I think it's a couple of years since I last saw you."

Mike put his right hand out right away and shook John's hand as he said, "Mr. O'Connell, it's nice to see you again, Sir." And then he sheepishly said, "I really want to thank you for helping my aunt and me. I really appreciate it." His eyes were looking toward the ground, trying to avoid John's eyes.

"Mike, I heard you were looking for a job," John said smilingly.

"Yes, Sir, I am," Mike replied.

"I can use a good strong young man like you. Come to my office tomorrow morning at eight o'clock and I'll put you right to work. How does that sound to you, Mike?"

"Great, Mr. O'Connell. Thank you so much. I'll be there!" Although Mike was tired, he was very happy at that moment. John had a good reputation as an employer.

As they walked toward the car, Nan wondered if John needed another worker or if he was hiring Mike for her sake.

Joseph, who was standing next to the car, opened the back door for Aunt Nan and Mike to get in, while John opened the front passenger side door and hopped in.

They dropped Mike off at his darkened house. As he hesitatingly opened the door, he was hoping everyone was sleeping. He just didn't feel up to a lot of questions.

Kitty, who was a very light sleeper, heard the turn of the door handle and came into the kitchen.

Mike looked at her as he whispered, "I'm sorry, Kitty."

Kitty rushed over and gave him a hug and kissed him on the cheek. She had a lump in her throat and a few tears surfaced as she said, "Oh, Mike, thank God you're home. Everything will be all right. You and I will work things out, like we always have."

"Yes, Kitty, things are going to work out because Mr. O'Connell has given me a job. I'm going to start working for him tomorrow."

"Oh, thank God," Kitty replied.

CHAPTER TWELVE

Nan was feeling exceptionally happy that Saturday morning, thinking of how she had been able to help her nephew Mike and at the same time alleviate her sister's unnecessary worry. She also felt a sense of satisfaction that she had been able to avoid Maurice all week.

Knowing that John had sent Maurice on a couple of errands, Nan felt confident as she went down the concrete steps to bring up the weekly supply of wine bottles from the cellar.

At one time this part of the cellar had been outside the house, but many years ago, when the kitchen was enlarged, John thought it was a good idea to extend the cellar area, too, so that there would also be an inside entrance to the cellar.

Although John owned a brewery, he preferred to drink wine and had quite a variety of wines in his cellar.

Before Maurice arrived, Nan and Joseph routinely had for years brought up the wine bottles on John's list, every Saturday morning.

Before John, who was slightly nearsighted, had started courting Victoria, Joseph Coleman was already working for him as a driver and all around helper. John always sat in the back seat of the vehicle, keeping track of all the details of his business, or reading papers and other things he considered important.

Joseph was about ten years older than Nan. They had great respect for each other. She considered him as being very dependable and one of the most unselfish people that she ever met. Many times they had shared a smile or a laugh over some cute things the children had said or done as she bundled them up and he helped them into the car and drove them to school or a variety of other places. Nan suspected that Joseph loved those children almost as much as she did. Over the years she had grown to love him like a brother.

When John hired Maurice, he informed him that he would be Joseph's assistant and to do whatever Joseph instructed him to do. Likewise, he instructed Joseph to keep Maurice busy by giving him some of his own chores to do.

Nan picked out the three wine bottles that were on John's list and put them on top of the counter. Her first thought was to carry two bottles up and come back down for the third bottle. But she assured herself that the bottles were not that big and she could easily carry the three bottles in one trip. She placed the three bottles in a row in her left arm and held them secure against her body and started up the stairs.

These concrete stairs were spaced higher than average steps. She did not clear the seventh step. Instead, her right shoe hit the step and threw her off balance. Everything happened so fast. She could feel the middle bottle slipping and heard the loud crash of glass. Her first thought was to make sure she didn't fall on the remaining bottles. Trying to catch her balance, her left wrist slammed into the corner of the step. She felt excruciating pain. Before she could catch her breath, she felt her ankle bang against a step further down the stairs. She cried out in pain, but no one was in the kitchen to hear her. Slowly she took the first bottle out of her left arm and placed it on the corner of the stone step above. Her knee felt wet. She assumed it was from the wine. It also felt kind of numb. She crawled to the top of the stairs and opened the door. She called out for Doris, the maid, who was dusting in the dining room. She came right away.

Doris looked at Nan in disbelief. "Oh my God, Nan, what happened?" she said with great concern in her shaky voice as she helped her over to a chair close by.

Nan sat down quickly, as she tried to catch her breath.

Doris' eyes widened and her mouth fell open as she exclaimed, "Nan, look at the blood on your dress."

At first glance, Nan had thought it was wine, but now she realized it was blood. She pulled her long skirt up over her knee and was shocked to see that although her stockinged leg had numerous bloody cuts, to the right of her left knee cap was an opening not only in her stocking, but in her knee itself, that was about two inches long and one inch wide. She could actually see the inside of her knee and the pool of blood sitting there.

John had heard the excited voices and came running into the room at that moment. He took one glance at Nan's knee and instructed Doris to stay with Nan while he called Dr. Spencer.

Dr. Spencer arrived quite quickly. He was a nice-looking man with hazel eyes and graying hair and a very pleasant manner. He was not only the O'Connell's family doctor, but also for all of those in the household. Nan always felt that he was so good with the children and that he was a very special, caring doctor. He gave her some pills for the pain. It took him quite a while to remove glass and stitch up her knee and other smaller cuts on her leg.

He confirmed what she suspected, that her left wrist was broken.

All the time he was trying to keep her in good spirits. He told her under the circumstances, it could have been worse, but he thought she'd be good as new within a few weeks.

CHAPTER THIRTEEN

It was a cool, sunny morning, a perfect spring day, as Mary started on her way to school. She had only gone a block when she saw a group of people standing around the end of the sidewalk and off the gutter into the road. They were laughing and making sly remarks. Her curiosity pushed her through the crowd to see what was so funny.

There, in the gutter was Pa, trying so hard to get up. Each time he would just manage to get so far up and then he'd topple over again. His body was so contorted that he couldn't seem to straighten himself out long enough to stand. He was mumbling a few incoherent words.

Compassion momentarily gripped Mary as she looked upon her Pa. Then she got angry as she thought, "How dare these people laugh at my Pa."

She went and stood next to him and looked up at the crowd. "My Pa is sick and you people are mean to laugh at him. How would you like it if people stood around gawking and laughing at you?"

As the crowd started scattering, a familiar face emerged. Mary felt relieved to see Officer O'Reilly. Her Pa's weight seemed even heavier than usual, and she had already begun to wonder how she was going to help him home and still carry her books.

As Officer O'Reilly started helping Daniel O'Neill to his feet, he smiled at Mary. "How are you today, Mary?"

"I'm good," she answered with a smile on her face. "But as you can see, my Pa is sick again. I was so glad to see you! Will you help me bring my Pa home?"

"Sure, Mary, I'll be glad to help you."

Mary looked at her Pa as she said, "Pa, it's Mary, are you all right? Officer O'Reilly is going to help me to take you home, Pa."

"Your Pa is lucky to have a little girl like you, Mary. And you did the right thing sticking up for him."

"They just don't understand. My Pa is sick." Her eyes searching his for a glimpse of understanding.

In a flash, Officer O'Reilly's memory took him back to his childhood, and the sad, heartbreaking stories his father had told him about the heartache and the many injustices he had seen in Ireland. Officer O'Reilly had heard the stories told over and over so many times since he was young, that he actually felt as if he had been there and witnessed the scenes first hand. It was as if he personally knew these people that he encountered many times in his Pa's memories.

Tears would come into his Pa's eyes as he recounted the true stories of what happened to a relative, a neighbor, a friend, and how strong and vibrant men and women, through hunger and disease, can sometimes be emotionally crippled. Always his Pa ended the stories with the unanswered question, "Why did they have to be so cruel?"

It seemed like but a few moments later that he answered Mary. "No, Mary, they don't understand." He glanced at his time piece. "Mary, you better run on to school or you'll be late. Don't worry. I'll get your Pa home safe and sound."

Mary kissed her Pa and thanked Officer O'Reilly and waved as she started running toward school. She usually picked Molly up on the way.

But they had agreed that if Mary wasn't there by a certain time,

Molly would start for school, so that they both wouldn't end up being late. Molly lived two blocks from Mary and two blocks from school, exactly halfway between Mary's house and St. Mary's school.

Most times, Daniel O'Neill was ashamed of his inability to control his drinking. He hadn't always been this way. He was an only child. His mother had him late in life. His father died when he was ten years old. When he was working he had to give his mother all his pay. He could not spend one penny without her permission. Maggie was barely twenty when he married her and brought her into his Mother's house to live. Although Maggie held her tongue, she considered his mother to be a very selfish, controlling, dominating woman who always wanted and got her own way.

As far back as Maggie could remember, her mother-in-law complained constantly about everything but she could not remember her ever saying one kind word to her. This went on for a number of years. Then she started getting very confused and forgetful. At first it was about little things and somebody was always around to help her so it wasn't so bad. Then she started getting up in the middle of the night and waking everybody else up, telling them that they had to get up or else. There was no arguing with her. Maggie tried to get her husband to talk to his mother about it and try to explain. But all his life he had never talked back to his mother and he couldn't bring himself to do it now, either. Things got progressively worse.

She started running off while Maggie would be out hanging the clothes, or was busy with the baby. Maggie would drop everything and go off looking for her. They were becoming concerned about her safety.

Senile is what people called it. Finally, one night when everyone was sleeping, she turned on the stove without lighting it. If it wasn't that the baby just happened to wake up a few minutes later, they all very likely would have been asphyxiated. The baby usually didn't wake up anymore through the night and Maggie always believed it was the hand of God that saved them.

Another day, she set the bed on fire. They realized that for her safety, as well as their own, they had to do something about the situation. They decided to take her to the "Little Sisters of the Poor" to live.

When Daniel went to visit her on Sundays it seemed at that time she had her narrow-minded memories and she berated him unmercifully, over and over again telling him what a good mother she was and how much she had given up and done without in raising him, and how ungrateful he was. How could he allow his wife to do this to her? She always believed it was Maggie's idea, because she didn't think he would have had the nerve. But that didn't still her vicious tongue – lashing out, in trying to make him feel guilty. "I did everything for you. I never thought that you would abandon me in my old age."

He got so unnerved that he started drinking after every visit. Before this time, he only drank sporadically. He felt as if he needed a drink to try to shut out her hateful words. Everybody told him that she was in good hands and not to pay any attention to her complaints, but the guilt gnawed at him.

Sometimes he would find her disoriented and confused, when she didn't even know him. But many times she was her old so-called sane, bickering self, and nagged and complained throughout the whole visit.

She missed her own bed. This one was too hard and lumpy. The food was terrible. The tea was cold. She was sure that the Sisters and other people didn't like her. Why couldn't he come every day? That's the least he could do when she had always been so good to him. She hopes he's satisfied that he made her last years so unhappy.

Her tirades started really fraying his nerves and wearing him down. There were days when he was already feeling low enough and couldn't help silently wishing that he'd find her out of it, but this kind of thinking made him feel even guiltier than ever. He got so that he dreaded going to see her and having to listen to her unrelenting anger. He started drinking before and after each visit.

Right up to the day she died, she lambasted him about his shortcomings and for forcing her to be at the home, managing to leave him with a very guilty conscience and a great sense of failure.

Maggie always wondered if she could have kept her mother-in-law at home longer, but everybody reminded her that she had to think of her children's safety first.

CHAPTER FOURTEEN

As Mary stood outside school waiting for Molly, she wondered what it was that Sister Mary Bernard wanted to talk to Molly about. She wondered if it had anything to do with Molly's mother marrying Mr. Gorman.

The Gorman's had lived in the same house since before Molly was born. Molly's parents had been very good neighbors and friends with Charlie Gorman and his mother as far back as Molly could remember. Mrs. Gorman had been like a grandmother to Molly. She really liked Molly's mother a lot and more than once she had said that she wished her Charlie could find a wife like Molly's mother.

Everything seemed to have been going so well and then Mrs. Gorman got sick. Molly's mother went over every day to take care of her and do the laundry, cleaning and cooking. Mrs. Gorman held on for about two weeks. The doctor said that she died of complications brought on by pneumonia.

Charlie had only one brother who lived in Virginia, so his mother's death created a great void in his life. He seemed to become even closer to Molly's parents. They invited him over every night for supper, pointing out that it was foolish for him to cook for himself when they had plenty. Charlie insisted on giving Molly's father money toward the groceries. Molly's father accepted, realizing that Charlie just wanted to pay his way. Charlie and Molly's father worked together at the railroad yard and seemed to become even closer friends. It was almost a year ago that Tom O'Connor was working as usual and was close to finishing the night shift when a heavy fog set in. In crossing the tracks he was killed by an oncoming train. Molly and her mother and Charlie were deeply shocked at his tragic death.

Charlie helped Molly and her mother every way he could. Molly thought of him as an uncle and her mother considered him like a brother. That idea, set so deep in Molly's mind, is what made it even harder for Molly to fathom the conversation she overheard that Saturday evening when she got home early. Molly's mother was explaining to Charlie that she didn't want to worry Molly, but her husband's insurance money was almost gone and although she'd been working part-time doing cleaning jobs and other odd jobs, that she now would have to get some kind of a factory job and they would have to move into a house with cheaper rent. Molly was stunned to hear Charlie tell her mother that he wished that she would consider marrying him. Then she and Molly could move into his house.

As Molly stood there dumbfounded, out of their view, Charlie continued telling her mother that he had loved her for a long time and would never have acknowledged it if it weren't for these difficult circumstances. "And you know how much I care about Molly. I would love her like a daughter. So please think about it, Nellie. I wouldn't..." he stammered, "expect anything, unless you..." and again he stammered, too shy to be able to put his thoughts into words.

Being an only child, Molly had really been very close to both of her parents. The idea that her mother would even consider marrying Charlie made her feel hurt and betrayed.

"No!" she hollered as she walked into the room. She looked at Charlie as she shouted, "My father was your friend and you've betrayed his memory." And then glancing over at her mother, she said, "You've both betrayed his memory. If you get married I'll quit school and run away." Then she turned and ran out of the room crying. She slammed the back door, wanting to give them the impression that she'd left the house. She hid in a back hall closet that she hadn't been in since she was a child.

After Molly heard Charlie leave, she got out of the closet and went into the house. Molly, who was usually a pretty easy-going person, was so shaken up by what had happened that she went into the living room where her mother sat, with her head in her hands, crying softly.

When she looked up, there were tears in her sad eyes. She felt a mixture of relief that Molly had come home but a feeling of sadness that Molly did not understand and, yes, even hopelessness that there were no words she could possibly say to Molly that would help her to understand.

For the very first time in her life, Molly felt very angry at her mother. She felt doubly mad at Charlie. She felt he had come between them. The idea that her mother might marry Charlie really disturbed her.

Molly stood there for a moment looking at her mother. She had always been a good mother and Molly didn't want to say things that would hurt her, but there were things that had to be said. She had to make her mother understand. She tried to explain to her mother that they didn't need Charlie, that she could leave school now and get a job. Her mother protested. "Your Pa always wanted you to finish school."

Molly angrily shouted back. "I don't believe that's important anymore, if it means you marrying Charlie." And then Molly went a step further and gave her mother an ultimatum that if her mother married Charlie, then she definitely was going to quit school and run away, probably to New York City, and get a job.

Molly's mother looked worried, as more tears came into her

eyes. "Oh, Molly, promise me that you'll never run away. I've lost your Pa and I don't want to lose you, too. Promise me you won't run away." Molly hesitated. Her mother looked sad as she continued. "I've sent Charlie away. I told him I couldn't consider marrying him as long as you were so much against it. I'll get a job and we'll move to a smaller place where it won't cost so much for heat. So don't worry anymore. I just want you to be happy."

Naturally Molly had told Mary all about what had happened. Mary thought that Molly would be much better off if her mother and Mr. Gorman did get married, especially since Molly and her mother had to move into that four-family house that was literally falling apart. Molly's mother had told her that was all they could afford. After Mary had observed a few cockroaches, she felt so uneasy that she would only stand at the door waiting for Molly. She couldn't bring herself to go into the house. Now, to make matters worse, Molly's mother suspected that somebody was stealing their coal.

Mary thought, how could she ever forget what had happened the other day. Just thinking about it made her face all twisted up as she literally shivered and shook all over again. She could actually feel her legs shaking uncontrollably as they had done that day.

Mary was aware that Molly and her mother had to go down to the cellar and bring up coal for the stoves. Mary hadn't thought anything of it until that day. Molly's mother was working for Mrs. Jordan and was called in early that morning. So after school Mary went with Molly to fetch the coal. There weren't any mice in Mary's cellar or any in her Aunt's cellar. Her heart started pounding rapidly as a group of mice scurried around her feet. She thought there must be four or five and wondered if any were rats, but she was too petrified to even turn her eyes to see, as she started shaking all over. She breathlessly whispered to Molly, "There's mice down here."

"Of course there's mice down here, but if you don't bother them, they won't hurt you."

But Molly's assurance did not calm Mary's fear, as her vivid imagination brought such terrible scenes into her mind of mice scampering up her stockings and rats baring their teeth and biting her, that she actually started shaking even more as she held tightly onto Molly. "Molly, wait, I'm sure we can loan you some coal. Let's just get out of here. I'll ask Mike to bring up your coal. I know he would do it if I asked him to."

"No, Mary, I've got to get the coal now so that my Mama won't have to come down in the dark. Besides, I have to start supper. You can wait here if you want to."

Either way was frightening to Mary. She was afraid to go forward with Molly. She was afraid to stand there alone, and she was afraid to go back without Molly. And God forbid, if anything happened to Molly because she didn't help her, she would never have forgiven herself. So, almost as if she were afraid that the mice could hear her, she whispered, "I'll go with you, but go slow, and let me hold onto you."

As Molly was putting some coal in the kitchen stove, Mary sighed loudly as she fell backwards onto the kitchen chair, oblivious to the cockroaches nearby. "Thank God that's over," she sighed. "I don't ever want to go through that again."

"Oh, Molly, I would think that you'd be glad to have your Mama marry Mr. Gorman and move into his house. Then you wouldn't have to go in the cellar anymore."

"I'd sooner go in the cellar every day and face the mice and even rats before I'd want to live in Mr. Gorman's house. I loved my Pa and I don't want Mr. Gorman to take his place. Why, I'd feel somehow as if I was betraying my Pa's memory, too."

Seeing how poorly Molly and her mother were living really bothered Mary. Believing that they would be so much better off if her mother married Mr. Gorman, Mary brought up the subject another day. Molly started to cry and couldn't seem to stop, Mary decided she would never mention it to Molly again.

As soon as Molly came out of the school and they had walked a little distance from it, Mary's curious mind forced her to ask, "What did Sister want to talk to you about, Molly?"

"My mother asked Sister to talk to me about her marrying Mr. Gorman."

"What did she say?" Mary impatiently asked.

"Well, she asked me if I thought Mr. Gorman was an nice man," Molly paused.

"Well, what did you tell her?"

"I said, yes, Sister, I think Mr. Gorman is a nice man, but I loved my Pa, and that I didn't want Mr. Gorman to take his place."

"So what did Sister say then?"

All of a sudden Molly's face began to look serene, as she calmly related to Mary her conversation with Sister. "Sister said, 'Your Pa will always have a very special place in your heart and no one could ever take his place. But God gave us big hearts so that we can love the many people who come into our lives.' Then she asked me if I thought that my Pa liked Mr. Gorman, and I said, 'Yes, Sister, my Pa and Mr. Gorman were very good friends.' And then she said, 'Your Pa was a good, kind man, who loved you and your mama very much. Don't you think that your Pa would be happy to know that the two people he loved the most were going to be taken care of by his good friend?' And it's funny, Mary, because when she said that, I could almost see in my mind, my Pa and Mr. Gorman smiling at each other as I had seen them smiling at each other so many times. Then Sister said, 'You have a very special Mama, Molly. She has told me that although she believes her marrying Mr. Gorman would be what's best for all of you, that she will not marry him without your approval. She's placing your happiness before her own. Perhaps you should also think of her, too. You're thirteen already, and the years go by fast, so it won't be long before you'll be going out with young men, and perhaps fall in love, and want to get married. Wouldn't it be nice to know that your Mama wouldn't be lonely, that she had a nice man like Mr. Gorman to take care of her? So Molly, you think about the things I've said and I'll pray that you will make the decision that God wants you to make. You're a good girl, Molly, and I truly believe that if you just give Mr. Gorman the respect he deserves, that in time, everything will work out for the best."

CHAPTER FIFTEEN

For the past three Sundays, Mike refused to go to Mass. "I'm old enough now Mama to make up my own mind, and I don't want to go to church anymore." This acknowledgement had made Maggie feel very sad. The first two Sundays Mike refused to go to Church, Maggie figured that maybe Mike was just not feeling well or overtired from working so hard, so she didn't persist. Now this morning he had refused again and this time she was greatly concerned. She had stopped in after Mass to ask Father to speak to him. She really believed that there was something that Father could do or say to make Mike change his mind.

They had just finished eating Sunday dinner. Aunt Mary and Aunt Kate had just left, with Pat walking them home on his way to a friend's house, and Kitty and Mary were clearing off the table full of dirty dishes. Mike had just gone into the living room to finish reading the Sunday newspaper when Father knocked on the door, hoping to catch Mike before he left the house for the day.

Maggie answered the door and seeing Father said, "Give me a moment, Father, to tell Mike you're here."

Kitty and Mary looked up a little surprised to see Father Duffy in their kitchen. Kitty said, "Hello, Father, how are you? I enjoyed your sermon at Mass this morning."

"Thank you, Kitty. That's always good to hear."

"I did, too, Father," acknowledged Mary.

"Thank you, too, Mary. And how are you young ladies doing on this beautiful spring day?"

Before they had a chance to answer, Maggie was back, and beckoned for Father to follow her into the living room where Mike was standing, waiting to greet him.

Mike looked a little sheepish as Father entered the room. "Hello, Father, you wanted to speak to me?"

"Yes, Mike, if you have a few minutes."

"Of course, Father. I think you'll be comfortable sitting on the sofa, and I'll just sit on this chair across from you."

Maggie, in the meantime, had quietly closed the door from the dining room to the kitchen behind her, and immediately went to talk to Kitty and Mary.

"Father is talking with Mike, and I don't want either one of you to say anything to Mike about what they talked about. Do you understand?" They shook their heads yes. "As soon as you finish cleaning up, you girls can go to the movies. I heard you tell Annie you were going to take her, so make sure she's clean."

Father Duffy was optimistic as he looked at Mike. He was confident in his Priestly training and his knowledge of the Bible.

"So, Mike, how have you been?"

"Good, Father."

"I heard you were working for Mr. O'Connell. Do you like your new job?"

"Yes, Father, very much so."

"I'm glad to hear that, Mike. Mr. O'Connell is a good man. Very generous to the church. Mike, what I want to talk to you about is that I haven't seen you in church in the past couple of weeks. Is there anything wrong?"

"No, Father, there is nothing wrong. But I have decided not to go to church anymore."

"Oh? Do you mind if I ask you why? Are my sermons that bad?" Father chuckled jokingly, trying to put Mike at ease, hoping that Mike would open up to him and tell him the main reasons for his decision.

"No, Father," Mike answered with a smile on his face. "In fact your sermons are better than most." Mike looked a little more serious as he said, "But I've been thinking about this for a long time now, even before you came here. In fact, at least this whole past year I've only gone to Church because of my Mother. I know how much it means to her, but now I'm beginning to feel like a hypocrite, going through the motions for something I just don't believe in anymore."

"You do believe in God, don't you, Mike?"

Mike sighed deeply and hesitated. He really didn't care to have this conversation with the Parish Priest on a Sunday afternoon. But, he was taught to tell the truth. And that's what he would do. "No, I don't, Father, not any more."

Father pondered for a moment. "Mike, I wonder if you would satisfy my curiosity?"

"I will if I can, Father."

"I would like you to try to remember what it was that turned you away from believing in God? Was it something someone said or did or something you read about?"

"Well, Father, now that you ask, there were a few things that I really wondered about, like the injustices in life. Not only because some people are selfishly unfair to other people but also the fact that some people are born into a life of pain and suffering, while others are born into the lap of luxury. How can you justify saying that God is all just? If indeed there is a God at all. And I for one find it hard to believe that there is."

"That is not a new question, Mike. Many people have asked that same question for centuries and all I can say is that we just don't know why. But, I can assure you, Mike, that a lot of the injustices in the world have to do with man's misuse of his God-given free will. God has told us that our ways are not His ways, and that He loves us, and He has promised us that if we seek Him, we will surely find Him. If we keep His Commandments, we will have eternal life. Someday He will wipe every tear from our eyes and we will see Him as He is."

Mike shook his head, "I'm sorry, Father, but those answers are just not good enough to persuade me to change my mind."

"Well, Mike, you said there were a few reasons. What else can you think of?"

"Well, probably the thing that made me question even more than ever was when I read Darwin's Theory of Evolution. That makes much more sense to me. Did you ever hear about that book, Father?"

"Oh yes. I read Darwin's theory quite a few years ago. While I have great respect for Darwin's work, I would have to point out that it is only a theory that has never been proven beyond a shadow of a doubt. Also, Darwin started his theory with the extension of life forms that had already been created by God. And although Darwin also questioned God's existence, he never, to my knowledge, became an atheist.

"Mike, there is much evidence to back up a belief in God. Right from the beginning and throughout the history of the Church, there have been thousands of miracles, the greatest of course being Jesus' Resurrection and Ascension into Heaven."

"Father, I have great respect for you personally, but there is nothing you could say that would convince me to believe. I don't want to be rude, but I really must go. I have somebody waiting for me right now."

"Of course Mike, run along, I understand. Thank you for being so candid. You'll be in my prayers."

"Thank you, Father."

As Mike walked away from Father and out of the room, he thought to himself, if it will make Father happy, then let him pray for him, but to him, it seemed like a waste of valuable time. He called in from the hallway, "See you later, Mama, I'm going to meet Frankie."

Maggie, who had been in the kitchen praying for Father to be able to convince Mike to go back to church, came into the living room. She asked Father if he would like a cup of tea. Father thanked her but said that he had a couple of sick calls to attend to.

As Maggie stood before Father, her questioning eyes sought an answer to his conversation with Mike. "Father, will Mike be going to Church?" She blurted out.

"I'm sorry, Maggie, but I'm afraid he won't be. Not for a while, anyway."

The disappointing news made Maggie feel so sad. She sat down in the chair and her body shook as she quietly sobbed, dabbing her eyes, and blowing her nose with the handkerchief she had taken from her dress pocket. She felt as if her whole world had crumbled about her. This was the most important thing in her life, her belief in God. She could suffer anything, the hard work, the drunken husband, being poor and doing without, but her son turning from God was too much for her to bear. How could she be happy in Heaven if this son she loved so much was not there? And with this thought, many more tears came forth and flowed down her wrinkled face.

Father Duffy thought and thought. What could he possibly say to console this saintly woman?

"Maggie, did you ever hear of Saint Monica?"

"Well, Father, I know that Monica is a saint's name, but I don't know why."

"Well, Maggie, Monica had a son, too, who didn't believe in God, and she prayed for many years for his conversion. Her son was

St. Augustine, who is one of the greatest of the Father and Doctors of the Catholic Church. Maggie, the Lord works in mysterious ways. Mike's a little mixed up at this time in his life, but he's had a good religious foundation and it's all in there rattling around. He's a good, kind, hard-working boy. With faith and patience, I believe that everything will work out. Take Jesus at his word, He said, 'And all things whatsoever you shall ask in prayer, believing, you shall receive.'"

Maggie looked up as she listened carefully to what Father was saying. She thought for a moment and then with a ray of hope and optimism in her voice she said, "Yes, Father, I do believe, and I will always pray for Mike and for all my children every day for as long as I live."

CHAPTER SIXTEEN

"I simply don't believe I was meant to be a housewife," Kitty said to Mike unapologetically. "I hate housework. I don't want to spend my days washing piles and piles of other people's dirty clothes, and then spending another whole day ironing them. I don't mind sewing and baking here and there, but I certainly don't want to have to do that every day of my life. Personally, I'd rather go out to work every day, just like I do now. It gets hectic sometimes, and there are certainly days I'd rather be doing something else, but considering the choices that are available to me, I'd much sooner be doing what I'm doing right now. Of course I can think of a lot more exciting things I'd rather do with my life if I didn't have to worry about making a living, but the point I'm trying to make is, if I choose to work, and I work hard, and I work my way up the ladder at the telephone company, then I should not be barred from a job I'm qualified for because that job is reserved for a man. Not because he's better qualified than I am, or because he's been there longer, but just because he's a man, he gets the job, and along with it, a lot of extra money. That's just not fair."

"I know you want the vote," said Mike, but now you want to be paid the same money as a man? Men have families to support. It sounds a little selfish to me."

"Selfish? Selfish? For wanting the same opportunity at a job, and the same pay for doing the same job as a man. For Heaven's sake, that's just simple fairness. Besides, not every working man has a family, you know. A lot of them are unmarried. And some men never do get married and have children."

"They may not have children, but I'll bet you most men out there are helping to support their parents or younger family members," said Mike.

"You mean like I am?" Kitty shot back. "I'm helping to support my younger brothers and sisters."

When Mike sighed and looked away, she knew she'd made her point.

"You know as well as I do that there are cases where a woman's husband has died or abandoned the family and she's left as the sole provider for that family. Take Mrs. Sullivan. She left a good job with the telephone company a few years ago to get married and raise a family, and we were happy for her. Then her husband died. A heart attack, out of the blue. She came back to work and she's the sole provider for her family. Three young children *and* her mother, who takes care of them during the day. She, alone, is supporting a family of five! And you know as well as I do that there are many cases like hers. Even strong, healthy people get sick all of a sudden and die. Don't you realize that if something were to happen to you, I could end up being the sole support of our entire family? Not counting Pa, I mean. And... well, frankly, we can't count on him, can we? And, God forbid, if that did happen, wouldn't you want me to be in a position to be financially able to do more for Mama and the children than I would be if I was kept back from a promotion or paid less than a man for doing the exact same job?"

Seeing that Mike was considering her point and had no reply, Kitty took the opportunity to continue before he had a chance to interrupt.

"I'm only trying to get you to see my point, Mike. If a woman wants to get married and raise a family, I think that's wonderful, and I'm the first one to wish her well. But if she chooses to remain single, she should be able to make that choice, too, and instead of being looked upon as a poor soul who couldn't catch a husband, and to add insult to injury, be called an Old Maid – which has to be one of the stupidest terms I've ever heard, and obviously made up by a man – well, that single woman should not only not have to justify herself for her choice, but she should not be financially punished for it, either. I just think that women should have the opportunity to be more than just wives, mothers, teachers, nurses and seamstresses, if they want to be. And Madam Curie, like many, had a husband and children. And you can be sure there would have been many more like her if they'd just been given the opportunity, the education, the encouragement. You think you're so fair-minded, Mike, but how would you like being denied the fundamental right to vote? How would you like to be paid less than a woman for doing the same job she's doing? You just have no idea what it's like to not have any control of the way you're governed. To not have any say at all about the laws that govern your entire country, that say what you can do and what you can't do in your home, even. The very laws that are used to prosecute you if you break a law you didn't even have a voice in making! Honestly, Mike, I don't understand how a man who speaks so passionately about the rights of working men, even to strike for better conditions, is unable to recognize the injustices this society does to the women in it. I guess some people who are quick to recognize prejudice in others just don't recognize it in themselves."

"Prejudice?" said Mike, as astonished at her use of the word as she had been only moments earlier at his use of the word 'selfish.' "Are you accusing me of being prejudiced? I'm not even slightly prejudiced."

"I say you are prejudiced," Kitty replied, "not against men of other races or religions, but against women. You're against giving women voting rights and promotional opportunities and equal pay, and that's discrimination. People who practice discrimination are prejudiced, plain and simple. You, who think rich employers are unjust by not giving their workers the right to unionize and vote on matters of importance to them, and not providing a livable wage and more time off, are just as unjust to women. The sad part about it is that you don't even realize that you're prejudiced. I can think of a number of women I know who would hate to be married to a man like you."

Mike's jaw dropped. "How can you say such an insulting thing to me? I'll be a very good husband and father. You of all people should know that by now. Haven't I always done everything I possibly could to help my family?"

"Yes, you have, and we're grateful for it," said Kitty. "But I'm not talking about that kind of help. I'm talking about men giving women real freedom and allowing them to be able to vote for the people who make the rules that control their very lives, and the lives of their children. I'm talking about encouraging women to speak up and give their point of view."

Mike said, "I believe a woman's place is in the home, raising a family, taking care of the children, being there when they come in from school, and when her husband comes home from work, like Mama always has been."

"Spoken just like the average man," Kitty sighed disapprovingly. "How would you like to have to stay home all the time, day in and day out, doing housework?"

"I can tell you there are days the average man would be glad to change places with his wife. It's no picnic working in the freezing cold, or the sweltering heat, like most men have to do, at some low-paying job for some demanding boss, especially when he's not feeling good and it's an effort to keep going because he knows there are people depending upon him. There are lots of ways women have it much easier than men, and they don't even know it. And women don't have to go to war."

"Well, if women were in charge in the first place, there would never have been so many wars."

"Well, I don't even think it's normal not to want to get married and have children."

"Oh, now who's insulting who?" said Kitty. "And what's 'normal,' anyway, just doing what everybody else does? What everybody tells you you're supposed to do, whether you want to do it or not? You mean it's not normal to you because that's the way you think, like a typical man with a limited vision. Choosing against marriage is perfectly normal for some people, male and female. Married life is definitely not for me! Why, I'd be afraid I'd end up like Mama, and that thought scares me. Besides, I know many women who never married and they're perfectly 'normal' and they've accomplished some wonderful things, including helping their families and their neighbors and their churches. And do you know who immediately comes to mind? Aunt Nan, Aunt Mary and Aunt Kate. And all the Sisters and teachers who taught me, and taught you, too, when we were young. And the Sisters and the nurses in the hospitals, and on the battlefields, tending to wounded soldiers. Queen Elizabeth was an unmarried woman and she ruled an entire country in the sixteenth century, and I can't have the vote in the United States of America in 1913?"

"All right, all right," said Mike. "You're getting away from the point. Let's get back to your original argument. Where are all these jobs for single women and all the money to pay them equal wages going to come from? Sometimes there aren't even enough jobs for men with wives and children, with all the immigrants coming into the country, not that I begrudge them and their families the opportunity for a better life. So you can call it prejudice if you like, but most men I know don't want to see a bunch of uninformed women jeopardizing important goals, like a fair hourly wage, shorter working hours and better working conditions for every hard-working man in this country. Until we have a decent job for every family man, we should keep women's right on the back burner."

"It's been on the back burner throughout history, and that's long enough! Oh, there's always going to be something you men think is more important than a woman's right to vote and be treated equally, but if not now, then when? Look at Aunt Nan. She's highly intelligent, yet she's denied the right to vote. Then compare her to Pa and some of his drinking buddies. It's just so unfair for you and your friends to treat women like third-rate citizens."

Mike said, "I agree that in her case it's unfair. But she's the exception to the rule – "

"And what about me?" said Kitty. "I got high marks all the way through eighth grade, and I'll bet I would have done well in high school, and even college, if I could have only had the opportunity. But in reality, I'm out there working every day, just like you. I read the same newspapers you do. I'm up on things. Am I another uninformed woman who's vote scares you?"

Mike smiled tightly and sighed. "You two are the exception to the rule."

"So that's two 'exceptions' to your rule. And how about Aunt Mary? Aunt Kate? Mama? Are they also a bunch of uninformed women who are going to jeopardize your goals, or are they actually informed women whose votes will *help* you to achieve your goals because your goals are also our goals?"

He stammered, flustered, and finally said, "You know as well as I do that most women aren't up on things like you are. I guess you could say I just don't trust the majority of women to vote responsibly. Some women might vote because a candidate is handsome. They may be charmed into voting for him instead of voting for the better candidate. So my answer to you is, you show me where there are enough women who are educated enough to vote intelligently without disrupting the country and then I'll talk about women voting."

There was a touch of anger in Kitty's voice as she responded, "How on earth can the United States call itself a democracy when half its adults are denied the right to vote? Honestly, just think about this a minute, Mike. What if you had to live your whole life in submission because a whole group of people who were stronger than you said so?"

Mike shook his head. "You just don't want to face reality."

"How funny you should say that," Kitty replied. "I was just thinking the same thing about you. But you might as well get used to one thing, Mike. People like me, men and women both, are not going to give up until women have the right to vote in this country. It's something we should already have. This is the twentieth century, and it's ridiculous that women are still denied the right to vote in the United States of America."

"You know, Kitty, if I were you, I'd be careful who I talked to about this. Some people just might think you have some pretty ridiculous ideas. You've certainly got the most radical views of any woman I've ever heard."

"Well, I'm not surprised by what you just said. I have some basic, normal, fair-minded, intelligent ideas, and I'm not afraid to share them with anybody. The problem is that when they enter your limited, narrow mind, they seem to you to be radical. But I'm not discouraged by people like you, because I know there will come a day when women will be allowed to vote and participate more in world affairs." She looked aggravated as she said to him, "I'm telling you right now, don't bother demonstrating those man-made courtesies like opening a door for me when at the same time you've closed your mind, and you continue to deny me my God-given rights."

They both suddenly turned at once as they heard their Aunt Nan's voice as she came into the kitchen. "Anyone home?"

Kitty optimistically exclaimed, "Oh, Aunt Nan, what perfect timing! I was just telling Mike that women have been waiting long enough for their rights, but I can't seem to convince him how important it is. Please help me!"

"Oh, dear," Aunt Nan sighed with a playful smile. "What have I walked into?"

Aunt Nan put her things on the table and took a seat. "Well now, you know that I normally don't like to take sides when two people are having a friendly disagreement. However, sometimes it's too important for the welfare of too many not to speak up."

It was unusual for Aunt Nan to stop in on a Sunday morning after Mass. Kitty couldn't help but feel pleased. She knew that Mike was trapped now. He had far too much respect for his aunts than to make up an excuse to leave, or refuse to listen to what they had to say, and Kitty knew that Aunt Nan was much more qualified than she to discuss the plight of women as to their overdue rights.

Aunt Nan explained, "But before I get started talking about Women's Suffrage, I want to see Mike alone for a couple of minutes about something else."

Kitty looked surprised but right away mentioned she had something to do in the living room.

Mike was also a little surprised and curious as to what his Aunt Nan wanted to talk to him about.

"Well, Mike, I'll get right to the point. Your mother mentioned to me that while I was recuperating, you had stopped going to Sunday Mass. From what she said, I put two and two together and figured it's because of Darwin's theory. Since I'm the one who lent you that book about evolution, I feel more than a little responsible." She sighed. "Mike, while I thought it was a good idea to open up your mind, I certainly didn't expect it to cause you to stop believing in God. I stopped in this morning to lend you this medical book for you to look over today and tomorrow. I don't even like to take this book out of our home library, but I know you'll take good care of it. I'll pick it up Tuesday evening. I want you to look in particular at the detail of a complex structure called the human body. It's hard for me to believe that such a complicated edifice could possibly have come into existence without a blueprint made by the master designer, God. I personally don't see how anybody could study the detail of the human body not believe in God. In fact, there was a Harvard professor that carried on a correspondence with Darwin, whom he respected greatly. But he wrote that he had a hard time believing that the human eye could have evolved. While it is a very interesting theory, we can't lose sight of the fact that a fish is still a fish and a man is still a man. I guess it's human nature to want instant answers. But that's not God's way. God must have His reasons, and we'll find out all the answers to the 'Why's' when we get to Heaven. I put these few thoughts down on this little card for you to think about." And she started reading what was on the card. "Although I can't prove to you that there is a God, there was a time when I couldn't prove to you that the earth was round, instead of flat, until somebody went around it. I couldn't prove that there were other planets and other suns and stars until somebody invented the telescope. I couldn't prove to you that there was such things as germs until somebody invented the microscope. In God's time, some day, everyone will realize that there is a God." She looked into his eyes, "Believe me, Mike, there is a God. The circumstantial evidence of God's existence is overwhelming. Now while you put this book on top of your dresser, I'll call Kitty and I'll give you a very brief history of the plight of women seeking their rights."

Aunt Nan began, "I don't have anywhere near the amount of time it would take to adequately explain the injustices to women, and consequently, to their children down through the ages. I will give you what I consider some of the main reasons why women definitely should be given the right to vote as soon as possible.

"From the beginning of time, there were so many injustices to women that they would be too numerous to mention. And there were so many laws enacted down through the centuries, some of them actually ridiculous, that gave women very little control of their own lives and those of their children, and even control over their own bodies. Fortunately, in some places, some of the injustices against women are slowly being corrected. The movement for removing unjust laws has progressed at different rates in various countries.

"Before the accession of Queen Victoria, there was no systematic education for English women. But as the first half of the nineteenth century drew to a close, broader views began to be held on the subject. Queen's College was founded in 1848. Out of its teaching grew nearly all the educational advantages which women enjoy today.

"Bedford College, Cheltenham College, the North London Collegiate School for Girls, the Girls Public Day School, are some of those which sprang into light in different parts of England and were filled as rapidly as they were opened, by girls in the middle and professional classes. From their teachings came the final stage which gave women the same academic advantages as men. In the Act of 1908 establishing the New Roman Catholic University in Ireland, it was provided that two members of the Senate should be women, and Queen's University, Belfast, had three women in 1910 in its Senate.

"The United States constitution did not say that women could not vote. The founding fathers already had enough differences to contend with, so they left it up to the states. Each state had its own qualifications or laws for how one could vote. At first, only white males who owned property were allowed to vote in most states.

Women in most states were not allowed to vote in most elections. Many felt that this was unfair. In 1814, Emma Willard established a boarding school for girls in Middlebury, Vermont. Rejecting contemporary theory on female education, she included in her curriculum a number of subjects such as mathematics and history, offered only in schools for boys. She was convinced that married life would be happier and on a higher plane if the wife was the intellectual equal of her husband. She knew that mothers whose minds and ideals had been strengthened by education would give the world better sons. One of her students was Elizabeth Cady Stanton.

"Women have been allowed to practice law in the United States and in a few other countries, but they still can't vote for the representatives who make the laws. There are women doctors and lawyers who can't vote while some men digging ditches, who can't read or write, can vote just because they are men. Does that honestly make any sense to you, Mike?" She paused as she looked into his eyes, waiting for an answer.

He looked back into her eyes, took a deep breath, and shook his head in the negative. "No, Aunt Nan, it doesn't make any sense at all."

Aunt Nan smiled. "Let me just finish by saying that since the very beginning of this country, women, alongside men, have struggled valiantly and endured all manner of hardship. I don't believe this country could have survived without the women. While the men were away at war, the women were planting the fields, harvesting the crops, managing the households, raising the children, besides tending the sick and wounded. So you can see, Mike, I truly believe women have already earned the right to vote."

Mike smiled as he answered, "So do I, Aunt Nan."

Kitty had been listening intently, always eager to learn more about her favorite subject. "Hooray!" she shouted. "At last, we have one more man who understands, and will no longer be fighting against us."

The medical book Aunt Nan had brought to Mike to look over sat undisturbed on his dresser until that Tuesday evening right before supper when he took a fast two minute glance through it.

When his Aunt Nan had handed the book to him on Sunday morning, he already had made plans for Sunday. Monday and Tuesday he had to work all day. Monday evening he was too busy to even think about it.

So there he was hurriedly trying to see if there was anything that would register on his mind, in case his Aunt Nan were to quiz him, knowing that she would never understand why he didn't take the time to study the book, especially since she had put herself out, to give him such an opportunity. So he was already thinking ahead about what he could say to her.

When he saw Joseph drop her off that Tuesday and tell her he would pick her up later, Mike felt relieved that he didn't have to walk her home, thus avoiding unnecessary questions.

CHAPTER SEVENTEEN

"I hope you made a wish," Kitty said to Mary as she plucked the smoldering candles from the cake around which they'd just finished singing "Happy Birthday."

"I wished I was seventeen," Mary smiled.

"For Heaven's sake, Sweetie, don't wish your life away," said Maggie. "Why, these are the best years of your life!"

"Not my life," Mary replied. "The best years of my life will be when I marry a rich man and have beautiful clothes and travel all over the world."

Maggie sang, "Dreams, dreams, be-u-tee-ful dreeeams..."

"It's just as easy to love a rich man as a poor man," Mary replied matter-of-factly, and of course the man she had in mind was Jack O'Connell.

Kitty said, "Mary, don't you know that a man who has money is looking for a woman who has even more money than he has?"

But Mary was too happy to give credence to naysayers, and she was too certain of herself and her dreams to be discouraged.

"And you enjoyed your trip to Albany on the train with your Aunt Mary and Molly on Sunday?" Aunt Nan asked.

"Oh, yes!" Mary smiled excitedly. "It was a perfect day. I always wanted to ride on a train. Molly and I agreed that one of these days we will take a train all the way to New York City."

Aunt Mary added excitedly, "After all the trains I saw go by in my lifetime, I finally had the opportunity to ride on one. It was a dream come true!"

Mike and Pat had both been late for supper. They had joined in singing Happy Birthday to Mary and were now finishing their meatloaf, mashed potatoes and the green beans Maggie had canned at the end of the previous summer.

Aunt Nan turned toward Mike and Pat as she said, "I know you'll both be leaving soon. John mentioned that there was a good turnout Saturday for the Johnny Evers Day. Did you both enjoy it?"

As usual, Mike answered first. "Oh, it was a terrific day," he said, smiling with the memory of it fresh in his mind. "You know it was Johnny's first trip east as manager of the Chicago Baseball Club. We lined up behind Doring's thirty piece band at eight in the morning at the hotel, including men from all walks of life, and we marched to Union Station in our straw hats. The streets were crowded with people, and everybody was so excited and happy. We boarded the train and as we passed through the south end, the factory workers came outside and gave us some loud cheers! When we arrived at 138th Street in New York City, we lined up again behind Doring's Band and unfurled this big banner that said, 'Troy, the Collar City.'

"After lunch, we marched to the Polo Grounds and went to a nice restaurant. Oh, you can imagine the attention we attracted as we strode down the street in our straw hats, bamboo canes with 'Troy and Evers' Pennants flapping in the breeze. In fact, I hung mine over my bed when I got home. There were over four hundred of us!" he exclaimed. "And marching right along with us were about forty young baseball players in uniform. When we got to the Polo Grounds, Johnny Evers himself was there to meet us! Then we marched into the stadium, the band first, then us walking eight abreast, the Chicago team, led by Johnny. Then came manager

McGraw and his men, each carrying a Giants' banner. Everybody in the stands jumped up and applauded. They were whistling and hooting and hollering. Oh, it was great!

"Then we marched to the home plate and presented the managers, Evers and McGraw, with a life-size ballplayer floral piece and a silver loving cup. Most of the people were impressed by what the Mayor said when he made the presentation to Johnny."

As Mike was talking he grabbed a newspaper page off his dresser and handed it to Pat as he said, "Here, Pat, read what the mayor said."

Pat began reading. "The Mayor said, 'In ancient times when a Trojan had performed some unusual feat, it was the custom of his fellow Greeks to adorn him with floral tokens of esteem and appreciation of his efforts. That Troy, said the mayor, has passed out. But there is another Troy to perpetuate the name, and like the ancient Troy, the modern ileum possesses athletes of extraordinary merit and accomplishment.' He then told manager Evers that Trojans generally believed that in him Troy, has produced one of the greatest exponents of the national game, and if it were proper for the ancient Trojans to honor their distinguished athletes, so it was for the Trojans of this age in presenting a silver loving cup to manager Evers. The mayor said, 'The city of your birth is proud of you and I have been delegated to present you this handsome silver loving cup, which is symbolic of our esteem for you, Johnny Evers. We wish you well, and may your success continue.' And then the mayor addressed manager McGraw and mentioned some of the early history of baseball in Troy, and told of the sale of the Troy team to a party of New York sporting men in order that New York might be represented in the national league. Since that time, said the mayor, Trojan fans have become partisan rooters for the Giants, notwithstanding their loyalty to their fellow townsmen.'"

As Pat finished reading the newspaper article, he looked up and said, "Besides all of us on the special train, there were quite a few that went down on the excursion boat and quite a few of all the former Troy residents that live in New York City now. Imagine, one newspaper estimated that there were twenty-five thousand spectators! It certainly was an outstanding day."

"Then, to top it all off," Mike explained excitedly, "it was Johnny who scored the first run and batted in the second to win the game for the Cubs by a score of two-to-one."

Pat said, "And he's so humble. You could tell he was really touched that so many came from his old home town to celebrate. At the end of it all, he said, 'I have figured in many big league events, but I will always remember this day above all others.'"

Mike added; "I think a lot of other people will, too! Coming home on the train, everybody was happy and most were too excited to be tired."

"What surprised me," Pat exclaimed, "was the large crowd there was when we arrived home and marched back to the hotel around eleven-thirty."

Kitty chimed in, "I was glad to hear that everybody had such a great time and that the weather was so good. No matter where you go around town, people are still talking about it."

"Mary, did you have a good time on your birthday today?" Aunt Nan asked.

"Oh, yes, it's been so very special," Mary answered with a beautiful smile on her face. "And thank you again Aunt Nan for the delicious chocolate birthday cake you baked."

"It was delicious," Annie added, the evidence still on her face.

Mike spoke up, "It's a good thing you're not superstitious, Mary, turning thirteen years old on the thirteenth of May, in the year 1913."

Aunt Nan piped in, "Oh, superstition is a lot of hogwash, anyway. Even the dictionary says that superstition is a belief founded on irrational feeling, especially of fear. Imagine somebody somewhere sometime made up the idea that Friday the 13th was unlucky, and that you shouldn't walk under a ladder, and that it was bad luck if a black cat crossed in front of you. Well, I refuse to consider such ridiculousness. Why, I feel for the nice little cats that everybody's trying to avoid just because they're black."

Aunt Kate added, "And speaking of fear, Jesus told us to fear not."

"And speaking of dictionaries," Aunt Nan mentioned, "I usually don't give gifts for birthdays, because there's just too many, but when I was at the bookstore this afternoon and I saw this dictionary, I thought of you right away, Mary, and all the times you've asked me the meaning of so many words. So I thought it would be good for you to have a copy of your own. My advice is to look up every word that you don't know and you will start reading faster than ever. Of course I know you'll share it with everybody."

"Oh, great!" Mary answered enthusiastically. "Just what I always wanted. My very own dictionary. And thank you again, Aunt Nan, for that great set of cyclopedias. We've all been reading those books often."

Kitty and Mike nodded in agreement as Pat added, "They are a wonderful help to all of us."

Mike said, "I hate to eat and run, but I know you'll all excuse me, because I have things to do, places to go, and people to see. It's great to have you back, Aunt Nan, and I can get back early to walk you home."

"Oh, I'm glad you mentioned it, Mike, because I almost forgot to tell you. Joseph is going to drive me home tonight so that I don't have to walk too far. My ankle is still a little swollen."

Pa, who had been for the most part sitting quietly and listening, said to Mike, "Wait up, Mike, I'll walk out with you. I wanted to ask you if certain people I know had gone to New York City."

As Mary looked at Pa, she remembered how, that morning, when she'd entered the kitchen, he had jumped up from his chair. He had walked over to her and kissed her on the forehead and said, "Happy Birthday, my Little Darlin'!" The thought of it made her smile.

Mike stood in the doorway for a moment as he said, "I hope everybody has a great week." And, turning to Mary, he added, "And I hope my beautiful kid sister enjoys the rest of her special day!"

Mary smiled as she answered, "Thank you, Mike."

As soon as Pa and Mike went out the door, Pat stood up, as he said, "I hope you ladies will all excuse me, because as usual, I have to go into the living room to study. I'll be looking forward to seeing you all another day."

"Good night, Pat," they all said in unison.

"And good luck, Pat," Aunt Mary said.

"Your mom told us you are getting wonderful grades in school," Aunt Kate added.

Aunt Nan turned to Maggie as she said, "And Maggie, you enjoyed your Mother's Day adventure?"

With a broad smile on her face, Maggie exclaimed, "Of course, it really started on Saturday afternoon when I answered a knock at the door to find a young man asking for Mrs. O'Neill. I was surprised, because I didn't recognize him. When I said, 'Yes, I'm Mrs. O'Neill,' he handed me flowers. Of course I said to him, 'No, there must be some mistake, I'm not expecting flowers.' But Annie was in the living room and overheard everything and she said, 'No, Mama, those flowers are for you. Kitty ordered them.' Well, you could have knocked me over with a feather. Two beautiful pink carnations!"

Delighted at her mother's continued excitement over the affair, Kitty piped up and said, "When I saw the florist advertise in the paper on Friday, I thought, 'Why not? My beautiful mother deserves flowers on Mother's Day, too!' I'd already told Pa and the boys that I was taking Mama and Annie to dinner on Sunday, so Mama wouldn't be cooking dinner, and they were welcome to join us, but they all said, No, you girls go and have a good time for yourselves, they'd just make do with pickups. But when I got home from work on Saturday, I couldn't believe my eyes. Mama had cooked their whole Sunday dinner and put it in the ice box so they could heat it up on Sunday! You know Mama, she couldn't enjoy her dinner unless they had a good dinner, too! Oh, but we did have a wonderful day and we were especially happy that Aunt Kate felt up to going with us."

Aunt Kate answered, "I thank God I really have been feeling better lately and I appreciate how you are all so thoughtful. Thank you again for inviting me. I had a really wonderful time."

Kitty continued, "We went to dinner at the hotel and then we went to the picture show to see the great comedy, 'The Prince Chap.' We laughed all the way through it. It was great!"

"What a coincidence!" Aunt Mary exclaimed, "at the same time you people were laughing in Troy, Mary, Molly and I were laughing in Albany. As you know, we went on the train, then attended the Bishop's Mass at the Cathedral. Then we had a very delicious dinner at a nice little restaurant close by, and proceeded to see what's been advertised as Brandon Thomas' screaming farce comedy, 'Charlie's Aunt.' And we couldn't stop laughing, right, Mary?"

"Oh, yes, it was really good. Molly and I are still laughing as we remember different scenes and dialogue."

Aunt Nan said, "One of these days, I hope to see both of those funny shows. Doctor Spencer said that laughter is good for everybody."

Kitty said, "I personally think we all ought to toast Anna Jarvis, who's worked so hard to do a great service for the mothers in our country, through her tireless efforts to see Mother's Day declared a national holiday. I for one hope it happens."

"We've all been so lucky this week," said Maggie, "it just makes me feel all the more sorry for other mothers and their families who are having hard times right now with all the strikes and riots going on in the country. I've been praying extra prayers that things will turn out right, very soon."

"Oh, I know just what you mean," said Aunt Nan. "I'd thought by now things would have gotten back to normal. I remember reading in the paper about three weeks ago about the silk mill strike in Patterson, New Jersey. There'd been clashes between the police and the strikers, and I just felt so sorry for them when I read that the strikers planned to send their hungry children to New York City, five thousand of them, to be taken care of by strike sympathizers. The same thing was done during the textile strike in Lowell, Massachusetts."

"Imagine having to send your children to strangers just to make sure they have food to eat!" said Maggie, shaking her head in dismay.

"The strikers themselves were getting their food in the bread line at the strike headquarters," Aunt Nan went on. "Friday's paper had a picture of troops on strike duty in Syracuse and it said they were concerned about other violent encounters between the police and soldiers and the strikers. Infantrymen from the state guard were put on strike duty in the city with orders to shoot to kill if necessary."

"Oh, my God, isn't that terrible!" Aunt Kate exclaimed.

"Yes, it is," Kitty agreed, "and it's enough bad news for any one day." She turned toward Aunt Nan and said, "Now, to change the subject, I know we asked after you when you first got here, but in all the hubbub, I don't think we got a real indication of just how you're feeling? We certainly missed you here the past couple of weeks, didn't we?" she said to the insistent agreement of the others around the table. "You're walking much better than the last time I saw you."

Aunt Nan answered, "I really feel great knowing I'm on the mend. It seems that every day I'm losing a little more of that stiffness, so now my mind is back thinking about that trip in July. I've been following the London Suffrage movement very closely. Last month the papers mentioned that the suffragettes tried to blow up a castle. Then another day the paper decried how they took possession of the monument which was near the northern approach to London Bridge that commemorates the great fire that destroyed London. Ascending to the top-most balcony, they displayed two flags and an inner banner. The suffragette colors, each of which was written in white on a black background saying, 'Victory or Death.' Having securely fastened the flags to the railing surrounding the balcony, the women locked themselves in to prevent the police from ascending the staircase. Then they took up their position in the iron cage and showered suffrage literature among the thousand people that had gathered at the foot. For a long time traffic was suspended in the immediate vicinity, which is one of the busiest districts in London.

"In last week's paper, an article went on to say that a ten thousand dollar Pekinese champion dog owned by a woman, was poisoned by the militants."

"A ten thousand dollar dog?" Annie exclaimed.

"A ten thousand dollar dog," Aunt Nan replied.

With concern in her voice, Annie said, "I feel so sorry for that poor lady. I'll bet she misses her dog."

Aunt Nan continued, "The owner received a post card yesterday saying something to the effect of, 'We're very sorry Choo-tai had to be sacrificed, but we are resolved to stop at nothing now.' They went on to threaten that valuable racehorses such as a 'derby' winner will be maimed or destroyed when the chance presents itself until they get the vote for women. 'You and other owners of valuable property can only enjoy peace by helping us to get the vote,' they said."

"That's just not right," said Mary. "They are so mean to kill animals because of what their owners do. The animals can't help it."

"I agree completely," said Aunt Nan. "But sadly, as we've seen, there are hot heads in most organizations, and some get to the point of becoming fanatics."

"Oh, it doesn't even make sense!" said Aunt Kate. "Those kinds of tactics usually backfire."

"A very good point," said Aunt Nan. "And yet it's getting even worse."

"The other day the paper reported that two more bombs the militant suffragettes are using to try to scare the British Parliament into giving them the vote, were discovered. One of the bombs was found in the waiting room at a railroad station in Liverpool and the other was in a post office sorting room at Redding. According to the paper, many historic edifices throughout the country, which during this season are usually visited by thousands of Americans and other tourists, have been ordered closed, except during the hours of service."

"I've said it before and I'll say it again," Kitty exclaimed, "when I read what's been happening over there, my heart just goes out to all of the selfless, dedicated women who've worked so tirelessly for such a worthy cause and now just because of the actions of a few fanatics, the whole cause is being damaged! The other day the Duke of Marlborough closed Blenthenheim Palace to the public following receipt of an anonymous letter revealing the existence of a suffragette plot to destroy the palace. The newspaper mentioned that threats of a real reign of terror to be conducted by the militant suffragettes, combined with daily outrages, are causing real alarm. It is estimated that five million dollars' worth of damage has been done and that Scotland Yard is taking extreme measures to stop the disorders. The newspaper stated that 'London is really in a panic...'

"The latest is they attempted to wreck Saint Paul's Cathedral with a bomb. Can you imagine? St. Paul's Cathedral! Not only is that clearly wrong – attacking a house of worship – but what kind of sympathy for the cause can anyone honestly hope to gain by doing something like that?"

"They're just going to make people angry."

"And they'll say, 'See? They're irresponsible and dangerous. They don't deserve the vote!'"

"Exactly!" Kitty agreed. "Thank goodness the man who conducts the site-seeing tours heard the ticking and found it underneath a chair beside the Bishop's Throne. They described it as a heavy parcel done up in brown paper, and he picked it up and carried it out and put it into a pail of water, and then he called the police. And a similar bomb was on the steps of a newspaper office. But on a much more favorable note," she smiled, "did anyone read about Philadelphia having two police women? Imagine that! Two women police officers were given the authority to make arrests in the two main railway terminals in the city. They've been given special police badges and are permitted to carry revolvers and blackjacks! That really surprised me."

"I did see that," said Aunt Nan, "and must admit, I was surprised, too. But very pleased."

As Mary got up to get ready for bed, she thought to herself, "Now that I'm thirteen, I should be able to stay up longer." But she caught herself, realizing that if she'd made the argument and won, Aunt Nan might not talk as freely about the O'Connells. So, instead, she said good night and prompted Annie to do the same, but as she lay in bed, listening anxiously, hoping that at any moment Aunt Nan would mention something about Jack and his family, she heard her aunt's voice on the telephone in the dining room, telling Joseph she was ready for him to pick her up. She really appreciated his offer and she didn't want to keep him up later than usual on her account.

Mary sighed quietly. It had been a wonderful day. Pa was doing well, and everyone had had such an exciting weekend. She counted her blessings as she said her prayers, and as she lay waiting for sleep in the dim light that sifted into the room from the kitchen through a crack in the curtains, she thought again of Jack, and of the adventures they would share together one day, and she smiled.

CHAPTER EIGHTEEN

In the weeks that had passed since Genevieve had begun visiting, she'd been able to tell Maggie about the anger and resentment she'd felt toward her husband, and the pain that his affair had brought her. She spoke of how often she'd felt overwhelmed by grief when thoughts of it all swept over her at any moment, leaving her lonely and sad. Sometimes, even though she was hungry, the reality of it all would surface again and suddenly she felt so sick to her stomach that she couldn't eat, no matter how hungry she was.

But, she told Maggie, as bad as the days were, the nights were even worse. Night after night, she had a hard time getting to sleep at all, and after only four or five hours, she'd wake up, unable to get back to sleep because her thoughts turned to what had happened and how he'd betrayed her, and it would overwhelm her again, and her stomach would knot up and her head would ache.

Maggie, who knew only too well the sorrows and disappointments of life, would reach across the kitchen table and hold her hand while she cried, and she always greeted and saw her off with a warm, hearty hug. But mostly, and most importantly, Maggie simply listened, sympathized, and tried to console her. Often Genevieve would begin crying as if her heart would break in two, and, seeing her newfound "sister" suffering so, moved Maggie to tears.

Over the course of time, Maggie learned from Genevieve that one night, instead of tea, the woman brought out a bottle of wine. After she and Genevieve's husband each had a couple of glasses, the woman took him by the hand and led him to her bed, and started taking off her clothes. He said he told her that he had never gone with anybody but his wife, and he just couldn't do anything because his conscience was really bothering him. She told him she understood, because that's the way she felt the first time she went to bed with that married traveling salesman. She tried to convince him that there wasn't anything wrong with their being intimate because they weren't hurting anyone, and nobody would ever find out. He said he didn't go there again for a few weeks and was trying to figure out what to do.

Genevieve pointed out to Maggie that while this was taking place, she was having a hard time trying to get her husband to face their responsibilities and do what was best for their family. She mentioned that she babied him, coaxed him and even pleaded with him, but nothing seemed to work. He refused to listen to any problems, sometimes cutting her short and walking out the door saying something sarcastic.

Then she'd confided one day, "I'm only human, too, and sometimes with all the problems, I just wasn't feeling very good. There were times that I had such terrible pains in my chest that I really thought I would have a heart attack. Sometimes my heart would race so fast that I couldn't catch my breath. Other times I remember breaking out in a cold sweat and feeling light headed and faint." She related feeling moments of panic, as if she wanted to just run up the street as fast as she could, just to get away. She felt so discouraged, not only because he wouldn't help, but because he just didn't seem to care anymore. It made her feel so sad. Nothing seemed to work. There were times he was really ornery.

She mentioned she remembered one evening so vividly, that he came in fairly early. She had such a terrible headache from trying to figure who they could pay that week. She tried to get him to help her figure it out. He'd said, 'If I knew this, I'd have stayed out later instead of coming home.' Then he just went to bed.

"See what I mean?" she said. "Why go home to your wife and family and face responsibilities when it's so much easier to go to this other woman and let her tell you how wonderful you are?"

Genevieve proceeded to tell Maggie that one evening she'd finally lost her patience and they had a big argument, and he'd left the house really angry. He said that he was so mad at her that nothing seemed to matter anymore. So this time when the woman led him to her bed, he went with her. Genevieve started sobbing softly, as fresh tears welled up in her eyes.

That same afternoon, Genevieve continued, blowing her nose in her handkerchief, she sighed as she said, "If I had refused him and turned my back on him, at least then he would have had some kind of an excuse, but every week without hardly any exceptions, I went with him, because I know that's important to a man. It seems almost ironic, but I never wanted to give him a reason to be unfaithful. Some of those times I was so tired and discouraged, and inwardly resentful because he wouldn't help me, but God knows for the sake of the family, I swallowed my pride, and tried hard to be a good wife."

Genevieve continued to relate to Maggie that the whole situation went on for months. Then he'd told her that when he finally did start thinking about it and rationalizing it, he started asking himself, "'What have I done? What have I gotten myself into? How do I get out of this?' Because by then he'd begun to see this woman in a different light. He began to realize that she wasn't as innocent as she had led him to believe. She had gone with another married man before him that she worked with, but it didn't last long. He didn't completely trust her anymore. He was afraid if he didn't keep going there, that she might call me up and tell me, and that I would put him out and the children would turn against him. He said he'd lie in bed, night after night, and think, 'What a fool I've been. I have such a wonderful wife and a good family, but now if my wife finds out I may lose everything. Today may be the last day I'll be able to stay here.'

"See, by this time the boys were back to work and paying board, and they were involved with other things that kept them busy. His business had picked up, so it was easier, and since we had a little more money to pay our bills, the bill collectors had stopped calling.

"He said as we became closer again, his conscience started bothering him terribly. He told her how he was feeling guilty about cheating on me, and she said, 'Why should you?' When she said that, it made him feel all the more that if he didn't keep going there, that she would call me, figuring I would throw him out and he'd go to her. He said he had started feeling so guilty that he felt as if he had a big knot inside his stomach, and he couldn't find peace.

"So he said he started considering very seriously of taking his own life, just to get out of the whole situation. He started rationalizing that when he went hunting, he could make it look like he fell on his gun and accidentally shot himself. Then we'd have the insurance money and nobody would ever find out.

"But around that time she had mentioned this older widowed neighbor who wanted her to go out with him. My husband said he tried to encourage her to do that, hoping it would lead to her marrying the man, and then she would finally be out of his life. He hadn't been to bed with her in months, and kept making excuses for not staying, just trying to appease her.

"He said he decided to go to the priest and confess everything because he couldn't shake the guilt he felt. He didn't want to go to our Parish Priests because when he saw them at Mass, it would be a constant reminder, so he went down to the Bishop's office and confessed everything to a Priest there. He said he was very understanding and he told him Jesus would forgive him of everything. The Priest advised him not to go to the woman's house anymore, keeping himself away from temptation and the occasion of sin.

"He said after Confession, he felt as if a great burden had been lifted from him, but he was still afraid if he stopped going there that she might call me. That was two months ago and he had gone there for the second time just to collect her insurance and encourage her to go out with that neighbor man.

"After that woman called and told me that she thought that I should know that the reason my husband wasn't home is because he was with another woman, I felt so shocked and hurt and angry at the same time.

"So when he came home we talked it all over. At first he denied it and then finally he said very discouragingly maybe it was just as well that I found out because he was feeling so guilty that it was eating him up inside.

"He teared up and said, 'I'm so sorry, please forgive me. I know it's all my fault. I was weak. I wouldn't blame you if you wanted me to go, but I want you to know I'll always love you, and if you'll forgive me, I promise to make it up to you.'

"And you know, Maggie, when he asked me to forgive him, all I could think of was that Bible story about the woman caught in adultery, where Jesus said, 'Let he who is without sin cast the first stone.' It seemed as if we've heard that gospel story at Mass every year as far back as I can remember. I could picture the scene and felt almost as if Jesus was saying that to me personally.

"And I guess I'm fully aware that in order to call myself a Christian, I have to forgive him. And I have to forgive her, too. But it's so hard. It's hard enough to say I forgive, but it's harder still to really mean it, when the heartache goes so very deep inside. It's as if there's an open sore inside of me that just won't heal.

"Sometimes I still feel sad and overwhelmed. I trusted him and believed in him. But when I needed him the most he ran out on me. She offered him an escape from reality, but I wish I could tell her how much harder she made my reality. He said she was lonely. Lonely? I was the one who was lonely. Do you know what it's like to have someone physically near but mentally so far away? Sometimes I felt almost desperate. I needed his help with our children but all I got was silence. It's a different kind of loneliness, but it is very lonely when this person who you've been so close to has now turned his back on you with complete indifference.

"One day I wrote him a little note to tell him just how bad I felt that he wouldn't help me. A little while later I heard him whistling. He didn't even care. It wasn't important to him. I wasn't important to him anymore. And then he left the house and I just cried and cried. I felt so dejected. So lost and alone. When I think back to times like that, I wonder if that evening he went to her house and smiled in her face.

"Here I was falling apart right before his eyes. There were so many people depending upon me that I didn't know if I would hold up under the strain without his help, and he felt sorry for her. There were times I felt like running away, too, but I had to put up with all the fights and complaints, no matter how bad I felt. I just had to keep on going and try not to feel sorry for myself. I felt so tired and discouraged, trying so hard to get him to face our responsibilities and help me. Many a night I cried by myself because I didn't want to upset the little ones. If it wasn't for my faith, I don't think I could have survived.

"In talking things over he said he always hated arguing and fighting. Well, who likes it? Does anyone really enjoy arguing and fighting and trying to persuade people to do what they should be doing in the first place, without being asked?

"Oh, Maggie, how could I have possibly competed against her? There she was appearing to be sweet and understanding and always available, making a big fuss over my husband, while on the other hand everything in our lives was so negative, with me at my worst, not feeling good half the time, and the boys fighting and the bill collectors calling. In comparison I must have really come across as the proverbial nagging wife, pleading with my husband to face our responsibilities, for the sake of the children. While her place was so quiet and peaceful, our house was like a zoo sometimes. How romantic. No problems, no responsibilities. At one point she even offered to loan him money that she had received from her aunt's insurance, while I, on the other hand, had to tell him about the bill collectors calling, and for the sake of the children, had to say things I'd sooner not have had to say.

"And I'm angry at a man I don't even know. Like that married man that first encouraged her to leave her husband and children. I wonder what kind of a man he was. Look at all the heartache he caused her husband. And there must have been lots of times her children needed her, and she wasn't there. If that didn't happen to her, and she had stayed with her family, then we wouldn't have had all this trouble, either.

"I can't help wondering. Did he really love her? Or was he just stringing her along and smooth talking her? Maybe he was even bragging to his friends about this married woman who was crazy about him. He really caused a lot of innocent people to pay a high price for his selfish choices. I can't help wondering if he learned a lesson from that experience. Or did he go on to another conquest, and break up other families?

"I feel such a great desire, almost like a yearning, to go back and relive that time, so I could change the results by stopping it before it began. I wish so much that somebody would have told me sooner. I feel so victimized. It's like she chose to be the other woman. And he chose over and over again to go to bed with her. But they made the choice for me to become an unsuspecting part of that unholy triangle. I would never have chosen to be part of such an arrangement. I would have definitely given him the alternative of choosing her or me and if he still found it hard to be faithful to me, then she could have him, because I really wouldn't want him. I would have gladly chosen to scrub floors from morning till night or taken in washings than to have been forced to be a part of such a degrading situation.

"My husband said that since he's seen how much heartache his actions have caused me, he's just sorry he ever met that woman and feels ashamed that he let her encourage him to deceive me.

"When I think of her now, I can't help feeling a little sorry for her because I think any woman who has lost the love of her children is to be pitied. No man is worth it.

"Since he pleaded with me to forgive him, I thought that he had found a certain amount of peace. I guess I didn't think he ever thought about it anymore at all. But he told me sometimes he feels so guilty about the way he treated me, and for what he's put me through.

"He said with tears in his eyes, 'I know I'm never going to forget, and that you're never going to forget. I try hard to block it out because it's so painful to remember how much I let you down, and how I almost lost everything.

"He woke up the next morning in a cold sweat, with tears in his eyes. He said, 'I had a terrible dream. I dreamt you left me. I said to you, 'I love you,' and you said, 'Well, I don't love you anymore and I'm leaving you.' It was a terrible nightmare,' he said. He was actually sobbing. I had to reassure him that I'm not going to leave him.

"I told him I married him for better or for worse, and now that the worst is over, we'll work together to try to recapture what we lost. And I guess at that moment I realized that he has paid a high price, too. He really is a good person. I always wanted to be a wife and mother. The great love and joy I have known far outweigh the disappointments. I do have a great sense of fulfillment that can't be taken away from me, no matter what.

"I've been trying to remind myself not to waste valuable time living in the past. After all, life is short, and we're not getting any younger. None of us knows how many years we have left. And, God forbid, if anything were to happen to him, I don't want to look back on this time and have a guilty conscience that I didn't completely forgive him and try as hard as I could to forget." She sighed. "I've really been trying hard to think of all the happier times we had before she got in the way. So many times I've said to myself, 'Don't let the past ruin the future. Thank God it's over.'

"Somewhere deep within me I hear a little voice whispering, 'You will conquer this and time will ease the pain.'"

This day Maggie noticed right away that Genevieve seemed much more calm and optimistic as she exclaimed, "The other day was our anniversary. Larry wanted to do something special to celebrate. He's been trying so hard to make it up to me. So he suggested we go out to dinner, and then go to the picture show. He brought me flowers and the most beautiful card. We had a delicious dinner at the restaurant, and then we went to the picture show.

"As we started walking home, I was thankful that the moon was not too bright, and that the trees shaded the stars. I know he's sorry, and I didn't want to ruin the evening for him, but I just couldn't help it, I cried all the way home. I turned my head so he couldn't see me, and when he heard me sniffling and blowing my nose, he said, 'Are you coming down with a cold?' I said, 'Yes.' I just couldn't help crying. I felt so sad and such a great sense of loss for what could have been.

"When he came home last night he took me in his arms and said, 'I love you so much. I was thinking all the way home how lucky I am to still have you. If you weren't so good, it might have been so different. Thank you, Darling, for being so kind and understanding'

"And speaking of kind and understanding, Maggie, makes me think about you. I thank God every day.

"No sister, even if she were related to me by blood, could have helped me more."

"I'm glad."

"I just hope that some day, I will be able to help you as much as you have helped me."

At that moment they heard the voices and laughter of the children coming in from school.

CHAPTER NINETEEN

"Fate!"

"Did you say 'Faith', Aunt Nan?" Kitty asked.

"No, I said fate, F-A-T-E. Mike just asked me if I didn't feel a little apprehensive about going to London after reading about the bombs on the train and all the other problems they're having over there."

The usual Tuesday evening group was still gathered around the kitchen table. Supper was finished and they were now enjoying a big plate of cookies which Aunt Nan had baked the day before.

"I have to admit it has crossed my mind," said Aunt Nan, "that after celebrating being one of the winners of the contest, then having my hopes dashed because of my fall, imagine after all that, I'm over there on a train or in a church and a bomb goes off and I'm hurt, or even killed. But while I certainly believe in doing as much as I can to try to stay safe in this world, and I wouldn't 'tempt fate,' as they say, I do believe that in the end, anything can happen, anywhere, at any time, and you can't live your life in fear, afraid to do the things you really want to do, or feel you should do, out of fear that something bad might happen if you do it. After all, the odds are in my favor that nothing bad will happen. And life is funny. I could cancel the trip out of fear of violence and at the exact same moment I would have been safely strolling down some boulevard in Paris, I could step off the sidewalk here in Troy and get hit by an automobile. Especially the way people drive those contraptions!" she laughed. "And *that* would be a sad irony I'd rather not suffer!"

"Still," said Mike, "it sounds like it's getting even worse. Last week they sent a mail bomb to the magistrate hearing the charges against the suffragette leaders. It was delivered right to the courthouse. You must have read it. I guess one of the court officers got suspicious and took it outside and plunged it into a pail of water, just like the one at the cathedral. Then another day the police found these tin canisters filled with combustibles, wrapped in suffragette placards on a train crowded with passengers on their way to work. It's pretty scary. Imagine how you'd feel if you were on that train, or knew one of the people that had to keep riding that same train back and forth to work every day. Maybe those women think they're just using scare tactics to get the vote, but fooling around with bombs goes way too far. I definitely agree with the paper that they are hurting their cause."

Aunt Nan spoke up. "While I agree with you completely, Mike, it doesn't seem to be any different with some other groups in this country, either. The paper mentioned the Cincinnati Street car strike situation is still deadlocked and in Patterson, the New Jersey silk mill workers are still on strike."

Aunt Mary added, "And because of my own job, I'm very aware that they are still having all kinds of problems with the Underwood Tariff Bill."

Aunt Mary spoke up. "While I believe that most people are good, kind, hardworking, law-abiding citizens, I am always amazed how some people become so dedicated to their cause that they can become blind fanatics, in believing that their particular cause gives them the right to break the law and endanger the lives of others, or hurt little helpless animals. I know a lot of people that just love their cats and dogs. A number of times this week I couldn't help thinking of little Choo-tie, that Pekinese that was poisoned. I thought to myself, no matter how much money the owner has, she probably loved that little dog. How could those women do such a heartless thing?"

Aunt Nan added, "I've been saying this for years. I am completely convinced that most people have a blind spot due to their own personal experiences, desires and prejudices. Many seem to start out as fair-minded, intelligent people with good intentions, but when they can't get their way, they deceive themselves and actually make excuses for their selfish behavior. And sometimes they even turn around and blame the people in charge for 'causing them' to break the law and cause innocent people to get hurt."

Aunt Mary said, "What annoys me are people who make jokes at other people's expense and embarrass them. Especially children."

Aunt Kate said, "Oh, yes! And speaking of embarrassing children. Every Saturday morning my heart just goes out to those two little boys up the street who wet their beds. Their mother wraps the wet sheets around them and makes them parade up and down the street! I feel so sorry for them. She's trying to shame them into stopping, but I've always believed bedwetting is the result of weak kidneys and it runs in families."

Mary could see those boys in her mind, and she too felt sorry for them. She was thankful that her mother hadn't done that to her. She would have died of embarrassment. She still remembered how awful she felt when she had wet the bed at the age of ten. But one day Pa had told her he and his brother were late bed wetters and she shouldn't worry. Mary had prayed and prayed to stop, and finally, she did. And she could still remember seeing her mother bent over the sink washing the sheets every day on the scrub board, but she never hollered at Mary, even once.

"Know-it-alls annoy me the most," said Aunt Nan. "People who think they're always right. And I hate to talk to people who are so opinionated that as you're talking, you realize they're not listening to you at all. They're thinking of what they're going to say as soon as they get the chance to interrupt you. I learned to be a good listener when I was very young. Circumstances demanded it of me. But it also gave me the opportunity to learn many things from educated people. Of course, one of the people I enjoyed listening to the most was Mr. Richardson, Victoria's Father. Only being ten when I went there and not having a Father of my own, I used to wish he was my Father, too! But as I was saying, to me it just isn't worth discussing things with people who really have a closed mind. Most times they become argumentative and shout other people down when somebody doesn't agree."

Kitty spoke up. "What annoys me are people who actually have the gall to call somebody else stupid. It's usually somebody who talks a lot and very seldom listens. And also, procrastinators drive me crazy. I'm so very independent that I hate asking anybody to do anything for me, anyway, but I just hate to ask anyone who procrastinates. I feel like shaking them and saying, 'Just do it!' It must be especially hard living with a person like that. But what can you do? It doesn't do any good to get upset over it. We can't control anybody but ourselves."

"Most times it's the same people who are late all the time," Mike said. "That really annoys me. I don't mind anyone that has a good excuse and is late once in a while, but I have no patience whatsoever with people who are always late. I think they're just plain selfish. They don't seem to care if they keep you waiting and waste your time, but you can be sure that if somebody was standing on a street corner giving out money, they'd be on time for that! I don't see why they don't just figure out that if they're usually fifteen minutes late and they're supposed to be someplace at seven-fifteen, they should figure they have to be there at seven and then they'd be on time!"

Aunt Mary said, "I hate to be around people with tempers. There's a simple misunderstanding or disagreement and they start arguing and shouting. They make me nervous. You just don't know if one will start shoving the other and then they're into a full-fledged fight. And half the time somebody else gets hurt."

"I know what you mean," Kitty added. "Some people's personalities just conflict. I say to myself, why don't they just do everybody a favor and stay away from each other until they learn how to control their tempers instead of getting other people all upset for nothing?"

Mary had been sitting there listening intently and really felt as if she couldn't get a word in edgewise. Finally she blurted out, "People who borrow your things and don't take care of them."

"That's a good one," Kitty acknowledged, and, catching her breath, she said, "And people who don't clean up after themselves. Remember when we moved in here? Oh, I'll never forget how filthy it was! Thank God everybody came over and helped us clean it up."

"Many hands make light work," Maggie added.

"But the people should have cleaned up their own mess before they moved out," Kitty said, with an impatient tone in her voice. "I'd be ashamed to leave such a filthy house."

"That's like people who don't follow the rules. They insist you do, but they seem to think the rules apply to everybody but them!" Mike exclaimed.

"I wonder if some people even realize that for every action there is a reaction," said Aunt Nan. "But even after listening and adding my own two cents' worth to this whole discussion about people's personality quirks and selfish behavior and blind spots, I can tell you from experience that there is no one that I've ever met or heard of who even comes close to The Old Lady. I couldn't count the times I've heard her mumbling or complaining to her friends about 'too many foreigners' and 'those no-good people with bad blood should stay where they belong' and 'the government should halt immigration to everyone' except the so-called 'better people.' She's so tuned in to breeding and upbringing and so-called etiquette that she puts her nose in the air and calls other people coarse and crude. But to me, etiquette isn't knowing which fork to use, it's good manners, and good manners is not being rude or out-and-out cruel to a fellow human being. To me, that's the height of bad manners!"

Nan looked at her sister Mary as she said, "I know you've always said, 'If you don't have anything good to say about somebody, don't say anything at all.' And while I think that's very good advice, I recognize that while you have the patience and easy-going, charitable personality to do that, I just don't. Talking about The Old Lady's selfish treatment of Mama and me and others has helped me not only to accept it, but to look beyond it. One day as I got a little older, I got a good look at The Old Lady and I thought to myself, 'Am I nuts? This is the most selfish, egotistical, demanding bigot that I've ever met. Why should I allow the likes of her to get me so upset?' I made up my mind right then and there that I wasn't going to, anymore. I couldn't answer her out loud, so I started making a game of it. Sometimes I'd just say in my mind what I felt like saying out loud. When she'd be feeling the dishes to see if they were dry, I could see myself throwing the dishtowel in her face and saying, 'If you don't like the way I dry the dishes, do it yourself!' I can remember more than one hot day when I'd be scrubbing the floor, perspiration falling down my face, and she'd come along and complain about some petty thing and I'd think to myself, 'Why, you old bitty, I'd like to stick this scrub brush right in your face.' Other times as she'd bark out her orders like a general in a war zone, I'd say to myself, 'Yes, Sir! And would you like me to do cartwheels and clean all the windows on the way?' And instead of getting upset, I'd get to laughing to myself. Oh, and she's always just raving about

England and complaining about America. I had all I could do to keep myself from saying, 'Why don't you just stay over there and give us all a break?' There were so many times I felt like screaming at her, 'Will you please shut up?' or, 'You don't know what you're talking about.' Well, like they say, we all have our crosses to bear, and I've always considered that old woman to be one of mine. You'd have to go far to find anyone that was any meaner than she is.

"When I fell on the stairs, John and Victoria couldn't have been nicer to me. They were so concerned. They had some furniture and whatnot moved into this little room off the kitchen and they even had my own bed moved down there so I wouldn't have to go up and down the stairs, and they made sure I had extra pillows and blankets and my books, and it was a nice, bright little room with a window that looked out onto the street, so I didn't feel quite so cut off from the world.

"But now, if you can picture this scene, there I was in bed with over fifty stitches in my leg. Most of them didn't bother me all that much, but I felt a real achy tightness in my knee and of course my wrist and my arm and shoulder were very tired and achy and heavy. But, the one thing that was bothering me the very most was my ankle bone. Other times it felt as if somebody had stuffed a big thick needle into the bone and was moving it back and forth and around and around and the pain was absolutely pulsating through me and it made me feel headachy and nauseated and the slightest movement was very painful.

"At that point, I'd not only given up hope I'd go to Europe, but I was honestly beginning to fear that I'd never walk normally again, without a limp or in pain. But I just kept saying to myself, 'This too shall pass,' and, 'Better days are ahead.' But I was still having a hard time trying to convince myself. One of my all-time favorite books is, 'As A Man Thinketh,' by James Allen, where he talks about cultivating 'the garden of the mind,' and about thinking positive thoughts.

"Since the mind can't think of two things at the same time, I was really trying hard to keep diverting my mind to that way of thinking. Now, while I'm going through this ordeal, The Old Lady comes along and she says to me, 'I don't feel one bit sorry for you. It's your own fault this happened. You should have waited for Maurice to help you with those bottles like John suggested. You're just lucky Victoria allows you to recuperate in her home.'"

"Well, I looked at her and I felt like shouting, 'This is my home, too, Old Lady! And I'm sure Victoria and John think it is, too! So get on your broom, you troublemaker, and fly away! And good riddance!' Then I went back to reading my book, and I thought to myself, 'Thank God I'm out of your clutches." She took a deep breath and then with a note of joy in her voice, she said, "I also thank God for Doctor Spencer's optimism. He really helped keep my spirits up. When he came to change the bandages a few days after the accident, I said to him, 'I don't suppose there's any chance now that I'll be able to go on that trip to Europe.' And I was surprised, and so happy, when he said, 'Of course you're going to Europe. You're in very good physical condition and the human body heals itself remarkably well.'

"Then when he took the stitches out and told me I could walk on it, I was so anxious that I guess I overdid it. My ankle swelled up again and I felt as if it had gotten worse instead of better. I was feeling a little discouraged, I'll tell you, but he said, 'Oh, it's only a little setback. You still have plenty of time. Before you go on that trip, I expect to see you running up the street!' He said the worst thing that might happen is that I'll have to take this cane with me. Heck, I think I'll take the cane with me anyway, just in case some big English Bulldog comes after me!" And she brandished the cane like a sword fighting off an imaginary foe, and they laughed along with her, glad of her recovery and the renewed sense of purpose it had brought her.

CHAPTER TWENTY

"Dreams, dreams, beautiful dreams! Will they ever come true?" Kitty wondered aloud.

"Absolutely!" said Mike. "And I for one intend to make my dreams come true!"

"Well, you certainly have the right attitude," Aunt Nan commended him.

"Probably from reading all those Horatio Alger books you always used to bring home for me, Aunt Nan. Like the 'Ragged Dick' success stories."

"Oh, my goodness, I'd almost forgotten," said Aunt Nan wistfully. "All those stories of underprivileged boys winning fame and fortune by practicing the virtues of honesty, diligence, and perseverance. And remember 'Pluck and Luck' and 'Tattered Tom' and all those dime novels?"

"Oh, sure," Mike smiled, "why, they were my heroes. I always figured if they could be successful, so could I. I still feel that way."

Aunt Nan's enthusiasm was infectious. "Horatio Alger did do a lot of good in helping and inspiring so many young boys. He had a good background. He was educated at Harvard College and Divinity School. After working in Paris as a journalist and tutor for several years, he returned and was ordained a Unitarian Minister. He went to New York City and became a Chaplain at a newsboys' lodging house. His books, most issued as dime novels, sold millions of copies, and he used the profits to help poor boys. It's amazing how one life can influence so many other lives."

Kitty asked, "Aunt Nan, you've read a lot of true stories and history. What do you think? Do dreams come true?"

"Well," Aunt Nan answered, "I believe what James Allen wrote in his book, 'As a Man Thinketh: He who cherishes a beautiful vision, a lofty ideal in his heart, will one day realize it. Columbus cherished a vision of another world, and he discovered it. Copernicus fostered the vision of a multiplicity of worlds and wider universe, and he revealed it; Buddha beheld the vision of a spiritual world of stainless beauty and perfect peace, and he entered it. Cherish your visions; cherish your ideals; cherish the music that stirs your heart, the beauty that forms in your mind, the loveliness that drapes your purest thoughts, for out of them will grow all delightful conditions, all heavenly environments of being, if you but remain true to them, your world will at last be built." Aunt Nan paused to take a breath and then said, "As you probably guessed, I memorized that. And it goes on to point out that 'Only the wise man, only he whose thoughts are controlled and purified, makes the wind and the storms of the soul obey him. Dream lofty dreams, and as you dream, so shall you become. Your vision is the promise of what you shall at last unveil."

"Oh, that's just beautiful," said Aunt Mary.

"The book is small, but full of insight," said Aunt Nan, sipping her tea. "It's one of my all-time favorites."

"But what about the dreams coming true? That's what I wonder about," said Kitty.

"Well," Aunt Nan continued, "while I certainly believe that dreams do come true every day, I also believe that it depends a lot upon the dream, and the dreamer, and, of course, the circumstances in which the dreamer is dreaming the dream, and trying to make the dream come true. I myself have seen where some people's dreams come true just because they have the money, the power, and the opportunity to realize their dreams. And I've also seen first-hand and read about so many instances where people did great, almost supernatural things, even though the odds were greatly stacked against them.

"History tells the tales of many real people who, because of their hard work, determination, and will to succeed, made their dreams come true. Perhaps they thought like Mike does, that it's possible, and therefore they can do it, so they try as hard as they can, and they do it. But then there are people whose dreams aren't practical to begin with. People who have 'pipe dreams,' you might say. Someone might even dream of going to the moon, but try as they may, how likely is that?

"But, now, God willing, one of my greatest dreams is about to come true. All my life, I've seen pictures of people and places all over the world in the cyclopedia and the newspapers and magazines, and now to realize that I may very likely be able to see some of those things in person... Well, it just goes far beyond my wildest dreams."

"And you deserve it!" Kitty added to the agreement of the others.

Mike exclaimed, "My first dream will come true when I buy a motorcycle. Ever since Frankie's brother got his motorcycle and has given us a few rides, Frankie and I are both saving for our own."

"I'd like to get a player piano!" said Kitty excitedly. "I've always wanted to learn to play the piano and Mrs. O'Brien said she'd teach me for free if I had one. I've always thought that people who can play a musical instrument are the luckiest people of all. Instead of sitting around worrying about things, they can divert their thoughts with happy music."

Mike continued, "After I get a motorcycle, I'll start saving for an automobile. I just read in the paper last week that on January first of last year, there were 670,000 automobiles in the United States! That's one automobile for every hundred and thirty-three people! When you figure five people to a family, that means there's an average of one automobile for every twenty-six families in this country. And *I'd* like for us to become one of those families!" he remarked with determination in his voice.

"Maybe after you get your motorcycle and I get my piano, we can save together toward a family automobile," Kitty suggested. "Then after that, we can save together toward a house! There was a good ad in the paper this week about purchasing property for a small down payment and having rents coming in every month. Maybe we could buy a four-family house and with rents coming in, we could pay it off that much faster, and actually have extra income! The ad said that less than one-tenth of one percent of people in America own enough land to live on. That has to be one of the most pitiable statements that could be made for a great free nation like ours."

Mike smiled and said, "Oh, I expect you'll be off getting married before then."

"Ha!" said Kitty. "We've already had that conversation. In fact, that's one of the reasons I get so impatient sometimes. If we could get the vote, then, just maybe, we could raise wages for everybody, and then if we could get women equal pay for equal work, why, we could all afford to live decently, and get those few extra things to really enjoy life!" She sighed contentedly just to think about it, and said, "It's not as if we all need to be rich, I just wish I had enough money not to have to worry so much about getting the rent together and paying the bills. And to be able to buy the things you need when you need them, instead of having to do without. And I guess someday I'd like to have enough to make Mama's dream come true. A nice little house with a front porch and a beautiful lawn filled with flower beds and a rose arbor, and white picket fence."

Maggie said, "Oh, don't fret over me. I always admired Mrs. Flynn's house, with all those beautiful flowers, but I'm perfectly content with what I've got and I thank God every day for giving me as much as He has, a loving family, a roof over my head, food on the table and clothes on my back. And also good health. That's all you really need in this life. And if I never get that house, I'll still be happy, and I'll never miss it."

Kitty said, "Well, you deserve more, Mama, and I'd like to see you get it. It must be wonderful to be able to buy the things you need and to help the people you love to be able to reach their dreams. I always feel as if my life is on hold."

"I don't think you're alone feeling that way, Kitty," said Aunt Mary, "but I agree with your Mama. We have to thank God we have food, shelter and clothing. And a bed to lie down on, huh, Mary?" she winked at her niece. "And we have to remember that there are some poor folks in this world who don't even have that much. They're the ones I really feel sorry for. Why, I was appalled to read in the paper the other day about the slums in Washington. I knew there were slums in New York City and other parts of the country, but in our nation's capital! I think it's disgraceful. But the article did say that a collection of $5400 was taken up by the society women of Washington to go toward cleaning up the slums. Apparently Mrs. Wilson contributed one hundred dollars herself. The article went on to say that she'd gone out on at least two occasions and quietly investigated the alleys and the narrow streets in which, apparently, thousands of people are actually huddled! Why, it reminded me of Dickens's 'Oliver Twist.' Could you imagine living with your family in such a horrible condition? While I don't see anything wrong in dreaming big dreams, I think at the same time we should thank God every day for His blessings and share whatever we can with the poor and disadvantaged."

"Of course, Aunt Mary, you know that if we had more, we'd

give more," said Kitty.

"Oh, of course I do, Honey. I just meant people in general."

"It's too bad we don't have a lottery like some of those other countries," said Mike. "There was a story about it a couple of weeks ago. Did you see it, Aunt Nan?"

"Oh, excuse me a minute, Mike but before I forget," Nan turned toward her sister Mary and said, "When I just mentioned Columbus a few minutes ago, and now Washington's name, it reminded me to give you what I wrote about America." She handed her the folder she had taken from under her purse. "It took me much longer to finish than I thought it would," she exclaimed. "After you finish reading it, maybe you could pass it on to Kitty and Mike, and it might even help Mary in her schoolwork.

"To get back to your question, Mike, Yes! I did read that article. But while lotteries still exist in Spain, Austria, Holland, and a few other countries, if you read that article closely, you'll notice it wasn't actually in favor of lotteries. In fact, it mentioned that Italy is abolishing its lottery because, although it's been immensely profitable for the state, it's a dead loss to the majority of people who participate in it. But worse than that, it encourages a gambling spirit among the people, with the hope of winning a living without working for it."

"Well, I know one whole group of people who'll never have to be concerned about winning or losing money," said Kitty. "All those lucky rich royals at Princess Victoria's wedding last Saturday."

Mary added, "At least they don't have to worry about what to wear."

Aunt Mary spoke up, "And we shouldn't, either. The Bible tells us not to be concerned about what we put on," adding with a smile, "Although I must admit to a weakness for hats," she chuckled.

"But I have to wear something to look half-way decent," Mary remarked.

"Oh, you always look half-way decent, Mary," Annie smiled mischievously.

"Well, you know you can always wear anything of mine that you want to. Just help yourself," Kitty exclaimed.

"Thank you, Kitty," Mary smiled quietly, and she did appreciate her older sister's generosity, but would never tell her that Kitty's browns and other dreary colors were not to her liking. Mary was lighter than Kitty and needed stronger colors to bring out what Pa always called her "peaches and cream" complexion, and she always felt she looked washed out in Kitty's hand-me-downs. Mary favored bright colors, especially blues and greens. Kitty also chose baggy clothes that certainly didn't do anything to enhance Mary's trim figure. In fact, she actually felt a little embarrassed in Kitty's clothes. But the royals, now that was a different matter.

"Listen to this," said Mary as she rushed back into the room with the newspaper clippings she'd saved. "'Brilliant sunshine and cloudless skies have set in for the wedding festivities of Princess Victoria Louise, daughter of the German Emperor and Empress, and Prince Ernst August of Cumberland. King George and Queen Mary, when they alighted from the train, were greeted with the customary cordial embraces by the Emperor and Empress and other members of the Imperial Family, King George and Emperor William then jointly passed in review the Guard of Honor drawn up on the platform. This complete, the two monarchs together and the Queen and Empress side by side, drove in open state carriages through the Avenue of Victory and Unter den Linden to the castle, each carriage escorted by a squadron of cavalry. The wide thoroughfares were lined with troops and behind them all Berlin seemed to have gathered to give the King a royal greeting to the city. The dirigible balloons, Sephlin and Harsa, flying the British colors, accompanied the royal train from about fifty miles away.' Oh, don't you just wish you'd been there?" Mary blurted out excitedly.

"No," Kitty quickly answered, "I don't wish I'd been there."

"Me, either," Mike added. "I can certainly think of better things to do with my valuable time than to watch a bunch of spoiled people prancing around in fancy clothes."

"Keep reading, Mary," Aunt Nan directed. "This is history in the making and yes, I also would like to have been there."

"Berlin's Streets Gay with Decorations and Brilliant Uniforms of Kaiser's Soldiery – Russia's Ruler Arrives. The gathering of three Emperors – those of Germany, Russia and the British dominions – for the wedding on Saturday of Princess Victoria Louise and Prince Ernst August of Cumberland has made the German capital the centre of interest.

"Besides the three great rulers, the only daughter of Emperor William at her marriage is to be surrounded by such a gathering of Princes and Princesses as rarely has been brought together," she continued reading excitedly.

"Extensive precautions have been taken for the safety of the royal personages, the Prussian police being assisted by large bodies of Russian and British detectives, while the soldiers at the stations lining the routes of the royal processions carry loaded rifles.

"The Russian Emperor was met at the station by Emperor William and King George of England and a great gathering of members of the various royal families. The Russian Emperor drove with his imperial host in state to the castle. Emperor Nicholas' journey from the frontier station to Berlin was made in the Russian Imperial armored train."

Mike spoke up. "Now there's something that I find interesting. The police, detective, soldiers with loaded rifles and an armored train, no less!"

"Shall I keep reading?" Mary asked as she looked over at Aunt Nan.

"Yes, go ahead. Continue, Mary," Aunt Nan answered.

"Very early in the day, the Dowager Duchess of Baden, the Emperor's aunt and the senior living member of the royal family of Prussia, arrived, followed shortly afterward by the Duke and Duchess of Cumberland. Besides the principal guests, a swarm of minor Princes and Princesses arrived at the other stations in Berlin. Many of them are related to each other," Mary paused to catch her breath.

Aunt Nan added, "Most of them are Queen Victoria's grandchildren. On February 10th, 1840, she married her first cousin, Prince Albert of Saxe-Coburgh-Gotha and they had nine children and forty-one grandchildren. Kaiser William is her oldest grandchild, son of her oldest daughter, Vicky, who became the wife of the German Emperor. In fact, Queen Victoria's mother was Princess Victoria Maria Louisa of Saxe-Coburgh-Gotha. Her father was Edward, Duke of Kent, fourth son of King George III. Her parents had been living someplace else but they purposely returned to London so their child would be born at Kensington Palace. You'll have to excuse me for getting carried away, everyone, but I always find the lives of the royals of all the countries to be fascinating and intriguing. So continue reading, Mary."

Mary continued, "Emperor William, Emperor Nicholas and King George of England after the customary embraces reviewed the guard of honor together. King George and the Emperor Nicholas are so remarkably alike in appearance that it was difficult even for those familiar with both monarchs to identify them except by the different uniforms they wore. Both were dressed as Prussian officers of the respective regiments of which they are honorary Colonels."

Aunt Nan added, 'I have seen pictures of King George and Czar Nicholas and they certainly do look a lot alike. Their mothers are sisters. Edward VII, who became king when his mother, Queen Victoria, died in 1901 after over sixty-three years on the throne, had married Princess Alexandra, eldest daughter of Christian IX of

Denmark. Her sister, Princess Dagmar, is the mother of Czar Nicholas II, who was the eldest son of Alexander III. He succeeded his father in 1894, and in the same year married Alexandra of Hesse, a granddaughter of Queen Victoria. Please excuse me, there I go again with my fascination of the royals. Please continue, Mary."

Mary answered, "I don't mind at all, because I find it interesting, too, the way they are all inter-related."

Mike answered, "Well I don't find them interesting at all, and wouldn't walk outside the door to see any of them. I definitely don't believe that the princes and princesses or the dukes and duchesses and earls, or for that matter the kings and queens are any better than me or anyone else. In fact, I consider them all a bunch of freeloaders. But I must admit, the one thing I would have liked to see are those two dirigible balloons."

Aunt Nan said, "I noticed the newspaper quoted King George of England saying, 'The preservation of peace is my fervent desire, as it was the chief aim and object of my dear father's life.' And people don't realize it, but when Princess Victoria Louise of Prussia and Prince Ernst August of Cumberland were married with the rites of the Lutheran Church in the royal chapel of the imperial castle, the ceremony signaled the reconciliation between the dethroned House of Hanover and the House of Hohenzollern. The newspaper article pointed out that the presence of the three most powerful sovereigns of Europe – the German Emperor, the Russian Emperor and the British King-Emperor – on terms of intimate friendship made the event a demonstration of international peace, and that there were a number of guests from the United States."

While Mike and Aunt Nan were talking, Mary quickly scanned and skipped over a number of paragraphs and then spoke up, "Listen to this," as she started reading again, "'Wedding gifts on display in the palace were estimated to be worth $2,000,000. Jewels, some of them almost priceless, furniture, ancient tapestries, rich Persian rugs, masterpieces of world-famous artists and sculptors making up the collection.' Can you just imagine all that pomp and two million dollars' worth of wedding gifts? It must be wonderful to be royalty," Mary remarked. "They certainly don't have to worry about 'making ends meet.'"

Aunt Mary spoke up, "Well, I for one don't envy them at all. I would never want to be of so-called 'noble birth.' All those gifts wouldn't tempt me one bit. I would much sooner live a simpler life such as we do."

Aunt Nan answered, "Besides, Mary, that's the good part of being royalty when everybody is getting along. I noticed in Friday's paper, while there were celebrations in Berlin, at the same time, in Athens, because of the consequences of the resumption of hostilities between the Bulgarian and the Greek troops, King Constantine of Greece, accompanied by Prince Alexander and the general staff of the army, left for Salonika that morning. Then Saturday's paper mentioned that severe fighting had resumed between the Greek and Bulgarian troops, that the forces are hotly engaged and that the situation was extremely grave."

Aunt Nan added, "And that reminds me of that element of danger. When Victoria was queen, there were, I believe, seven assassination attempts on her life. The first when she was in the family way. I noticed the attempt was made in June, 1840, on her and Albert, as they were arriving in an open carriage. She had her daughter Vicky in November of the same year. There's always been some problem or other. According to the Encyclopedia Britannica, when Victoria was less than thirty years old, there were revolutions in Paris, Vienna, Berlin, Madrid, Rome, Naples, Venice, Munich, Dresden and Budapest, and panic-stricken princes and princesses wrote to Victoria and Albert for political assistance, or 'pecuniary aid.' Perhaps this is the hope of world peace, that the leaders meet at a happy, joy-filled celebration where there is mutual respect for each other and their countries."

Aunt Mary added, "And speaking of leaders, it mentioned in Friday's paper that President Wilson had received a cablegram from Emperor Yoshintro of Japan. Apparently the President had inquired about his health and he wrote back expressing his sincere thanks to the President, the government and the people of the United States. So that also was a nice exchange between two world leaders."

Kitty spoke up, "The papers were so filled last week about the royal wedding that they hardly mentioned anything about the militant Suffragettes in England. But I did notice in yesterday's paper it mentioned in St. Andrews, Scotland, where the opening of the matches for the amateur golf championship of the world, that during the night before, two militant suffragettes tried to damage the links and interfere with the opening of the play, but were intercepted by night guards. On the other hand there was a piece of good news about the suffragette movement in this country. It seems that there's a woman lawyer who is planning to take an active part in the international suffragist congress at Budapest, Hungary, during the summer. So that's great news," Kitty enthusiastically proclaimed.

"And speaking of good news," Mike mentioned, "I think most people are really looking forward to the Memorial Day Policeman's picnic this Friday at Rensselear Park. I know I sure am. It really sounds like it's going to be terrific. They are going to have horse racing, aeroplane flights and motorcycle racing. Then fireworks at the end."

"That's quite a good-sized park," Kitty exclaimed.

"Forty-two acres," Aunt Nan advised. "During the Civil War, which of course is before our time, the area was a training center for soldiers."

Mike got up to leave, "I better get going or Frankie will be wondering what's keeping me." He said the usual goodbyes as he walked out the door.

Maggie looked over to Annie as she said, "Come on, Annie, it's time for you to go to bed. I'll come in and hear your prayers."

"All right, Mama," Annie replied.

Mary jumped up as she said, "Let me kiss everybody good night now. I have to look over some school work." She started with her mother and went around the table and into her room.

"Kitty," Aunt Nan exclaimed, "I brought you a copy of the Sunday Knickerbocker Press that you were inquiring about last week, when you read their ad in the paper. You said you were surprised to read that a newspaper could contain fifty-two pages, but it does. Here it is: The first news section has sixteen pages, the second news section has sixteen pages, the Capitol District News section, eight pages, the magazine section, eight pages, and the comics section has four pages. So after you read this week's, if you want me to, I can bring it every Tuesday. There's no sense in you spending your hard-earned nickel for it when I can give it to you free two days later."

Aunt Nan turned toward her Sister Mary as she said, "When you were talking about living a simpler life, it reminded me of what Mr. Richardson had said to me in the library that evening, a short time before he was reported missing. He said, 'I'm sorry, Nan, that you have had to put up with my wife's childish outbursts. You may have even wondered why I don't speak up even when they're directed at me. People like my wife don't listen. They don't want to listen. They think that they know everything and that they're right and that's all there is to it. I made up my mind years ago to try to keep peace for the sake of my sweet little Victoria. I'm sure you've noticed my wife is very class-conscious. People like her like to take credit for something their ancestors did years ago, as if that made them better than other people. She looks down upon the lower classes, as if it were their fault for their poor circumstances. My wife is what I would call a 'Street Angel, House Devil.'"

Nan continued, "Mr. Richardson told me how he had grown up in a beautiful peaceful little village in England, where there was farmland, fishing, and honest, kind people. Nobody ever got mad or tried to outdo anyone else. In contrast, he said, 'some shallow people like my wife just don't care about people. They can't ever seem to get enough material possessions for themselves, spending their whole lives collecting things. It seems the more they get, the more they want, so they can laud it over their so-called friends. They never seem to enjoy or appreciate what they have. They just always seem to be jealous of those who have more. They seem to be under some delusion that somehow the more material possessions they have, the more important they are. But to me, it seems like such a sad way to live. To me, material possessions are worthless. Some people call this the good life, but as far as I'm concerned, that was the good life, in that little village where I grew up. The people back there were really helpful and caring. There wasn't any competition over stupid things of no real or lasting importance.' He looked a little sad as he said, 'So many times I've really missed that simple life with its carefree days.'

"He was one of the kindest and most honorable men I ever knew. From what I understand, he collided with the bank policy more than once in his being very lenient towards the poor, and they were breathing down his neck about foreclosures. But it really bothered him, putting people out on the street. It went against his principles, and I think he just didn't want to be a part of it any longer."

"But do you think that he would have embezzled the bank's money?" Kitty asked.

"No, he was a very honest man and I don't think that he would have taken any money that didn't belong to him. But he was brilliant, a financial wizard. I wouldn't be a bit surprised if he figured out how to camouflage the books and take out his own money, even though it appeared otherwise at the time. The Old Lady has always had a lot of money of her own. So there was plenty of money left for the family. He was a kind, gentle man. Maybe he reasoned that if he didn't foreclose, how could he keep his position? If the bank let him go, what would he do? How much public humiliation would the family have been put through?

"The day after that attempted burglary, which was the week before he left, he came into the kitchen for a cup of tea. He confided in me that he was having a hard time sleeping because it really bothered him that hard-working people were losing their homes and he couldn't do anything about it. 'My hands are tied,' he said. I think he felt helpless and just wanted to set the record straight. It seemed as if he needed somebody to talk to who he thought might be able to understand how he felt. He certainly couldn't tell his wife and probably didn't want to worry Victoria or John. And in business, who can you really trust?

"I think that he got tired of putting up with her bickering, and he knew that Victoria was happily married. John was so good to her and the children. Even if it dawned upon him that they would miss him, he would probably have convinced himself that they would get over it. Because, after all, they had each other. I've always thought that with that break-in, he saw the best opportunity that he could ever have, and he took it, believing that they would connect his disappearance and the break-in. He longed for that simple life that he knew as a boy.

"Victoria still misses him terribly. Her being an only child, they were very close. After her father left, Victoria missed him so much that she went through a great depression and took to her bed for months. Her headaches just got so bad. I think not knowing what happened to him just made things so much harder for her.

"John, of course, has always been so understanding, but even after all these years, Victoria will be sitting at the table having lunch, and she'll glance over at the door, and I'll bet she's thinking of him and remembering all the times he came home to have lunch with her and the children."

As usual, Mary overheard everything that was said. She did have school work to do, but, as always, her main reason for leaving the room was to give her Aunt Nan time to talk about the O'Connell family, particularly Jack.

Mary was in the habit of just scanning the daily newspaper. She didn't want to take the time away from the interesting books her Aunt Nan always brought for her to read.

Besides, she knew every Tuesday she would get an edited version of all the happenings in Troy and around the world.

But, one thing she did keep track of was the comings and goings of the more affluent people, the schedule of all the latest travel choices, and lists of entertainment that was available in Troy and Albany. Not that she was able to go to Albany to see anything, but to imagine she could, was a happy part of her daydreams.

Mary's aunts had just left and Mary started thinking of the boat trip the previous Saturday that she wished so much she could have been a part of, especially when she heard her Aunt Nan say that John and Victoria and the family were aboard. John had met his brother and his family at Kingston Point.

Mary had cut out the advertisement and put it in her scrapbook fully aware there was no chance she could go this time, but, maybe in the future, she hoped.

She reread the ad – "Go to Kingston Point Saturday, May 24th, to meet the New Day Line Steamer, 'Washington Irving.'

'This new floating palace of steel and glass will make her first trip up the Hudson River to Albany, Saturday, May 24th.

"An unusual chance to see the finest and fastest river steamer in the world as she enters regular service. The fifty oil paintings by famous artists illustrating the Irving period will be on view. The decorations include reproductions from the Alhambra; the Old Cock Tavern of London; Irving's study at Sunnyside, and from many other interesting historical places.

"Leave Albany 8:30am on Steamer 'Robert Fulton.'

"Return on Steamer 'Washington Irving.' Round Trip, $1.00. Holding's Orchestra.

"Hudson River Day Line."

And as she put the advertisement back in her scrapbook, Mary thought, I'm never going to throw this away. Some day I am going to go on that boat.

In fact, some day I'm going to take a boat or a train all the way to New York City to see the 100 tall buildings I read about in last weeks' paper. It mentioned one building was thirty-five stories high. She couldn't even imagine a building that high.

As Mary drifted off to sleep, her head was filled with beautiful dreams, mostly about Jack and her. And one after the other, like a moving story, she reviewed them.

Somehow, some way, she was optimistically convinced that at the right time, she would marry Jack and all of her dreams would come true.

CHAPTER TWENTY-ONE

The sun was bright and the air was warm in Washington Park as the young girls in their white dresses walked slowly through, two by two, carrying bouquets of mixed flowers, their eyes sparkling, their lips pursed in little smiles. It was the annual May Procession, and everyone watched and smiled as the girls made their way in a circle around the park.

Washington Park was a privately-owned park that came into being when several prominent citizens and businessmen developed a tract of land just south of Troy's thriving downtown.

They laid out a residential square with a landscaped green space at its center. They named it Washington Park and started building their houses around it.

It is one of only two privately-owned parks in the country, the other being Grammercy Park in New York City.

The park was owned in common by the owners of the houses in the immediate vicinity, who comprise the Washington Park Association, as established in the original deed or partition of 1840. Saint Mary's Church was at the northeast corner across the street from the park.

The young girls followed Father Duffy and the altar boys while singing,

"On this day O Beautiful Mother,

On this day we give thee our love.
Near thee, Madonna, fondly we hover
Trusting thy gentle care to prove.
On this day we ask to share, Dearest
Mother, thy sweet care; Aid us ere our
Feet astray, Wander from thy guiding way."

Mary was carrying the lilacs from the lilac tree in her backyard, and lilies of the valley that grew along the side of her house. At the end of the line was a girl carrying a satin pillow, upon which was a flowered crown. Behind her was the eighth grade girl whose name had been chosen for the honor of crowning the statue of the Blessed Virgin Mary.

As Mary walked around the Park singing those beautiful, loving words to the Mother of Jesus, she was feeling especially happy.

As far back as Mary could remember, there was a statue of the Blessed Virgin Mary on the mantelpiece in the dining room of their house.

From her mother and her aunts and the Sisters at school, she had learned about Jesus' mother and from the time she was a little girl had grown to love her.

As she continued in the Procession singing the words she knew by heart, Mary's mind wandered, as it so often did.

Thanks to Kitty, she really enjoyed wearing this beautiful new dress, and felt special in it. She could still remember how upset she had been to learn that her mother had given her dress pattern to the lady next door so that she could make the same dress for her daughter, who was in Mary's class.

"But Mama, I don't want to be dressed just like Joan. I want a nice pretty dress that's just mine, so I'll look just as nice as everybody else."

"Oh, Mary, it's a sin to be so vain. What difference could it possibly make as long as you both have nice dresses?"

"It would make a lot of difference to me. Somebody would probably notice it and say something, and I would feel very embarrassed. It just isn't fair."

"Mary, you're making far too much of this. Mrs. Delaney asked me if she could use the dress pattern so she wouldn't have to waste money buying one. It seems to me you're being selfish, not wanting to share what you have. I think maybe you should think about what I'm saying."

Mary had gone into her room and sat on the bed. But the more she thought about wearing the same dress as someone else in her class, the more aggravated and disappointed she felt. And she didn't think it was fair of her mother to be so generous at her expense. She was always wearing other people's castoff clothes and she had been so looking forward to the new dress her mother was making for her. The pattern was really nice and the material beautiful. But now, this disappointing news brought a scowl to her face, and tears to her eyes. "It's not fair," she kept thinking.

"It's time to set the table, Mary," her mother's voice rang out.

As Mary had gone through the boring motions of setting the table, Kitty had come in from work and right away noticed the forlorn look on Mary's face. "What's the matter, Mary?"

As Mary poured out what to her was a tale of woe, Kitty listened intently. Even as Mary was telling Kitty she figured she was probably wasting her time, because Kitty usually always sided with her mother. She was very practical and circumstances had forced her to be thrifty. But, when Kitty said, "I don't blame you," Mary looked up with a surprised look on her face and hope in her heart.

As Kitty went into the living room to speak to her mother, Mary moved closer to the doorway so as to hear what was being said. After Kitty kissed her mother hello, she asked her how everything was going. Maggie answered most things were good, but she told

Kitty about loaning the pattern out and Mary's reaction to it.

Kitty was careful in choosing her words, because as always she didn't want to hurt her mother's feelings. "You know, Mama, I think I understand how Mary feels. She has always had to wear so many of my clothes and other castoffs that she was really looking forward to this new dress. I certainly agree with you, Mama, that we should be generous, but I think there's also a time when there is nothing wrong with a young girl wanting to have a pretty dress to help her feel extra happy on such a special occasion. I don't blame Mary for not wanting to have the same dress as Joan Delaney. I know I wouldn't want to have the same dress as somebody I worked with."

"Well, Kitty, what could I do when Mrs. Delaney asked me to borrow the pattern? Should I have told her that I didn't care that her daughter didn't have a nice dress to wear? I felt that as a good Christian it's only right that I should share it with her. Now I can't very well ask her for it back."

"No, Mama, you can't do that. I agree that most times, if it's necessary, we should share what we have. But Mrs. Delaney could certainly afford to buy her own patterns. Let's face it, she's always been cheap, and has always put herself and her family first." Kitty's voice softened as she said, "How is Mary's dress coming along, Mama?"

"I just finished the basic dress today, and now I just have to get the trim." As she said this, she had gone in and taken the dress from the bed, where she had laid it out to show it to Kitty.

"Oh, that looks real pretty, Mama. You always do such a good job. I've got a good idea. How about letting me decorate it? I picked up some really good tips on decorating at that sewing class."

Maggie looked over at Kitty, surprised by her words. "Of course, Kitty, if you want to."

Mary had heard most of the conversation, and as she realized that Kitty was coming back into the kitchen, she moved fast over to the sink to get a drink of water, and to try to make it appear as if she had not been eavesdropping.

Kitty came through the door. "I've got good news for you, Mary. Mama said that I can finish your dress. I'll talk over the ideas I have with you and we will decorate your dress so special that it won't look anything like Joan's," she smilingly said. "In fact, it will be the prettiest dress of all."

Mary smiled as she felt the joy come forth within her. "Oh, thank you, Kitty." She had seen some of the clothes Kitty had altered, and she felt very hopeful. Now, remembering, Mary smiled to herself. To her it really was the most beautiful dress of all.

They were going around the park for the second time, singing,

"Bring flowers of the fairest,
Bring flowers of the rarest,
From garden and woodland and hillside and vale.
Our full hearts are swelling,
Our glad voices telling
The praise of the Loveliest Rose of the Vale."

They had just gotten to the entrance of the church when they started singing,

"Oh Mary. we crown thee with
Blossoms today. Queen of the Angels,
Queen of the May,
Oh Mary, we crown thee with blossoms today.
Queen of the Angels, Queen of the May."

They paraded down the middle aisle, and when they got to the altar they placed their flowers in vases to the right and to the left of the three foot statue of the Blessed Virgin Mary that was set upon a table covered with a beautiful white cover, in front of the altar railing.

They then proceeded going to the right or to the left and into the church pews in an orderly fashion.

And then the young lady placed the floral crown on top of the statue of the Blessed Virgin Mary. She then took her place and everyone in the church sat down.

The organist started to play the Ave Maria and within moments Pat was singing, "Ave Maria."

"A-ve, Ma-ri-a, gra-ti-a-plen-na
Do-me-nus te-cum, be-ne-di-cta-tu
In-mu-li-e-ri-bus, et be-ne-di-ctus
Fru-ctus ven-tris tu i-Je-sus
San-cta-Ma-ri-a, Ma-ter-De-i
O-ra pro no-bis pec-ca-to-ri-bus
Nunc et in-h-ra- mor-tis no-strae. Amen"

Pat's heart and soul were in his voice. For he loved the mother of Jesus with more mental passion than most men would ever know. And when the listeners were sure his voice was stretched to its capacity, he reached even higher notes.

Pat's vocal tribute was so moving that the church was hushed except for the organ music and his voice. Maggie and some of the older women even had tears in their eyes.

His voice made people forget their cares and worries and in their place feel peaceful and joyous and happy beyond words.

Maggie couldn't help remembering that weak, sickly little boy and how she had prayed and prayed the rosary to ask our beautiful Blessed Mother to intercede and heal the delicate little son she loved. Then when he started singing with such a beautiful voice, she actually believed that not only her prayers had been answered, but that an actual miracle had taken place.

When Pat finished singing, Father Duffy stepped up to the lectern, smiling at them all.

"This," he said, "is a very special day for us all, as we give to Mary, the Mother of Jesus, the honor that she so justly deserves. In God's plan of Salvation, He chose Mary to fulfill a very unique destiny. Our Heavenly Mother Mary was the only human being, besides Jesus, who was born without sin. Because God did not want the tiniest speck of sin to touch His Divine son, Jesus. And she was the only human being present both when Jesus was born, and when He died. In between those two very important events in the life of Jesus, her son, we read about the love, faith, patience and humility of our Blessed Mother Mary. I pray that as we journey with our Mother Mary through the joyful, sorrowful and glorious Mysteries, that we will be drawn even closer to her, and to her Divine Son, Jesus Christ.

"In the Gospel of St. Luke, we read, 'Now in the sixth month the angel Gabriel was sent from God to a town in Galilee called Nazareth, to a Virgin betrothed to a man named Joseph, of the house of David, and the virgin's name was Mary. And when the Angel had come to her, he said, 'Hail, full of grace, the Lord is with thee. Blessed art thou among women.'

"When she had heard him, she was troubled at his word, and kept pondering what manner of greeting this might be. And the angel said to her, 'Do not be afraid, Mary, for thou hast found favor with God. Behold thou shalt conceive in thy womb and shalt bring forth a son, and thou shalt call his name Jesus. He shall be great, and shall be called the Son of the Most High, and the Lord God will give him the throne of David his Father, and he shall be King over the house of Jacob forever, and of His kingdom there shall be no end.'

"But Mary said to the angel, 'How shall this happen, since I do not know man?'

"And the angel answered and said to her, 'The Holy Spirit shall come upon thee and the power of the Most High shall overshadow thee; and therefore the Holy One to be born shall be called the Son of God.' And behold Elizabeth thy kinswoman also has conceived a Son in her old age, and she who was called barren is now in her sixth month; for nothing shall be impossible with God."

"But Mary said, 'Behold the handmaid of the Lord; be it done to me according to thy word,' And the angel departed from her."

Father paused, and looked out upon the congregation as he said, "The Blessed Virgin Mary is the only person in the Bible that was addressed by an Angel of the Lord, as being filled with God's grace." Then he continued reading the Bible account.

"Now in those days, Mary arose and went with haste into the hill country, to a town of Judah. And she entered the house of Zachary and saluted Elizabeth. And it came to pass, when Elizabeth heard the greeting of Mary, that the babe in her womb leapt. And Elizabeth was filled with the Holy Spirit, and cried out with a loud voice saying, 'Blessed are thou among women and blessed is the fruit of thy womb.' And how have I deserved that the mother of my Lord should come to me? For behold, the moment that the sound of thy greeting came to my ears, the Babe in my womb leapt for joy. And blessed is she who has believed, because the things promised her by the Lord shall be accomplished."

Father paused again, and as he looked out upon the congregation he said, 'Of course we know that the Babe in Elizabeth's womb was John the Baptist."

"And Mary remained with Elizabeth about three months."

"Behold an angel of the Lord appeared to Joseph in a dream, saying, 'Do not be afraid, Joseph, son of David, to take to thee Mary thy wife, for that which is begotten in her is of the Holy Spirit. And she shall bring forth a son and thou shalt call him Jesus, for he shall save his people from their sins.' So Joseph arising from sleep, did as the angel of the Lord had commanded him, and took unto him his wife.

"In the Gospel we read that a decree went forth from Caesar Augustus that a census of the whole world should be taken. Joseph went from Galilee out of the town of Nazareth into Judea to the town of David, which is called Bethlehem – because he was of the house and family of David – to register, together with Mary his espoused wife, who was with child. It came to pass while they were there that the days for her to be delivered were fulfilled. And she brought forth her first born son, and wrapped him in swaddling clothes, and laid him in a manger, because there was no room for them in the inn.

"And there were shepherds keeping watch over their flock by night. Behold, an angel of the Lord stood by them and the glory of God shone round about them, and they feared exceedingly.

"And the Angel said to them, 'Do not be afraid, for behold, I bring you good news which shall be to all the people; for today in the town of David a Savior has been born to you, who is Christ the Lord. And this shall be a sign to you. You will find an infant wrapped in swaddling clothes and lying in a manger.' And suddenly there was with the Angel a multitude of the Heavenly Host praising God and saying, 'Glory to God in the highest, and on earth peace among men of good will.'

"So the shepherds went with haste, and found Mary and Joseph, and the Babe lying in the Manger. When they had seen, they understood what had been told them concerning this child. And all who heard marveled at the things told them by the shepherds. But Mary kept in mind all these things, pondering them in her heart. And the shepherds returned, glorifying and praising God for all that they had heard and seen, even as it was spoken to them."

He looked out again at the congregation as he summarized.

"Then a short time later, when in obedience to the Law of Moses, they presented the child in the Temple where the Holy Prophet Simeon, taking the child in his arms, offered thanks to God for sparing him to look upon his Savior. Simeon blessed them, and said to Mary his mother, 'Behold this child is destined for the fall and for the rise of many in Israel, and for a sign that shall be contradicted. And thy own soul a sword shall pierce, that the thoughts of many hearts may be revealed.'

"There was also Anna, a prophetess. She was of a great age and never left the temple, with fasting and prayers, worshipping night and day. And coming up at that very hour, she began to give praise to the Lord, and spoke of Him to all who were awaiting the redemption of Jerusalem.

"And behold the Magi coming from the east followed the star until it stood over the place where the child was.

"And when they saw the star they rejoiced exceedingly. And entering the house, they found the child with Mary his Mother, and falling down they worshipped him and opening their treasures they offered him gifts of gold, frankincense and myrrh. And being warned in a dream not to return to Herod, they went back to their own country by another way.

"But when they had departed, behold, an angel of the Lord appeared in a dream to Joseph saying, 'Arise, and take the child and his mother, and flee into Egypt, and remain there until I tell thee. For Herod will seek the child to destroy him.' So he arose and took the child and his mother and went into the land of Israel and settled in a town called Nazareth. And the child grew and became strong. He was full of wisdom and the grace of God was upon him.

"And when Jesus was twelve years old they went up to Jerusalem according to the custom of the Feast of the Passover. And after they had fulfilled the days, when they were returning, the boy Jesus remained in Jerusalem, and his parents did not know it. But thinking that he was in the caravan, they had come a day's journey before it occurred to them to look for him among their relatives and acquaintances. And not finding him, they returned to Jerusalem in search of him.

"And it came to pass after three days they found him in the temple, sitting in the midst of the teachers, listening to them and asking them questions. And all who were listening to him were amazed at his understanding and his answers. And when they saw him, they were astonished. And his Mother said to him, 'Son, why hast thou done so to us? Behold in sorrow thy Father and I have been seeking thee.'

"And he said to them, 'How is it that you sought me? Did you not know that I must be about my Father's business?' And they did not understand the words that he spoke to them; and his Mother kept all these things carefully in her heart. And Jesus advanced in wisdom and age and grace before God and men.

"And Jesus' mother Mary was present at the Marriage Feast at Cana, along with Jesus' disciples, when Jesus performed his first miracle. We are told that it was Mary who called to Jesus' attention that, 'They have no wine.' And Jesus said to her, 'What wouldst thou have me do, woman? My hour has not yet come.' His mother said to the attendants, 'Do whatever he tells you.' And as we know they filled six stone water jars with water and Jesus changed the water to wine. And we realize that even though Jesus had said that his time had not yet come, Mary believed that he would do something, and indeed we know that he did act upon Mary's concern, by performing his first recorded miracle.

"After that, we are told that she went down to Capernaum with him and his disciples. Over the course of Jesus' public life, I would not be surprised to learn, although it is not recorded anywhere in the gospels, if many times Mary saw Jesus make the blind see, the deaf hear, the lame walk, the dumb speak, the lepers healed, and that she heard many of his Parables.

"And when Jesus was arrested, there are no words that could possibly describe how Our Blessed Mother must have felt, looking upon Jesus after he had been beaten and crowned with thorns. Then watching the soldiers place that heavy cross upon his scourged, bloody back. Helplessly watching him fall on the way to Calvary. To see nails pierce the hands that she had once kissed and hear the taunts of those who mocked him. Yet by Faith, know that Jesus was our Redeemer, and by her resignation to the will of God, accept this as the fulfillment of our Redemption.

"When Jesus therefore saw his Mother and the disciple standing by, whom he loved, he said to his Mother, 'Woman, behold thy Son,' then he said to the disciple, 'Behold thy Mother.' And from that hour the disciple took her into his home."

Father looked out at the congregation as he said, "And we believe that when Jesus gave his Mother to John, that he gave her to all of us. Just as he wanted to share with us, God his Father, he also wanted to share with us, his Mother Mary.

"And as they took Jesus from the cross and placed him in her arms, her anguish must have been unbearable.

"Then we know that Jesus was buried and that three days later he arose from the dead and appeared to the women and then to the Apostles on a number of occasions and then forty days later, before their eyes, he ascended into Heaven.

"The last thing we read in the Bible about the Blessed Virgin Mary is in the Acts of the Apostles. It says that when they returned from the Mount called Olivet and went to the Upper room, all these with one mind continued steadfastly in prayer with the women and Mary, the Mother of Jesus and with his brethren.

"And as we know, when the Blessed Virgin Mary died in this life, she was taken up Body and Soul to Heaven. We call it the Assumption of the Blessed Virgin Mary. Because God did not want this Holy Body that had borne, nurtured and protected His son, Jesus, to decay.

"God chose the most perfect Mother of all for His Son Jesus. So it is only right that we think of her as being first among all God's Saints.

"And next to God and Jesus, and the Holy Spirit, who loves us the most but our Heavenly Mother Mary.

"And when we pray and ask her what we should do, she will tell us the same thing that she told the attendants at the Wedding Feast at Cana. 'Do whatever he tells you to do.' And we know from the Bible what Jesus wants us to do.

"When the Blessed Virgin Mary appeared to St. Bridget, she said, 'No matter how many sins a man has committed, if he comes to me with a desire to change his life, I welcome him. I am more interested in the sincerity of his desire than in the hatefulness of his sins. I am always ready to soothe and heal the gaping wounds of his soul. That is why my name is 'Mother of Mercy.'

"The Blessed Virgin Mary is the most loving, gentle, patient, forgiving Mother that was ever born. Next to Jesus himself, we could not have a better role model.

"Yesterday being Memorial Day reminded me that the first Catholic Bishop of the United States, John Carroll, declared the young nation to be under Mary's protection. And in 1847, Pope Pius IX proclaimed the Blessed Virgin Mary 'Patroness of the United States.'

"As we close our special tribute to our Blessed Mother Mary, let us sing the hymn 'Holy God We Praise Thy Name." The organ started playing and everyone started singing:

"Holy God, we praise they name,
Lord of all we bow before thee!
All on earth thy rule acclaim.
All in Heav'n above adore thee.

Infinite thy vast domain.

Everlasting is thy reign."

They arrived home from church. Maggie, Kitty, Aunt Mary, Aunt Kate and their Aunt Alice were sitting at the kitchen table drinking coffee. Mary and Molly were in the living room, chatting.

Their Aunt Alice was saying although she did think it was a beautiful service and was glad to be there to see Mary in the procession and hear Pat sing, she still believed the Catholics' worship of the Blessed Virgin Mary took away from Jesus.

Aunt Nan quickly, but patiently, answered, "Aunt Alice, that's a misconception. We don't worship the Blessed Virgin Mary, we just give her great honor and respect because she was the mother of Jesus and suffered greatly with him. And this may come as a surprise to you, Aunt Alice, but Martin Luther had a great devotion to the Blessed Mother. For after all he was originally an Augustinian Priest."

Just then Pat walked into the kitchen.

They all complimented him on how good his singing was, when he took everybody by surprise by announcing that he was going to become a Priest.

He went on to explain that he had intended to wait until he finished La Salle in two more years, but he had decided that he would leave at the close of this school year. "I'm sure God wants me to go now." He mentioned the new Franciscan Seminary in Rensselear, and that he had been going there after school. He was sure that he wanted to be a Franciscan Priest.

After they got over the initial shock that he would be leaving so soon, they were all very happy about him becoming a Priest, and after hugs and kisses they all told him they'd help him in any way they could.

CHAPTER TWENTY-TWO

After Mass and dinner, the girls hurried to get the dishes out of the way fast, so that they wouldn't be late for the picture show. They tried unsuccessfully to talk Maggie into going with them, but Maggie said she wanted to talk over some things with her sisters.

Mike anxiously waited for them all to leave. His anger toward Pat had been building up all week, ever since he found out Pat was neglecting his chores and returning home late every day.

He'd just been waiting for the right moment to have it out with him, without the interference from his mother and sisters taking sides.

Mike felt justifiably angry at Pat's complete lack of family concern. Yesterday's announcement that he was going to be a priest was the final straw. He wanted to tell Pat, in no uncertain terms, why he considered his plan to become a Priest ridiculous, but at the same time he didn't want his mother to hear what he had to say. He felt his heart beating impatiently, watching his mother just poking along, as he kept both his eyes on Pat to make sure he didn't get away. He knew this opportunity would not come again soon, if at all.

The outer door had hardly closed behind Maggie when Mike started his tirade of words. He tried to hold his voice down and not exhibit the anger that he was really feeling. All he needed was for his mother to hear him, knowing that she would have returned and scolded him for his unkind words to Pat.

Pat and Mike were probably as opposite as two brothers could possibly be. Mike, who was two years older, was sturdily built. He, along with Kitty, felt a great sense of responsibility toward the family. From the time he was young, Mike was a hard worker, and took on any job he could to help the family financially. Consequently he had become very strong and was a very good athlete. He was only twelve years old when he first started working for Mr. Stewart six days a week. Sometimes he even helped him deliver furniture. Mike figured he could finish his education in his spare time through the interesting books his Aunt Nan provided him. Good school grades didn't mean much in comparison to making money that was desperately needed at home.

Pat, on the other hand, was from the very beginning smaller and thinner. When Pat was seven years old, he got pneumonia and almost died. After a long, sometimes painful recovery, he seemed prone to sickness. It was only the past few years that he even began to look a little healthier.

Maggie had a good relationship with all of her children, but because of Pat's condition, she had gotten in the habit of shielding him from overwork and what she considered unfounded criticism.

Mike very angrily began, "Well, I couldn't believe my ears this morning when I woke up to hear the girls talking about you becoming a priest. Are you out of your mind? I know you've always wasted a lot of extra time at church, but I had no idea it had gone this far. Why, I've just been waiting for you to graduate from La Salle so you could get a job and help with the family finances. I could never understand why you had to go to high school for four years anyway, when most people go to work after eighth grade, if not sooner. Two years ago I mentioned to Mama that you should quit school and help the family. But she convinced me at the time that you were not real strong, and would need more schooling to get an easier job. Well, okay, I've been patient, but enough is enough. Why should I knock myself out, pouring my hard earned money into this house, while you run off following an illusion? As far as I'm concerned, you're running out on your family obligations and I resent you for it. It's time for you to forget childishness and pay back for all the things you've been given. Why, you're even deserting your own mother. How can you justify that?"

Pat calmly answered, "I don't expect you to understand. But one thing I know for sure is that I have to do what I know God wants me to do. Besides, Mama understands and told me that she'd prayed for years that one of us would become a priest. I'm really sorry, Mike, that you don't understand. But this is not something I've just recently thought about. As far back as I can remember, I've thought about becoming a priest. Then when I had pneumonia, I used to wake up in the middle of the night and I would see the lit candle and the reflection of the statue of the Blessed Virgin Mary on the wall, and even though I was in pain, I felt as if she was guiding and protecting me, and I still believe that. When I was recuperating, I read the book about the lives of the saints, and felt inspired by them. They're my heroes, doing everything for God's greater glory. I realized then I wanted to be like them and do all the good that I personally could to make this world a better place, by helping people and spreading Jesus' message of love and peace, and charity."

Mike retorted, "Well, you know what they say, charity begins at home. You could start by spreading some of that love and caring for your own family first. In fact, you might just be able to make some good money singing, maybe even on stage. I didn't want you to get a swelled head, but when you sang on St. Patrick's Day for the Hibernians, Joe was bartending. He told me that there was a New York City talent scout there who was in Troy visiting his cousin. He said you were good enough to be on the New York stage."

Pat said, "Yes, he came backstage to talk to me, and told me he could get me a good job singing, making at least twenty dollars a week to start."

"And you passed that up?" Mike said angrily. "Why that's almost twice what Pa makes in a week as a blacksmith! And did you say *'to start'?!*'"

Pat answered, "I only sang that night to earn money to give to Mama. God gave me this voice to sing holy hymns and songs that will make the poor people happy. I want to sing for the people who can't afford the price of the ticket."

Mike shook his head. "That's so typical of you, putting your own family last. Did it ever occur to you that your working could ease the burden that Kitty and I have had to share since we were young? I realized long ago that the old man would never be very dependable. It won't be long before the girls will all end up getting married. I always thought that you and I could some day buy a two-family house together and help take care of Mama and Pa in their old age. I can see now that all along you've been selfishly thinking of what's best for you and you're running out as usual leaving me holding the bag."

"I'm sorry, Mike," Pat proclaimed, "But I can't live my life the way you want me to, any more than you would be willing to live your life my way. I must follow God's calling. I really have no choice. Besides, Kitty will be of much more help than I would ever be."

"Oh, she'll be like the rest of them and run off someday and get married," Mike replied.

Pat shook his head, "No, not Kitty. She knows what she wants out of life, and her plans include staying single and taking care of Mama. And even though she's impatient with Pa, I'm sure she wouldn't put him out on the street."

Mike said, "Well, anyway, good intentions can only go so far. How much help can she possibly be when women don't make anywhere near the pay a man makes. That's why in order to get ahead we need another man's pay around here."

Pat smiled. "Well, maybe if you'd listen to Kitty a little better, you'd have realized that is one of the main reasons she wants women to have the same opportunities as men, so that they will be able to earn more money. So there's your answer. You help the women get the right to vote and get more pay, and then Kitty will make more money and be in a position to share more of the responsibilities with you."

Mike, obviously annoyed, very angrily answered, "Oh, how can I talk intelligently with someone who refuses to help his own family?"

Pat smilingly said, "And I wonder how I can talk to somebody who is so close-minded on certain subjects and won't even listen or try to understand."

Mike quickly said, "What do you mean? I'm a very open-minded person."

Pat calmly answered, "Maybe on most subjects, but not when it comes to God, Jesus, the Catholic Church or women's rights. Mention any of those words and you put up a mental barrier."

Mike commented, "That's because I keep hearing the same thing over and over again. Empty words that don't help anything or anybody. If I didn't agree with them the first dozen times I heard them, how could anybody possibly believe that I'd ever agree with them? Besides, I heard all that church rubbish every Sunday and many mornings when I was an altar boy."

Pat questioned, "Yes, excerpts taken from here and there, but were you really listening, or was your mind on the baseball games and all the other things you were going to do that day? You've never read the Bible from cover to cover, or studied about the background of the Bible, or all the historical facts that it contains. I wonder how many other books, of no lasting importance, have you and so many other people read, while ignoring what millions of people consider the most important book of all time. You're always reading history books, and yet you've chosen to ignore the most historical book of all. The Old Testament of the Bible is a documented history of the Jewish nation. If you don't believe Abraham and all his descendants, then how can you believe the history of any nation? Greece, Egypt, Rome, etcetera? Aunt Nan has read the whole history of the world, and she believes in the Bible. Some day you're going to find out that the Bible is the most important book in the world. I can assure you that there is a great body of evidence to substantiate this claim, but most people haven't even tapped the surface. In fact when it comes to religious matters, I'd be willing to bet that most people don't even have a third grade education."

Mike impatiently answered, "Well, your studying of what you call the body of evidence, has, in my opinion, made you become a religious fanatic. I'm just trying to talk some sense into you before it's too late, and you end up throwing your life away. When I look at you I think, what a fool, reciting words that go up into the air into nothingness."

Pat confidently exclaimed, "No, it is I who look at you and feel sadness for you, because you have closed your mind to the God that loves you. You are denying yourself a great spiritual awareness and consolation that will comfort you throughout any tribulations that you may experience in life. In fact, I challenge you to read the little over three hundred pages of the New Testament of the Bible, and really encounter the dynamic Jesus of Nazareth, and his friends, who gave up everything to follow him and bring forth his message. Jesus said, 'Seek and you will find,' but, if you refuse to seek, then you've only yourself to blame for the absent void within you."

Mike angrily replied, "If there's anybody who has a void within them, it's you, being so totally unrealistic."

Pat said, "You don't just understand that because I trust God completely, I know He will provide in all things. So I step forward in faith, and proceed one step at a time. I cannot explain it any better than this to you, because I cannot transfer to you the inner peace I feel. I cannot turn back and I cannot separate myself from God's calling. I must follow God's call all my life and beyond to the grave and to eternal life with Jesus."

Mike quickly retorted, "Well, some of us have to face the realities of this life. I'm glad I'm not living in that twilight zone. I would never want to lose sight of the reality of this life, for a flimsy belief in the hereafter. That's the way I feel."

Pat quietly responded. "Mike, it might surprise you, but I do understand how you feel. Be under no illusion, I am well aware of the realities of this life. I've never lost sight of them. But if you really face reality, then you'd realize that this life will fly by fast and then what? Will you be prepared for Judgment Day?"

Mike replied, "Well, I don't believe all that rubbish."

Pat hurriedly answered, "Mike, just because you don't believe it doesn't mean it isn't going to happen."

"Well, just because you do believe it doesn't mean it is going to happen," Mike said. "And if God wants me to believe in Him, then let Him speak to me about it."

Pat replied, "God is speaking to you, but you're not listening. You have filled your mind with many insignificant things of no lasting importance and you've chosen to shut God out of your life."

Mike confidently questioned, "Okay then, explain to me where this God of yours came from? Do you really believe like your church teaches that God always was, and always will be? Now to me that's ridiculous."

Pat exclaimed, "Perhaps it's hard for you to believe, but what's your explanation? To believe that this whole universe, with the planets, stars, sun, moon, earth, all the people, and so many different kinds of plants and animals, that all this developed out of nothingness? With no plan? Now to me that's absurd. It makes much more sense to me to believe that there is an Almighty God of wisdom, that designed the universe and its people and that He set everything in motion, but that we just aren't intelligent enough to understand this God of love. In the Bible, we read that God said, 'My ways are not your ways.' To me it's utterly ridiculous to believe that haphazardly out of nothing the first form of life came to be, and then at some magical moment, this life force developed into a man and then a woman. And then just by coincidence they happened to fit together to reproduce? Besides there were the Prophets in the Old Testament of the Bible, that foretold hundreds of years ahead of time about the coming of the Messiah and Jesus fulfilled those prophecies. There were many other things foretold about his life and death."

Mike said, "Jesus knew those things too so he could have just done those things so that it would appear as if it was about him."

Pat confidently replied, "Oh, sure, that he would be betrayed by a friend for thirty pieces of silver. That he would be given vinegar and gall. They would cast lots for his garments. Not a bone would be broken. His side would be pierced. Think what you will, but Jesus had no control over those prophecies."

Mike impatiently replied, "Well, I for one am just sick of hearing about the Prophets. From now on the only prophets I want to hear about is spelled *P-R-O-F-I-T-S*. Besides, they don't even have the originals."

Pat explained, "That's true, but if you had an important document and you wanted to preserve it, and it was becoming worn, wouldn't you copy it, before it was too late?" And without waiting for an answer, Pat acknowledged, "Well, that's exactly what they did."

Mike quickly answered, "But if the documents were so important, why didn't God preserve them so there wouldn't be any question at all? And there were others besides Jesus that did wondrous things and made the claim that they were the Messiah, and they had many followers."

Pat replied, "Yes, and when they died, their followers disbanded. But no other followers but Jesus' made the claim they had personally witnessed him bringing people who had died, back to life. And you are also ignoring the fact that down through the centuries there have been hundreds and hundreds of miracles. People from all over the world healed of all kinds of infirmities and diseases."

Mike said, "Well, I believe that's Catholic propaganda. I don't know of anybody that was healed and I've seen a lot of disabled people. Why aren't they healed? And I'll bet you don't know anybody that was healed, either."

Pat agreed, "I don't know anybody personally, but I have read about a number of healings. That's part of your problem is disbelief. Unless you personally see something, you don't believe it. You've always said that history was your favorite subject, but the whole history book is filled with happenings that you never personally saw. How do you know they're true?"

Mike questioned, "If there is a God, then in all honesty, how could you possibly believe that He's all just? When some people have been given every advantage and opportunity, with servants to wait on them, all kinds of fancy foods, plenty of money to travel abroad and purchase everything that their little hearts' desire. Others live with rats and cockroaches, wearing rags and going to bed hungry. They spend their whole life in abject poverty, enduring overwhelming heartache. Where is this God of yours? Is He blind and deaf? Maybe if you could explain to me why this God of yours would allow that selfish conniving Old Lady Richardson to live in the lap of luxury, while a saintly lady like Mama is forced to do without, and why that jackass Edgar, who never worked a day in his life, is given the best of everything? Your God seems to give more to the hypocrites. Is that just? Maybe if I had what people like the O'Connells have, then I could believe, too. But all I've ever seen is constant struggle just to make ends meet and people like Mama working by the sweat of their brow just to have the meager necessities of life. And how can you expect me to love a God that would command the Israelites to destroy a whole group of people, including women and children, and take their land? How can you justify the Israelites following God's command, when they had to break His Commandment, 'Thou Shalt not Kill,' to do it? How can somebody be right and wrong at the same time? And what about Noah and the flood? And why did this all-knowing, all-loving and all-powerful God of yours stand by and allow all those early Christians to be fed to the lions, and all the martyrs put to death for their beliefs? So if there is as you claim a God, as far as I'm concerned He's very unfair and not doing a very good job. I find it hard to believe that this unjust God of yours loves me, and it's even harder for me under the circumstances to love Him in return. I'm just being honest about it."

Pat listened intently and then replied, "I don't have all the answers, and I'll be the first one to admit it. What you want is for somebody to give you a precise, analytical, logical explanation of the mysteries of life. But like everyone who ever went before us and all those who will come after us, no one has the answers. God will give them to us when He's ready. Maybe God had to allow certain things to happen for the greater good."

Mike said, "Well that answer's not good enough for me. I'll believe in your God when you can explain to me why this God of love allows innocent people to suffer, especially children!"

Pat explained, "Many people suffer because of the selfishness of their fellow man."

Mike questioned, "Then why does God allow it?"

Pat answered, "Because He gave man the gift of free will to choose for ourselves right or wrong."

Mike said, "Another thing. It's just not normal for a man to go his whole life through without ever having been with a woman, or to not want children to carry on after him."

Pat replied, "It's not normal for you. But what you call normal and what I call normal are miles apart. My love for God and Jesus is much stronger than my desire to marry and father children. But I just don't think you can understand. And speaking of what's normal, to me it's not normal for a man not to have a relationship with the God who gave him life and the very breath he breathes. Believing in God brings a great peace of mind, a very warm feeling of God's love and an overwhelming awareness that no matter what goes wrong in this life, that some day when you die you'll experience the greatest happiness of all, seeing God face to face and being reunited with all the people you loved in this life. In comparison what does not believing do for anyone?"

Mike quickly answered, "I say you believe it because you want to believe it."

Pat pointed out, "Well, you can think and say whatever you want to. But to set the record straight, I believe because I have seen, heard and read so much evidence to prove that it's true. But if you choose to ignore God and refuse to study the evidence, then naturally you won't advance in the spiritual dimension. It's hard to explain to someone who is so in tune to the physical side of the human body, who actually denies the very existence of the spiritual side, but I'll try anyway. You're my brother and you are standing before me. But Jesus is my brother too, and just because I don't see him in the physical presence doesn't mean that he isn't real. It's as if Jesus lived in another state and we correspond through letters."

Mike responded, "But he doesn't answer you."

Pat quickly answered, "Oh, but he does. Through the Gospels, Jesus has communicated, and is still doing so. He has told us in no uncertain terms who he is and what he wants his followers to do. So we really hear his voice through the Scriptures and from within. To each one of us he is saying, 'Follow me.' And that is what I must do. Follow this Jesus of Nazareth, this 'King of Kings' and 'Lord of Lords'. I will read Jesus' words and pray that I make the right choices. And I believe I will."

Mike impatiently replied, "What's really hard to explain to someone is reality when their head is in the clouds."

"I didn't think you'd understand," Pat replied. "How could I possibly make you understand the love I have for Jesus? When I read about how good, kind and caring he was when he was on the earth and how much he suffered for the sins of mankind, it just causes me to want to do all that I personally can to encourage and help people turn to Jesus. Not only for their own sake but also because he deserves it."

Mike shook his head as he said, "Well, I don't want to hear anymore about your imaginary God who doesn't seem to give a damn about the world that you believe He created."

Pat almost prayerfully replied, "I'm really sorry you feel that way, Mike. I hoped even though we disagreed that we could still remain friends. All my life I will pray that some day you will return to the God who loves you. You see even though you have chosen to turn your back on God, God will not turn His back on you, because He loves you."

Mike very impatiently replied, "Well, you can waste your time as much as you want to, with idle empty words, going nowhere. It's your life. But don't expect me to waste mine when there are so many important things to do. You're right about one thing, I don't understand such nonsense. Such complete disregard for your family.

As far as I'm concerned, the day you leave for the seminary, I'll consider that day as the day you died. If anybody asks me how my brother is, I will say, I have no brother."

The door opened and Maggie came in quickly, closing the door hurriedly behind her. "Shhh. My goodness, what will the neighbors think? I never saw such an opinionated family in my life. I suppose I should at least thank God that you don't get into a fist fight like some brothers. I hope you haven't been arguing since I left and I hope you're going to end it now. You know how I hate arguments. They make me so nervous and they never do any good. Nobody ever changes their mind. So what good comes of it? You both must have better things to do with your time. So I don't want to hear another word from either of you."

Mike looked disgustingly at Pat as he shook his head and walked into his room feeling angry that nothing he had said helped in any way to alter Pat's course.

CHAPTER TWENTY-THREE

It had been a busy Monday and the O'Neills had just sat down to supper. Kitty was saying how wonderful it felt to be working only nine hours a day instead of ten, as the phone company had just instituted its new forty-five hour work week.

"That extra hour of sleep this morning was so wonderful! I think this is the wave of the future. People work better when they're well-rested."

"Maybe you could add that to your list of causes," Mike replied, dunking a piece of bread into his soup. "We could use that at the brewery, too."

"Give me the vote, and I will," she smiled, spooning into her bowl.

Annie said, "Forty-five hours a week! And I thought school was bad! Maybe I'll be able to go through one or two years of high school and not be bound for the factory after eighth grade like most. I do have really good grades. That way I'd not only be guaranteed a better job, but also have the opportunity to meet and marry someone on a higher financial level."

"Well," said Kitty, "if and when you do get married, you'll be working all day long and into the night keeping house for your family."

Annie answered, "But if I marry someone with money, I can

hire someone to help me."

Maggie smiled as she said, "Besides, it's not the same as a job when you're in your own home and you're doing the things you want to do for the people you love."

Mary thought to herself, Annie is beginning to think just like her.

"Enjoy these days while they're here, girls," said Kitty. "These are the most carefree days of your life."

Suddenly there was a pounding at the door and a voice called out, "Mrs. O'Neill! Mrs. O'Neill!"

All at once they dropped their spoons and ran to the door. Mike pulled it open and there stood a boy Kitty recognized as one of the Sweeneys, who lived next door to Aunt Mary and Aunt Kate.

"Mrs. O'Neill! My Pa said to come quick! Your sister Miss Fogarty has had some kind of a spell and they sent for Doc Taylor!"

Mike immediately put his hand out to help his mother up off the kitchen chair. Kitty grabbed her mother's shawl and put it around her as the three of them went out the door and down the stairs.

Kitty called to Mary to put out the stove and leave a note for Pa and Pat before following them. Then they ran out of the house and up the street, with Annie breathlessly trying to catch up to them.

Mary checked the stove to make sure everything was turned off and then proceeded to her room for a pencil and paper.

Ripping a page from her notebook, she scribbled:

Pa and Pat –

Aunt Kate had a spell! We all ran over there! Your food is on the stove.

Love, Mary

She dropped the pencil on the table and rushed out the door. Holding her dress up, she ran up the street as fast as she could.

Finally she reached the house, where already a group of people gathered around the doorway and on the porch. Breathless, she shouted, "Let me through, let me through, it's my Aunt's house!"

Mike met her just inside the door and the look in his eyes told her all she needed to know.

"She's gone, Mary," he said quietly. "Doc Taylor said it was most likely a heart attack. She went fast. She didn't suffer."

"Oh... Poor Aunt Kate," said Mary.

"Mama and Kitty are with her," he whispered.

"She was always so sweet. How is Aunt Mary taking it?"

Mike stared into her eyes, confused. "Aunt Mary?"

"Yes, how is she? I'll go talk to her, too."

"Mary," said Mike quietly, holding her gently by the arms before she could move any further into the house. "Aunt Kate is all right. She's very upset, naturally, but," he paused, searching for just the right words.

Mary's eyes were blank for a moment. It was hard for her to understand his words. They seemed not to make sense. "Mike, are you telling me that it was Aunt Mary who died, and not Aunt Kate?"

"Yes, Honey, I know it's hard to believe, but it's Aunt Mary who died."

All of a sudden, the full reality of the situation hit Mary. "Oh, Mike," she exclaimed sadly. As she started sobbing on his shoulder, he held her tightly.

CHAPTER TWENTY-FOUR

Mary laid in bed listening to the voices of her mother, Kitty and her Aunt Nan drifting in from the kitchen. It was the Tuesday evening after her Aunt Mary's funeral and they were still talking about the wake, funeral and other things related to her Aunt Mary's death. She had gone to bed early. She was still missing her Aunt Mary a lot and talking about her still drew tears to her eyes.

Kitty was saying, "Aunt Kate said that she just didn't feel up to coming over today, so I brought her dinner over there and told her I'd be back early to stay over tonight."

Maggie said, "Of course. Although we're all going to miss Mary, she's going to miss her the most. Just the two of them living together for so many years, and Mary helping Kate so much."

Kitty spoke up. "In fact, Aunt Kate mentioned to me exactly what did happen that day. You probably already know, but I was so busy taking care of things and still had to work. Aunt Kate mentioned that when Aunt Mary came home from work that day, she looked so tired. Aunt Kate said to her, 'Sit down at the table and I'll get you a bowl of this delicious soup that Maggie brought over this afternoon.' She said Aunt Mary nodded smilingly at her. Aunt Kate said she filled the soup bowl and when she turned back, Aunt Mary was already slumped over the table. At first Aunt Kate thought that she was so tired that she had fallen asleep. But when she couldn't wake her up she called Mr. Sweeney and he called the doctor. Mr. Sweeney told me afterwards that he didn't want to alarm Aunt Kate, but he thought right away that Aunt Mary was dead. Heart attack, the doctor said. She died instantly."

Kitty continued, "Did you know that when people heard Miss Fogarty died, they all assumed it was Aunt Kate? She was sickly all her life, while I can still remember Aunt Mary saying that she'd never been sick a day in her life. She was always so healthy and so vibrant. Who would ever think she'd die so young? Only forty-two years old. I still can't believe it."

Nan said, "She was always so aware of the preciousness of life, especially after Robert, her fiancé, died so young of tuberculosis. He was only twenty-four. I remember after he died she said, 'Now I have to live for the two of us.' She'd say every day is a gift from God. I don't think I know anybody that was more unselfish than she was. I can still remember when we were young, Mama working, and Mary taking care of us. She was the one that taught all of us our ABC's and how to read and tie our shoelaces and tell time and all the basics. She was so patient and enthusiastic. She always made you feel as if you could do anything. She always had so much faith. Remember how she always used to say that she had enough faith for any ten people?"

Maggie added, "In fact, I think she just wore herself out helping everybody. I was amazed at all the people at the wake. Each one had a story to tell about how she'd helped them or their families in some way or another. I was just so surprised that she even knew so many people. And all those flowers and all those Mass cards. I never saw so many in my life."

Aunt Nan exclaimed, "Mike told me that the line was all the way around the block both nights of the wake."

Kitty mentioned, "Mrs. Patterson told me that whenever she heard the words, 'They will know we are Christians by our love,' that she always thought of Aunt Mary."

"Yes," Maggie added, "she was such a good person, I don't know what I would have done so many times without all her help and without all your help, too, Nan. I just like to think that she's up in Heaven with Mama, Papa, Aunt Rose and all those other wonderful people who unselfishly did their best to make life easier for the rest of us." Her eyes misted over as she thought of it.

After a moment, Maggie continued. "Kate and I talked it over about what to do with Mary's clothes. They don't fit any of us so I gave them to Mrs. Foley. She has a large family and was very thankful to get them. We thought that Kitty being the oldest should get the ring that Robert had given to her."

Mary started remembering the wake. Aunt Mary had been laid out in their parlor in a beautiful blue lace dress. Mary was also amazed at how many people were at the wake. She noticed her Aunt Mary's colored friend Joan that walked to work with her every morning. She and her Aunt Mary had to be to work a half hour earlier than everyone else. She was quietly sobbing as she moved through the line. Mary couldn't help but remember that when she was a few years younger that Joan's son had accidentally drowned. She had seen the funeral procession go by, and among the sea of dark faces, one white face stood out. It was her Aunt Mary's. Through love and humility, her Aunt Mary and Joan had been able to go beyond the barrier of skin color and had become good friends.

Everyone said how beautiful she looked, almost as if she were sleeping, but when Mary looked at her, she didn't think so. She wasn't laughing or smiling anymore, and she never would.

Mary continued listening as she heard her Aunt Nan remark, "Her funeral Mass was beautiful too, with Pat singing all of her favorite hymns, and Father saying such nice things about her. I'm glad he included the twenty-third psalm. I told him it was her favorite," and she started reciting it, "The Lord is my shepherd, I shall not want.

He maketh me to lie down in green pastures. He leadeth me beside the still waters. He restoreth my soul. He leadeth me in the path of righteousness for His name's sake. Yea, though I walk through the valley of the shadow of death, I will fear no evil, for thou art with me. Thy rod and thy staff, they comfort me. Thou prepares a table before me in the presence of my enemies. Thou anointeth my head with oil. My cup overflows. Surely goodness and mercy shall follow me all the days of my life and I shall dwell in the House of the Lord forever."

CHAPTER TWENTY-FIVE

It was Friday the 13th and Mary was on her way to Aunt Kate's, carrying their supper and a paper bag in which she'd packed her overnight clothes and the copy of "Pride and Prejudice" which Aunt Nan had brought on Tuesday.

"It is a truth universally acknowledged that a single man in possession of a good fortune must be in want of a wife." From that opening line, Mary had been hooked, and already she was fifty pages into the novel, which both fascinated and amused her to no end. In her mind's eye as she read, Mary could see Mr. Darcy at the ball, tall, handsome and refined. She could feel the palpitations of the hearts of the many young ladies who tried to woo him with their charms. Mary was glad that, unlike Mr. Darcy, Jack was not prideful or prejudiced against those who had been born with less than he had. And at a certain moment in time, he would know that she was deserving of his heart, in marriage. She giggled to herself to think of it, and sighed again at the fact that she was only thirteen. Oh, she wondered, why does time have to drag on so slowly? Oh, if only she were a few years older.

She continued along her path toward Aunt Kate's wondering what was in store for Mr. Darcy and Elizabeth Bennett, and her sister Jane, who had just accepted Mr. Bingley's proposal of marriage to the delight of Mrs. Bennett and the Bingley sisters. Mary could just imagine such a wedding party in their finery, the women sparkling with diamonds, the silverware sparkling on the tables. One day, she told herself, one day...

Since Kitty had to get up early for work on Saturday, it was decided that Mary would stay over on Fridays from now on and help Aunt Kate by doing some household chores. Mary was glad to do it, not only because she knew how hard Kitty worked and was anxious to help in any way she could, but she knew that Aunt Kate needed them, and she knew it was the sort of thing Aunt Mary would have done, and would have wanted her to do. She imagined Aunt Mary was proud of her for it, and even now smiling down on her.

Even though Aunt Mary and Aunt Kate's house was just two blocks away on the same side of the street, Mary was in the habit of crossing the street not far from her house, and crossing back again close to their house. She tried at all costs to avoid that man who hung around the saloon in between their houses. He made Mary feel very uncomfortable and embarrassed at the way he stared at her, looking her up and down, giving her that creepy grin. She felt as if he knew that he made her nervous and enjoyed it. She tried to hide from him her developing figure. He was usually all dressed up. Even though she tried to keep alert and not let her guard down, eyes wide open to catch a glimpse of him beforehand, so as to avoid him, every once in a while when she and Molly were walking home, he'd step out of the shadows into the light of the lamp post and really startle them. They nicknamed him Blackie, because even his flaming red hair could not distract from the fact that his eyes were black as coal. They'd heard he was suspected of knifing a man in the back in a dark alley, but it could never be proved. Thankfully, tonight he was nowhere to be seen, and she breathed a sigh of relief.

Aunt Kate was tired but in better spirits than she had been lately. As they ate, they chatted about school and Pat's decision to go into the priesthood, Mike saving up for a motorcycle, which Aunt Kate said made her nervous but which Mary assured her was perfectly safe, Kitty's work for women's suffrage, and how appreciative of their help Aunt Kate was. "Mary replied, "We love you, Aunt Kate, and we are all glad to be able to help." After Mary had finished putting away the dishes and Aunt Kate had finished her tea, Aunt Kate led her niece into Aunt Mary's bedroom and took the statue of the Blessed Mother off of the dresser, where it had stood vigil for as long as Mary could remember, and she placed it into Mary's hands and closed them around it. Holding Mary's hands in her own, Aunt Kate had misty eyes and a gentle smile as she said, "This is for you, Mary. I know that she would want you to have it."

"Thank you, Aunt Kate," said Mary quietly, holding onto it tightly. "I'll put it on my dresser so it'll always remind me of Aunt Mary, and you." She hugged Aunt Kate and kissed her gently on the cheek.

Years ago, Aunt Nan had accompanied John and Victoria and the children to Cape DeMadeline at Three Rivers, north of Montreal, and had brought back four statuettes of the Blessed Virgin, one for herself and one for each of her sisters. Mary smiled as she remembered herself as a little girl no more than six years old, sitting on that very bed, propped up with pillows and covered in double blankets because of the cold, Aunt Mary alongside her, reading stories from a children's book Aunt Nan had loaned her, or relating with joyful emphasis stories of bygone days. Mary especially loved to hear the stories about when Mama and her aunts were little girls themselves. They had even less than Mary and her own brothers and sisters, but they had each other, and they had fun.

Mary had started staying over on Saturday nights after Danny died, and Annie was still a baby. Aunt Mary had told Mama she'd be happy to keep Mary over Saturday nights and give her sister more time to rest. Mary enjoyed it so. Aunt Mary would take her over to the store with her store book and get some kind of a treat, ginger snaps or a licorice stick. Then they'd walk back to the house and Aunt Mary would tuck her in and read to her. The Blessed Mother smiled down on them from the dresser. Mary had never felt so warm and comfortable and safe as she had back then, and she was grateful to Aunt Mary for the memory of it.

In the morning, Aunt Mary would brush her hair and dress her up and she and Aunt Kate would take her to Mass. From there they'd walk through the park on their way back to Mary's house for dinner. Sometimes Aunt Mary would pick her up earlier on Saturday and take her shopping with her. On those days, she would always treat Mary to an ice cream. It was Aunt Mary who taught her how to tie her shoelaces and how to tell time. It was Aunt Mary who helped her with her homework when she needed help. Mary always got good grades, and thought it was because of Aunt Mary's help as well as the books Aunt Nan brought for her to read.

Dorothy was a very nice girl who went to school with Mary and Molly. She always got the lowest marks in the class, and they felt sorry for her because her parents were immigrants who didn't know the language. She had to drop out of school in sixth grade to help with her younger brothers and sisters. Mary remembered thinking, if only Dorothy had had someone like Aunt Mary to help her, she probably would have gotten good marks, too.

"Aunt Mary," she remembered asking when she was still a little girl, "Why do some people have so much more than others? Like Gail O'Connell. She lives in a big beautiful house and has such nice clothes and good food. She has beautiful dolls and she even has a carriage *just for the dolls!* And servants! And one of the girls at school has *dessert twice a day!*" She paused a moment. "Aunt Mary, does that mean that God loves them more than he loves me?"

Aunt Mary seemed surprised by the question and immediately she said, "Oh, no, Mary, you must never think that. God loves us all exactly the same. But we just don't know why some have so much more than others. It's a mystery. But we do know that when we get to Heaven, we'll find out the answers to all of our questions, and everything will fall into place," she smiled lovingly.

Mary exclaimed, "Well, I can't help it, Aunt Mary, I just wish I was rich! Then I could help everybody."

Aunt Mary laughed lightly and said, "There's nothing wrong in daydreaming, Sweetie, as long as you do your best, don't neglect your work and keep everything in the proper perspective. Some people get resentful and angry at God when their own unrealistic dreams don't come true. Life is an adventure, Mary! Every day we must remember to thank God for all our blessings, no matter how big or how small. Even a beautiful day is a gift from God. And always take time to notice the beautiful flowers in the spring and the colorful leaves in the fall. Why, most of my happiest memories had nothing to do with money. In fact, I truly believe that money is only as good as the good that comes from it. Many people are very rich, but they're not happy. Happiness is a state of mind. It comes from the wisdom to love God and Jesus and to appreciate what you have, no matter how much or how little it seems to be. Naturally, if you're basically a happy person, money can allow you to do the things you want to do. But if you're basically an unhappy person, well then, no amount of money will ever make you happy. And if you ever did have money, it would be a wonderful thing to help others. It would not only be very unselfish, but it would be the true Christian thing to do. Why, helping others is the most wonderful thing in the world, Mary. Remember what Jesus said, 'That which you do to the least of my brethren, so you do unto me.'"

Aunt Mary paused and allowed the words to sink into her niece's young mind, and when she was satisfied that Mary understood, she continued. "I've always been very aware of the preciousness of life, Mary, maybe more so than most people, because my Pa died when he was only thirty years old, and my darling Robert was only twenty-four when the tuberculosis took him from me. So I've learned to thank God for each day I have on this earth with the people I love. So I try to enjoy it and to do as much good as possible. If we have food, clothing and shelter, we should appreciate it, because that's more than some people have. And we should realize that if we have the important things like faith, health and peace of mind, everything else is secondary. So you just do your best and try to be happy and help other people to be happy. And never envy anyone, because at some time in life, it seems that each person suffers pain, sorrow and their own disappointments."

It was then that Mary realized she did envy. She envied Annie for getting all of Gail O'Connell's beautiful hand-me-downs that looked like they'd just come from some expensive store, while Mary was ashamed of some of the things she had to wear, especially that brownish-orangey coat that had belonged to Kitty. She appreciated the fact that it was warm, but it made her look like a little old lady, and the color clashed with her red hair. Thinking back on it now with an embarrassed smile, she realized how little those things had really mattered, so long as Aunt Mary was there to help her through it.

And how well she remembered that day she'd been feeling so down. She must have been about eight then, and Mama was playing with Annie and kissing and hugging her and smiling and laughing and saying, "Who is the sweetest little girl in the whole world? Who's the sweetest girl? You are, that's who!" And Annie squealed with delight. And Mary thought that Mama must love Baby Annie the most and probably Kitty the second, because she was always talking to her like a grown-up and asking her opinion on things instead of just telling them what was what, as she did with Mary and the boys. And of course she figured that Pa must love Mike and Pat the most because they were boys. And where did that leave her? So that night, when she was staying over she said, "Aunt Mary, Don't you love me more than the others?"

Aunt Mary seemed perplexed and said, "I love you all the same."

But Mary tried to coax a more favorable answer. "But don't you love me just a little more than the rest?"

"No," Aunt Mary answered, "I love you all the same."

And then, almost pleading, Mary said, "But don't you love me just a tiny little bit more than the others?"

Now Aunt Mary looked closely into Mary's eyes as she realized not only how important her answer was to Mary, but for the first time, she also realized that it was true. She whispered, "Yes, I do love you the most, but don't tell anybody." And that happy acknowledgement made Mary feel so much better that she hugged Aunt Mary tightly and quickly went off to sleep with a smile on her face.

Now as Mary lay on Aunt Mary's bed in the dark, tears came into her eyes thinking of how much she still missed her. She couldn't seem to stop thinking of how much life could change in such a short time. It was only two weeks before that she had gone to sleep with Aunt Mary right here next to her. Everything seemed so wonderful then. She remembered the next morning how happy Aunt Mary seemed as she told them about two happy dreams she'd had through the night. In the first dream, she said, she'd seen her mother looking through the window, smiling at her. In the second dream, she'd seen Robert standing at the bottom of the bed with a beautiful smile on his face and his right hand extended toward her as if beckoning. Thinking of it now, Mary wondered if it was possible that it could have been a premonition. Mary wondered if there could be a deeper meaning to dreams. When Aunt Nan heard about it, she said she believed it was simply a product of the subconscious mind. Mary started thinking about her birthday celebration less than a month before. She and Molly were so excitedly happy to be going with Aunt Mary and this was only her second trip to Albany, even though it was only seven miles away.

She remembered in particular how very happy her Aunt Mary was telling them that for her it was a dream come true.

Her Aunt Mary talked about her Darling Robert, who grew up next door to her. She mentioned that many times they had talked about taking the train to Albany, but they always needed the money for more important things. He was the oldest in his family too, and was always concerned about helping his family.

Mary noticed that her Aunt Mary seemed to talk about her Darling Robert more that day than ever before.

As Mary continued thinking of her Aunt Mary, she remembered that a couple of weeks before that, Aunt Nan had given Aunt Mary a pretty hat that had belonged to Victoria. Aunt Mary, who was really good at decorating, fixed it up to look even prettier than it had been. Then Aunt Mary had taken the hat box, covered it with beautiful blue felt and added ribbons in just the right way to make it look like a beautiful treasure box, and inside she put a selection of happy thoughts, pretty pictures, poems, the words of some happy songs, and three of her favorite Bible quotes, Psalm 118:24, "This is the day the Lord hath made, let us rejoice and be glad in it;" Mark 11:24, "Therefore I tell you whatever you ask in prayer, believe that you have received it, and it will be yours, says the Lord;" and Philippians 4:6-7, "Have no anxiety at all but in everything, by prayer and petition, with thanksgiving, make your requests known to God. Then the peace of God that surpasses all understanding will guard your hearts and minds in Christ Jesus." And she gave the box to Mary. She called it a "Happy Memory Box" and she told Mary, "I started your collection by writing down some of my own happy, favorite thoughts, and I hope they'll help to keep you happy, too. Now *you* collect some happy things to add to them, and some day if you're feeling sad or disappointed, you just go to your Happy Memory Box and relive those happy memories and thank God for them."

Now Mary started to think of some of the things in her Happy Memory Box. And as she drifted off to sleep, she started dreaming.

Thinking of Aunt Mary and her Happy Memory Box helped to remind Mary of what a very special day they had in Albany. She had worn her Easter clothes that Aunt Mary had made for her. She felt a little more at peace as she started to think of some of the things in her Happy Memory Box. As she drifted off to sleep she started dreaming.

Mary dreamt that she saw a staircase about fifty feet away from where she was standing. A horse-drawn carriage pulled up to the staircase and her Aunt Mary stepped out, wearing that beautiful blue lace dress that she was laid out in. She started climbing up the stairs. She had a radiant smile on her face. Mary started running toward her as she called to her, "Aunt Mary, wait for me, I want to go with you."

Her Aunt Mary still smilingly looked over at Mary as she continued ascending the staircase. "No, Mary, you can't come with me now." As Mary was almost to the bottom of the staircase, her Aunt Mary had reached the top. She was still beaming as she took one last look at Mary and then went through the door.

Mary woke up and started crying. But from that day on, she took it as a sign that her Aunt Mary was in Heaven. She made up her mind, that even though she would miss her terribly, she would be happy for her.

CHAPTER TWENTY-SIX

It was already 10:00pm that dark, cloudy Saturday evening as Mary left her Aunt Kate's house. As she walked along, she was in deep thought trying once more to analyze the dream she had the night before. Within seconds, those thoughts were pushed out of her mind as an eerie feeling swept over her. Panic gripped her as she realized that she had made a mistake and walked too far. She was already almost in front of that saloon. Standing right there before her eyes was Blackie. And as she quickly observed, not another soul in sight.

Oh, how she wished that she had been more careful and crossed over to the other side of the street. But it was too late now. Her best bet, she thought, was to walk closer to the road and ignore him. As she passed without turning her head, she let her eyes turn slightly toward the right, for she did not trust him at all. She saw his hand reach out for her. Her confidence wavered as she felt her knees tremble. By instinct, she turned fast toward him. For a split second her eyes were transfixed on his. They were even blacker and harder and more arrogant than they had looked from afar. A shudder went through her as she gasped. And with every ounce of strength and courage that she could muster, she pushed him as hard as she could. He sailed through the swinging doors. She heard a thud as his head hit the floor. She was so gripped by fear that her heart was pounding rapidly and she was trembling all over. She started running as fast as her shaky legs would go, and every second she thought that she would have a knife in her back. Then she felt a sense of terror as she thought about her door being stuck. What if he caught her before she could get it open?

Recently the door kept sticking and was hard to open. Everyone was after Mike to fix it. "Oh, my God," she thought, "what if I can't get the door open?" She jumped up the two steps as she turned the door handle back and forth and tried to push the door open. It was stuck at first, but finally she opened the door. At the same time, she felt a hand over her mouth as she was pushed inside the dark hall. She could hardly breathe as she struggled to be free. Her mouth was slightly open as the hand around her mouth tightened. She could feel a tiny lump of skin between her teeth. She bit down as hard as she could. His hand swung away from her mouth as he swore in some foreign tongue. He was still wrestling with her when at the top of her lungs she screamed, "Mama, help!" She could hear her Mother yell, "That's Mary's voice," and within seconds the hall light went on as a figure tore down the stairs rapidly.

She felt the weight of his body taken from hers, and she heard a thud as he was lifted up and slammed against the wall with such force that the house shook.

Maggie believed in modesty and up to that point, Mary had never seen Mike without a shirt on. Now for the first time she beheld the power of his might. The wide shoulders, the huge arm muscles, the small waistline and the massive back muscles that rippled with every movement, greatly surprised her. Then she saw fear grip those black evil eyes as they stared into Mike's angry face. He was pleading as he tried to catch his breath, "Mike, I'm sorry. I didn't know it was your sister."

Maggie called from the top of the stairs, "Mike, stop, for the love of God, or you'll kill the man."

Mike's face was still red, with anger, as he stared at this shaking man. "If you see me coming, turn and run the other way, because if I see your face again, I'll be reminded of this day, and my Mother won't be there to plead for you, and I'm not sure that I'd be able to control my anger."

"Okay, Mike, okay," he exclaimed as he ran out of the door.

Mary was still shaking all over, and breathing unevenly as Mike helped her up the stairs and tried to comfort her. "Oh, Mike, I was so scared and the door was stuck and I couldn't get it open!" she breathlessly exclaimed.

Mike tried to comfort her as he said, "It's okay now, Mary. You don't have to be afraid. He won't bother you anymore."

Mary felt drained as she started drifting off to sleep. She could hear Mike and Maggie talking in the kitchen. "Oh, Mike, it's too bad that you didn't get that door fixed sooner, so that it wouldn't have been so hard for Mary to open."

Mike answered, "I fixed it yesterday, Mama, but the poor kid was probably so frightened that she wasn't turning the handle right."

When Mike came home the next day, he told Mary that he had heard from a reliable source that Blackie had left town that morning for good. But it would be a long time before Mary would feel relaxed enough to stop looking over her shoulder.

CHAPTER TWENTY-SEVEN

As she sat on the bed and flipped hurriedly through the cyclopedia to the section on Paris, waiting impatiently for Kitty, and maybe Annie, to join her for their recent morning ritual, Mary smiled again at the memory of the scene at the train station. Aunt Nan in her smart new navy blue tailored linen suit with a pink silk bow at the neck and a carnation on the lapel, smiling more happily than she'd probably ever seen her smile in her entire life, turning for one last wave as she boarded the train bound for New York City from Albany, Mary and Annie and Kitty and Mama and Aunt Kate all in a jumble smiling and waving back and calling out the last "Bon Voyage" and "God Bless!"

The family had only just gotten to the station when Joseph had pulled up alongside them right on the dot to drop off Nan and unload the rich dark brown leather luggage set which Victoria and John had loaned her for the trip. Aunt Nan had exited the car like a society matron all dolled up in that one of the several new outfits to which Victoria had treated her for her big trip. Mary could still hear her exclaim in a whisper (lest the neighbors should hear) at the table the previous Tuesday evening, "Can you imagine? Victoria took me on a shopping spree downtown to her favorite stores on Saturday! She just kept saying, 'Oh, look at this, look at this,' holding dresses and suits up to me for size, putting hats on my head to check in the mirror. Why, I told her, Victoria, it's just too much, and do you know what she said to me? She said, 'Nan,' and here I get a little misty, I just can't help myself, she's so sweet to me, she said, 'Nan, for thirty years you've been right alongside me through thick and thin. You're the closest thing I have to a sister and you're like a second mother to my children. A lifelong dream has come true for you – you're making your European debut,' she joked, 'you simply *must* have a new wardrobe.' And she just kept saying, 'Put this on my account, put this on my account.' Why, I'll bet she spent over a hundred dollars on me!" And Mary's and Annie's jaws had practically dropped open at the thought of it. "And loaned me some very nice pieces of costume jewelry to top it off!"

Although they hadn't been able to actually see her off at the dock in New Jersey, Mary had imagined the scene a dozen times, and as she did so again now, she imagined herself in Aunt Nan's place, and Jack at her side: Dusk just beginning to descend on what had been a hectic but beautiful, warm and sunny summer day, a perfect evening for a lifelong dream to come true as her family watched from the pier while she made her way carefully but gingerly up the boarding ramp after a sweetly sentimental scene with her sisters and Mama and her aunts in New York City for the send-off, turning alternately back and forth for one last hug and hoorah followed by quick admonitions to get going, get going, before you miss the ship, Jack's waiting for you, but oh, one last hug... The Fogarty Goodbye, as Pa called it, was a notoriously drawn-out affair of last-minute kisses and confidences before the final leave-taking was taken. And once aboard the massive ship with its mile-high rigging and tall smokestacks already belching coal dust into the darkening pink and red sky, she and Jack scrunched in between dozens of other departing passengers gathered at the railing, Mary would continuously wave her white lace handkerchief up and down, smiling a smile so wide that everyone would know that the dreams of her childhood had, indeed, come true.

"Paris, France!" Kitty exclaimed as she swept into the room with her last bite of toast and sips of coffee. "Imagine Aunt Nan in Paris!"

"Is Annie coming?" Mary asked, holding the book open on the bed as Kitty sat on the other side.

"I doubt she'll make it this morning – she's not even at the breakfast table yet!" Kitty chuckled good-naturedly while rolling her eyes at her baby sister's lackadaisical locomotion. "I told her we were starting, and she knows how serious I am about punctuality. If she comes in, she comes in. If she misses it, she can look through the book herself after school. Now," she said, excited as a schoolgirl herself, "what is Aunt Nan going to do and see in Paris today while I'm at work and you're at school?"

For weeks now Mary and Kitty, sometimes with Annie, sometimes without, had gotten up and eaten breakfast twenty minutes early so as to sit on the bed with the cyclopedia books and follow Aunt Nan's progress across the Atlantic Ocean and through Europe, reading up on the places she'd visit and poring over the pictures of the places she'd see.

They'd started excitedly but had gotten a tad bored the first few days, reading and re-reading the Hamburg-American Line brochure during the twelve day crossing from her June 26th departure from America to her July 8th arrival in Germany. After all, even if the Hamburg-American was the largest transatlantic shipping line in the world and its passenger liners among the most luxurious, no matter how exciting it was, how many different ways on different days could they imagine Aunt Nan walking the decks in the ocean's breeze, arm-in-arm with a fellow contest winner, perhaps, or reclining on a deck chair reading a book; playing a game of shuffleboard or bingo; delighting in yet another roast beef or sirloin or capon dinner in the state dining room, or even roast duck, as Pa had suggested; perhaps finished out another evening enjoying an ice cream over a game of gin rummy? But once she'd landed and the trip through Europe itself had actually got going, they couldn't help but delight in reading up on her planned activities and re-imagining it throughout the days as they plodded through their lives, Mary always wishing these years away so that she could get on with the business of adult life, which she just knew would bring her everything she'd ever dreamed of.

Already they had followed Aunt Nan from her arrival in Hamburg, Germany's cosmopolitan port city of almost a million people on the banks of the Elbe River, and on by train to Berlin, where she and her companions had spent five days visiting museums, galleries, churches, cathedrals, parks and palaces such as the Gemäldegalerie, which the cyclopedia translated from German into English as, literally, "Picture Gallery," with paintings from artists such as Albrecht Dürer, Lucas Cranach, Titian, Peter Paul Rubens, Rembrandt, Vermeer, and one room with five different "Madonnas" by Raphael; the Friedrichswerder Church, which the book described as "the first Neo-Gothic church built in Berlin, finished in 1831, as designed by Karl Friedrich Schinkel, for whom it is known" and showed a stately rectangular brown brick building with two tall square towers on either side of the high wide front doors; the Berlin Cathedral, known as "The Protestant Saint Peter's," a massive, ornate and beautifully carved Baroque basilica built just 8 years earlier on the site of an original construction from the 15th century; and, no doubt, on the island of Berlin-Wannsee in the River Havel, both the Glienicke Palace, originally a cottage that was later turned into a summer palace, all white with tall columns and porticos "in the late classical style," also designed by Schinkel for Prince Carl of Prussia in 1826 with two large gold gilded lions in front and antique "objects d'art" inside, which the Prince had brought back from his many trips around the world.

The following Monday morning, July 14th, Aunt Nan and her compatriots had gone to Dresden, home of the medieval Dukes and Electors of the Duchy of Saxony and, as of 1806, the capital city of the Kingdom of Saxony, which had joined the German Empire in 1871. There they had spent two days touring the Kathedrale Sanctissimae Trinitatis ("Cathedral of the Holy Trinity") one of the city's most famous landmarks, which the cyclopedia reported as having been designed by architect Baetano Chiaveri as commissioned by Frederick Augustus II, Elector of Saxony and King of Poland in 1738 as a "Roman Catholic counterbalance to the city's Protestant Frauenkirche ('Church of Our Lady')." They had marveled at the beauty of the cathedral in the photograph that showed the great oval-shaped Baroque structure in all of its finely carved marble grandeur with statues along the rooftops and a huge four-story cupola-style steeple at the front. The travelers were then to go on to visit the Green Vault, which the girls had at first imagined to be a park, perhaps, or some sort of natural structure but were surprised to find listed in the book as "Grünes Gewölbe," a historic museum "founded by Augustus the Strong in 1723 featuring a rich variety of exhibits from the Baroque to Classical periods." Then it would have been on to what was listed in Aunt Nan's brochure as "parks and promenades." Doubtless they would also have visited or at least seen the factory that produces the world-famous Dresden China (actually, Meissen China, as they were surprised to learn) a "hard-paste porcelain" developed in 1708 by Ehrenfried Walther von Tschirnhaus in the city of Meissen, right next door to Dresden.

On that Wednesday, they had gone on to Frankfurt ("Do you think they'll have frankfurters?" Annie had giggled to Kitty's mock-serious assurance that they'd probably have several during their two-day visit since the hot dog was named for the city, after all) where they were listed as being scheduled to visit churches (no doubt) such as the Frankfurt Cathedral (formally, the Cathedral of Saint Bartholomew), a Gothic church located in the center of Frankfurt, and Saint Paul's Church, the seat of the German Empire's first democratically elected Parliament in 1848) and "other attractions" which they thought doubtless included "Landmarks of Frankfurt" listed and pictured in the book, such as the Frankfurt Opera House, "reportedly designed by the Berlin architect Richard Lucae and financed by the citizens of Frankfurt, among whose invited guests on opening night, October 20th, 1880, was Kaiser Wilhelm I", and the Eschenheim Tower, a large round tower "erected at the beginning of the 15th century" which had served as part of the late-medieval fortifications of Frankfurt, "the oldest and most unaltered building in the Innenstadt district."

On Friday, July 18th, Aunt Nan and the group were scheduled to "proceed by express steamer on the Rhine River to Cologne, to view a cathedral, bridge of boats, and St. Ursula's." The girls agreed that the cathedral referred to was probably Cologne Cathedral, which was listed in the cyclopedia as "the city's most famous monument and the Cologne residents' most respected landmark, a Gothic church started in 1248 and completed in 1880 which houses the Shrine of the Three Kings that supposedly contains the relics of the Three Magi" (at which they marveled). Try though they may, however, they could not figure out what the "bridge of boats" was supposed to be, and figured they'd ask Aunt Nan when she returned. St. Ursula's, however, they did find listed in the city's Landmark's Section as "The Basilica church of St. Ursula, located in Cologne in the Rhineland, Germany... built in the 17th century upon the ancient ruins of a Roman cemetery where the 11,000 virgins associated with the legend of Saint Ursula were said to have been buried." Curious, they had then looked up Saint Ursula, whose entry read, "Saint Ursula ('Little Female Bear' in Latin), a British Christian saint traditionally held to have been a 4th century Romano-British princess who, at the direction of her father, King Dionotus of Dumnonia in southwest England, set sail to join her future husband, the pagan Governor Conan Meriadoc of Armorica, along with 11,000 virginal handmaidens. A miraculous storm reportedly brought them over the sea to a Gaulish port, where Ursula declared that before her marriage she would undertake a European pilgrimage. After setting out for Cologne, which was besieged by the Huns, all the virgins were beheaded in a dreadful massacre, and Ursula shot dead."

"Eleven *thousand* handmaidens?" Kitty frowned. "Sounds like a bit of an exaggeration to me."

Mary shrugged.

The next morning, the girls opened the first book in the cyclopedia set to the entry headed "Amsterdam," where the travelers were to proceed by train and take in such sites as "old and new churches, royal museums, picture galleries and numerous monuments." Kitty pointed out that Amsterdam is the capital city of The Netherlands, which is often referred to as Holland, one of the originally independent founding regions of the modern-day Kingdom of The Netherlands. Mary identified several landmarks which Aunt Nan and the others would no doubt tour during their three-day stay, such as the Museumplein, which Mary translated from the book as, "Museum Square."

"'Created in the last quarter of the 19th century on the grounds of the 1883 World's Fair,'" she read aloud, "the northeastern part of the square is bordered by the very large Rijksmuseum ('State Museum'). In front of the Rijksmuseum on the square itself is a long, rectangular pond. This is transformed into an ice rink in winter."

"Oh, imagine ice skating on a little pond in an old European square on a winter day," said Kitty wistfully.

"I can," said Mary, "and some day I'll do it."

"Someday, maybe," Kitty smiled indulgently. "But back to the present, please."

"Someday, definitely," Mary smiled confidently to no one in particular as she resumed reading while Annie rolled her eyes in Kitty's direction. "The square is bordered by the Van Gogh Museum, Stedelijk Museum, Diamond Museum, and Concertgebouw (literally, 'Concert building'). The southwestern border of the Museum Square is the Van Baerlestraat ('Van Baerle Street'), which is a major thoroughfare in this part of Amsterdam."

"Oh, Aunt Nan will just *love* visiting all those museums," said Kitty.

"Museums, museums, museums," Annie yawned. "I might as well have stayed in bed."

On Monday, July 21st, they opened the book to the section on The Hague, where the European visitors were scheduled to spend the day in the city where the first international peace conference was held in 1899.

"The Hague is the capital city of the province of South Holland in the Netherlands," Mary read.

"The entire city is called 'The Hague'?" Kitty asked.

"I guess so."

"Huh," she said curiously. "I've heard of it but I always thought 'The Hague' was a government building or something. I guess you do learn something new every day."

Mary smiled and continued. "The Hague is the seat of the Dutch government and parliament, the Supreme Court, and the Council of State – there you go, no wonder why you thought it was a government building – but the city is not the capital of The Netherlands, which constitutionally, is Amsterdam."

"Oh, that *is* interesting," Kitty thought aloud.

Just the day before, Mary had opened the book to read about Brussels, where Aunt Nan and the others were to travel by train to see "Royal Museums –"

"More museums?" Annie sighed.

"The Palace de Justice," Mary continued, "in English, 'Palace of Justice,'" holding the book toward the others so that they could also see the picture of the huge ("Larger than St. Peter's Basilica in Rome") building ("in the eclectic style") by Dutch architect Joseph Poelaert ("begun on October 31, 1866, and inaugurated on October 15, 1883, after Poelaert's death") with its dozens of columns all around the exterior ("housing eight courtyards, twenty-seven large court rooms and two hundred forty-five smaller court rooms and other rooms") and its 340 foot high dome "situated on a hill with a level difference of 65 feet between the upper and lower town, which results in multiple entrances to the building at different levels."

"Wow," said Kitty, "that *is* big. And beautiful! Aunt Nan will *love* it!"

That had brought them to this morning, and as Mary began to review and recite the cyclopedia listing for Paris, Annie finally made her way into the room with her two pieces of toast put together like a sandwich and her glass of milk in hand.

"Did Mama say you could eat that in here?" Mary inquired with a raised eyebrow.

"Why, yes, she did," Annie replied dryly, "thank you for asking."

Kitty shook her head in amusement at the two of them. "Paris," she said to Mary, who shook her head at Annie, not in amusement, but at Mama's endless indulgence of the baby of the family, who got away with doing things which none of the rest of them would even dare to attempt.

Mary cleared her throat and began.

"Paris," she announced, "is the capital and largest city of France. It is situated on the River Seine, in northern France. Paris was the largest city in the Western world for some 1,000 years, from the 9th to the 19th centuries. The earliest archaeological signs of permanent settlements in the Paris area date from around 4200 BC, and the city gets its name from that of the Parissi, a Celtic tribe which inhabited the area from around 250 BC through Rome's conquest of the region in 52 BC."

"Isn't Celtic, Irish?" Annie inquired.

"Yes," said Kitty, "but apparently the early Celts were in Europe and kept getting pushed west by Germanic and Italian and French tribes until they eventually ended up in Ireland."

Moving on to the Landmarks Section of the listing, Mary said, "Oh, my goodness, there's so much here! No wonder they'll be there for six days. Listen to this!" And she went on excitedly reporting on the various sites which Aunt Nan and the American entourage would see:

"The Place de la Bastille is a square in Paris where the Bastille prison stood for four hundred years before the July 14th, 1789 'Storming of the Bastille' at the start of the French Revolution and its subsequent physical destruction by the end of 1790 – no vestige of it remains."

"Imagine that," said Kitty, "I always assumed it was still there."

Mary nodded and continued. "In the center of the square stands the July Column, a monument to the Revolution composed of twenty-one cast bronze drums, weighing over 163,000 pounds. It is 154 feet high, containing an interior spiral staircase, and rests on a base of white marble. The column is engraved in gold with the names of Parisians who died during the revolution, atop which stands, on a gilded globe, Auguste Dumont's Génie de la Liberté (the 'Spirit of Freedom'), who is crowned with stars and depicted perched on one foot while brandishing the Torch of Civilization and the remains of his broken chains.

"The Avenue de Champs-Elysées is one of the most famous streets in the world. A 17th century garden promenade-turned-avenue lined with cinemas, cafés, luxury specialty shops and clipped horse-chestnut trees, the avenue runs for 1.18 miles from the Palace de la

Concorde in the east to the Arc de Triomphe in the west. The name is French for 'Elysian Fields,' the place of the blessed dead in Greek mythology.

"The Place de la Concorde is one of the major public squares in Paris. Measuring 21.35 acres in area, it is the largest square in the French capital. Designed by Ange-Jacques Gabriel in 1755 as a moat-skirted octagon between the Champs-Elysées to the west and the Tuileries Gardens to the east, and decorated with statues and fountains, the area was originally named Place Louis XV to honor the king at that time. During the French Revolution, the statue of Louis XV was torn down and the area was renamed 'Place de la Révolution.' It was here that the revolutionary government erected the guillotine used to execute King Louis XVI on January 21st, 1793, Queen Marie Antoinette on October 16th, 1793, and hundreds of others, often to the acclamation of cheering crowds. A year later, when the revolution was taking a more moderate course, the guillotine was removed from the square and it was renamed 'Place de la Concorde' as a symbolic gesture of reconciliation.

"Montmartre is a hill almost one mile high which gives its name to the surrounding district in the north of Paris and is the location of the Saint Pierre de Montmartre Church, which, according to the earliest biography of Saint Ignatius Loyola, is the location at which the vows were taken that led to the founding of the Society of Jesus."

"The Jesuits," said Kitty.

Mary nodded again and continued. "'The Avenue Montaigne boasts numerous stores specializing in high fashion, such as Louis Vuitton and Coco Chanel, as well as jewelers such as Bulgari.' Oh, can you just *see* yourself *shopping* there!" she exclaimed.

"Me?" said Kitty. "No."

"Well, *I* can," Mary smiled widely, continuing on.

"Avenue de l'Opéra ('Avenue of the Opera') is situated in the center of Paris and runs from the Louvre to the Palais Garnier, an elegant 1,979-seat opera house built from 1861 to 1875 for the Paris Opera."

"Oh, Aunt Nan was especially excited about going to the Louvre," said Kitty.

"Yes, I remember," said Mary, flipping forward to that section in the book while holding her place with a finger. "Here it is. 'The Louvre is one of the world's largest museums, the most visited art museum in the world and a historic monument. A central landmark of Paris, France, it is located on the Right Bank of the Seine and houses objects from prehistory to the 19th century over an area of 652,300 square feet."

"Is that big?" Annie asked.

"Very big," said Kitty. "To give you an idea, Prospect Park is 80 acres, so the Louvre Museum would be, let's see, something like *8,000 times* larger than Prospect Park."

"So, 8,000 Prospect Parks would fit into the museum?" Mary asked, astonished at the thought of it.

"Yes."

"Wow," said Annie, eyes wide open, "that really *is* big!"

Mary continued. "'The museum is housed in the Louvre Palace, which began as a fortress built in the late 12th century under Philip II. Remnants of the fortress are visible in the basement of the museum. The building was extended many times to form the present Louvre Palace. In 1682, Louis XIV chose the Palace of Versailles for his household' – Oh, Aunt Nan mentioned Versailles, too – we can read up on that tomorrow morning – 'leaving the Louvre primarily as a place to display the royal collection. During the French Revolution, the National Assembly decreed that the Louvre should be used as a museum, to display the nation's masterpieces, now including such famous paintings as 'The Mona Lisa' by Leonardo da Vinci, 'The Death of the Virgin' by Michelangelo

Merisi de Caravaggio, 'The Crowning with Thorns' by Titian, and 'The Astronomer' by Joannes Vermeer. Sculptures include the 'Venus de Milo,' and ancient Greek statue, one of the most famous works of ancient Greek sculptures, created sometime between 130 and 100 BC, and Michelangelo Buonarroti's 'Dying Slave,' as well as thousands of prints and drawings.' Oh, she'll enjoy that."

"I'll say," Kitty agreed, "but meanwhile, it's getting late. Put a bookmark in the section on Paris and we'll continue tomorrow morning, how's that?"

"That's perfect," said Mary, "I still have to finish getting ready for school. And so do you," she said to Annie, who yawned and ignored her as best she could.

In the days to come, they would continue to follow Aunt Nan's progress through Paris and on to London, where she would see, and they would read about, Buckingham Palace, the 18th to 19th century home of the royal family, the 19th century Palace of Westminster, home of the British Parliament and Westminster Abbey, historical site of coronations and burials of the kings and queens of England, and of course, St. Paul's Cathedral.

And finally, in the last week of her six-week adventure, the Emerald Isle: Ireland, the land of the Fogarties not-so-distant forebears, a hearty and proud people who'd made the island their home for thousands of years before the many millions, forlorn in famine, had in the middle of the 19th century been forced to leave the country of their ancestry and heritage, a land they'd loved, to brave the Atlantic crossing which itself often brought death, in order to make a new life for themselves and their descendants in America. It had been the one place that Aunt Nan had marveled most at visiting, the old country, as second and third-generation Americans so often called the land of their grandparents, a sort of second homeland, and the girls could only imagine the delight in Aunt Nan's eyes at the view as her ship entered Dublin Bay in the capital city of Ireland, its most populous city, situated near the midpoint of the island's east coast, at the mouth of the River Liffey. There she and her companions would visit such landmarks as Dublin Castle, originally built by order of King John of England in 1204 as a defensive fortification for the city, and which later evolved into a royal residence and seat of government for the representatives of the English monarchs; Trinity College, Ireland's oldest university, founded in 1592 by Queen Elizabeth (for whom Aunt Nan had always had a particular interest and admiration) which houses the Book of Kells, an illuminated Latin Gospel manuscript created by Celtic monks around 800 AD; and Saint Patrick's Cathedral, originally founded in 1191, the largest church in Ireland with a 140 foot spire that can be seen from anywhere in the city.

Then on to Killarney in Southwest Ireland, home of St. Mary's Cathedral, "completed in 1842," Mary read, "and considered to be one of the most important Gothic Revival churches of 19th century Ireland."

Next would come Blarney Castle, "a medieval stronghold in Blarney, near Cork, Ireland, and the River Martin, originally dating from before 1200. At the top of the castle lies the Stone of Eloquence, better known as *the Blarney Stone*," Mary announced with the accompaniment of Kitty and Annie as Mama hurried to the door to listen, smiling broadly with the girls.

"Tourists visiting Blarney Castle may hang upside-down over a sheer drop to kiss the stone, which is said to give the gift of eloquence. There are many legends as to the origin of the stone, one being that it is the Lia Fáil, a magical stone upon which Irish kings were once crowned."

At which point the book was closed and they would marvel at the fact that five weeks had passed since Aunt Nan had gone. The day after, she and the rest of the tour group would return to Queenstown, England, and embark on the transatlantic journey that would bring them back to America, first to Philadelphia, and then home to Troy, where the Forgarties would await her return on Sunday, August 24th, impatient to hear all about her great adventure and to pore over the picture post cards and pamphlets and booklets she'd promised to bring home, which Mary would see in her mind's eye again and again through the weeks and months of these years of her youth, always envisioning herself one day in such photographs, standing in front of the landmarks and monuments of Europe, smiling broadly in her happiness, with her husband, Jack O'Connell, smiling happily right alongside her.

CHAPTER TWENTY-EIGHT

After Aunt Mary's death, it was decided mainly by Aunt Nan and Kitty that Mary should stay overnight with their Aunt Kate to help her in any way she could. Kitty would have liked to bring Aunt Kate into their house, but there was not only a shortage of room, but worse was Pa's drinking problem, and she knew Aunt Kate was just too fragile to endure that.

At first they had been concerned about how they were going to keep paying the rent, but when Aunt Nan had asked John for an advance on her wages, and he found out what it was for, he insisted upon paying for Aunt Kate's rent, food and medicine.

"Besides," he told her, "I'm glad to be given the opportunity to pay you back for all those good stock market tips you have given me over the years."

Mary got in the habit of getting up very early every morning and getting breakfast for her and Aunt Kate. After school, she would stop at Aunt Kate's house to do what she could. Then she would go home for a couple of hours and then bring supper back to Aunt Kate's for the two of them. In between, Maggie went over at least twice every day and the neighbors looked in on Aunt Kate in between.

Sleeping in her Aunt Mary's bed each night made Mary miss her even more. Mary loved her Aunt Kate, too, and she had always felt sorry for her, but she couldn't help it that Aunt Mary had always been her favorite, and she suspected that Aunt Nan was Kitty's favorite aunt. To Mary, her Aunt Mary had just the right type of personality. She seemed to have the instinct to speak up when she should and to be quiet and listen under other circumstances. Mary considered her Aunt Mary one of the best listeners she had ever known. People were always telling her their problems and she always helped everybody she could no matter how tired she was. And in between that empathy and caring balance she was very optimistic, laughing and smiling quite often and was a joy to be with.

Pat completed his second year at La Salle High School and left for the seminary.

In 1914, Montana and Nevada adopted women's suffrage.

Frankie's brother purchased a newer model motorcycle and Mike and Frankie bought his. The year flew by. The highlight of her weeks was seeing Jack at Sunday Mass, and listening on Tuesday evenings for Aunt Nan's update on Jack and his family, and of course daydreaming about him the whole rest of the week in between, and reading the interesting books Aunt Nan supplied her with.

And before she knew it, it was June of 1914 and Mary and Molly graduated from the 8th grade and got jobs at Earl and Wilson's factory on the outskirts of town, along with some of their classmates. The only students who went on to high school were the few whose parents were better off financially.

Mary and Molly started working at 7am and they made sure they arrived early because after the workers went into the building at 7am, the door was locked and not reopened until 8am. So if anyone was late, their choice was to either go back home or to stand out freezing in the winter cold or sweating in the summer heat, and everyone needed their meager wages. Rarely was anyone ever late.

There was great political and economic rivalry among the nations of Europe, which had fostered the development of two hostile military alliances. On June 28th, 1914, at Sarajevo, capital of the Austro-Hungarian province of Bosnia, the Archduke Francis Ferdinand, heir-presumptive to the throne of Austria-Hungary, was assassinated by a Serb nationalist. That same day, Austria-Hungary declared war on Serbia. Within days, Germany declared war on Russia, France and Belgium. By August 5th, the New York Times headline read, "England Declares War on Germany; British Ship Sunk; French Ships Defeat Germans; Belgium Attacked; 17,000,000 Men Engaged in Great War of Eight Nations; Great English and German Navies About to Grapple; Rival Warships Off This Port as Lusitania Sails."

On August 6th, President Wilson's wife Ellen died of Bright's Disease.

On August 14th, Pope Pius X died. His successor, elected by his fellow Cardinals, chose the name Benedict XV. He was known as a man of peace during a time of war. He put forth several peace proposals to end the war, but his efforts were largely ignored.

Probably what he would be most known for was the canonization of St. Joan of Arc, and promoting the wearing of the brown scapula. Not too long before he died, he said, "We offer our life to God on behalf of the peace of the world."

In the fall, Congress passed a bill that effectively ended the alley slums of Washington, D.C.

With Mary working and most of her pay going into the family fund, Kitty figured she had saved enough to put down on the player piano, and could afford to pay the rest in installments. Evening after evening, a whole group of friends and neighbors would happily gather and play the piano rollers and sing its tunes.

War reports continued to dominate the newspaper headlines. Then, on May 7th, 1915, the British steamship The Lusitania was torpedoed by a German submarine ten miles off Kinsale Head, Ireland. The ship sunk in less than twenty minutes, with the loss of 1152 persons. 114 of the casualties were U.S. Citizens. The vessel was unarmed, but the Germans asserted that she was carrying contraband of war, and that Americans had been warned against taking passage on British vessels in a notice signed, "Imperial German Embassy," which had appeared in American morning newspapers on the day the vessel sailed from New York City.

In the US, strong sentiment developed for declaring war on Germany immediately. President Woodrow Wilson, who still tried to maintain a policy of strict neutrality for the United States, sent Germany a note asking for reparations. The Germans refused to take the blame for the deaths of the Americans, but finally agreed not to sink passenger liners without warning.

40,000 marched in New York City's Suffrage Parade, the largest parade ever held in that city.

Women suffrage measures were defeated in Pennsylvania, New Jersey, New York, and Massachusetts.

On October 29th there was a full page ad for an Anti-Suffrage Rally, which read, "Grand Anti-Suffrage Rally, Music Hall, Troy, tonight at 8:15pm. Famous orators will tell why women should not be given the ballot. All Welcome."

On November 3rd, the Troy Record reported the Rensselear County Election Results: More than 15,000 citizens expressed themselves on the proposition, the cause losing by about 4,000.

U.S. President Wilson tried to bring about negotiations between the two groups of powers for a peace that would, in his words, bring "Peace without victory."

A conference was held in Europe with Wilson's confidential advisor Colonel Edward M. House and leading European statesmen attending. Some progress was at first apparently made toward bringing an end to the war, but although Wilson continued his mediary efforts, the terms set forth from each group were irreconcilable.

Thirty-six National American Woman Suffrage Association State Chapters endorsed NAWSA President Carey Chapman Catt's "winning plan," a unified campaign to get the amendment through Congress and ratified by the states.

On October 25, 1916, Maggie O'Neill opened her parlor door and started down the stairs. Halfway down, she stiffened up and unconsciously toppled down the remaining steps. She'd had a stroke. For days, her life hung in the balance. Kitty decided that Mary would have to quit her job and stay home to take care of their mother and do all the household chores. Kitty would have preferred to do it herself, but she made so much more money than Mary did, and they really needed the money. So during the day, Mary took care of her mother, and at night she still slept over at her Aunt Kate's while Kitty was home at night with their mother. Kitty and Mike gave Mary spending money.

Mary didn't mind doing the work. She felt so sorry for her mother and her Aunt Kate and tried very hard to be encouraging so that they wouldn't think that they were a burden to her. She could still remember her Aunt Mary talking about someone she knew whose family made her feel that she was a burden to them. Aunt Mary had said, "It's so hard for that person to be sick, but it's even worse when the people she loves make her feel so much worse with their selfish attitude."

In November, 1916, Woodrow Wilson was re-elected President of the United States.

In January, 1917, Germany announced that beginning on February 1st, it would resort to unrestricted submarine warfare, not only against the shipping of Great Britain, but also shipping to Great Britain.

The United States had already expressed its strong opposition to unrestricted submarine warfare, which it claimed violated its rights as a neutral country. Consequently, on February 3rd, Wilson dismissed the German ambassador, cutting off diplomatic ties. At Wilson's request, a number of Latin American nations, including Peru, Bolivia and Brazil, followed his example.

In February and March, several American ships were sunk.

Alice Corbett Fiacco

BOOK TWO

**March 25, 1917
Troy, New York**

CHAPTER TWENTY-NINE

Mary awoke that Sunday morning to Annie's sobbing voice.

"She's dead. She's dead." Mary's heart was pounding and she was thinking of her Mother as she leaped out of bed and ran to the kitchen.

"Who's dead?" She pleadingly asked. But Annie was crying too hard to reply. She seemed oblivious to Mary's presence or her voice.

Mary thought of her Mother again and ran into her room silently praying on the way that she was all right. She felt relieved to see her Mother breathing. Her next thought was that it could be Aunt Kate. She'd been sickly all her life. Aunt Nan and even Kitty came into her mind, realizing that Aunt Mary had died young. Mary went back to where Annie was still sitting. She shook Annie by the shoulders and demanded an answer. "Annie, if you don't tell me who died, I'm going to slap you in the face." At this Annie stopped crying momentarily, believing that Mary probably would do it. Annie looked at Mary as if she were seeing her for the first time. "It's Mickey Moo Moo, Mary, she's dead."

As Mary looked at Annie, within seconds her face changed from bewilderment to relief to anger. "Do you mean to tell me that you got me all upset like this over that cat?" Mary heaved a big sigh of angry relief.

Mickey Moo Moo was the name that Annie had given the kitten that Mike had found about three years before. Mike was on his way home one blizzardly cold winter night when he heard a frail little kitten barely meowing. The kitten was pure white and blended in with the snow. He picked her up and cuddled her in his overcoat.

Mike tried to keep Annie from becoming too attached to the kitten because he wasn't sure she'd make it. But between him and Annie, the kitten thrived. Mike thought of naming the kitten Snowball, but from out of nowhere Annie wanted to call it Mickey Moo Moo. Even though it was a female, Mike realized how much Annie loved her, and let Annie have her way.

For about a month now the cat had been missing. They looked all over for it. Mike thought maybe somebody might have taken the cat because she was really pretty.

Mary did not feel bad that the cat was missing. She didn't like cats. When she was seven years old she heard Mrs. Decker tell about how she had gone into her baby's room one morning to find the cat was sitting on her baby's chest and the baby was turning blue. She said that she picked up the cat and threw it out the open window. She believed that if she hadn't gone into the room at that moment, that her baby might have suffocated. Ever since hearing that frightening tale, Mary never trusted cats.

Then there was the O'Reilly cat. Their baby was just barely crawling around when she pulled their cat's tail and the cat turned around and scratched the baby on the face. Everyone said they were lucky that the cat didn't scratch the baby's eyes and blind her.

At first Annie tried to get Mary to like the kitten and play with her, but Annie had scratches all over her hands from the kitten. When Mary pointed them out, while keeping her distance, Annie insisted that the kitten was only being playful and that they didn't hurt at all.

Some people say that cats have their own personalities. Others say if you give them love, they'll give you love in return. Some say that a cat can tell if you like them or not the minute you enter the room. Mary wondered if this was true and if the cat really knew that Mary wasn't overly fond of her.

Mary wondered, if the cat could talk, would she say, "The feeling's mutual?"

Mary noticed that when she entered the room, the cat would keep an eye on her, but when Annie entered the room, the cat was obviously happy as she ran over to her for lots of affectionate pets, hugs and kisses.

Mary was always after Annie to wash her hands after playing with the cat, especially at dinner time. She was not convinced when Annie told her that Mike said that cats are very clean animals. Mary considered the cat very sneaky. More than once she had come into the kitchen and found the cat sitting on the kitchen table and it sickened her. She'd yell scat and grab the broom. The cat would run into the bedroom and under the bed. And the cat was smart enough to know that Mary wouldn't try to get her out from under the bed. Mary was afraid the cat would scratch her. And then Mary would take a cloth with hot soapy water to clean up after her. To her, the cat was a nuisance.

But the topper of all was that if the cat's dish was empty and she was waiting for her food, but Mary happened to be busy at the kitchen sink, the cat would walk up behind her and lightly bite her on the back of the leg, startling her. So, when the cat was first missing, Mary not only didn't miss her, she thought to herself, good riddance to bad rubbish.

At that moment, Mary looked up to see Mike coming through the door. He looked sad and he had tears in his eyes. She was surprised, as she thought to herself, how can a big, strong man like Mike cry about a cat?

Kitty walked in behind Mike as she said, "Oh, Mike, did you see her nails? She must have walked miles to get home." And then even Kitty got choked up and wiped a tear from her eyes, as she announced that she had to help Mama get ready for church.

Mike went to the kitchen sink and washed his hands and got a drink of water. Then he turned around and noticed Annie sitting at the kitchen table, still looking sad and lonely.

He exclaimed, "Annie, do you want to help me? I know where there's a nice wooden box that will be just the right size. Go ask Kitty if she has any soft material we can use." Annie jumped off the chair and headed for the dining room to ask Kitty.

A little while later when Mary looked out the window she noticed that Mike had dug a hole, down by the back fence, where the flowers grew. He put the box in the hole and covered it over with dirt.

Annie knelt down and put a little wooden cross she had made at the top of the little pile of dirt. Then she beckoned for Mike to kneel down too, as she said some prayers for Mickey Moo Moo.

Later in the day when Annie still seemed to be moping around looking sad, Mary, who usually considered her to be very spoiled, couldn't help feeling sorry for her. Finally she said, "Why Mickey Moo Moo is probably already in Heaven." Annie looked up wide-eyed. "Do cats go to Heaven?" She asked, seemingly holding her breath for a favorable answer.

"Sure," Mary retorted confidently. "Why wouldn't there be a nice place for good cats and dogs and other loving pets to always be happy?"

For the first time that day Annie looked up hopefully. "Gee, if I thought she was happy in Heaven, then I wouldn't feel quite so bad."

CHAPTER THIRTY

The women were still sitting around the kitchen table that Tuesday evening slowly savoring the delicious apple pie Nan had brought for dessert. Annie was tucked into bed, and Mary as usual was listening intently.

"Well, I couldn't believe my ears when Nellie told me what Victoria's cousin's maids were saying about Victoria," Nan said with an exasperated concern in her voice.

"Victoria went to New York for the spring fashion shows and to do some shopping last week. Since the jarring of the train has at times made Victoria nauseated, she asked John if it would be alright for Maurice to drive her, and of course he agreed.

"Apparently, the gossip is that there's hanky-panky going on between Victoria and Maurice."

"Victoria and Maurice?" Maggie said, shocked at the suggestion of it.

"Yes, now isn't that ridiculous?" said Nan.

"You don't think there could be any truth to it?" Kitty asked.

"I'm astonished you'd even ask," Nan sighed disapprovingly. "Of course it's not true. And it's all based upon the fact that they were seen out dining together at a high-end restaurant the night before they left for home, and Nellie was quite emphatic that she knew for a fact that they had unlocked the door between their rooms at the hotel.

"She said, 'It seems mighty suspicious to me when she could stay at her Aunt's house and visit with her cousins, why she would choose to stay at a hotel and get an adjoining room with her chauffeur.'"

"Well, I told her although Victoria would definitely visit them, she just doesn't feel comfortable there. Her cousins have always been jealous of her and not only talk behind her back, but they enjoy nothing more than spreading around unfounded, vicious gossip. As for being out in a restaurant together, well, they had to eat, didn't they? She probably took him out someplace nice as a thank you for his help through the week. Victoria's very sweet like that, and would never think anything of it. As for the door between their rooms being unlocked, it makes sense to me in case someone tried to break into her room, he'd be there to help her.

"Well, Nellie threatened to tell John."

"Being convinced it was true, she said to me, 'I feel that my first loyalty is to the master of the house. I suspect that to you, the missus could do no wrong. You wouldn't want to believe it, no matter how much proof you had. I think you're being naïve.'

"Well, I answered her emphatically, 'I am most definitely far from naïve, but this is all hearsay. There is no proof, no evidence to make such an outrageous accusation.' I told her, 'You'd better think this through and don't dare bother Mr. O'Connell with such a stupid thing.'

"Now you know that John is a very calm and soft spoken man, but it wasn't too much later when I heard his voice, loud and angry, that I knew she'd told him. I've known him for well over twenty years and the only other time I ever knew him to get that mad and raise his voice was the time The Old Lady hit Jack with a horse whip.

"John and Jack and Gail never liked Victoria's aunt or her

cousins, and he was angry when he said to her, "My wife is the mistress of this house. It is not your place to judge her or to pass on idle gossip about her. I would expect you, as a member of this household, to defend her honor when it was so viciously tarnished by hypocrites with their unfounded accusations and their lying tongues. I want you out of this house before my wife returns. You pack your things immediately and I will give you your wages."

"Well, Nellie came downstairs red-faced and started crying. 'I should have listened to you,' she said."

"Even though I think Nellie was wrong in telling Mr. O'Connell, I can't help feeling sorry for her," Maggie said. "I'll pray for her."

At just that moment, Mike appeared in the door to walk his Aunt Nan home. On the way, Aunt Nan waited for Mike to talk, hoping he'd confide in her about the latest news she'd been shocked to hear. She'd intentionally avoided the subject at the house, but as they'd already gone a few blocks and he hadn't said anything about it, she felt compelled to speak.

"Mike," she said, "what's all this I hear about you and the men forming a union?"

Mike was stunned by her words. "Who told you that?" he asked.

"Never you mind who told me. Is it true?"

"Well," he stammered, not knowing quite what to say.

"Well, is it?" she asked again.

Mike thought for a moment. He'd need to choose his words carefully. He was fully aware of his Aunt Nan's way with words and her unconditional loyalty to Mr. O'Connell.

She saw his hesitation and said, "If it is true, it's just like biting the hand that feeds you. And I can't help but feel responsible, because you got that job through me. I can tell you there's nobody fairer than Mr. O'Connell. If anybody deserves a raise, he'll give it to them. You know I'm all for unions, but in this case, I just can't see a need for it."

Mike turned slightly and looked her in the eye and said, "I was going to tell you about it shortly, Aunt Nan, because I didn't want you to hear it from somebody else. But I didn't want to put you in an awkward position. I figured you wouldn't feel comfortable knowing, and being obligated not to tell. But before I explain the reason we're talking about a union, I want you to tell me how you heard about it. We're sworn to secrecy in fear of being blacklisted. You know what that would mean. Nobody would hire us."

Nan ignored his question as she exclaimed, "Well, I simply cannot understand how you could all turn against John O'Connell."

"Believe me, Aunt Nan, this has nothing to do with Mr. O'Connell. And at the right moment, I'll explain that to him. It's about Edgar."

"Edgar?" Nan said, confused. "How could it possibly have anything to do with Edgar?"

"We've been thinking of the future," he said, "and what would happen to our jobs if anything happened to Mr. O'Connell. Aunt Mary died so unexpectedly and all the people we know who died young of tuberculosis, scarlet fever, pneumonia. Then there was that typhoid epidemic. We just feel we'd be better off if we had a little job security. We have to face reality, Aunt Nan. All the men like Jack. He's a nice guy and down to earth, but he's not interested in the business. Who can blame him? If I was in his shoes, I'd rather do something else, too. But none of us want to be at the mercy of Edgar. He's so pompous and self-righteous. He's never done an ounce of work in his life, but he thinks he's an authority on everything. He has that attitude like he's better than everybody else, and even his voice conveys the fact that he looks down on everybody. You should know that even better than I do."

"Yes," Aunt Nan said, shaking her head. "He takes after his grandmother. Jack is more like his father and his grandfather."

Mike continued, "But Edgar comes in every now and then. We

know he's not interested in the business, but he just likes to boss us around and try to show how important he is. Last summer we were working as hard as ever, just dripping from the heat, and along comes Edgar with his fancy clothes and his shiny shoes and *he* tells *us* that if we worked a little different, we'd get more work done. Something about a time study he learned in college. He had the gall to follow some of the men around with a pad and pencil and timepiece, timing them, and making notes. I for one felt like pushing the little pipsqueak off the dock. But naturally we can't say anything. Why, if he was in charge, he'd be a slave driver. He has a mean streak in him. He'd never understand or acknowledge that it's people like us that built that place and keep it running by the sweat of our brows. We made it the success it is today. Mr. O'Connell recognizes that. And he's a fair employer. But if anything happened to him, especially if jobs were scarce, that'd be our tough luck. Edgar would have us over a barrel, and he'd do just as he pleased. So we're just trying to be a little more prepared for the future."

"Well, I'm glad you explained it to me. But be very careful. Edgar is very sneaky."

They got to the O'Connell house. Nan got on her tiptoes and pulled him forward to kiss him on the cheek. "God Bless you, Mike, you've always been such a good boy."

CHAPTER THIRTY-ONE

Maggie was sitting in her rocking chair in the parlor, enjoying the peace and quiet of the evening, when all of a sudden she heard a woman's screams coming from the apartment across the hall from them.

Just a week before, a new family had moved in. A man and wife and three young children. The husband was of average height and weight and didn't smile much. The wife was small and as thin as a rail and had a frightened look about her. The week before, they had heard the woman screaming and Kitty said it sounded as if the husband was abusing his wife. Kitty was furious. When Mike came home, Kitty told him about it.

Mike said, "Maybe she should keep her mouth shut. Some women do get their husbands all riled up."

"I don't believe my ears. Are you saying that if a wife says something that her husband doesn't like, that he has the right to hit her?" Kitty impatiently asked.

Mike hurriedly spoke up, "No, of course not. I don't mean that. But I have known some nice guys that just have bad tempers, and if their wives were more patient, they wouldn't get hit."

Kitty, obviously annoyed, answered, "Well, apparently your definition of a nice guy and my definition of a nice guy are not the same. As far as I'm concerned, no nice guy would ever, under any circumstances, hit a lady, especially his wife. He's no nice guy. He's a coward. And furthermore, in this case, he's a big bully and she's like a scared little rabbit. You can be sure she didn't say anything to make him angry."

Mike answered, "Well, even so, I don't have the right to walk into his home and interfere with his family. He could get me arrested for trespassing. Then what? I've got to work and think of this family. If I'm in jail, how can we pay the rent and the other bills? And while I was in jail, he'd beat her up, anyway. Maybe even worse. So what can I do about it?"

Kitty impatiently replied, "Well, if I were a man, I can assure you, I'd do something about it. It's disgusting letting him get away with that."

Now this evening, more screaming brought Maggie to her feet. There was a hurried rap on her door. She rushed over and opened it right away. Her neighbor was standing there looking wide-eyed and scared to death. Maggie noticed right away that her nose was bleeding.

"Oh, Mrs. O'Neill, I'm so glad you're home. Please hide my children from my husband. He's been drinking badly today and he's out of his mind. I'm afraid for their safety. He might hurt one of them."

Maggie looked at the children huddling close together and clinging to their mother. They looked scared and were crying softly. Maggie opened the door wide, pulled them all in, shut the door fast, and locked it behind them.

Then there was a pounding on the door and a man's loud voice demanding that the door be opened and that his wife come out of there. The wife was shaking, as she pleaded with Maggie to let her go out and maybe she would be able to calm him down.

Kitty came in from the kitchen and yelled at the husband, "Stop that pounding immediately or I'll call the police."

But the pounding got louder, as the husband shouted, "It's none of your business. Let my wife out of there. I just want to talk to her."

Kitty didn't trust him and hollered back. "She'll go home when you calm down. She's only visiting us now."

Just then Mike came in the back way. When he saw the wife with a bloody nose, a red mark on her cheek and the scared children huddled in the corner of the room, he got angry. He opened the door half-way as his angry eyes faced the surprised bully. "What's going on here?" he demanded.

"I want to talk to my wife, and your sister won't let her come out to talk to me," the husband belligerently stated.

"My sister won't let her out because she don't want her to get punched again," Mike yelled. "And let's get one thing straight. We will not stand for wife-beating in this building. You ought to be ashamed of yourself. You got your wife and kids all upset and scared. What kind of a so-called man are you, anyway?"

The husband continued to excuse his behavior as he answered, "It's my wife's fault for getting me mad. I only pushed her a little. I can't help it because she fell over."

Mike, apparently aggravated, replied, "No, I think what got you mad is the men at the bar teasing you and trying to get your goat. Apparently they did. Since you weren't man enough to stand up to them you came home to take it out on your wife. That's undoubtedly what happened."

The drink still in him gave the husband the nerve to say, "It's none of your business. It's between my wife and me."

Mike quickly responded, "Well, I'm warning you right now, I'm making it my business. Your family is spending the night with us. It'll give you some time to cool off and think over what I've said. Because if this ever happens again, you'll answer to me." As Mike slammed the door in his face, the pictures on the wall shook, and the things on the mantelpiece rattled.

CHAPTER THIRTY-TWO

It was Saturday afternoon and Mary, Molly and Grace were sitting on Mary's back porch watching the festivities that were taking place two doors away and listening to the music.

Frankie's sister Ruth had just gotten married that morning at church and now friends and relatives had gathered at their home. They would most likely be serving sandwiches and salads, milk, beer, tea and coffee. And of course a homemade wedding cake would be on display in a prominent place.

It was a beautiful spring day, warmer than usual, and some of the family and guests were singing, and even dancing to the music in the back yard.

Frankie's father played the fiddle at square dances. His uncle played the accordion and Frankie was a pretty good guitar player. People seemed to be having a good time.

Grace was a girl who worked at Earl and Wilson's with Mary and Molly. She had gone to the public school and lived several blocks from them, so that they didn't know her before they started working with her. Grace had to quit school after the sixth grade, so she had already worked there for two years when they met her.

Mary and Molly both felt very sorry for Grace. She was tiny and very, very thin. She had olive skin and very deep-seated brown eyes surrounded by deep, dark circles.

Grace came from a very poor family. She was the oldest of five children. Her father had died a couple of years before. Her mother was not very healthy herself, but had always worked very hard. She took in washing and did ironing and sewing and any other kind of work she could get to make ends meet. Grace gave her mother her whole paycheck. Then finally a month came when they just couldn't scrape together enough to pay the rent. They knew that they would be thrown out into the street.

Grace's mother had no place to turn to. She had come from a poor family. Both of her parents had worked hard all their lives and died before their time. She couldn't get any help from other relatives because they all had troubles of their own.

A woman on the next block had just died, leaving her husband with four young children to raise. He told Grace's mother that she and her family could move into his house if she would be willing to do the washing, ironing, cooking, cleaning and take care of his children while he worked. His only other choice was to put his children in an orphanage. But some people talked about them living together, so they got married.

Mary and Molly both liked Grace right away. She had such a loving, sweet, unselfish disposition, and never complained. She was just as good and kind to her step-brothers and sisters as she was to her real brothers and sisters. Being extra kind and very unselfish was a big part of Grace's nature. She always gave the appearance of being tired and hungry, and Mary and Molly suspected that besides being overworked at home, that she probably gave some of her food to the other children.

Molly was very thoughtful, and being an only child, would bring an extra sandwich and fruit and cookies. Then she would tell Grace she had too much and she hoped Grace would help her eat it.

Mary would never forget that fall, the year that she met Grace. When the weather started turning cold, Grace was still wearing an old sweater, full of holes. Even though Grace was shivering, she kept saying she wasn't cold. Mary and Molly kept suggesting that she wear her winter coat, when she admitted that she didn't have one.

When Mary got home from work and told Kitty about Grace not having a winter coat, Kitty immediately thought of Gail, and called Aunt Nan to see if Gail had an extra winter coat. After she explained the situation, Aunt Nan said she would talk to Victoria. A few minutes later, she called to say that she would bring the coat with her the next night, which was Tuesday.

One night Mary and Molly stopped on their way to a dance to pick up Grace. Her mother had told her that she would be able to go with them that week. Grace was really looking forward to it. Mary and Molly had gotten some things together for her to wear.

As they approached the house, they could see through the ripped shaded windows that Grace's stepfather was drunk and hollering at her Mother. They knocked on the door, hoping maybe it would shame him into acting right. As Grace opened the door slightly, they could see that some of the children were huddled in the corner, noticeably scared.

Grace's mother was trying to calm him down. As Grace was hurriedly trying to tell them that she couldn't go with them, her stepfather pulled the door open widely and pulled her by the hair. Grace winced. It forced her to turn sidewise and then he lifted his right foot and kicked her.

Mary had all she could do to keep from grabbing Grace and knocking him down. But when she saw Grace's face and heard her say, "Please go, it will be all right," she was afraid of making things worse for Grace and her family. She thought maybe he would kick Grace harder, so she kept her mouth shut. Later, Grace would tell them that her stepfather was usually very nice and kind, and that he worked very hard, but sometimes things would go wrong and he'd get so discouraged and overwhelmed and start drinking again and then sometimes he'd be mean.

They always invited Grace to go with them to movies and dances and shopping or even for long walks, but most times Grace would have to mind her brothers and sisters. Grace always seemed to cough a lot and Mary and Molly thought that she was probably overworked and rundown.

Since Mary had to quit working and stay home to take care of her mother and do all the household chores, she didn't see Grace very often anymore. But Grace and Molly walked to work together every day and became even closer friends. Mary was really glad that Grace had a friend like Molly.

Grace made a great impression on Mary. She made her feel a little guilty about her own fancy daydreams and wild expectations, when Grace had so little and yet was so thankful and appreciative for all the little things that most people took for granted.

Even though Mary and Molly had both agreed to invite Grace to everything, to give her a much needed chance to get away from her family, Grace rarely came with them. Mary was so happy to see Grace that day that she went over to give her a hug.

"Grace, it's so good to see you," she happily exclaimed. She hadn't seen Grace in months and was very surprised at her continuous, uncontrollable cough.

The music was great and people were still singing and dancing in the yard when Molly noticed the people passing their back fence. They were over by the back yard where the music was playing. "Why, it's the Gypsies." Molly exclaimed excitedly. "I didn't know they were in town again."

"Neither did I," Mary happily replied.

They looked at each other with adventurous smiles on their faces and at the same time blurted out, "Let's get our fortunes told."

Then Mary thought, "I don't have any money and I don't want to go in the house to ask somebody and have to explain what it's for."

Molly put her hand in the pocket of her dress. "Look at this, it must be fate," as she showed them three pennies. "Come on, let's do it."

"I couldn't take your money," Grace responded.

Molly replied, "Oh, come on now. If you had the money, you'd pay for me, wouldn't you?"

"She's right, Grace," Mary added, "She really wants to pay, so we should let her."

Mary was thinking in her mind that she would pay Molly back the penny another day, but she didn't want to say that and make Grace feel bad, because they knew Grace just didn't have any money.

On the way down to the back fence, Molly whispered to Mary and Grace, "Now remember that they say you shouldn't look into their eyes because they can cast a spell over you."

They waited at Mary's back yard fence until the Gypsy finished telling fortunes to the few people who wished to hear them. Then they stopped at the back fence of the house next door where two other people were gathered. Mary had already talked Molly into going first and Grace second.

The Gypsy saw them waiting. She came over to them. She was dark and very pretty, with deep penetrating brown eyes. She looked from Molly to Grace to Mary, just as they were lined up by the fence. It looked as if for a moment she was studying their faces. "You would like your fortune told," she said this more as a statement of fact than a question. "For only one penny I can tell you all about your future."

Molly gave her a penny and put out her hand. She held Molly's hand and looked at her palm.

"Somebody that you loved, died." Molly was surprised and exclaimed, "Yes, my father died." Then she said, "He wants you to know he's happy." Molly had a somber face. The Gypsy looked back at Molly's hand. "You are going to have a long life and be married twice. Yes, I see two husbands in your future." And then she let go of Molly's hand and looked at Grace. Grace handed her the penny that Molly had given to her.

The Gypsy looked into Grace's face, then down at the palm of her hand, "I can see you work very hard," she said.

Grace impatiently asked, "Will I get married some day, too?" The Gypsy looked at her palm again as she said, "I see you in a white dress, in between two windows," Grace was happily excited as she told her friends, "See, I told you I was going to get married some day."

Then it was Mary's turn to have her fortune told. The Gypsy held her palm and then for a split second looked into her face. "Somebody you know is going on a trip," she exclaimed. That news did not mean much to Mary. She really didn't care that somebody she knew was going on a trip. She was impatiently waiting to find out about Jack. Then the Gypsy opened her hand a little wider as she said, "I see you in the near future trying to decide between two men. One is light and the other is dark." And then she paused as she continued looking at Mary's hand. It was only seconds, but to Mary it seemed like many minutes, as she eagerly waited for the Gypsy to tell her more. Finally her curious mind forced her to look into the Gypsy's eyes with the question, "Well, which one will I choose?"

The Gypsy gave her a knowing look as she smiled and answered, "You will choose the right one and have a very happy life."

Later, as Mary thought about the fortune the Gypsy had predicted for her, she felt more determined than ever that Jack would be the dark man the Gypsy spoke of and that she would marry him.

Later, when Mary told Kitty about the fortune teller, Kitty said, "Oh, Mary, you didn't fall for that. They don't know any more about the future than you or me. In fact, I'll bet I can tell your fortune just as well as she can."

"I'd look into your eyes and I'd think, what would a young girl like this want to hear? And then I'd proceed to tell you that you were going to meet a handsome young man, that was going to fall madly in love with you and ask you to marry him, right?" And without waiting for an answer, Kitty continued. "And then she told your friends a little different version of the same thing. They just tell what they believe people want to hear. I wish I could be invisible for a little while and follow her around. I'd be willing to bet that she has a certain amount of fortunes, then repeats the same ones with a little variation. Am I right? Didn't she tell you and your friends that you were going to meet a man who wanted to marry you?"

Mary told Kitty about the predictions the Gypsy had made. When she told her about the Gypsy telling Molly that she would have two husbands, Kitty started laughing. "Miss Monroe is a good age now, but she mentioned one time that she'd had her fortune told twice. Each time they told her she'd be married twice, and she's still not married even once yet."

When Mary told Kitty about the Gypsy's predictions about her, Kitty said, "Mary, you're attractive and intelligent. I could have told you that you'll meet a lot of young men. Naturally some will be dark and some will be light. So choosing between two men, one dark and one light, doesn't say anything. You notice she was smart enough not to tell you which one you'd choose, because she doesn't know anymore than you do, but this increases her chances of appearing right. If you ask me she's a good saleswoman. She predicts for you a great future and you're a happy customer and now you'll tell your friends. Most people remember the few guesses that were right, but they forget all the predictions that never come out. As far as I'm concerned, fortune tellers are clever, and that's just a gimmick they use. They let other people earn their money by the sweat of their brow, and then they convince gullible people like you that they have the power to tell the future. I'll bet you girls were hanging on to every word she said. Well, you won't catch me wasting my hard-earned pennies. Why, I'd sooner put that penny toward the ticket for the picture show. And by the way, Mary, are you aware that fortune telling is against the Church and you're going to have to tell that in Confession?"

Mary answered, "Oh, gee, I never thought of that."

Kitty continued, "Father will probably remind you that if God wanted us to know the future that He would have told us."

One week later, Grace died of consumption. Mary and Molly were shocked when they heard the news.

On the way to the wake, Mary started thinking of the things she intended to say to Grace's stepfather about being mean to her, but she was surprised to see that he had tears in his eyes. She remembered Grace's words, "He's really a very kind person when he's sober, but sometimes he gets overwhelmed by problems and then he drinks and becomes mean. When he sobers up again, he cries and says he's sorry. Many times he doesn't remember what he did."

As Mary and Molly knelt on the kneeling bench praying in front of Grace, they both noticed that she was in a white dress, in between two windows.

On the way home from the wake, Mary and Molly questioned the unfairness of life. Molly mentioned about Grace always wanting a white dress and they both felt so sad that she had to die to get one.

When Aunt Nan heard about Grace's death, she spoke to John, who provided the white dress for her to be laid out in. He made arrangements with the undertaker to send him the bill and he had Nan send boxes of groceries to the house.

Grace's unselfishness made a great impression on Mary. She found it hard to understand how someone could always be so kind and so thankful for so little.

When Mary mentioned to Kitty about the Gypsy's prediction coming true, "I see you in a white dress in between two windows," Kitty analyzed it by saying, "Most young ladies I know have a white dress, and every parlor I've ever been in has two windows."

But Mary and Molly had a hard time believing that it was just a coincidence.

CHAPTER THIRTY-THREE

Kitty was elated as, during supper that Tuesday, she shared with everyone the good news that at last a woman had ben seated as the first Congresswoman of the United States.

"Listen to this," she excitedly exclaimed as she proceeded to read aloud the descriptive scene that had taken place the previous day. "Miss Rankin takes seat. Elaborate prelude of ceremony. First woman member of Congress. Her entrance signalized by uproarious cheering and applause. Representative Janette Rankin of Montana, first woman member of Congress, took her seat in the House today after an elaborate prelude of ceremony in which women suffragettes predominated. The principal occasion was a breakfast for 'The Honorable Janette Rankin of Montana' under the auspices of Suffragettes of all factions. Mrs. Carey Chapman Catt, President of the National American Suffrage Association sat at Miss Rankin's right and, 'The day of our deliverance is at hand,' was the keynote speech to the notable gathering of women. Miss Rankin's entrance to the House was signaled by uproarious cheering and applause. Every member on the floor and everybody in the crowded galleries rose as, accompanied by Representative Evans of Montana, she walked to a seat in the rear center of the hall. Miss Rankin carried one of the scores of bouquets of flowers which had come to her office. She wore no hat and was attired in a dark dress. Members rushed from all parts of the chamber to congratulate her. Another ovation. A second outburst of applause greeted Miss Rankin when her name was called on the roll and she replied, 'Present', rushing furiously the oration continued until she rose from her seat and bowed.

"Hooray! We've finally got a woman's voice in our government. And this is only the beginning," Kitty confidently announced.

Mike patiently listened to Kitty's enthusiastic presentation, and then finally piped up.

"Well, that's just dandy, but let's not lose sight of the really important news that President Wilson has addressed a joint session of Congress. This has been called the most serious crisis since the Civil War."

Aunt Nan spoke up with concern in her voice, "It sounds like our Capitol was a busy place yesterday. According to the paper, while Congress waited to hear the President, pacifists and anti-pacifists besieged Congress toward their respective views of impending war with Germany. Both called for unorganized sidewalk processions to the capitol where Senators and Representatives might be canvassed for their peace or war ideas. Simultaneously, thousands of telegrams from all parts of the country poured in upon the Capitol and White House, either praying for peace or urging drastic action to uphold American rights and honor."

Aunt Nan continued, "According to the paper, most pacifists went there from New York and other cities under the direction of the Emergency Peace Federation, and when they assembled at their headquarters they were given white armbands bearing in large black letters an inscription, 'Keep out of war.' The anti-pacifists, calling themselves 'Pilgrims of Patriotism', come from a number of eastern cities, marshaled by a New York Citizens Committee to neutralize the effect of the anti-war forces."

Mike exclaimed excitedly, "Did you hear what happened when

several men and women from the pacificist delegation called a Massachusetts Senator to the door and asked him to vote against a declaration of war with Germany?"

Kitty answered, "No, what happened?"

Mike replied excitedly, "The Senator said that if President Wilson asked for such a declaration, he certainly would support it. 'That is cowardice,' retorted one of the group. 'National degeneracy is worse than cowardice,' replied the Senator. 'You are a coward,' said one of the men. 'You are a liar,' retorted the Senator.' According to the account, the man advanced and struck the Senator, who then, despite his sixty-odd years, launched a blow that sent the man sprawling on the hard tiles of the corridor. 'The man and several of his friends were taken in charge by the Capitol Police.'"

Aunt Nan added, "The pacifists told the Capitol Police that he was not the aggressor and contended that the Senator had struck the first blow, so who knows. There's at least two sides to every story. But the paper also mentioned that after overnight consideration of the President's address, most of the so-called pacifist groups declared that if war came, they would stand by the president and that a war resolution is expected to pass both Houses of Congress overwhelmingly."

Aunt Nan shook her head as she said, "I still have a hard time believing that after that beautiful wedding ceremony last year when the Kaiser's daughter got married and those world leaders celebrated together, how such a thing could possibly have happened. It's a shame all these conflicts taking place in so many places in the world and all the extra heartache and suffering so many innocent people have to endure. But I do think the President did the best he could to keep us out of war for as long as he could, and in so doing, saved thousands of American lives. But now what can he do? Between the Zimmerman telegram and the German government's announcement that it would use its submarines to sink every vessel that sought to approach either the ports of Great Britain, Ireland, or the western coast of Europe or any of the ports controlled by the enemies of Germany within the Mediterranean."

Mike asked, "Aunt Nan, what exactly was the Zimmerman telegram?"

Aunt Nan replied, "The German diplomat Arthur Zimmerman sent a coded message through telegram to the German minister to Mexico. It was intercepted and decoded by British cryptographers. Anticipating US entry into the war on the allied side, Germany invited Mexico to join the Central Powers. In return for its efforts toward winning the war, Germany promised to reward Mexico with the return of land previously lost to the United States, namely, Arizona, New Mexico and Texas. It was shown to President Wilson in late February of this year and it was revealed in the American press on the first of March. The coded message said, 'We intend to begin on the first of February unrestricted submarine warfare. We shall endeavor in spite of this to keep the United States of America neutral. In the event of this not succeeding, we make Mexico a proposal of alliance on the following basis: make war together, make peace together, generous financial support, and an understanding on our part that Mexico is to reconquer the lost territory in Texas, New Mexico and Arizona. The settlement in detail is left to you. You will inform the President of the above most-secretly as soon as the outbreak of war with the United States of America is certain, and add the suggestion that he should on his own initiative invite Japan to immediate adherence and at the same time mediate between Japan and ourselves. Please call the President's attention to the fact that the ruthless employment of our submarines now offers the prospect of compelling England in a few months to make peace. Signed, Zimmerman."

Aunt Nan continued speaking, "So it's obvious that we have been unwillingly drawn into this conflict and at this point have no choice.

But I admire the President's speech to the Congress. I have a copy right here and I'd like to read it to you. Part of what he said was, 'The present German submarine warfare against commerce is a warfare against mankind. It is a war against all nations. The challenge is to all mankind. Each nation must decide for itself how it will meet it. The choice we make for ourselves must be made through the moderation of counsel and temperateness of judgment befitting our character and our motives as a nation. When I addressed the Congress on the twenty-sixth of February last, I thought that it would suffice to assert our neutral rights with arms, our right to use the seas against unlawful interference, our right to keep our people safe against unlawful violence. But armed neutrality, it now appears, is impracticable. Because submarines are in effect outlaws when used as the German submarines have been used against merchant shipping, it is impossible to defend ships against their attacks as the law of nations has assumed that merchantmen would defend themselves against privateers or cruisers, visible craft giving chase upon the open sea. It is common prudence in such circumstances, grim necessity indeed, to endeavor to destroy them before they have shown their own intention. They must be dealt with upon sight, if dealt with at all. The German Government denies the right of neutrals to use arms at all within the areas of the sea which it has proscribed, even in the defense of rights which no modern publicist has ever before questioned their right to defend. The intimation is conveyed that the armed guards which we have placed on our merchant ships will be treated as beyond the pale of law and subject to be dealt with as pirates would be. Armed neutrality is ineffectual enough at best; in such circumstances and in the face of such pretensions it is worse than ineffectual: it is likely only to produce what it was meant to prevent; it is practically certain to draw us into the war without either the rights or the effectiveness of belligerents. There is one choice we cannot make, we are incapable of making: we will not choose the path of submission and suffer the most sacred rights of our Nation and our people to be ignored or violated. The wrongs against which we now array ourselves are no common wrongs; they cut to the very roots of human life.

With a profound sense of the solemn and even tragical character of the step I am taking and of the grave responsibilities which it involves, but in unhesitating obedience to what I deem my constitutional duty, I advise that the Congress declare the recent course of the Imperial German Government to be in fact nothing less than war against the government and people of the United States; that it formally accept the status of belligerent which has thus been thrust upon it, and that it take immediate steps not only to put the country in a more thorough state of defense but also to exert all its power and employ all its resources to bring the Government of the German Empire to terms and end the war.

"What this will involve is clear. It will involve the utmost practicable cooperation in counsel and action with the governments now at war with Germany, and, as incident to that, the extension to those governments of the most liberal financial credit, in order that our resources may so far as possible be added to theirs. It will involve the organization and mobilization of all the material resources of the country to supply the materials of war and serve the incidental needs of the Nation in the most abundant and yet the most economical and efficient way possible. It will involve the immediate full equipment of the navy in all respects but particularly in supplying it with the best means of dealing with the enemy's submarines. It will involve the immediate addition to the armed forces of the United States already provided for by law in case of war at least five hundred thousand men, who should, in my opinion, be chosen upon the principle of universal liability to service, and also the authorization of subsequent additional increments of equal force as soon as they may be needed and can be handled in training. It will involve also, of course, the granting of adequate credits to the Government, sustained, I hope, so far as they can equitably be sustained by the present generation, by well-conceived taxation.

"I say sustained so far as may be equitable by taxation because it seems to me that it would be most unwise to base the credits which will now be necessary entirely on money borrowed. It is our duty, I most respectfully urge, to protect our people so far as we may against the very serious hardships and evils which would be likely to arise out of the inflation which would be produced by vast loans.

"In carrying out the measures by which these things are to be accomplished we should keep constantly in mind the wisdom of interfering as little as possible in our own preparation and in the equipment of our own military forces with the duty - for it will be a very practical duty - of supplying the nations already at war with Germany with the materials which they can obtain only from us or by our assistance. They are in the field and we should help them in every way to be effective there.

"I shall take the liberty of suggesting, through the several executive departments of the Government, for the consideration of your committees, measures for the accomplishment of the several objects I have mentioned. I hope that it will be your pleasure to deal with them as having been framed after very careful thought by the branch of the Government upon which the responsibility of conducting the war and safeguarding the Nation will most directly fall.

"While we do these things, these deeply momentous things, let us be very clear, and make very clear to all the world what our motives and our objects are. My own thought has not been driven from its habitual and normal course by the unhappy events of the last two months, and I do not believe that the thought of the Nation has been altered or clouded by them. I have exactly the same things in mind now that I had in mind when I addressed the Senate on the twenty-second of January last, the same that I had in mind when I addressed the Congress on the third of February and on the twenty-sixth of February. Our object now, as then, is to vindicate the principles of peace and justice in the life of the world as against selfish and autocratic power and to set up amongst the really free and self-governed peoples of the world such a concert of purpose and of action as will henceforth insure the observance of those principles.

"Neutrality is no longer feasible or desirable where the peace of the world is involved and the freedom of its peoples, and the menace to that peace and freedom lies in the existence of autocratic governments backed by organized force which is controlled wholly by their will, not by the will of their people. We have seen the last of neutrality in such circumstances. We are at the beginning of an age in which it will be insisted that the same standards of conduct and of responsibility for wrong done shall be observed among nations and their governments that are observed among the individual citizens of civilized states.

"We have no quarrel with the German people. We have no feeling towards them but one of sympathy and friendship. It was not upon their impulse that their government acted in entering this war. It was not with their previous knowledge or approval. It was a war determined upon as wars used to be determined upon in the old, unhappy days when peoples were nowhere consulted by their rulers and wars were provoked and waged in the interest of dynasties or of little groups of ambitious men who were accustomed to use their fellow men as pawns and tools. Self-governed nations do not fill their neighbor states with spies or set the course of intrigue to bring about some critical posture of affairs which will give them an opportunity to strike and make conquest. Such designs can be successfully worked out only under cover and where no one has the right to ask questions. Cunningly contrived plans of deception or aggression, carried, it may be, from generation to generation, can be worked out and kept from the light only within the privacy of courts or behind the carefully guarded confidences of a narrow and privileged class. They are happily impossible where public opinion commands and insists upon full information concerning all the nation's affairs.

"A steadfast concert for peace can never be maintained except by a partnership of democratic nations. No autocratic government could be trusted to keep faith within it or observe its covenants. It must be a league of honor, a partnership of opinion. Intrigue would eat its vitals away; the plottings of inner circles who could plan what they would and render account to no one would be a corruption seated at its very heart. Only free peoples can hold their purpose and their honor steady to a common end and prefer the interests of mankind to any narrow interest of their own."

"Now, to purposely change the subject, John was telling me about the new Chinese Restaurant that has just opened up, serving Chinese and American food. He went there yesterday to a special businessman's lunch. That is one thing he and I share in common, we both love Chinese food."

Mike enthusiastically exclaimed, "Thanks Aunt Nan for reminding me. Speaking of restaurants, I'm inviting everybody out to dinner this Sunday to the Trojan Hotel to celebrate Easter. I hope you'll be able to join us too, Aunt Nan. Listen to this advertisement," he said as he took a piece of paper out of his pocket.

"Easter greetings from the Trojan Hotel. Sunday, April 8 is Easter. We have arranged to give the people of Troy something out of the ordinary. From twelve-thirty pm to two-thirty pm we will have a trio of well-known local voices, together with Nofler's celebrated orchestra, who will entertain the people with a sacred concert. We will also endeavor to excel all our previous Sunday dinners. A five course dinner with white wine will be served for the usual price of fifty cents. Signed, W. H. Wyatt, Proprietor."

Mary spoke up. "Oh, Mike, that sounds great, but I already promised Molly that I'd go with her to the picture show on Sunday to see 'Joan the Woman.'"

Kitty chimed in, "I know a number of people that are planning on going to that movie."

Aunt Nan added, "That was quite the advertisement, 'Because she loved her country, they killed her. Because she saved her country, they worship her as a Saint. Joan of Arc chose to be burned at the stake rather than to deny her faith. Geraldine Farrar as Joan in the Cecil B. DeMille cinema masterpiece."

Mike laughingly said, "Well, of course I wouldn't want anybody to miss out on such an exciting picture show as that. But the answer is simple, Mary, invite Molly to come with us and we'll get there early so as to beat the crowd and you'll have plenty of time to get to the picture show." Everybody happily agreed.

Before leaving the house, Mike called Kitty aside and whispered, "Kitty, try to get everybody to go out to dinner Sunday. With this war coming upon us fast, we can't be sure when we'll have the opportunity to celebrate again. And Mama will really enjoy the dinner and music and the memory of it will be with her forever."

Kitty looked into her brother's eyes with concern as she answered, "Oh, Mike, I've been so distracted with the news of the Congresswoman that up until now I haven't thought about the war. I guess I've just been unrealistically hoping it could be avoided. But I guess now we'll have to just hope for the best, but be prepared for the worst."

"Something like that," Mike smilingly answered as he went over to give his mother and his Aunt a kiss and hug before going out the door.

CHAPTER THIRTY-FOUR

Each day the newspaper was filled with war plans that came from Washington. Plans that were necessary to defend America. Mary and her family read in their Troy paper on Thursday, April 5th, "Request for immediate appropriation of $3,400,000 for the Army and Navy were made to Congress by the executive departments. Provision is made for increasing the enlisted strength of the navy to 150,000 men and to increase the Marine Corps to 30,000. Of the great sum, a little more than $2,930,000 is asked for the army. Tax measures for the war. It is believed that a bond issue at 3.5% would raise $2,000,000 at once. Present internal revenue taxes will obtain approximately $750,000 this year. Suggested increase in inheritance tax rate alone is estimated would increase the return from that force to $500,000. One plan being considered is to raise the rate on large income. One of the proposals under consideration would swell the sum to vast figures as to the aggregate of which there are widespread differences of opinion. Increase taxes on distilled liquors, beer and tobacco are also under consideration."

Friday, April 6th, "War becomes an actuality today. Wheels of the government's newly-planned machinery begin to whirl. War document signed by the President. German-armed ships in American ports seized. The first act of war – House adopted war resolution. By a vote of 373 to 50 – Members talked all day. And all night – 17 weary hours absorbed in debating. Signing of the war resolution by the President and Vice President. The final step – flock of German submarines reported waiting in Mexican waters – President's Proclamation, Cuba also may fight Germany. Washington, April 6th, President Wilson today signed the resolution of Congress declaring a state of war between the United States and Germany. The War Resolution was signed by the President at 1:11 o'clock. All naval militia and naval reserve were called to the colors with the President's signing of the war resolution.

"The new army bill. The government plans to raise a war army of a million men within a year, and two million within two years. Expansion of regular army and national guard – many new regiments – under the principal of universal military service. Selection conscription. A bill prepared by the general staff and approved by the President for submission to congress provides for the immediate filling up of the regular army and national guard to war strength of more than 600,000 by draft unless enough volunteers enlist quickly and for bringing into the service by late summer of the first 500,000 of the new force of young men between the ages of 19 and 25 to be called to the colors by selective conscription. In drafting its program, the staff recognized the fact that the United States first starts at the beginning and trained an army of 100,000 officers and non-commissioned officers to undertake the training of the thousands of youths who will enter the service with no notion of military duty or life.

"In New York Harbor. German ships seized – men and officers transferred to Ellis Island – officials do not know what to do with the women found aboard the seized ships. Aggregating more than 275,000 tons gross from the 54,000 ton liner Vaterland down to the 1,468 ton bark Matador was completed early this morning and their 1500 men and officers were transferred under military guard on government barges to the immigration station on Ellis Island. Later today, Navy experts are to begin an examination of the ships to determine the amount of damage it has been reported the crews inflicted on them when diplomatic relations severed with Germany. Problem – what shall be done with the 100 or more women found aboard the seized ships. They are wives and daughters of the officers who, for the most part, left Germany after the war began to join the men during their enforced stay in the United States.

"The Japanese press hailed the entrance of America into the war as the death-knell of Germany. The papers print articles praising the nobility of President Wilson's motives and congratulating him on the stand he has taken.

Saturday, April 7th, "Soldiers in the trenches glad to hear news of America into the war. It was hailed with cheers, especially the Canadians with whom many thousands of Americans are already serving. Many Canadian and British companies were busy preparing signs to hold up over the trenches telling the Germans the tidings from Washington.

"The United States War Loan. The federal government will raise for war purposes over three billion dollars. Bonds will be sold bearing interest at three and a half percent. Neutrality will not characterize this loan. Citizens through patriotism will seek participation in large and small amounts."

And then it was Sunday – Easter Sunday, and it was as if the war news had been put on hold for a day. It was a beautiful day and many of the people in Troy dressed up in their Easter finery and proceeded to a number of area churches to celebrate the "Good news that Jesus had risen from the dead." Many people felt spiritually uplifted sitting in St. Mary's church observing the altar so beautifully decorated with an assortment of flowers and plants, especially Easter lilies. And the beautiful organ music playing traditional Easter hymns.

Mary felt elated singing her favorite hymns, "Alleluia, alleluia, let the holy anthem rise, and the choirs of Heaven chanted in the temple of the skies; let the mountains skip with gladness and the joyful valleys ring with Hosanna in the highest to our Savior and our King. Alleluia, alleluia, like the sun from out the waves, Christ has risen up in triumph from the darkness of the grave. Glorious splendor of the nation on the land an endless day; Christ the very lord of glory who is risen up today."

Even Mike went to Sunday Mass with the family. Not that he believed in God, but he knew that it would make his Mother happy. Mike had a fairly good idea of what lay ahead. He knew it would only be a matter of time before he would be leaving, and he wanted this to be a perfect day so that his Mother and Pa and his Aunts and the family would have this special happy memory to look back upon when he was gone.

Seeing his Aunt Nan at the Mass reminded Mike of the medical book she had dropped off that Sunday morning a few years before. He still felt justified that between work and prior commitments he really was too busy and just couldn't get to it. He knew his Aunt Nan would never understand, especially since she had gone out of her way and actually limped into their house so he could read it. She was known for saying, "Put first things first," and she never would have believed the things he had to do were as important as his taking the time to read that book, so he had just let her assume that he had read it and avoided getting into a discussion with her.

After Mass, they had all gone to the hotel for a delicious dinner and beautiful music. They had a very special, memorable time, after which Mary and Molly were inspired by the courage of Joan of Arc as portrayed on the movie screen.

CHAPTER THIRTY-FIVE

As they gathered together that Tuesday evening for their usual supper-sharing session, they were discussing all the happenings since the previous Tuesday, and about the big parade that had taken place the night before. It had created a patriotic optimism. The paper mentioned that the big patriotic parade that had taken place was primarily for the purpose of stimulating recruits for the navy to bring the nation's naval forces up to the number required for active duty.

The paper article estimated that there were between 7,000 and 10,000 marchers and that most every marcher carried a flag. Most of those sitting at that table had witnessed the parade and knew many people marching in it.

"There were flags everywhere," Mike said, "not only in the parade, but all around the parade and a few of the fellows I know have decided to go into the Navy. In fact, they're going down today to sign up.

"If it was up to me, I think that's the branch of service I would go into, too. Frankie and I have agreed to go together, and ever since that time he fell or accidentally got pushed into the Hudson River, he's been afraid of water and can't swim. I hate to think of what might have happened that time if his brother hadn't been close by to dive in and save his life."

"Thank God he was there," Maggie said, "Frankie has always been such a nice boy."

Kitty mentioned, "There is something about our flag with its red and white stripes representing the thirteen original colonies and its forty-eight white stars on a navy blue background representing the total number of our United States today that arouses a deep sense of patriotism in most Americans. I thought the parade was great."

"Me, too!" Mary and Annie echoed together.

Aunt Nan offered, "I think our President Wilson made a good observation about the flag when he said, 'The meaning of that flag is up to each generation. It has to be perpetuated and carried on, and the responsibilities are ours. That flag is not permanent unless we make it that way.'"

Maggie said, "And to that I say, Amen."

Mary asked Mike if he would do her a favor by picking up something she had forgotten to get at the store that day, before he went out for the evening. While he was gone she sat at the kitchen table listening to Kitty and her Aunt Nan chatting. Kitty mentioned that the Lafayette Flying Squadron composed of Americans at the front would change from the French to the American military uniform and hereafter carry the American flag, but that they will still be under command of the French Army. Kitty also pointed out that she found it interesting that the monthly pay of privates would be increased to $33 a month for overseas service and a payment of $20 a month for the wives of enlisted men, and $2 a month for each minor child. But, she remarked, what surprised her the most was when she read that one of the Vanderbilts was selling his yacht to the government for a dollar.

Aunt Nan replied, "Yes, I noticed that our newspaper mentioned that there were many yacht owners donating their vessels and that to make the transfer legal they had to be sold for $1 to the government."

Mary piped up, "What surprised me the very most was reading in tonight's paper about the American warship being fired upon one hundred miles south of New York City."

Aunt Nan answered, "I was surprised at that, too. It mentioned that a torpedo hurled at the destroyer Smith missed the ship by about thirty yards and that the wake of the missile was plainly seen across the bow – then the submarine disappeared."

New York City was only a little over a hundred miles south of Troy. When Mary had first read the article, she had dreamed of submarines coming up the Hudson River and surfacing in Troy, but, she felt too embarrassed to mention it to anyone.

Just then, Mike came in. "Aunt Nan, your name just came up at the store."

"What?" Aunt Nan responded. "My name? What are you talking about?"

Mike answered, "Don't worry, I listened to make sure nothing bad was said. Actually you were paid a compliment."

"What?" she asked again as she looked at him, quite bewildered.

Mike replied, "Well, Mr. Picket, Mr. Moore and Mr. Higgins agreed with each other that you were pretty smart for a woman. One of them said you were even as smart as some men."

Aunt Nan shook her head in obvious disbelief as she replied, "They think that's a compliment, but believe me I consider it an insult. They think they know everything, but in my opinion, between the three of them, they don't have a half a brain. They are like three peas in a pod. They stand around in the store and only agree all the time with each other. Heaven forbid if they were to listen to another point of view. As far as I'm concerned, they have closed minds and take things out of context. Most times I've been able to just ignore them, but every once in a while I've had to speak up, like the other day, for instance. They are so insensitive. I notice that they don't say anything about the war in front of Mr. Hess because they're probably afraid he'll put them out, and that seems to be their favorite hang-out. But they don't mind what they say in front of Mrs. Hess. Sometimes they talk as if she was invisible or a non-person.

"I went over to them and I said, 'For Heaven's sake, if you must talk about the war, do it someplace else. Mrs. Hess is a wonderful woman and she's worried enough about her family in Germany without your stupid comments. In fact, I'd like you to know that on my trip I met a lot of nice German people, but if your country goes to war with another country, any country, what can the average person do about it? People are just caught up in circumstances they have no control over.' I don't know if it did any good, but at least I gave them a piece of my mind, and didn't let them get away with it."

CHAPTER THIRTY-SIX

The month had flown by so quickly. Mary's 17th birthday had come and gone. It was already May 19th and she was in a good mood, getting ready for the Saturday night dance.

Most importantly, her mother seemed to be getting better every day and she was optimistic that it wouldn't be much longer before she was almost completely well. Except for all the war talk, everything else seemed to be going really good, and the war being so far away, at times even seemed unreal to her.

As Mary stood in front of the mirror in the beautiful blue dress that Kitty had given her for her birthday, she couldn't help smiling at herself. She felt extra confident as she got ready, that she really did look pretty.

The dress, Kitty had pointed out, was the same color as her eyes, and it wouldn't be right for her not to have it. Mary really appreciated Kitty's unselfish generosity. This was not the first time that Kitty had passed up buying a better dress for herself in order to buy Mary a dress too.

The happiness Mary felt at that moment about wearing the dress and also the beautiful gold and pearl dangling earrings that Molly had given her, went beyond words. She had seen these beautiful earrings in the store window and couldn't help going over to look at them every time she and Molly passed the store, even though she never thought that she would ever be able to have them. How surprised she was when Molly gave them to her for her birthday. Molly was very generous, too.

At that moment, Mary realized more than ever before, just how lucky she was to have a sister like Kitty and a best friend like Molly.

Mary started thinking of who she might see at the dance. Tonight they would go to St. Mary's. Last week they had gone to St. Peter's and the week before to St. Lawrence's dance. They had agreed that they would only show up at the same place every third week, so it wouldn't appear that they didn't have a Saturday night date. And if either of them met a young man who wanted to walk her home, he had to be willing to walk them both home. They never split up.

Mike hollered in from the kitchen, "Mary, Molly's here." Mary took one last glance, smiling at herself in the mirror, and left the room.

As soon as Mike saw her, he smiled and said, "Why, Mary, you look so pretty. I don't know if I should let my little sister go out unchaperoned, looking so pretty."

"Oh, Mike, you're just teasing me," Mary smilingly replied.

"No, Mary, I really mean it, you look beautiful," as he went over to her and kissed her on the cheek. Hearing Mike say that really meant something to Mary.

In leaving the house in the dress and those earrings, with Mike's words still echoing in her mind, Mary really felt extremely happy and very special.

Mary and Molly were in their usual carefree, silly mood and they laughed on and off all the way to the dance. The music was already playing as they walked to the door.

That was another one of their little secrets. They never arrived too early, so as not to appear too anxious.

Right away Mary's flirting eyes surveyed the room. She smiled her coy, inviting smile a couple of times at the young men that she knew. She analyzed that she was sure of at least two or three dances.

She was soon proved right as two of the young men came over for the first and second dances. They said politely that they would appreciate a dance later and Mary smilingly agreed.

Molly also was invited to participate in both dances. Soon they started chatting with a couple of old school friends that they hadn't seen in ages. They all started laughing as they got reminiscing about some old school day happenings.

The music started for the fourth dance, a waltz. Mary looked across the dance hall and her heart momentarily stopped beating. There, striding across the dance floor toward them, was Jack O'Connell. She was very surprised to see him there. She had thought that he was still away at college. She hadn't seen him in months and then only at Mass one Sunday morning.

She wondered who was standing behind her, or farther down the line, that he would ask to dance with. "Oh, Jack," she whispered in her mind, as just looking at him aroused all those feelings that she had always felt for him. They were still there, just below the surface.

Mary was so surprised when Jack stopped right in front of her and put his hand out and said, "May I have this dance?" As she looked into those eyes, it was all she could do to contain her composure. She literally thought that she must be dreaming. She smiled shyly as she stepped into his arms. As they were dancing he asked her if she was from Troy, and she realized that he had not recognized her. But then again, she thought, why should he have? If he had ever noticed her before at all, it would have been as Pat's skinny, straggly red haired, freckled faced kid sister.

She smiled again sweetly as she said, "I'm Mary O'Neill and I believe you went to school with my brother, Pat." He flashed that most beautiful smile she had ever seen and her heart started palpitating as he answered, "Oh, yes, of course, you're Aunt Nan's niece. Well, you've certainly grown up to be very pretty, Mary."

She blushed slightly as she smilingly said, "Thank you."

Their dance was over so quickly, and as he escorted her back to where he had picked her up. To Mary's disappointment, he didn't say he'd come back again for another dance.

She stood there debating with herself if she wished that other young men would ask her to dance, so that she would give the appearance of being popular, or if she should wish that no one asked her, so that she would be available if he came back again. But she was asked and she did dance most of the evening.

The night flew by and Mary caught sight of Jack dancing a few times with other girls, mostly the girls that came from better families and were very well dressed.

It was time for the last dance of the evening. It would be the moonlight waltz, where the lights would be dimmed and everyone would change partners over and over again. It was Mary's favorite.

She started dancing and one by one changed partners and then came the moment when she looked up and there was Jack dancing with her again. She smiled happily as he hastily asked, "Mary, can I walk you home?" She nodded approvingly as she hoped he heard her say yes.

He was waiting for her at the door and they again exchanged smiles. She introduced him to Molly and asked if he would mind if they walked Molly home first. He smiled at Molly. Of course he would be glad to.

She started thinking ahead. Like any other proper young lady, she would never allow any young man to kiss her goodnight on the first date. She agonized, should she let Jack if he tried? God knows how much she wanted him to. But if she did, would he think less of her? Maybe she could let him kiss her, and then try to explain that she normally never would, but that he had taken her by surprise. Or would that explanation only make things worse? She wished she knew just what to do, and what to say, so that he would ask her out on a date. This was a magical evening. The night she had waited for her whole life, and she didn't want anything to spoil it for her. They got to Molly's house and she said her goodbyes and went in. As they walked along, Mary tried to think of interesting things to talk about. He asked her about Pat and she asked him about school and polite questions about his family.

It was hard for her to just small talk about insignificant things when she wanted so desperately to touch him. He was the only person she had ever felt this way about. She realized this was the closest that she had ever been to him and she hoped that he wouldn't hear her heart pounding. She had made up her mind that if he tried to kiss her, she would not protest. On the contrary, she really wished that he would take her into his arms and kiss her passionately as she had seen in the movies and read about in so many romantic novels.

She could hear within her mind her mother's voice. "Don't give a man the impression that you're easy. Men don't marry that kind of girl. Act a little hard to get and they'll like you better."

They were on her street already. The time had gone by so fast. Mary almost gasped out loud. She couldn't believe her eyes. Right in the gutter a few feet from her house, was her Pa.

What could she do? Sometimes, no matter how drunk he was, he would recognize her. She didn't think Jack would know what house she lived in so she decided to go to the nicest house on the block, which was a little past hers, and hope her father wouldn't see her. The other houses were much more likely to have people going in and coming out of them.

Mary smiled embarrassingly at Jack as she beckoned him past her Pa by whispering that the man was a neighbor who lived in that house. As she hurried by, she pleaded, "Oh, God, don't let him see me," but before she had finished her prayer, she heard, "Mareee? Is that you, Mareee?" She didn't answer as she whispered to Jack, "His wife's name is Mary."

Mary felt very embarrassed over the whole thing, especially in front of Jack. If it had been some other young man, she might very likely have said, "He's my Pa, and he's sick," but she just couldn't say that in front of Jack. She just hated to lie, it went against everything she believed in, but what could she do? What choice did she have? She thought of Jack's father. She had seen him in church so many times. He was such a gentleman and Aunt Nan was always saying how kind he was.

Oh, why did her Pa have to be there? Why did he have to ruin the most important evening of her whole life? She wanted to sit a while and talk to Jack and maybe he would ask to see her again. There was nothing in the whole world that she wanted more. But now she felt as if she dare not spend too much more time with him, in case someone came by and wondered what she was doing on that porch instead of her own. Or worse yet, if they pointed to her father acknowledging that it was her father.

She tried to be as polite as possible, looking into Jack's beautiful eyes, that still stole her heart away. She exclaimed, "Oh, Jack, it was so nice seeing you again, and thank you so much for walking me home. I hope I see you again soon." That's all that she could say without being too forward.

Jack smiled into her deep blue eyes as he said, "I really enjoyed your company, Mary. I'll call you sometime and we can go to a picture show or something."

She nodded. "Yes, I'd really like that. And thank you again for walking me home," and then he was gone. She waited in the hallway an extra couple of minutes to make sure he was out of sight. She wondered if there was anything she could have said that would have encouraged him to ask her for a date on a specific evening. She couldn't think of anything. Oh well, she thought, he said he'd call. Maybe that's the way the young men from better families did things.

She hurried over to her father and tried to shake him awake. She still felt very guilty that she had denied knowing him. "Pa, Pa, it's Mary, come on, I'll help you upstairs." But his drunken weight was too much for her, so she left him and ran upstairs hoping that Mike or Kitty could help her. Oh, why did he have to be there, she thought, as she ran up the stairs. And for the first time in her life she was ashamed of her father. Kitty, who had no patience with Pa at all, helped Mary and mumbled all the way up the stairs about what a cross God had placed upon them all.

Sunday and Monday seemed to drag as Mary waited impatiently for Aunt Nan's Tuesday evening visit, wondering if Jack would have said anything to her.

After they ate supper Tuesday night and the dishes were out of the way, they all got to talking as usual at the kitchen table. Aunt Nan just casually said, "Mary, I forgot to tell you, Jack mentioned he had met you at the dance and how nice and pretty you are." And that's all she said. Nothing about him walking her home or saying he'd call. Mary was disappointed, but was still far from ready to give up her dreams.

Then Aunt Nan started talking about how Mrs. Ferguson's sister and her daughter were visiting from Boston and how beautiful her niece was and raved about her musical ability. Mary didn't want to hear about Mrs. Ferguson's niece, and as Aunt Nan continued talking, Mary's mind went back to Saturday night, reliving as she had so many times already, the warm feelings she had felt just being so close to Jack.

For days, Mary hung around the phone, hoping so desperately that Jack would call. Even if she had to go out she hurried back. Many times she'd ask her mother if anyone called. She felt as if her whole life's dreams were being held in mid-air just waiting for a phone call from Jack.

The following Saturday evening, Molly agreed with Mary that

this once, they'd go again to St. Mary's dance, just in case Jack went again. But of course he wasn't there.

Over and over again in her mind, she agonized over everything they had talked about, wondering if she could have said or done anything differently so that he would have called. She started wondering if there was any chance that he knew it was her father and that she had lied. And that was the reason that he didn't call. She reproached herself. That's what she would deserve for lying and being so unkind to her own father, who had always been so good to her. She was ashamed of herself, but quickly reassured herself that it was only ten days and maybe he was still busy with his family and friends.

The following Tuesday, when Aunt Nan came, she didn't say anything about Jack at all. All she talked about was what an extraordinary pianist Mrs. Ferguson's niece was, and that she had come to the house the past couple of days to help Gail with her piano playing. She added that she seemed like a very sweet girl.

CHAPTER THIRTY-SEVEN

Mary felt uneasy as she waited in line to go to confession. Even though she believed in confession, she did not like to go. And even though there was a screen in between her and the priest, she usually felt nervous and embarrassed. She did believe that the God-given power had been passed down from the apostles to the priest so that the priest represented Jesus in the confessional and that it was Jesus who was actually forgiving each one's sins. And just as much as she disliked going to confession, she really enjoyed the feeling she had after going. There were times that she felt as if a great weight had been taken right out from within her conscious mind. When she was young and preparing for her First Confession, Sister had told her and her classmates that when they were baptized, their soul was pure white, and that sinning put black marks on their soul. Then, when they went to confession, all those black marks were erased and their soul was pure white again. Mary always imagined her heart, because she couldn't see it, as a red heart-shaped thing a little less than two inches in diameter that was on the top-left side of her body, and that her soul was round and about the same size not too far away from her heart. As she stood there examining her conscience, Mary was still ashamed of herself for lying about her father. She had lied three times, she estimated. The first for telling Jack that her father was a neighbor. Second, when her father had called her by name, telling

Jack that this neighbor man's wife's name was Mary. And third, for leading Jack to a different house and claiming it to be hers. And she didn't feel any less guilty, although she did believe they were white lies, the kind that wouldn't hurt anyone or tarnish their reputation.

When she was in St. Mary's grammar school, each class was taken over to church every first Friday for confession, but when she went to work and couldn't always make it on the first Friday, she tried to go about every two or three months or whenever she had done something that disturbed her peace of mind.

Finally, it was her turn.

Mary walked into the confessional and knelt down on the kneeling bench. She made the sign of the cross as she said, "Bless me, Father, for I have sinned, it has been two months since my last confession, I accuse myself of the following sins. I told three lies and I had my fortune told by a Gypsy fortune teller. For these sins and all the sins which I cannot now remember, I am heartily sorry, humbly beg pardon from God, and penance and absolution from you, Father."

The priest replied, "If God wanted us to know the future, He would have told us so," as he emphasized the word He. "How much did it cost to have your fortune told?"

Mary whispered, "One penny, Father."

Father said, "For your penance, say three Our Fathers, three Hail Marys and put a penny in the poor box. Now make a good Act of Contrition."

Mary started praying, "Oh my God I am heartily sorry for having offended thee, and I detest all my sins because I dread the loss of Heaven and the pain of hell. But most of all because they offend thee, my God, who art all good and deserving of all my love. I firmly resolve, with the help of thy grace, to confess my sins, to do penance and to amend my life, amen."

Father replied, "God the Father of mercies, through the death and resurrection of His Son, has reconciled the world to Himself and sent the Holy Spirit among us for the forgiveness of sin; through the ministry of the church, may God give you pardon and peace." The priest then made the sign of the cross toward her as he said, "and I absolve you in the name of the Father and of the Son and of the Holy Spirit, amen. Now go in peace to love and serve the Lord."

Mary replied, "Thank you, Father."

Mary walked down to the front of the church and knelt down at the altar railing in front of the statue of Jesus to say her Our Fathers and Hail Marys.

Then she took a penny out of her purse and put it in the poor box in the back of the church.

As Mary walked out of the church, she felt a great sense of peace, that a heavy burden of guilt had been lifted from her. She always thought of God as the kind, loving father that Jesus had portrayed him to be, and she was determined to do better to please Him.

CHAPTER THIRTY-EIGHT

War news dominated the newspapers. On June 5th, the newspaper included this notice: Register, between 7am and 9pm. Attention all males between the ages of twenty-one and thirty years must personally appear at the polling place in the election district in which they reside. In accordance with the President's proclamation, anyone failing to do so will be subject to imprisonment in jail or other penal institutions for a term of one year.

Shortly after this, Mike and Frankie enlisted. It wasn't too long after, that everyone huddled around them at the station to see them off. Maggie kissed, hugged and blessed Mike, as she handed him a Blessed Miraculous Medal. On it was a picture of the Blessed Virgin Mary and the words, "Oh Mary conceived without sin pray for us who have recourse to thee."

Maggie hurriedly and prayerfully requested, "Mike, promise me that you'll keep this medal in your pocket at all times. You can keep it in this," as she handed him a little black pouch. "I would feel so much better knowing that you were in her care."

Mike looked at his mother as he thought. She was such a perfect mother who had such a hard life, especially putting up with their Pa. At that moment, Mike glanced over at his Pa, who had tears in his eyes. Mike noticed that since his mother had the stroke, her face was still a little twisted. He felt sorry for her. He didn't believe at all in this medal she was asking him to always keep with him, but if it would make her feel better, how could he possibly refuse her? "Okay, Mama, if it will make you feel better, I promise that I will always carry it in my pocket."

CHAPTER THIRTY-NINE

In the weeks that passed after Mike's departure, Mary tried to write to him often to tell him what was going on at home. She knew he'd enjoy news about the family and the neighbors. She tried to include some funny happenings or jokes that she heard or read to keep his spirits up. His letters home were full of self-confidence and predictions of success. The weeks dragged by with Mary still pining for Jack. He was in her thoughts constantly as she waited and hoped and dreamed and prayed that he would call. Her days were filled thinking of the special places he would take her and the interesting conversations they would have. But always, all her day dreams ended up the same, with her in Jack's arms. She tried to figure out some way that she could meet him without being obvious. She thought maybe she could go visit her Aunt Nan on some pretext, but what? She knew Aunt Nan would not encourage that. And she would have to go through the side door and probably wouldn't see him, anyway. She wasn't even sure that he was still home.

On July 4th, as all Americans celebrated their Independence Day, the newspaper announced that American troops had arrived in France.

Then came the Tuesday night that Mary was very unprepared for. As Aunt Nan flew in through the kitchen door, she announced that the O'Connell household was in an uproar. Jack had eloped with

Mrs. Ferguson's niece, Julie!

Mary stood at the table as if in a state of shock.

She pondered slowly, Jack eloped? Jack married? How could it be?

Aunt Nan exclaimed, "Married! Less than six weeks after they met! Everybody's in shock!"

Suddenly, Mary could hardly breathe. She felt a little light-headed as her knees went weak. It was as if someone punched her in the gut and snatched out of her grasp a thing of immeasurable value, which she'd had in her possession all her life. She felt a sadness deep within her heart, and that nothing in life would ever fill the great emptiness she was feeling at that moment. She did not believe she would ever find anyone to love as she had loved Jack. If only Jack had asked her for a date the night he walked her home, he would have fallen in love with her, before this Julie arrived. She hadn't felt so sad since her Aunt Mary died and it was just as if Jack also had died, taking with him all those hopes and dreams she'd carried in her heart since she'd first caught sight of him in that hallway so many years before. Her eyes filled with tears as she moved toward her room. She didn't want anyone to see her crying. This girl Julie would never love Jack as much as she did. Oh, why did she have to come along and ruin everything? Why didn't she just stay in Boston, where she belonged?

CHAPTER FORTY

It was Sunday afternoon and Mary and Molly were walking around Prospect Park listening to the Band Concert. As usual, there were many people, old and young. Some people were sitting while others were walking around, some pushing baby carriages. Most of the people looked quite happy, many singing the songs out loud. Mary was doing her best to feel happy with them, while trying to chase out of her mind the thought that Jack had married Julie. She was still having a really hard time believing the heartbreaking news.

It had only been seven weeks before his marriage to Julie that Jack had walked her home from the dance and had told her he'd call to make a date to take her out. Every one of those days were filled with the hope that he would call that very day. Now she had to face the reality that all those precious daydreams she'd had of Jack, over and over again, since she was a young child, were all shattered, never to be lived, never to come true. And those thoughts which she was having such a hard time shaking, made her feel very sad. Every night since hearing the news, she cried into her pillow. Finally, she made up her mind that she was not going to sit around, wasting time, feeling sorry for herself, thinking of what might have been. She would try harder to keep busy and make her mind think of other thoughts.

It was such a beautiful day, and Mary, trying to lift up her spirits, was wearing her favorite dress. As she left the house, her mother had called out to warn her to take an umbrella, that the forecast called for showers in the afternoon. But it was too beautiful a day, without the slightest hint of rain, and she didn't want to be bothered carrying an umbrella all afternoon for nothing.

The concert was over and Mary and Molly started down the hill, with the intention of walking to Manory's for some ice cream, and then on to the picture show.

It was starting to rain. A car pulled over with two young men in the front seat. The one in the passenger side called out, "Girls, would you like a ride?" Molly said to Mary, "Come on, Mary, that fellow driving the automobile is Don Spencer, who used to live next door to us, before he got married." The young man who had called to them jumped out to open the back door for them, suggesting one of the girls might like to sit up front. They both jumped into the back seat fast, ignoring his words. He jumped into the automobile and it took off turning right at the corner, instead of left toward the city. Mary spoke up hurriedly. "We appreciate the ride, but we're going the other way."

The young man who had opened the door for them said, "Oh, we'll just go for a little ride and stop someplace for a couple of drinks. Don't worry, we'll get you home in no time at all, safe and sound."

Mary and Molly glanced at each other with obvious concern, realizing that these men had been drinking already. "But we don't drink and we don't go out with married men," Mary quickly answered.

The fellow driving answered, "We're not married. What made you think we were married?" As both men looked at each other and started laughing.

This time it was Molly who spoke up, quite excitedly, "Because, Don Spencer, about six or seven years ago, I went to your wedding."

He was shocked at her reply and started making up excuses, but still showed no sign of stopping and turning the automobile around. By this time, Mary and Molly also realized that the men had been drinking even more heavily than they at first had realized, and that it wasn't going to do any good arguing with them.

Mary knew exactly where they were, so she fast whispered to Molly, and when the car slowed down to make the steep downward turn, Mary opened the door fast and the two of them, holding hands, jumped out. Within seconds they were on their feet, limping into the bushes, scared to death that at their first opportunity the men would turn the car around and come back looking for them. As Mary and Molly hobbled about thirty yards into the woods and hid behind a wide tree, that's just what those two young men did do.

Mary and Molly clutched each other, almost afraid to breathe. They could hear the men arguing over where the car was when they jumped out. One thought it was further up and the other thought it was further down. The girls were silently praying that they wouldn't compromise and come into where they actually were.

The young men called in, "Girls, come out, we're sorry. We promise to take you right home." Mary looked at Molly and they both shook their heads no. Neither Mary nor Molly trusted them.

Molly held on to Mary even tighter, her eyes and mouth opened wide in terror, as she heard a dog howling in the not too far off distance. Molly had been bitten by a neighbor's dog when she was only five years old. She was terrified of dogs. Mary looked at her and moved her mouth without speaking, to form the words, "Don't worry, he's tied up," but Molly was still shaking in disbelief.

The men walked back and forth for a few minutes in the drizzling rain, still calling out the same message, and finally appeared to give up looking. As Mary and Molly heard their automobile drive away, they felt a little more relaxed. But Mary with her suspicious mind whispered, "What if they're only trying to fool us and they're waiting a short ways away for us to come out?"

Molly answered softly, "What can we do? We have to get out of here. Why, I'm soaked and I'm even getting cold."

At that moment, the dog howled again and Molly gasped out loud, "Oh, Mary, I'm so scared and I don't have your confidence in believing that dog is tied up. What if he isn't tied up and he starts coming after us?"

Mary tried to sound confident, as she said, "I'm sure he's tied up or he would have gotten here by now. Okay, this is what we'll do. We'll go that way," as she pointed in the direction of an open field, away from the road, and away from the sound of the dog. "I'm practically positive that if we go this way, that in a couple of minutes we'll be out on Brunswyck Road."

So they started walking and walking and walking. Molly didn't say anything, because she realized that when they had jumped out, Mary's body actually cushioned hers a little and Mary had gotten the worst of it. Mary's elbow was cut, she was limping, and her favorite dress was torn, wet and full of stains.

When they finally found their way out of the woods, it was Mary hanging onto Molly for the extra help she needed to walk. Her ankle had already started to swell. It was starting to get a little darker. Neither one of them knew where they were. It wasn't Brunswyck Road, or at least, if it was, it was further out than either of them had ever been before.

They were hardly aware that they had come out of the woods into a lot, full of automobiles, which were parked in front of what looked like a night club and hotel. They had stopped to catch their breath, and were leaning on a beautiful black shiny automobile. They were pondering what to do, when they heard a man's voice asking, "Excuse me, Miss. I couldn't help but notice that you hurt your ankle. Could I be of assistance?" They looked up at once. The first thing Mary noticed was the steel green eyes and beautiful smile, that displayed the perfectly shaped teeth of a very attractive man in his forties. His black hair was slightly graying at the temples, and this added to his handsomeness.

Mary tried to think fast, to make up an excuse for her and Molly's shameful appearance. She smiled shyly, "Oh, thank you, sir, we appreciate your concern. We were at the Concert at Prospect Park, and it was such a beautiful day that we decided to go for a walk. We got talking and walked much further than we had intended to. Then I twisted my ankle and it started to rain and an automobile went by and splashed mud all over us. Now we're trying to think of how we could notify my brother to pick me up."

Even though Mike was in the war and Pat was at the seminary, Mary thought that by mentioning she had a brother, if this man's intentions weren't as honorable as they sounded, that the thought of an enraged brother might keep him in line.

Mary had already fastly gone over in her mind their choices. She knew that she couldn't walk a block, let alone all the way home. They weren't even sure which direction home was in. Actually, the only choice they had was to go into this strange place and ask to use the telephone and call Kitty to pick them up. But maybe Kitty wouldn't be home. Anyway, where could they tell her they were? And Kitty, who already didn't have the best sense of direction, could very easily get lost in the dark looking for them.

He looked deeply into Mary's face, almost as if he were studying her, as he said, "I am Daniel Packard and this is my car. I'm going into the city right now and I would be very happy to give you a ride home." He smiled again as he opened the back door of the automobile.

Mary looked at the automobile. It was a very deluxe model, and he was dressed so impeccably that she assumed he was probably a well-to-do gentleman. But, just to make sure he wouldn't get the wrong idea, Mary hesitated and looked at Molly and then at him as she said, "Well we usually don't take rides from strangers, but under the circumstances, we do appreciate your offer."

Mary and Molly got into the back seat of the automobile. Mr. Packard closed the door, got into the driver's seat, started the automobile, and took a left turn onto the main road as Mary and Molly prayed silently that that was the right way. Within a few minutes they started seeing familiar sights and looked at each other, acknowledging their sigh of relief.

On the way home, Mr. Packard asked where they lived so he could drop them off. Mary still didn't completely trust him, so she told him he could drop them off at the corner of Hoosick Street and Fifth Avenue, acknowledging that they lived close by.

Then Mary asked him where he lived, and he said it wasn't far from where they met. Her next question was, did he and his wife have a very big family. She and Molly were surprised to hear that he not only wasn't married and had no children, but that he had no family at all. No brothers and sisters, or aunts and uncles. He was an only child, and both his parents, now deceased, had been the only child in their families also.

The following Sunday afternoon, Mary and Molly again went to Prospect Park for the concert. Mary was still slightly limping, so Kitty dropped them off, but she told them that she wouldn't be able to pick them up. Mary felt confident that if she sat on a bench to listen to the music that her ankle was strong enough for her to walk home on afterward. Also there was always the possibility that they might meet somebody they knew they could trust, who would give them a ride.

The concert was over and they started slowly walking down the road. Most of the people were already ahead of them. They were very surprised to see Mr. Packard approaching his automobile, which was parked half-way down the hill, just off the road. He was going down the hill on the grass, as if he had taken a short cut, from the concert. When he looked over and saw Mary and Molly he had that same beautiful warm smile as he said, "Well, hello there, how is your ankle?"

Mary smiled back as she said, "Oh, much better, thank you. But I must say, what a coincidence meeting you here."

"Oh, I come here often. I love music. I notice that you are still limping a little. Could I give you a ride home again?" he inquired.

Mary questioned, "Are you going our way?"

He answered, "Well, to tell you the truth, I'm going out to Burden Lake to watch the boat races, but I'd be glad to ride you home first. Unless of course you'd like to come for the ride. It's a nice day for a ride and I won't be gone long. I'd really appreciate the company."

As Mary looked at him, she remembered that he had no family. She thought to herself, he's probably lonely. Mary looked at Molly with that okay let's go look. Molly knew she wanted to go and said, "It's okay with me as long as we get back by seven o'clock."

While Mr. Packard took out his pocket watch to check the time, Mary again noticed how well-dressed he was and what a beautiful silver chain went from his vest pocket to his pocket watch. He looked at the timepiece. "It's only a little after five now, so we have plenty of time to be back by seven."

Mary was in a happier mood than she was the previous week, and as they drove along, the tune they had just played at the concert was still in her mind and she couldn't help but hum it. When she realized that she was humming out loud, she felt a little embarrassed and she laughingly said, "I just can't seem to get this tune out of my mind."

"Isn't that Daisy, Daisy?" he said.

"Yes," she answered.

He enthusiastically replied, "That's one of my favorites, too. Let's sing it. I love to sing, don't you?"

Before Mary or Molly could answer, he had started singing in a very good baritone voice. "Daisy, Daisy, give me your answer true, I'm half crazy all for the love of you." He stopped and turned slightly to the right, speaking over his shoulder so they could hear him in the back seat. He smiled as he laughingly said, "You're not going to make me sing all by myself, I hope." He continued and they joined in. "It won't be a stylish marriage, I can't afford a carriage, but you'll look sweet upon the seat of a bicycle built for two."

Within seconds after they sang that song, he said, "How about singing 'In the Good Old Summertime'?" Without waiting for an answer he began to sing and they joined in. "In the good old summertime, in the good old summertime, strolling down the shady lane, with your baby mine. You'll hold her hand, and she'll hold yours, and that's a very good sign, that she'd your tootsie wootsie in the good old summertime." They hardly caught their breath when he said, 'What about 'The Man on the Flying Trapeze'?" They said okay and he began with much gusto. "He flies through the air with the greatest of ease, the daring young man on the flying trapeze..." They sang one song after another, all the way to Burden Lake. In between the singing, they told him their first names and answered a few friendly questions he asked.

They watched the boat races and drove around part of the Lake and then he pulled up a short way from a refreshment stand where he bought them some ice cream and sarsaparilla. They wanted to pay for their own, but when he said, "Please let me treat," he looked as if they would be doing him a favor by allowing him to, so they smiled and thanked him.

After eating the ice cream, they sang all the way back to Troy. Before he dropped them off, he told them how very much he had enjoyed their company and he hoped they'd meet again. He wished them both good luck and then drove off.

The following Sunday, Mary and Molly went to the concert again. Afterward, coming down the road, they saw Mr. Packard's automobile parked in the same place. He was standing next to it, ready to get in. When he turned to the right to make sure there were no automobiles coming down the hill before he opened the door, Mary and Molly waved to him. He waited until they reached his automobile, and then with that same beautiful smile, he greeted them by name. "Well this is a pleasant surprise, Mary and Molly, the sweet young ladies with the beautiful voices. Where are you girls off to this beautiful day?" He questioned. "Any place special?"

They smiled back at him. "No, we're not really going any place special, just taking a little walk," Mary replied.

He said, "Well, I'm headed out to Crystal Lake to watch the boats. Have you ever seen the beautiful Merry-go-Round they have out there now?"

Mary and Molly both shook their heads no. "We've heard about it, though," Mary added.

"Well, if you'd like to see it, I'll be back way before dark, and I can't think of anything more pleasant than sharing the journey with you two. We can sing all the way again if you'd like to." He smilingly said. "Since you got me started singing last Sunday, I've been singing all week." So they agreed to go.

This was the beginning of an unusual Sunday afternoon friendship. As he dropped them off each Sunday, he'd tell them where he was going the following Sunday. They were interesting places, in all directions, not too far from Troy, and he always got them home before dark.

CHAPTER FORTY-ONE

Kitty came home from a women's rights meeting and announced that she had met Jack's wife, Julie, who had come to the meeting with her aunt, Mrs. Ferguson. "She seemed very nice," Kitty was explaining.

Mary couldn't help but ask, "Is she pretty?"

Kitty thought for a minute and answered, "Yes, she really is very pretty, and between that and the beautiful clothes she was wearing, she just stood right out in the crowd."

"What was she wearing?" Mary asked.

Kitty answered, "She wore a lovely light blue linen suit with a long peplum, mother-of-pearl buttons and an elegant ruffle at the bottom of the full skirt. She had a stunning blue silk hat covered in pink flowers and simple ballerina flats." She paused for a second. "Oh, yes, she was also wearing a beautiful sapphire broach."

"It sounds like a beautiful outfit," Mary answered.

Kitty continued, "But aside from how pretty she is and the beautiful clothes she was wearing, I was more impressed by how down-to-earth she is. Mrs. Ferguson took her around and introduced her to the group. When she met me, she said, 'My aunt told me that I should ask you in what way I could help,' I said to her. 'We know you are from Boston, so if you have any suggestions, we'd be glad to hear them.' She replied, 'My aunt has filled me in and it sounds like you are all doing a great job.' So see what I mean about how nice she is? Now, Mary, I'm tired and I'm going to go to bed as soon as I check on Mama. Remember that interview I mentioned a couple of weeks ago about being considered for a promotion? Well, it's tomorrow. The supervisor is coming up from Albany to interview Margaret and me. I want to be at my best."

Kitty had just drifted off to sleep when she heard the commotion in the dining room and realized it was Pa at his worst. He was preaching to who-knows-what and talking about evil spirits. Finally, after listening to it for almost an hour, Kitty felt exasperated as she whispered to Mary, "I think if I had a gun, I'd shoot him." They knew from experience if they said anything to him, it'd wake him even more and he would just preach longer. Finally, after another hour, it got quiet. So Kitty had Mary tiptoe out and turn the lights out. She warned her, "Don't try covering him because it's liable to wake him up again. Besides, the drink he's got in him will keep him warm all night."

Kitty sent Mary because she knew if he ever woke up again, Mary could soothe him, whereas he'd get angry at Kitty. Before long, everyone in the house was sleeping, except Kitty. She was just too angry at her Pa to be able to get back to sleep. All she could think of was, how was she going to be at her best the next day for that important interview. The promotion meant a substantial raise in pay and Kitty actually felt as if she worked harder than Margaret and deserved it more.

CHAPTER FORTY-TWO

"It was ten o'clock when the phone rang. "Hello," Mary said. "Oh, Kitty, how are you? Mrs. Powell? Yes, she told me she would be here about eleven-thirty with some homemade soup for Mama." Mary paused and then answered, "Sure, I could do that." She repeated Kitty's message, "Bring you any kind of a sandwich and empty a soda pop bottle and fill it with the wine that is in the bag on the floor in the back of our closet. Yes, I know where it is. Also bring you some spearmint gum."

Mary paused again and then repeated Kitty's message, "I'm not to say anything when I hand you the bag except to say, "I'll see you later, and leave, so it just appears that you forgot your lunch. Okay Kitty I'll see you around noon and I'll keep my fingers crossed during your interview this afternoon."

Even though Maggie had gotten so much better, Mary still didn't want to leave her all alone.

As Mary hung up the phone, she couldn't help feeling sorry for Kitty, who had told her that morning that she hadn't gotten any sleep at all. Now she had just informed her that she was not only lacking her usual self-confidence, but actually had the jitters. Kitty believed drinking a little wine would make her more calm, and the gum would cover the wine smell and make her breath more appealing.

Mary never questioned Kitty because she knew from years of experience that whatever Kitty did, it was for the family. Even if something might not have sounded quite right, Mary knew that Kitty would have a good reason for doing whatever she did. Mary would always consider Kitty one of the most unselfish people she would ever know. She had always worked very hard and used to say, "When opportunity knocks, I'm going to be ready." Mary thought Kitty really deserved a promotion.

Mary was also so thankful for Mrs. Powell's help. She came to visit most Mondays, Wednesdays, and Fridays around noontime. Many times she would bring homemade soup for Maggie, and Mary, or a pie she had baked that morning. She always encouraged Mary to go out to get some groceries or to at least take a walk and get some fresh air. When Mary tried to thank her she'd say, "Oh, your mother's like a sister to me. In fact, you are all just like family."

Mary at first felt guilty thinking back to when she used to come in from school and was anxious to tell her mother something exciting that had happened at school that day or a good grade she had gotten and she would be disappointed to see Mrs. Powell there. She remembered thinking to herself, "Doesn't she have a home of her own? Does she have to be here so often keeping Mama from getting her work done?" But now she was so thankful for all her help. Mrs. Powell would always say, "Now remember, Mary, no matter what time it is, or what day it is, you just call me if you have to go someplace. I'm just thankful I can help in some way."

Mary quickly got ready and made Kitty's lunch. She was thankful that there was a bottle of soda pop left and she usually always had a couple sticks of spearmint gum in her purse. She always liked the way it made her purse smell sweet.

As soon as Mrs. Powell came in the door Mary kissed her mother goodbye and walked down the seven blocks to Ferry Street to catch the ferry that would take her over the Hudson River to Watervliet.

As she stepped off the ferry at Sixteenth Street, Mary only had to walk one short block to the telephone office where Kitty worked.

Later that day, Kitty excitedly rushed up the back stairs and flung open the kitchen door, shouting, "I got the promotion!"

CHAPTER FORTY-THREE

As Mary and Molly were walking along, Mary was not happy hearing Molly's news that her step-cousin Veronica and her parents were coming for another visit. They were expected to arrive on Thursday.

At her last visit four years before, they had found her to be spoiled, self-centered and rude.

Molly was trying to convince Mary that it wouldn't be too bad because she'd only be there for a week. "Maybe she's changed and will act better this time," Molly unconvincingly stated. Mary gave a look that said, you don't believe that any more than I do. "Well, please, Mary, for my sake, don't lose your temper with her. My mother has made me promise that no matter what she says or does, to just ignore it for the sake of harmony. She pointed out that Charlie has been very good to us, and it would really please him to be able to have a nice pleasant visit with his only brother. Especially since they don't have the opportunity to see each other very often. So Mary, please promise me that you won't get into any arguments with her, either. We can put up with her for just a week. The time will go by fast."

"Well, I promise for your sake that I'll really try hard. But if she's still as self-centered and obnoxious as she was on her last visit, it'll really be hard to do."

How could they ever forget Veronica's last visit? Before she had arrived, Molly and Mary were made aware that Veronica and her parents had a lot of money and lived in a beautiful house in Virginia. But they were completely unprepared for her terrible disposition.

Charlie's brother Don and his wife Edith only had the one child. From the time she was young, they had pampered her and given her everything she wanted. She even had her own outdoor playhouse, pony and cart. Neither of them, it seemed, could bring themselves to say no to her, or to punish her in any way.

Veronica had found out at an early age that by throwing temper tantrums, she could always get her own way. She was a year older than Mary and Molly, but in many ways, was selfishly immature. They had found her to be spoiled, demanding, manipulative, and very egotistical, self-centered, rude and stingy.

Mary and Molly were aghast the first time that they observed her hollering at her parents. "I don't want to and you can't make me!" she shouted.

Her mother tried to soothe her. "Now, now, calm down dear. Nobody will make you do anything that you don't want to do."

Then there was the day that she demanded that they get her the new coat she wanted. Almost apologetically her mother said, "We just bought you a new coat."

Veronica pouted, "That old thing? I don't like it anymore. You certainly don't expect me to wear something that I don't like, do you?"

Her mother answered, "Of course not, dear."

At every opportunity, Veronica belittled her parents and hollered at them. She was very demanding as she ordered, "I want this or I want that," and with a mad face threatened, "And you had better get it for me." Mary nicknamed her, "I want."

Mary and Molly felt so sorry for her parents. No one that they knew had ever talked so hatefully disrespectful to their parents.

Veronica's mother actually seemed afraid of her. And her father kept quiet as she complained about everything, especially their shortcomings. It was as if she were the parent and they were the children. She'd angrily say things like, "I've told you and told you." Or, "Now see what you've done? You've got me all upset." They'd end up giving her her own way, every time.

There were a few times that she would start out nice enough, but if she didn't get her way, in a matter of seconds, she'd turn to threatening them again. If anyone dared to call to her attention something she'd done wrong, right away she'd try to blame someone else. "Well, it certainly wasn't my fault," she'd say in a threatening voice. Veronica was also a very bad sport. She pouted if somebody else got ahead of her or won a game. On more than one occasion, they caught her cheating. Mary had considered her a little nasty spoiled brat and finally refused to play any games with her.

But what had made Mary the most aggravated was the way Veronica downgraded Troy and the people who lived there. When she saw the factory that she and Molly worked in, she actually laughed out loud. "I don't know how you could lower yourselves to work in a place like that. I wouldn't work there if I was starving." Mary quickly and angrily retorted, "Well, that's easy for you to say when you get everything handed to you. But if you were on your own, you'd sing a different tune. Besides, it's honest work and nothing to be ashamed of. Aunt Mary always said, 'No matter how insignificant it may seem, you should feel proud to do an honest day's work and be independent enough to pay your own way and help the family.'"

Mary and Molly, working at Earl and Wilson's, were used to handing in their whole paycheck, and were given a very small amount of spending money. They were amazed at the amount of money that Veronica was allowed to waste on frivolous things.

There was no end to her extravagant demands. She had the attitude that she was better than other people and deserved more.

Mary was finding it hard to put up with this airy, uppity, shallow person who thought that she was better than they were, when her self-confidence told her otherwise.

Veronica was not only lazy and didn't lift a finger to help in any way, but demanded to be waited on. Esther, their colored maid, accompanied them everywhere and took care of Veronica's clothes and things, and got hollered at unmercifully if they weren't done to Veronica's unrealistic expectations.

It was Saturday morning when Molly called to invite Mary to have dinner with them that evening. Mary asked Kitty if it was all right, and Kitty very cheerfully told her to go and enjoy herself, that she herself had no plans and would be glad to stay home and take care of things.

Molly's mother cooked the dinner, with Esther assisting her. Molly and Mary set the table and then they all sat down to eat, with Esther waiting on them. Mary and Molly and her mother and Charlie were informal people and would have preferred if Esther had sat down with them, but for Veronica and her parents, such familiarity would have been unheard of.

After dinner, when the others took their pie and coffee into the living room, Mary and Molly started to clean up the dishes and insisted that Esther sit down and eat her own supper and pie.

Veronica not only didn't lift a finger to help, but had complained all through dinner about one thing or another. But what really aggravated Mary the most was the pie incident. Molly's mother had made an apple pie for dessert and cut it into eight pieces, one for each of them.

Veronica had gone into the living room to eat her pie with her parents and Molly's mother and Charlie. Molly put her piece of pie to the side and said she would eat it after she finished what she was doing. Mary and Esther were sitting at the kitchen table eating their pieces of pie when out came Veronica. She spotted Molly's piece of pie and as she was reaching for it, Mary quickly exclaimed, "That's Molly's pie." But before Mary could get to it, Veronica picked it up and in between gobbling the pie up, said rather sarcastically, "So what? She won't mind."

Mary sat there in disbelief as she thought to herself, Well that's enough for that idea, that this spoiled brat had changed. Apparently she's just as selfish as ever.

Mary said to Molly later, "You should say something to her about the pie," but Molly said, "I can have pie anytime. I'd sooner keep the peace and avoid any unnecessary trouble."

"I'll call you tomorrow for Mass," Mary stated as she was leaving. "And by the way, what are you going to do about Veronica when we meet Mr. Packard at 2pm?"

"Well, we'll just have to invite her to go with us," Molly responded.

On the way to meet Mr. Packard, Veronica showed Mary and Molly a picture of a handsome young man and a letter she said that he wrote to her, expressing his love and wanting to marry her. She went on and on about how crazy he was about her.

They really wondered if it was all true. They had already caught her in a few lies and the handwriting actually looked as if she had tried to disguise her own penmanship, without being too convincing. Then she showed them an expensive-looking gold bracelet that she said he had given her.

As she looked at the gold bracelet, all Molly could think of was the conversation that she had innocently overheard. She still felt guilty about it. But she tried to console herself with the knowledge that she wasn't deliberately eavesdropping. Even now, looking back, she didn't know what she could have done differently.

Veronica had gone to a concert with her mother and Molly's

mother. Molly was extra tired, having stayed up later than usual entertaining Veronica. It had been a tiring time, with Veronica turning the light on in her face at all hours. After all, Veronica could sleep late, but Molly still had to get up very early for work.

It was probably about nine o'clock as Molly lay in her bed, trying so hard to tune out the voices drifting in from the back porch.

Molly's bedroom was a converted back hall with three windows, two of which faced the large enclosed back porch. It had been a warm day and Molly had opened the windows. When she went to bed she had decided to just pull the drapes and leave the windows open. It was a very safe neighborhood, so she certainly didn't have to be concerned about her safety.

It only took Molly a few seconds to realize that the voices she was hearing were those of Charlie and his brother Don.

Don was four years older than Charlie. They had been very close when they were young. Don had been a traveling salesman who had settled in Virginia and married his boss' genteel daughter. When his father-in-law died, Don and his wife inherited not only a very successful business, but a beautiful home and many valuable possessions.

Molly thought Charlie must have thought that she wasn't home yet, or that her windows were closed and she couldn't hear them. She felt very uneasy listening, but what could she do? Wouldn't they feel more embarrassed knowing that she had heard them? She tried in her mind to think of something else and block out their voices, but she was unsuccessful.

Don was explaining to Charlie. "Of course it's only natural that under the circumstances, Veronica has always had extravagant taste in clothes and jewelry and we have always allowed her to charge expensive purchases to us. At first, we couldn't bring ourselves to tell her just how bad things really were. We tried to shield her from the truth, so as not to worry her, but finally we had to warn her not to make any more unnecessary purchases, because even quietly selling some of Edith's family possessions, we would just about be able to afford to have her finish at the exclusive school she had become accustomed to."

Molly thought that Don was talking quite loudly. In fact, she actually wondered if he had a hearing problem, or if it was just that he was anxious to tell his story to Charlie, hoping that he would understand and sympathize with the situation.

Don was saying, "And I wouldn't tell this to anyone but you, Charlie, but things haven't been going good at all for our poor little Veronica. It seems that there were a few things misplaced by a few students and finally there was an expensive gold bracelet missing. Someone said that they saw Veronica leave the room just before it was missing. Veronica said she was just in the room looking for her fellow classmate, but they took the other girl's part on that flimsy evidence, the poor kid was unfairly accused. Then to make it worse, her fellow students turned against her. Veronica said that the girls were just plain jealous and wanted to get rid of her because she was so popular with the boys. That convinced us that it would be a good idea to take her out of there and just get away for a while. I've already borrowed more money than I should have against our home and business. In fact, when we get back, we may even be forced to close down the business and sell Edith's old homestead."

Charlie, with concern in his voice, replied, "I'm sorry to hear that, Don. If we can help in any way, let us know."

Molly wondered. Was that gold bracelet just a coincidence? Especially since Veronica didn't wear it until they had already left the house. She thought to herself, that's not very nice, thinking badly of someone on circumstantial evidence. But when they arrived home much later, and Veronica took the bracelet off before going into the house, Molly's suspicions peaked again.

As Mary and Molly walked along with Veronica on their way to meet Mr. Packard, they explained to her how they had met him, and had continued to go out riding with him on Sunday afternoons. They told her about him not having a family and how they had assumed that he was probably lonesome.

Right away, Veronica started asking them questions, many of which were personal. They answered as much as they could, figuring that she was just being curious. They were flabbergasted when she suggested that they could get more out of him than ice cream and soda pop.

Mary and Molly looked at each other in disbelief, and almost in unison said to Veronica, "Why would we want to do that?"

"You could tell him a hard luck story," Veronica suggested.

Mary, with a look of disbelief upon her face, said, "Why, that would be deceitful."

Veronica replied, "Well, what's the difference, as long as you get what you want? The way I look at it, if he has no family, he has extra money. He has to spend it on something or somebody. It might as well be us. It's just obvious that you're missing out on a perfect opportunity by just being too honest. You should at least get some nice perfume or jewelry."

Mary couldn't wait to disagree with her. "Well, I don't agree with you at all. Aunt Mary used to say, 'You tell a little lie today, and tomorrow you'll tell a bigger one to cover it up. Then you won't know who you said what to. First thing you know, nobody will believe you even when you're telling the truth." Mary was hoping Veronica would take the hint because she meant it for her.

Mr. Packard was waiting at the usual place. Molly introduced her cousin to him as Mary slid into the back seat behind him, leaving plenty of room for Molly and Veronica. Molly followed Mary into the automobile and sat next to her. Veronica batted her eyes at Mr. Packard, gave him her fake smile and proceeded to lift her skirt quite high, showing off her legs, as she jumped into the automobile next to him.

To say that Mary and Molly were surprised would be an understatement. Their mouths fell open and they looked at each other in complete disbelief. They were hardly in the automobile when Veronica, complaining about the heat and turning toward Mr. Packard, proceeded to open the top buttons of her blouse, revealing far more skin than any decent young lady would. Mary and Molly were in shock. To say that Veronica had a lot of nerve was putting it mildly.

Mary hoped that they wouldn't be seen by any of their friends or acquaintances who might get the wrong idea about them. After all, Veronica would be leaving in a few days, but they had to live there. Sitting in the back seat of Mr. Packard's car had never before caused them concern, because they figured if anyone saw them, they would just assume he was a relative or family friend.

As usual, they went for a ride and sang on the way. When they stopped for ice cream, while Mary and Molly got out of the automobile to get it, Veronica insisted on keeping Mr. Packard company.

When Mr. Packard dropped them off, he waited until they walked about thirty feet away from his car, and then he called Mary back. "Mary could you come here a minute please?" Mary was surprised, but returned to the automobile.

Mr. Packard said, "Mary, I want to warn you and Molly to watch out for that one. She's not your type of person. She's been around. She could buy and sell you two. In fact I think she would if she got the opportunity. And I'm not kidding."

Mary innocently asked, "What do you mean, 'been around'?"

He replied, "Never mind, you just be extra careful."

Mary was surprised to hear Mr. Packard say such things about Veronica. She told him. "She's supposed to leave Thursday and I'll be glad when she does. But I don't think we have anything to worry about while she's here. We'll see you next Sunday," she shouted, waving good-bye. As she walked away, unfamiliar thoughts came into her mind. She pondered for a moment. "He couldn't mean – No, of course not," she thought. "Yes, Veronica is spoiled, selfish and self-centered, but nothing to be concerned about. Mr. Packard must have just misunderstood something that she said or did."

Over and over again, Mary and Molly couldn't believe just how horrible Veronica really was. They were in the habit of taking long walks in the evenings, so Veronica started walking with them. They found her to be very prejudiced, laughing at other people and their problems. She'd lie and take credit for things she didn't do. Her insincerity really annoyed Mary.

Veronica would sleep very late in the morning. No one would dare bother her. She was always primping in front of the mirror and had no respect whatsoever for other people or their time. She was so inconsiderate that she always kept them waiting. Mary complained to Molly, "I could have kept reading my book instead of wasting time waiting for Her Highness. If we ever kept her waiting like this, we'd never hear the end of it." Mary was impatiently exclaiming to Molly. "I'd like to give her a swift kick and tell her to grow up."

Veronica was always bragging about her trips and her clothes and her jewelry. She tried in every way to make other people feel inferior. Mary kept on her toes and said in answer to her, just as much as she felt that she could to bring her down a peg or two, without making things any harder for Molly.

Veronica was also in the habit of downgrading everything. It was for at least the third time that she was commenting on how glad she was that she didn't have to live in Troy. "I don't know how you can stand it here, etc. etc." The first couple of times, Mary tried to consider the source and ignore her by making believe that she didn't even hear her, but now it was beginning to get to her. Mary answered, "Aunt Mary said it shouldn't matter where you live, as long as you have food, clothing and shelter, and people who love you."

Mary believed that by quoting her Aunt Mary's philosophy, perhaps Veronica would learn something, and take the hint. Perhaps then she would be nicer to other people, especially her parents. But Veronica only half-listened to people anyway, and she was so selfish that the words just went right over her head. She had no idea what Mary was talking about.

Mary felt as if she were wasting her breath. But she wasn't at all prepared for Veronica's answer to her. "Your Aunt Mary said this, and your Aunt Mary said that. Don't you ever get tired of quoting what a dead person said?"

Well, that did it. In a flash, Mary's anger flared up to its highest peak. All the aggravation she had felt toward Veronica came pouring out. "No, you don't want to hear about my Aunt Mary, because my Aunt Mary was one of the kindest, most thoughtful, considerate and unselfish people who ever lived. While you are the rudest, most self-centered, lazy, egotistical, insensitive, deceitful so-called human being that I have ever met in my whole life. You complain about everything and appreciate nothing. You're far too selfish to understand what I'm even talking about. All you care about is yourself and what you can get out of other people. We had hoped that you would have changed, but you're even a worse brat than you were four years ago. I feel sorry for your parents. They don't deserve a little sneaky snot like you. They should give you the swift kick that you deserve. And you're a pig, too. Gobbling up Molly's pie!"

Mary finally stopped to catch her breath. She looked over at Molly, who rolled her eyes. "I'm sorry, Molly. I really tried. But enough is enough. When I hear the likes of this one belittling what my Aunt Mary said, that did it. Give me a call when her highness leaves." Mary walked away.

Veronica was surprised by Mary's outburst. "Well, my goodness Molly, your friend certainly is high strung."

Molly thought of answering Veronica and even defending Mary. But she thought. What good would it do? Besides, she had promised her mother. Instead she prayed, "Please Lord, give me the patience I need for the next few days."

CHAPTER FORTY-FOUR

As Jack's wife Julie sat waiting for her only brother Matt to arrive, she started thinking of her mother and father and the disappointing circumstances that had prompted this visit to Troy. When Matt called, he said he wanted to see Julie and meet Jack. But Julie knew Matt too well for him to be able to cover up the obvious main reason he was coming. There was no doubt in Julie's mind that Matt was trying to reconcile her with her father. Knowing this, Julie was going over in her mind what she thought Matt would say, and how she would answer him.

Thinking of her father these days made Julie feel very sad. She had always had a very good relationship with her father and knew that he loved her very much. She remembered when she was a little girl, asking her father why he called her Jewel instead of Julie, like everybody else. "Because you're my beautiful little jewel, more precious to me than diamonds or pearls," he exclaimed.

"What about gold or silver?" She questioned.

"Next to you, they're worthless," he answered smilingly.

Yes, Julie's relationship with her father had been so perfect – until that day – three months ago, when she felt her world tumble in around her. Julie would never forget that day.

Being the only girl, Julie was very close to her mother. It was not unusual for them to go shopping together not only in Boston, New

York City and Philadelphia, but Paris, London and Rome as well. They were a lot alike and really valued each other's opinions. Julie's parents were very generous to her and she was able to purchase just about anything she wanted.

That particular day, while Julie's mother was trying on hats, Julie was looking at gloves. She had bent down behind a counter and was not able to be seen by the two sales-ladies conversing a short way from her. As she proceeded to look for a certain style and color of gloves to match her new coat, she could not help but overhear what they were saying. "That's the woman right there, trying on hats," the one whispered to the other. "She's the one whose husband is seeing Vivian. In fact, from what I hear, he's always been known as a womanizer. I think Vivian is foolish to get mixed up with him, and I told her so. But she's too tempted by the beautiful gifts he's given her, and the special out-of-town places he's taken her to. In fact, he's taking her to the Hide-A-Way tonight." All of a sudden something clicked in Julie's mind. She looked over toward the millinery department only to realize that they were talking about her mother. She was stunned. She could feel her face reddening as conflicting thoughts rushed through her mind.

Julie's first thought was to go over there and tell them they were wrong. That they had mistaken her mother for someone else, and that she would make sure their gossiping tongues cost them their jobs. That was it, she thought, they had mistaken her mother for someone else. But they were still talking when she heard the name Mrs. Van Patten mentioned as she saw her mother approach them. Julie thought it just couldn't be true. Then, trying to convince herself, she reiterated it again, "Of course it couldn't be true," she analyzed. Her father was very handsome, friendly and outgoing. This Vivian very likely misunderstood something he had said. Or, she angrily thought, maybe this Vivian was the type of person who brags about things that are not true, just to get attention. Of course it's not true. She would prove it for herself that evening.

Her mother had just finished charging her purchase and was beckoning to Julie. But Julie didn't want to go anywhere near those two sales-ladies, so she called over to her mother that she'd meet her in the next department.

That evening, Julie sneaked out of the house, got into her automobile and drove to the Hide-A-Way. She was so thankful that she had her own automobile, and that she had insisted on learning to drive. She was much too independent to have to wait around for others to take her places at their convenience.

As Julie drove along, she kept telling herself how foolish she was being to pay any attention to idle gossip. She knew she would not find her father there with another woman. She kept thinking, later I'll be sorry I wasted my time.

Julie could have called one of her friends to go with her, but she didn't want to explain it all to anyone. And if there was the slightest chance that it were true, she would have felt even more humiliated in front of a friend. Besides, if it did turn out to be true, she wasn't sure yet just what she was going to do about it. She got there early and encircled the parking lot, but did not see her father's automobile. She pulled over to park the automobile where she would have a good view of approaching automobiles, without at the same time, be able to be seen.

After about a dozen automobiles went by, Julie spotted what she thought was her father's deluxe Studebaker. Then she recognized her father's chauffeur. What should she do? She thought as the automobile came to a stop. The chauffeur walked around to open the door. Her father and a woman got out. Julie rushed over and called. "Vivian!" An attractive woman, not much older than her, turned around and answered questioningly, "Yes?"

Julie's father was shocked to see her. He was obviously flustered and started to explain, but Julie was not listening. She had turned to run to her automobile, with her father running after her. She wanted to get into her automobile, lock the doors, and get out of there as fast as she could. Julie's father got to the driver's seat first. Julie was shaking. Her head was pounding. She felt so angry and so disappointed in him.

Julie's father was explaining that Vivian was a new secretary and they had worked late. Julie looked right at him and shook her head as she angrily shouted, "Stop lying to me. I know all about Vivian." He put his head in his hand as he said, "I'm sorry, Jewel, so very, very sorry. Please forgive me." He tried to comfort her but she pushed him away.

Julie replied, "Sorry? Well, those empty words don't mean anything to me." As she looked at him with contempt.

"Please don't look at me that way, Jewel. I'm really sorry," he pleaded. Julie justifiably answered, "You should have thought of that sooner. How can I have any respect for you? I hate cheaters and hypocrites. It's completely against everything I believe in."

Julie's father pleadingly suggested, "I'll drive you home, Jewel, and we'll talk about this in the morning."

Julie disgustedly replied, "I'd sooner drive myself home, and you can go back to your little playmate. And you're wrong, we won't talk about this in the morning. I never want to see you again. In the morning, I'm telling my mother – remember your loyal, faithful, true-blue wife? But no, you seem to have forgotten all about her."

Julie's father pleaded, "Oh, no, Jewel, don't tell your mother. You'll only hurt her. Believe me, Jewel, I love your mother. I promise this will never happen again."

Julie shouted angrily, "Promises? How could I possibly believe a liar? It seems to me you made my mother a promise years ago to love, honor and cherish her and forsake all others. Why should I possibly believe you would keep any promise?" Her words stung, he winced, making his handsome face momentarily distorted.

Julie replied, "Besides, my mother has a right to know, and to decide for herself what she wants to do. And let's put the blame where it belongs. You're the one that's hurt her, not me."

Julie spent a sleepless night, thinking, thinking, thinking, realizing that things would never be the same. Several times her father knocked softly and called out her name, but she didn't answer or open the locked door.

In the morning, Julie's father left late for the office, after knocking at her door several more times. He had slipped a letter under her door, begging her to wait until he came home, before she did anything rash. He explained again how much he loved her and her mother. And tried to offer convincing words. But before she read the letter, Julie had made up her mind, and there wasn't anything new in the letter to change it. No matter how many times she had gone over things in her mind, the only thought that dominated over all the others was that she believed her mother had the right to know. Julie knew that she would want to know if this happened to her, and she believed her mother would, too.

Julie waited until after breakfast, and then told her mother as gently as possible. Her mother listened intently as Julie proceeded to tell her everything she had learned. Tears came into her mother's blue-gray eyes as she asked what the woman looked like, and Julie related how young she was. Julie, trying to comfort her mother as best she could, asked, "Mother, did I do the right thing in telling you?"

Julie's mother convincingly reassured her. "Yes, Julie, you did the right thing. We've talked about this before in the women's rights movement. As you know, there have been, what I would call, many other casualties. Somehow, you just don't think it could possibly happen to you. I don't want to be here when he comes back. I just don't ever want to see him again. I'm going to pack right away and leave."

Julie questioned, "Where are you going? I'll go with you."

Julie and her mother went to Troy to visit her mother's sister. Of course, her father had tried to get in touch with them. He called, but they refused to talk to him. He sent letters and they refused to read them. They were returned unopened to the sender.

Julie's mother in the meantime contacted a couple of friends. Finding out that Julie's father would be out of town on business for a few days, Julie and her mother returned to the house for one last trip, to take what they considered of value to them.

The maid came in to tell Julie her brother had arrived. Julie ran excitedly out to meet him. He was, after all, her only brother, and what their father had done wasn't his fault. Knowing Matt, Julie was sure he, too, would have been saddened by what had happened.

Julie enthusiastically called out to the young man standing before her. "Matt! I'm so glad to see you. I missed you so much."

"Julie! I really missed you, too!" He optimistically answered, as they rushed into each other's embrace. After the usual, How have you been? What's new? How is Grace? How is Jack? And Julie's questions about a few of their friends, a few observations, and then, Matt studied Julie's face intently for a moment. He looked deep into her beautiful emerald green eyes, and said.

"I was so glad to see that mother looked good when I saw her recently."

Julie answered, "Yes! I'm proud of her adjusting so well."

Matt replied, "But Julie, I must tell you Dad isn't doing so well."

"Matt, I don't want to talk about him," Julie defensively answered.

Matt pleadingly replied, "Oh, Julie! I know you don't want to talk about him, but I feel as if I have to. So please, Julie, please listen, not for his sake, but for mine. Being a go-between is an awful position to be in, and I'd like to just say what I have to, and get it over with. It isn't easy."

"First, I'd like to ask you," Matt began, "Julie, is what I've heard right? Is our mother keeping company with Bob Hilliard?"

Julie answered calmly. "I don't consider a few dinner-theater dates, keeping company. You know very well, Matt, that Elizabeth Hilliard was one of mother's dearest friends. Mr. Hilliard always marched with them for Women's Rights and continues to do so in memory of his wife and for the future of his daughters. So since Mrs. Hilliard's death last year, Mr. Hilliard has been kind of lonely. I think it's wonderful that he and mother are helping each other through painful times in both their lives. Mr. Hilliard's a wonderful, kind, considerate man. I for one hope something does develop. Why should our mother have to pay the price for your father's indiscretions? Making it look as if there is something wrong with her. Even supplying the ammunition for those wagging tongues. Don't ask me to waste my pity on a man who cheated on his wife."

Matt defensively answered, "Julie, men are different. They're more, well, more passionate."

Julie impatiently replied, "How do you know? Have you interviewed every man and woman who ever lived? As far as I'm concerned, that observation was undoubtedly made by a man to cover up his own indiscretions. Some men are different. There are many more honorable men who would never think of cheating on their wives. They practice self-control. And there are women who cheat on their husbands, too, but no alibies are going to make it right. Above everything else, I believe in equal rights in every way, especially marriage. Of course people are attracted to other people. But, under no circumstances do I believe that cheating in any form is acceptable. As far as I'm concerned, people who cheat are just plain selfish. They don't care who gets hurt as long as they get what they want.

"Our mother is a beautiful woman. Did it ever occur to you that she might have been attracted to other men? But the main difference between him and her is that she has integrity. I wonder how open-minded you'd be if you came home some afternoon and found your best friend Larry in bed with your wife, Grace. Can you even imagine that scene? Think about it for a minute and tell me how you'd feel then. Maybe you'd understand what it's like to be betrayed by the person closest to you. Oh! But that would be different." She said sarcastically. "Why, you'd be the first one to throw her out of the house. But of course you see his point because you're a man, born into a man's world of double standards, with rules made by men, for men. Well, what I see is another woman, this time who happens to be my mother, victimized by that male chauvinistic attitude. I think it's even worse than the average case, because she's always been a Women's Rights advocate and he knew how strongly she felt not only about immorality, but deceitful, hypocritical behavior. I can't help wondering if the shoe was on the other foot, if you'd be pleading her case as strongly as you're pleading his. In fact, if anything, he's lucky she doesn't get even with him and take him for all he's worth. As it is, she doesn't want the house or anything else from him. I don't know if you're aware, Matt, but she left all the jewelry he ever gave her, including her engagement ring. She threw her wedding ring in the empty waste basket and put it on the vanity chair in their room to make sure he'd see it. She doesn't want to ever hear his name again or ever see anything to remind her of him. In fact, she gave me all the pictures and albums and wants me to divide them and just give her pictures of her with us and take what I want, and give you the rest for you and him, making you promise that you won't give him her picture."

Matt ignored the animosity in Julie's voice as he pleaded. "Julie, he's your father and he wants to see you. Don't you have any respect for him at all?"

Julie answered defensively. "Respect? What respect did he have for my mother? It seems to me, Matt, that you're so busy feeling sorry for him that you ignore the fact that it's our mother who is the victim, not him. He was in control and he made the choices and gambled and lost and now this is the result of those choices. Let this be a lesson to you, too! And I'll tell you right now, Matt, I'm making you this promise. If I ever hear of you cheating on Grace, I'll definitely tell her. And I hope you'll have the decency to tell me if you ever hear that Jack is cheating on me."

Matt impatiently replied, "Oh, Julie, why must you be so bitter and judgmental? I wish you could have seen the tears in his eyes as he explained to me that his whole world has always revolved around mother, you and me, and that the house is so empty and lonely without you and mother. He's having a hard time sleeping. He feels as if he's lost everything that ever meant anything to him."

Julie unsympathetically answered, "Well, he should have thought about that sooner. The tears I saw were in Mother's eyes. Could you possibly imagine what it's like for her, to have to move out of the home she's known for over twenty-five years and start making a new beginning for herself?"

Matt replied, "But Julie, he's really sorry. If you could only see how sad he looks, and how tired and discouraged. He said he never meant to hurt Mother or us."

Julie answered, "But Matt, we did get hurt, didn't we? And no amount of remorse is going to change that. Maybe he's just sorry that he got caught."

Matt replied, "What about all the good things he's done for us, Julie? Doesn't that count? As far back as I can remember, he's always been there for both of us and did hundreds of things right. Julie, as long as I live, I'll never forget how embarrassed I was, when he brought you to the baseball outing with us, just because you wanted to go. You didn't think it was fair for him to take me and not you, just because you were a girl. You kept saying, 'Why? Why?' And you would not accept any explanation. So he brought you. I'm the one who had to listen to the complaints of my fellow teammates. You always got your own way with him. Why, you could always wrap him around your little finger. I could go on and on. But, Julie, you know as well as I do that he's always been a good father. Okay, he's made a mistake and he's admitted it and tried to make up for it. Everybody makes mistakes. Haven't you ever made a mistake, Julie?"

Julie said, "Yes, Matt, I admit he always has been a good father. He was helpful and kind and always encouraged me. Those memories I will always be grateful to him for. When I was a little girl, I thought my father was the most handsome, wonderful, kind and honorable person I knew. I must confess, I loved him even more than I loved mother. He was the very center of my world. Maybe it wasn't fair of me to put him on such a high pedestal, but that's because that was the image he portrayed to me. Now it breaks my heart to find out the truth after all these years, that he is just like the other men with double standards and the hypocrisy that I most despise. It is very hard to accept. And now all of these current realistic thoughts push all of those good thoughts to the back of my mind."

Matt pleaded, "Dad really wants to see you badly, Julie. It's hard enough that mother won't speak to him. He feels even worse that you won't even let him explain."

Julie impatiently replied, "Explain what? What is there to explain? That he cheated on my mother and then lied to me about it?"

Matt said, "Julie, he knows it was wrong, but he mentioned that he was just so deeply attracted to this girl. He's promised me that it will never happen again."

Julie answered, "Oh, Matt! Mother has found out from reliable sources that over the years there were others. She was always honest with him. He should have been honest with her. He owed her that much. He enjoyed introducing her as his wife because she's beautiful and talented and never caused him a hint of scandal. But that wasn't enough for him. He wanted the best of both worlds."

Matt looked surprised to hear that there were others, but raced on in his father's defense.

Matt suggested, "But, Julie, just talk to him."

Julie replied, "I can't, Matt. I feel too angry and disappointed in him to talk to him."

Matt pleaded, "But, Julie, he's having such a hard time adjusting."

Julie retorted, "Matt, we're all having a hard time adjusting. The only difference is, he deserves it."

Matt looked sadly at her as he said, "Oh, Julie, I don't know how I can tell him that you refuse to see him."

Julie just as sadly replied, "Think of it this way, Matt. I'm no actress. It would be worse for him right now to see the disgusted look on my face. No matter how hard I tried, I know I just couldn't hide it."

Matt questioned, "What can I tell him?"

Julie answered, "Tell him whatever you like. Tell him I'm having a hard time adjusting to all that's happened. Maybe time will help. But Matt, I don't want to talk about him anymore. I've got a headache."

Matt looked at his timepiece. "I'll come back later, Julie. I have some others things to take care of."

When Matt left, Julie started thinking of his and Grace's wedding last year. Grace looked so beautiful, escorted down the aisle by her father. And Matt never looked more handsome and happy. Everybody told Julie how pretty she looked as a bridesmaid, and that it wouldn't be long before she, too, would be walking down that same aisle getting married.

Julie had always wanted a big wedding with lots of bridesmaids.

She dreamed many times of walking down the aisle on the arm of her father, to meet the man of her dreams. But her father had ruined that dream for her. She could not very well walk down the aisle on his arm, with people talking about how he had cheated on her mother. She wouldn't put her mother through that. Feeling such anger towards him, and such disappointment because of him, she especially didn't even want him at her wedding. Eloping seemed like the only way of settling the conflict.

 Julie felt annoyed at Matt for minimizing the damage that had been done by their father to their mother. She wondered, was it because she, being a woman, saw their mother's point of view more clearly and Matt, being a man, saw their father's position more clearly? Or was it because she had seen first-hand just what her mother was going through, and the tears she'd and the reddened eyes, while these scenes were hidden from Matt? Or was it that she had heard so many true stories of wife and child abuse and neglect by dominating, egotistical, thoughtless husbands, that she hated this male chauvinistic mentality and vowed long ago to do all she could to change it? She believed that educated women of influence had a duty to make things better for women and children and guarantee women the right to vote. How could Matt possibly understand that, to Julie, her father had not only failed to live up to her expectations, but had seriously damaged her trust in all men? If her father was like that, then who could she trust? She really missed the relationship they used to have, and felt very sad for what might have been.

CHAPTER FORTY-FIVE

Unbeknownst to Julie, Matt had not come to Troy alone. Realizing how angry Julie still felt about her Father, he didn't dare tell her that their father was at a local restaurant, waiting for Matt to return, hoping either Julie would be with him, or that he would bring with him an invitation to Julie's home for a reconciliation.

After Matt convinced his father that to force himself on Julie at this time could cause irreversible damage to their relationship, he decided to try once more to see his estranged wife at her sister's home.

Estelle Ferguson was alone in her sitting room when the butler came to announce that Richard van Patten was at the door, and wished to speak with her. She sighed deeply, thought for a few moments, and then said, rather reluctantly, "Show him in."

Estelle did not want to be in this position, and about the very last person she wanted to see right then was Richard. Considering the circumstances, she had complete sympathy for her sister, and felt Richard's behavior was very unacceptable. Knowing Richard for well over twenty-five years, Estelle still found all that had happened very hard to believe. If it hadn't been for Julie's eye witness account, she still wouldn't have believed it. He had always appeared to be so devoted to her sister.

"Estelle, thank you so much for seeing me. I really appreciate it,"

Richard said.

As Estelle put out her hand to Richard, the first thing she noticed was the deep circles under his darkened eyes and all the weight he had lost. It shocked her to realize that in less than one year since she had seen him last, at his and Marion's twenty-fifth anniversary party, that he looked as if he had aged ten years. This realization made her feel sorry for him, and no doubt, more open to his suggestion that followed.

Richard had but one goal in mind, and that was to convince Estelle that she would be helping not only him, but Marion too, by persuading her to see him. He gave Estelle his solemn promise that if Marion would see him just this once, he would never bother her again or try to see her or write to her, unless Marion wanted him to.

After much persuasion from Estelle, Marion agreed that even though he didn't deserve it, she would see him this one last time. Just to be rid of him, once and for all, and to not find his letters mixed in with her mail, would be worth this trying inconvenience she felt.

Marion entered the room as Estelle left, closing the door behind her. Richard started toward her, but she yelled, "Stop!" putting her hand up in front of her. "If you come any closer, I'll turn around and leave."

Richard sadly answered, "I'm sorry, Marion. It's just that I've missed you so much." As he moved back toward the fire place.

Marion, too, noticed the deep circles under Richard's eyes and the weight he had lost. But her reaction to it wasn't the same as her sister's. What it reminded her of was her own reflection in the mirror, day after day, night after sleepless night, finding it so hard to adjust to this extra burden he had placed upon her. Marion was not by nature a vindictive person, and felt overwhelming pity for people who were the victims of other people's selfish choices, but she had no pity whatsoever for the people who had caused that pain.

As Marion and Richard sat in front of the fireplace on twin settees, facing each other, she waited for a moment for him to speak. She felt his eyes upon her, but no words came forth.

Marion began speaking, "Richard, I must tell you that I really didn't want to see you. I've only agreed so that you can get all of this out of your system once and for all, and stop calling and writing. It's time that you, too, got on with your life."

"Oh, Marion, don't say that. Don't tell me that there's no hope at all of our reconciling. After all the years we've been together and all the things we've meant to each other. I've been so lonesome for you. Please don't tell me that you don't feel anything at all for me," with a pleading in his voice.

"Richard, you wouldn't want to know how I feel," she said. "You've never really cared how I felt."

"I'm sorry, Marion. I know I've taken you for granted and I've made mistakes. I'm truly very sorry. But I really have always loved you and always will. And I do care about your feelings. You must believe me."

Marion calmly replied, "Believe you? No, Richard, I don't believe you. Oh, I don't doubt that sitting here right now, you believe that. But as I look back, I realize everything I ever told you I believed in was falling on deaf ears. Before we were married, I went out of my way to be honest with you. I poured my heart out, telling you why I believed so strongly in women's rights and why I would spend my married life still involved in this cause. I gave you actual cases of the injustices that women and children were forced to endure because of obsolete laws which unjustly favored tyrannical men, but apparently you were only humoring me. Your mind must have been miles away. Since I left you, Richard, a number of my friends have rallied round, not only to tell me how sorry they are, but to let me know that they weren't surprised. They pointed out that over the years, especially when I was out of town, they or someone they knew well had seen you out laughing and dancing with pretty women, looking happy and carefree. They said they had their suspicions, but no concrete evidence, and didn't want to cause me any trouble. You would probably say they were secretaries or business associates or clients, but you see Richard, it not only hurts your credibility and caused unnecessary gossip, but it puts you in an unfavorable light. Am I supposed to think a few innocent laughs and dances and drinks and then in every situation you went home to bed alone? I think if it was so innocent, you would have mentioned it to me. Or was it 'out of sight, out of mind' and 'what she doesn't know won't hurt her?'"

Richard pleadingly replied, "Marion, I swear to you that she was the only one, and I haven't seen her since that night. I can't tell you how deeply sorry I am. You're my whole life. I don't want to lose you. I admit in the face of temptation, I was weak, but I never meant for you to be hurt. It had nothing to do with you. You were always the best. I've always loved you."

Marion calmly answered, "Oh, Richard, you think just by saying you're sorry, it erases everything, as if it never happened. But that's not the way it is. It did happen. And it does hurt more deeply than you'll ever know. Naturally, under the circumstances, you'd say she was the only one. Oh, I suppose I could hire a detective, but what good would it do? As far as I'm concerned, she was one too many. Maybe it's just as well not to find out for sure how many others there were over the years, because it would only add to the sadness and the heartache and embarrassment that I've already had to endure. It wouldn't help me in any way to know for sure that you had such little respect for my feelings that you made such a mockery out of our wedding vows. The way I feel is that the first time you reached out for another woman, you lost the right to ever touch me again. When I look at you now, Richard, I no longer see that special, wonderful man I loved and promised to spend my life with. The man

I loved for over twenty-five years, I believed to be honest, fair, gentle, kind and loving. Just the touch of your hands aroused in me a passion I did not know I possessed. But now I couldn't stand for you to touch me without being reminded that those same hands greedily fondled and caressed other women, while at the same time with your eyes and lips you were deceiving me. I just couldn't love a man who could smile in my face while sneaking around behind my back with another woman."

Marion felt at peace as she explained her feelings to Richard, "I know for sure, Richard, that this latest escapade had been going on for a couple of years. What hurts me the very most is to realize that even after we celebrated our 25th wedding anniversary, that you went back to her. There just aren't any words that could possibly describe just how sad that made me feel. You just don't put someone you love through such mental anguish. From outside appearances, you were thoughtful, attentive and generous with your gift-giving. But what you didn't give me was the greatest gift any man could give his wife – faithfulness! I wanted a man I could trust and look up to. I would have stood beside you through any storm, facing any obstacle, mental, physical or financial. Even if we had lost everything, or if you were forced to spend the rest of your life in a wheelchair, I would have been by your side, helping you. But lying and cheating are two things I just couldn't and wouldn't live with. When I married you, Richard, I was hoping and praying for the kind of marriage that I saw my parents had. A marriage of complete love and trust, that went beyond the sexual dimension to a mental and spiritual level that few attain. But such a marriage demands that the love the two people have for each other is greater than their love of self, making their eyes turn toward each other in a loving, caring, sharing way so that each is always trying to please the other until finally their very souls touch and just by a glance, one knows what the other is thinking. But one person alone can never attain that, and some people wouldn't even know what I was talking about."

As Marion explained with a calmness brought about only by her complete determination to put these heartaches into the past and make a new life for herself, Richard was looking down, unable to look at her through his tear-filled eyes. He hadn't understood, and now he felt overwhelmed with the realization that he had lost everything in life that he held dear, for something that in the long run, was not very important to him.

Marion continued speaking, "What I feel toward you now is anger, resentment and disappointment in the only person I ever allowed to be intimate with me. The person I should have been able to count on for loyalty. I think I deserved better. But you know, Richard, I never could justify feeling sorry for myself for very long, and I'm glad to say that I've already started a new life without you. I've really been trying hard to forgive you. I don't wish you any bad luck, but I know I can never forget. I feel even sorrier than ever for the women who are forced by circumstances to have to put up with such unjust behavior, and I thank God that I don't need you financially."

Marion glanced at her timepiece. "And now I must go. I've made other plans for this day. Of course, I expect you to keep your promise and not call or write again." And she was gone, taking with her all the plans he had hoped for their future, leaving behind a shattered man, holding his head and sobbing softly, huge tears rolling down his face.

CHAPTER FORTY-SIX

The summer had flown by. It was already the first day of September. Mary was getting ready for the dance at St. Mary's. She was still having a hard time completely forgetting Jack and facing the reality that all those special day dreams she'd had for so long, were never going to come true. She tried hard to keep busy and not let it get her down.

At the dance, Molly met a young man named Herman, who seemed nice. She felt sorry for him because he wasn't very good looking and she had noticed a couple of girls had refused to dance with him. That only made Molly feel even sorrier for him. So when he asked to walk her home, she accepted, mentioning to him about walking Mary home first. To which he said, "Better yet, I have a friend that I can bring along for your friend if it's okay." Molly said she'd check with Mary and let him know during the following dance.

Mary hadn't met anyone she was interested in, so she agreed. What's the difference, she thought, it's only a walk home.

Mary was very surprised that when they all met at the dance hall door, Herman's friend was quite nice-looking with blond hair and blue eyes. His name was Jim.

The four of them walked a few blocks together and then Molly and Herman walked toward Molly's house, while Mary and Jim continued on to her house.

The thought went through Mary's mind that she hoped this wasn't the night that her father would choose to have a repeat performance of the night that Jack had walked her home. Her father was nowhere in sight, so she sat on the porch with Jim for a few minutes. He seemed very nice. She found out that his father had died and that he lived with his mother and two younger sisters.

Mary could tell that he kept staring at her, but she really didn't mind. In fact, she felt flattered. Every once in a while, she'd look up at him and smile. She felt very much at ease with him, so when he asked her to go out with him the following Friday evening, she quickly agreed. She reasoned that keeping busy would keep her from thinking of Jack.

As Mary and Molly walked to the ten o'clock Mass at St. Mary's the next morning, they talked about the night before.

Molly usually let Mary talk first. All Mary had to say was that Jim seemed very nice and she made a date to go out with him the following Friday evening.

Mary couldn't believe her ears as Molly recounted how forward Jim's friend had been. He had practically pushed her into the dark hallway. At first he tried to coax her to kiss him goodnight and balked at her refusal. Her concern that people were sleeping and her quiet pleading with him to be a gentleman fell on deaf ears. Only her threat to scream brought him to his senses, as he swore under his breath, turned and ran out the door and up the street.

"And here I had felt sorry for him. That's the only reason I let him walk me home in the first place." Molly tried to warn Mary to be careful of Jim. "You know what they say, 'Birds of a feather flock together.'" Mary reassured her that Jim was a perfect gentleman and, on the contrary, seemed quite shy.

Molly offered her opinion. "Well maybe he's just appearing to be that way, and then when you're relaxed, he'll pounce on you."

Mary responded confidently. "Well, thanks anyway for the warning. I will be on guard. But I really do think Jim's a gentleman."

CHAPTER FORTY-SEVEN

That Wednesday, September 5th there was a picture in the paper showing American soldiers in formation, marching behind a large American flag. Underneath the picture were the words: "Our Soldier Boys March Through London. Piccadilly Throngs Expressed Joy Over American Reinforcements With Cheers And Waving Of Small American Flags."

Friday night came and Jim picked up Mary and they went to Proctor's Theater to see what was advertised as "The Great Vaudeville Acts," and as an added attraction, William Desmond in "The Master Of His Home." Afterward, he invited her to go to Manory's for a dish of ice cream. As they sat there, she still noticed out of the corner of her eye that he was still staring at her, and every once in a while Molly's words came into her mind.

At first Mary was on guard to make sure that Jim couldn't take advantage of her. But as she started going out with him twice a week, she began to realize just how shy he really was. He didn't even attempt to kiss her until the fifth date. Best of all, while she was with Jim, she rarely ever thought of Jack.

One night when Mary and Jim were at Manory's, Officer O'Reilly came over to their table. Mary was very surprised when Jim called him Uncle Tom, because they had different last names. Jim would explain later that Officer O'Reilly was his mother's brother and that he had helped them so much, especially since Jim's father had died.

Later, as they were walking home, Jim mentioned that he always wanted to be a policeman from the time he was a very young boy, and that his uncle had recently put his name on the list. After becoming aware that Jim's uncle was Officer O'Reilly, Mary completely believed that Molly's suspicions about Jim were unfounded. One night as they were sitting on her porch, Mary's curious mind finally caused her to ask Jim about his friend. She waited until she had gone out with him a number of times and tried to word her questions so as not to embarrass Molly.

Jim was surprised to hear how Herman had treated Molly, and he and Mary laughed together as Mary explained to him how she had been on guard so as to avoid a similar fate. Jim explained that he also had just met Herman that night. Herman was a cousin of one of his friends. He would further explain that it was his friend who asked him to go with Herman, because he had already asked another girl to walk her home.

Mary mentioned, "And while we're talking about that night, I would like to know why you kept staring at me?"

Jim answered, "Because I just couldn't believe how beautiful you are."

"What?" She surprisingly questioned.

Jim took her hand and looked into her blue, blue eyes, and explained. "When my friend asked me to walk home with the girlfriend of the girl his cousin was walking home, frankly, Mary, I was just expecting to see a girl that wasn't very good-looking. When I saw how pretty you were, I just couldn't believe it. I still can't believe that a beautiful girl like you is still going out with an ordinary guy like me."

As Mary looked at Jim, she realized that he was not only kind, warm, and sincere, traits that had already drawn her closer to him, but also that he was humble. Through Mary's eyes, Jim was much nicer looking than he realized. She really enjoyed his company and as time went on, she rarely thought about Jack.

CHAPTER FORTY-EIGHT

Julie sat at her piano practicing her music as she did every day. Chopin was by far her favorite composer, and his Etude in E Major, No. 3 was her all-time favorite melody. Now, whenever she played it, she always immediately thought of Jack. She had just finished playing that tune the night they met. But today, sitting there, Julie was feeling angry and frustrated. No matter how she tried she couldn't force herself from the negative thoughts that dominated her mind.

Julie had been in a good mood as she accompanied her mother to the afternoon tea, looking forward to meeting more of her Aunt Estelle's Troy friends.

Mrs. Foster had come over to their table and, with her loud, boisterous voice, began to relate to Julie about seeing Jack in a secluded corner of the restaurant with a very beautiful woman. "You better keep your eyes on that good-looking husband of yours," was the way she had begun, and continued to rattle on. Julie tried not to listen, for she felt extremely embarrassed and taken by such surprise that her mouth fell open and she did not know what to say. She was glad to hear her aunt retort, "Well, Julie certainly doesn't have to worry, because the girl couldn't possibly have been as pretty as she, and I never saw a young man more in love than Jack is with Julie." Julie tried to smile and act nonchalant, as if she didn't care, but it was hard. Even though her aunt had leaned over to whisper to her, "Don't let that busy-body get you upset, Julie," she couldn't help it, she was upset. Inwardly, she was seething. How dare he embarrass her like this? It was so typical of his careless, inconsiderate behavior, putting her in such an awkward situation. After all she had explained to him about her mother and father, how could he be so insensitive to her feelings? And now, as she sat pounding on the piano, she was hoping that this pent-up anger and frustration would seep through her fingertips onto the keyboard. Who was this woman, she thought? Were her suspicions true? Was Jack tired of her already? Had she fooled herself into believing that she could be enough for him? And added to the anger was a great childlike impatience. She wanted him home, so that she could accuse him, and see what he had to say about it. She wondered if he would deny it. If he did, could she believe him? Or had he already concocted some absurd story?

Julie had such a hard time concentrating as she routinely began playing all of Chopin's Etudes. She did not want what had happened to her mother to happen to her. She could still remember how angry and hurt her mother had been. Trusting her father completely, her mother never suspected a thing, and was taken by such complete surprise that she had a hard time adjusting. Julie could still hear her mother's voice. "I don't ever remember seeing any signs that there could be anything wrong. Oh, I always knew that he had an eye for a pretty woman, and he had to be away on business, but he was always there for anything important. I never in my wildest imagination ever dreamed that he could cross over the line and be such a deceitful hypocrite as to sleep with another woman. What I don't understand is how he could look at himself in the mirror every day, living such a lie? I feel so angry at him for putting me in such a degrading position. If we were in a war and he were in a foreign country and lonely and didn't know if he'd ever see me again, I wouldn't think it was right, but that, I could at least understand. But when I'm right here and I've been fair and never turned my back on him, it's just plain selfish and egotistical. I always made sure my involvement in the Women's Rights Movement never interfered with my family. Thank God, Julie, that the Women's Suffrage work has come as far as it has. Do you realize that if this had happened before they passed the New York State legislation of 1860, that everything I owned and inherited would have automatically belonged to him? Can you imagine how hard it must have been for those poor women back then, trying to raise their children while putting up with their drunken husbands, and very little money?"

Julie could still remember that even weeks later, when she had become so wrapped up with Jack that she had almost forgotten about her mother's problem, overhearing her mother and her Aunt Estelle talking.

"How are you doing lately, Marion, is it getting any easier?" Estelle caringly questioned.

Marion sadly answered, "Not much, Estelle. I still wake up in the middle of the night so frustrated and angry at him that I could scream. I feel so violated and humiliated to think that he went from her bed to mine, and who knows how many others. I'm still having such a hard time sleeping that sometimes I wonder if I'll ever have a good night's sleep again. I know they say time heals all wounds. Well, I certainly hope so. I'll tell you one thing, after all the heartache, I hope no one ever asks me to feel sorry for the 'other woman', unless of course the man lied and she didn't know he was married. I just hope all cheaters get caught and have to pay the price for all the heartache they've caused other people. As far as I'm concerned, she can have him, because I certainly don't want him. The sooner I'm free of him, the better. It's hard to forgive someone when their actions are so far from your own. At least I've gotten to the point where I've kept myself busy during the day so that I don't have as much time to waste thinking about him. And I've made up my mind that I'm not going to allow this devastating situation to defeat me. I'm determined to push on and keep reminding myself that I'm one of the lucky ones who's financially independent."

Julie began playing, as she did every day, three of her grandparents' favorite hymns, "Rock of Ages", "Amazing Grace", and "Nearer My God To Thee". Playing the hymns always reminded her of happy times and of going to church with her grandparents in Long Island. But today her mind felt so clouded that the music didn't seem to be able to penetrate it.

Julie looked at the clock again. It was already after 5pm and her patience was long gone. As she continued playing the music of some of her favorite composers, her mind wandered back to her mother and the trip from Boston to Troy. She could hear her mother's voice so plainly, as if she were in the room with her at that moment. "Learn from this Julie, and don't let it happen to you. Don't marry a ladies' man. He'll only break your heart. It's a long life. Don't be distracted by good looks. Hold out for a good, decent, faithful man, whose world revolves around you." And Julie agreed that she didn't want to spend some of the best years of her life with a man, only to find out that he had been cheating on her all along. If Jack was cheating, she'd sooner know now, end it and go on without him. But she realized that she had forgotten all about her mother's advice when she first set her eyes upon Jack.

Julie could still remember every detail of her and Jack's first meeting. Shortly after she and her mother arrived in Troy, they were invited to a party at the O'Connell home. The Fergusons were in the same social circle with Jack's family.

Estelle, having no children of her own, was very close to her sister's children and her friends were well aware of her talented niece from Boston, who was recognized by her teachers as being an outstanding pianist, having studied abroad and given several concerts. It was only natural that she was invited to play and graciously accepted.

Julie had just completed her program and was taking her customary bow when she noticed that standing a short distance from her was the most handsome man she had ever seen, and for a few fleeting moments their eyes collided. She felt her heart beating faster and her knees buckling as a faint feeling swept over her and she turned to the side, to hide from him the flush that was rushing to her face.

Coming up to Julie at that moment was the small, very thin, dark haired, olive skinned young girl with timid brown eyes, that she had noticed staring intently at her throughout her performance. She was shyly saying how much she had enjoyed Julie's playing and that this piano had never sounded like that when she played it. "I'm Gail O'Connell," she said, smilingly, "And I've heard so many wonderful things about you, Julie." Before Julie could say a word, Gail was motioning to someone and saying, "Julie, I don't believe you've met my brother, Jack."

Julie turned around and there he was, standing even closer, extending his hand to her. She was glad she had regained her composure, as she smilingly extended her hand to him. The touch of his hand aroused in her feelings she had never known before. As she looked into those beautiful brown eyes, she did not dare allow her eyes to tarry, afraid that they would be unable to ever turn away again. For Julie, it was a magical moment that was too soon, rudely interrupted by so many people. People were congratulating her and telling her how much they had enjoyed her playing and the selections she had chosen, while many beautiful young ladies were swarming around Jack, distancing him from her. For the rest of the evening there were many, many people in between them, and although Julie, out of the corner of her eye, saw Jack watching her a few times, she purposely did not acknowledge his glances. She was already trying to figure a plan that she would use to win him.

Gail had come back to sit next to Julie and started talking about piano lessons and the teachers she had, but still needed more lessons. Julie remarked at how much more she liked Gail's piano than her Aunt Estelle's, mentioning that Gail's piano was just like her piano in Boston. Gail was excited as she extended an invitation to Julie to come over to practice anytime. Julie agreed that she would like to come over, if Gail would in exchange allow Julie to help her with her lessons. For already a plan was forming in Julie's mind.

Julie went to bed that night with her head full of beautiful thoughts of Jack and a confidence that he would some day be her husband. She made up her mind that she would play hard to get, while all the other girls were throwing themselves at him.

Julie started going to visit Gail almost every afternoon and found that she really enjoyed Gail's friendship. Gail had a shy, quiet sweetness about her that blended with Julie's outgoing, confident, headstrong personality, causing them to become good friends. When Jack would come in, Julie all but ignored him, almost to the point that he would think he was bothering her. Coyly finding out from Gail where Jack would be, she paraded other young men on the scene, whenever possible, to arouse his interest. Finally, one Friday afternoon, he asked her to go out with him on Sunday. Not wishing to appear anxious, she told him she already had an engagement for Sunday. On the other hand, not wanting to discourage him altogether, she said she would be free the following Sunday, if he would like to take her out then. He quickly agreed.

On their first date, as they talked about many things, how surprised Jack seemed to be when he heard Julie mention that she probably would never marry, but go on with her musical career. She related to him about her current teacher, who wanted her to come back to Boston to be prepared for a world concert tour, as soon as the war was over. Remembering this happy time brought a peaceful smile to Julie's countenance, but it was soon erased when she heard the outside door open, and Jack approaching. He was whistling.

Julie started playing again, Etude in E Major, No. 3, hoping it would draw him to her. He stopped whistling, as he came to sit beside her on the piano bench (she had gotten into the habit of leaving room for him at her right side). Julie stopped playing and as she looked at him she felt annoyed, realizing that he was in such a good mood, after his actions had caused her such aggravation and humiliation.

Jack leaned over to kiss Julie, but she turned away. "What did I do wrong now?" Jack patiently asked.

Julie subtly started questioning him. "Anything happen while I was away last week? Did you meet anyone interesting?"

Jack thought for a minute. "No, not really."

Julie asked, "What did you do?"

Jack answered, "Oh, this and that, nothing special."

"Did you have lunch with anyone?" Julie further inquired.

Jack thought again. "I suppose so. In fact, it's hard to remember just what I did do last week. Julie, what is the matter? Why are you asking me all these questions?"

Julie, noticeably annoyed, remarked, "Well, I'll ask you one more question that will help refresh your memory. Who was the beautiful woman you were having lunch alone with last week, while I was away?" She looked at his face intently, hoping it would betray him, giving her the evidence that he was lying.

Jack thought and thought, trying so hard to remember the details of an insignificant week. He replied, "I didn't have lunch alone with any woman last week or any other week for that matter."

Julie angrily answered, "You're a liar. A deceitful liar," she shouted. "You were seen."

Jack questioned, "Seen? Where? By whom?"

Julie proceeded to tell him about what had happened that afternoon at the tea.

Jack impatiently answered, "Well she was wrong. I didn't have lunch alone with any woman. The only thing I can think of that she could possibly have misunderstood is last Tuesday, I believe it was, that I went to lunch alone. I purposely chose a booth toward the back of the restaurant, hoping no one would notice me. I was seeking peace and quiet. I wasn't sitting there more than five or ten minutes when along came George and Anne Brent. George insisted that no one should eat alone. I couldn't very well tell them that I preferred to eat alone, and wished that they would go away. I was even tempted to lie about it, telling them I was meeting someone there. But I couldn't do that. So they joined me. As soon as we had placed our order, George noticed John Foley had come in and he said he had to talk to him about business, so he excused himself, and was only gone a few minutes. I suppose that's when Mrs. Foster saw me with Anne Brent. But I wouldn't be a bit surprised if she saw George there, too. The truth never stopped her from spreading lies. She and my Grandmother gossiped all the time and never had a good word to say about anybody. They were two of the biggest trouble-makers in Troy. They didn't care who got hurt. In fact, they were two shallow people who laughed at other people's misery, and added to it."

Julie questioned, "Well, if it was so innocent, why didn't you tell me about it? I would have been prepared."

Jack replied, "It wasn't important. I just forgot about it. So it looks like you got yourself all worked up again for nothing. Oh, Julie, when will you stop these possessive, jealous tirades?"

At that moment, Julie's anger mounted. There was nothing to justify his careless lack of concern for her feelings. She hated him with a passion and wanted to do something to hurt him as he had hurt her, and Julie, who had always taken such pride in her self-control, caught sight of his hand resting on top of the keyboard and she lifted the cover and banged it down hard on it.

Jack uttered a cry of pain. "Uh!" as he freed his pain-filled fingers. He looked at her with a mixture of disbelief and anger. He shook his head. "I should have known better than to come in here in a happy mood." He walked toward the door and then turned toward her. "I wish I could understand you. You're either hot or cold."

Julie retorted. "You should talk. You're the moody one."

Jack ignored her words and stood in the doorway shouting, "If you don't believe what I said about Mrs. Foster, then ask Gail." And off he went, slamming the front door behind him.

CHAPTER FORTY-NINE

"Oh, Mrs. O'Connell, I heard a loud noise and I was just checking to make sure everything was all right," the young maid exclaimed in a rather hesitant, timid voice, feeling as if she were intruding.

Julie answered, "Yes, everything is fine."

The maid inquired, "Will Mr. O'Connell be back for dinner?"

"I don't believe so. And I won't be having any dinner, either. If anyone is looking for me, I'll be up in my room," Julie exclaimed as she walked toward the stairs.

As Julie lay face down on her bed, with her head leaning on her arm, the uninvited tears started to stain the beautiful satin coverlet. She felt a burning, churning, ache in control of her stomach, as she started thinking. Why couldn't he have been more sympathetic and told her he was sorry that she had been caused such mental anguish, instead of making such flippant, derogatory remarks, making the whole situation even worse? She wanted him to hold her close and kiss the tears from her eyes. Oh, how much she needed his arms around her, and to hear once more his passionate voice so filled with love. And she thought, how hard it is to be in love with someone you don't trust. Was it really all just jealous imaginings? What had happened to them? Everything had been so perfect! And Julie started remembering happier times.

The first time that they had gone out together, Julie realized that they had a lot in common. They both loved music, dancing, boating, swimming, horseback riding, tennis and quiet walks on the beach. They were both avid readers. She knew world history and how it had been forced to record such flagrant injustices to women. And she was angered by it. Other times she would lose herself in romantic novels, always admiring the heroine whose personality personified her own. Jack preferred adventure stories, and for years entwined them with his daydreams. Becoming the hero, and displaying in them, the courage that he knew he lacked. Escaping at times from a life that he found hard to face. They talked about the schools they had gone to and some of their friends, and it wasn't long before they confided to each other that they did not like to be among large groups of people, but preferred intimate dinner parties with close friends. The love that Julie had first felt for Jack was moment by moment, magnified. She could feel his sensitivity and knew for sure that he was, literally, "the man of her dreams."

Julie continued to go out not only with Jack, but two of his friends, hoping that their attention to her would make Jack jealous, increasing his desire for her. But it became harder and harder for her to act as if she were enjoying their company while thoughts of Jack filled her with a longing to be with him. Soon, she gave up trying.

For the next few weeks Jack and Julie were constantly together, breaking all other ties. They enjoyed every moment of every day, smiling, laughing, and doing all the things they both loved to do. They welcomed the quiet times, in secluded places, holding each other close, looking deep into each other's eyes, refusing to allow the world to come between them. Finally came the day when Jack asked her to marry him and she hesitatingly accepted. She thought of telling him of all the plans and dreams she had made that were so very important to her, but she figured they had plenty of time to talk about those things in the future. She was confident that Jack would do what he had to do to make her happy.

Jack and Julie decided to elope the following Saturday, July 7th, and go on a month-long honeymoon. When Julie told her mother her plans, she helped her get ready, tearfully agreeing to respect Julie's wish not to have a big wedding. They were married in a little church in New York City, spending their first night at a hotel there, where Julie completely surrendered herself to him. The next morning, they left by train for Atlantic City. Their honeymoon was more perfect than even Julie could have imagined. He was so attentive, his eyes overflowing with love. How often he had reached for her, never seeming to be able to get enough, as together they reached peaks of ecstasy that went beyond description.

Night after night, Jack and Julie stayed up late, dancing, talking, laughing, holding each other so close. Every morning they slept late, being in no hurry, with no worries, just enjoying the peace and joy of true love fulfilled. They went swimming, laid on the beach, and walked hand in hand on the Boardwalk. Their eyes were so locked together that they were oblivious to the heads that turned as they passed. She with her blond hair, green eyes and a golden tan that rested upon her perfectly shaped body, and he, who was the very epitome of the adage, "tall, dark and handsome."

From Atlantic City, Julie took Jack to Long Island to meet her grandparents, and then back to New York City, and on to Niagara Falls. They had been so happy! Why couldn't everything have stayed the way it was? What had happened? How could they have lost something so beautiful, so quickly?

Looking back, Julie realized that, right from the beginning, when they arrived back to Troy from their honeymoon, that many people were guilty of keeping them apart. Their first major decision was where to live. Because they hadn't talked about it, Julie assumed that Jack would allow her to make that decision. They went first to her aunt's house, because Julie was anxious to see her mother.

While Jack was in visiting with her uncle, Julie's mother and aunt tried to convince her to stay there, but Julie told them she wanted to stay at the hotel so that she and Jack would not be distracted from going out each day, looking for a place of their own. But when they got to Jack's house and his father insisted it was foolish staying at a hotel when they had so much room, Jack agreed. Julie felt annoyed, but didn't want to make a big scene their first night back. She silently went along with it, even though she knew she would feel uncomfortable there. Day after day, things kept coming up to keep them there.

Julie's aunt and uncle hosted a party for her and Jack, and Julie was annoyed that so many women still crowded around Jack, as if he were still single, many all but ignoring her. But there was no doubt in Julie's mind that the two people who had done the most damage to their relationship were his two so-called best friends.

Julie met Roger Collins the same night she met Jack. He was tall, very blond, a golden tan clinging to his muscular body, with compelling blue eyes that enhanced a broad smile. But from the first moment he opened his mouth, Julie realized that standing before her was the most arrogant, conceited, obnoxious, chauvinistic man that she had ever met, with a caveman philosophy that women, like children, should be seen and not heard. His words, his manner, his attitude reeked of chauvinism, all that Julie hated. She took an instant dislike to him, and felt the feeling was mutual.

Julie and her friends had started smoking in college, and of course Roger did not approve of women smoking, so when Julie would light up a cigarette, Roger, to show his disapproval, wouldn't talk until she put the cigarette out. Julie found it amusing, and welcomed the opportunity to be able to shut off his egotistical bragging, smoked more than ever.

The very first night Jack and Julie returned, Roger stopped in, "The men are getting together, if the little woman will let you out ha ha ha." Jack did not look at Julie, as he agreed with Roger to meet them later. Julie, who had planned for their first night back at the hotel alone, felt very, very disappointed. This was the beginning of many calls from Roger, "Jack, we need you for this or that, you can't let everybody down," and each time he went, Julie felt as if it were she he was letting down instead. If it wasn't bowling, it was cards or pocket billiards or basketball or trap shooting or something, always something to keep them apart. It wasn't that Julie minded Jack being with his friends, but she resented the fact that it was interfering with their plans and becoming more and more frequent. So that by the time they did move into a place of their own, she felt that the damage to their marriage had already been done.

Julie normally was very disciplined. The type of person who valued her time and planned ahead, how she would spend it, while Jack was lackadaisical. It aggravated her greatly to make plans for them, that Jack agreed to, perhaps a day together at the beach or horseback riding or just a quiet lunch together out of town, only to have Roger or one of Jack's other friends, who Julie always believed Roger put up to it, interfere with their plans. There was always the excuse that they could go the next day or another time. She felt as if Jack tried much harder to please Roger and his friends than he did to please her. She felt as if they were losing something precious. She really missed the closeness they'd had. She resented Roger's constant interference, but couldn't seem to free Jack from his grip. Jack was beginning to go out too many nights, drinking and gambling and who knows what else. And Julie didn't trust Roger at all.

And if it wasn't Roger calling, it was Sally. Sally's mother and Jack's mother were best friends. Jack explained that Sally was just as close as if she were an older sister, being three years older than he. She had gotten married fresh out of high school to an engineering graduate of RPI, originally from New York City. He was away quite often and Jack was in the habit of visiting with Sally a few times a week. He really enjoyed the children, who called him Uncle Jack. They were always talking together and Julie had a hard time understanding why Jack had to keep visiting Sally when it seemed he hardly had enough time for her, and she resented him for it.

Julie was beginning to realize that they could never be happy in Troy as long as these people had such a hold on him.

Julie started thinking, Why was it expected for the wife always to follow her husband? What was she doing here in this little town? This was not what she wanted in life. She missed the excitement of a big city and her former way of life. Why couldn't they make a new life for themselves somewhere else? It didn't have to be Boston. Maybe they could move to Philadelphia or New York City. Her uncle would give Jack a job in Philadelphia and she was sure Mr. Hilliard could find room for him in New York City. Or he could start a business of his own, she thought. She would help him.

Julie started thinking again of their honeymoon and how close they had been. She wondered if there was any chance of capturing that again. She was trying hard to concentrate on the book she was reading when she heard Jack coming in. She quickly turned out the light to make him think she was asleep and that she didn't care anymore what he did.

Jack quickly readied himself for bed, quietly trying not to disturb her. He crept in beside her.

His closeness to her aroused a desire for him within her. If only he would reach for her. She longed to feel his arms about her, his strong body pressed to hers, his warm breath in the hollow of her neck. She longed to lay her head upon his chest and feel his hands caressing her, molding her to the contour of his body. She wanted to touch him and invite him to touch her. But how could she let him know how she felt, when he was so unconcerned, and showed no sign at all of wanting her. For if he refused, she would not be able to endure the humiliation.

Jack laid in the bed thinking. Why had he said such mean things to her? Maybe if he had been more patient, then she would have welcomed his arms about her, and allowed him to satisfy this aching yearning he felt for her. If only he dared reach over to touch her warm body. The smell of her perfume filled his nostrils and tantalized his senses. He loved her with a passion he could not subdue. He longed to cradle her in his arms, to press her warm body to his was like a compulsion he could not still. How desperately he wanted to wrap her in his arms, to kiss her eyes and ease the sting of jealous tears, to lay his head upon her breast and free his pounding heart. But he would be crushed if she refused, when he had purposely stayed out late to shield himself from her whipping words, that always wounded his bleeding pride.

They might have been able to close the door on the world, to find in each other's arms comfort from the daily anxieties of life, to live a moment of ecstasy, as two hearts beat as one, but for the wall that lay between them. A wall of pride. And although it was invisible, it was just as impenetrable as if it had been made of granite.

CHAPTER FIFTY

It was Saturday, and Mary went shopping with Kitty. They had come out of a store when Mary looked across the street and saw Mr. Packard coming out of a restaurant with two men. Mary said, "Wait a minute, Kitty, there's a man I know that I want to say hello to." She ran across the street to where he was. She walked up to him with a warm smile on her face. "Hello Mr. Packard, how are you?"

He looked right at her, and without batting an eye, he said, "I'm sorry Miss, but you've mistaken me for someone else," as he walked on past her.

Kitty had gotten across the street just in time to hear his words. Mary was noticeably aggravated. "Of all the nerve. Who does he think he is, pretending he doesn't know me?" One of Mary's pet peeves was people who thought that they were better than other people.

"He's right, Mary, you've mistaken him for someone else," Kitty exclaimed. "You couldn't possibly know him. That's Lucky Dan Donovan, that runs that gambling casino/hotel on the outskirts of the city. Why, it's even been rumored that there are New York City prostitutes there."

"No, Kitty, I'm sure that's Mr. Packard, the man I told you about, that has no family, that Molly and I have been going out riding with on Sunday afternoons."

Kitty answered, "Well maybe he looks like Mr. Packard, Mary, but it's definitely Lucky Dan Donovan, because he's come into the telephone company a number of times to have more phones installed."

The minute Mary got home, she ran to the telephone to call Molly to tell her what had happened, and how angry she was at him for pretending in front of his friends that he didn't know her. She also pointed out that he had lied in not telling her and Molly who he really was. Molly agreed. "Maybe he just doesn't want to be seen with us. Now that I think back, it does seem kind of funny that he avoided being seen with us in public. Think about this, Mary, he always parked the automobile over to the side, away from other automobiles, and he either got out himself to go get us refreshments while we sat in the automobile, or he sat in the automobile and sent us."

Mary's voice acknowledged her annoyance. "Well, who does he think he is, putting on airs? Apparently he thinks we're good enough to take out riding, but not good enough to be introduced to his friends." Molly agreed.

Molly had been sick the past few days and still wasn't feeling good enough to go out. When Mary told her she intended to meet the man they knew as Mr. Packard the next day as usual, and tell him off, once and for all, Molly pleaded with her to wait another week, so she could go with her. Mary pointed out to Molly that she didn't want this hanging over her head all week. She wanted to get it over with. Molly knew that when Mary made up her mind to do something, it was practically impossible to change it.

Mary had a hard time sleeping that night. Thoughts of what she was going to tell the man she knew as Mr. Packard, aggravated her, and interfered with her usual peace-filled night's sleep. Since the summer concerts had ended, he would pick her and Molly up just before the entrance to Prospect Park.

All the way walking up the Congress Street hill, Mary rehearsed in her mind just what she was going to say to the alias Mr. Packard. It was two o'clock and he was there waiting for her. She was no sooner in the automobile when the words started pouring out of her mouth. She hardly stopped to catch her breath. She was so angry that she was hardly aware that he had driven up the Prospect Park entrance, crossed the park, and stopped on the hill overlooking the city. He listened patiently without interrupting her. Finally, her tirade of words was over, and although she was out of breath, she felt very justified, believing he deserved it.

He looked at her and waited to make sure that she had said everything she wanted to say. Then, very calmly, he said, "You have the wrong idea, Mary."

She was taken back by his calm retort. "What do you mean, I have the wrong idea?" she asked.

He looked into her questioning eyes as he softly answered, "You see, Mary, it wasn't that you weren't good enough to introduce to them, it was that they weren't good enough to introduce to you. Believe me, Mary, when I say they're bad news. They wouldn't understand this friendship. To me, you and Molly are happy, innocent young kids, but they'd never understand that. Just as it would be hard for you to understand men like that, who would sell their own mother, if the price was right. You see, Mary, living in this nice little city with your family and friends, you really live a very sheltered life." He looked kind of pensive, as if he was thinking of something he just didn't know how to explain. "How could you possibly understand that some people, just in order to survive, have to rub elbows with the scum of the earth. Or that sometimes you can just drift into a bad situation, find it really hard to get out of, and end up being forced to choose the lesser of two evils. But, like I said, Mary, it would be hard for you to understand. So just take my word for it. I have no choice. I have to do business with these people."

"Your word. How can I take your word for anything, when you lied to us about who you are?"

"Mary, if I told you who I was, would you have gone for rides with me?"

"Well, probably not."

"Have I ever been less than a gentleman? Or said anything out-of-line?"

"No," she finally smiled, "you've always been very nice and gentlemanly."

And he smiled, "Haven't we had a lot of fun?"

She was very calm now as she smiled again, shaking her head in the affirmative, "Yes, we certainly have had a lot of fun and have seen a lot of interesting things."

"So you see, Mary, no harm was ever done or ever intended."

"But you did deceive us, nevertheless. Why, we went out with you in the first place mainly because you told us you had no family. We felt sorry for you. We thought you were lonesome." And then her curiosity forced her to ask the question now uppermost in her mind. "Or was that a lie, too, that you have no family?"

"Well, Mary, in answer to the first part of what you said about being lonesome, maybe I was a little lonesome. Sometimes there can be people all around, but you can still be lonesome. Especially when you don't know who you can trust. In answer to your question about having a family, I can honestly tell you that I don't know. I wish I did know."

"How can someone not know if they have a family or not?" She asked, as she stared at him with a very inquisitive look on her face.

He was a very cautious man, and as he looked into her beautiful blue eyes, he pondered for a moment, made up his mind, and then slowly said, "I'll answer that question for you, Mary, if you can promise me that you will never tell anyone what I tell you." He looked very serious as he waited for her answer.

She looked into his trusting eyes as she shook her head, "I promise I will never tell anyone what you tell me."

"You see, Mary, at one time I had a wife and daughter. In fact, my little daughter had red hair and blue eyes. But I haven't seen her since she was five years old. At that time, my wife and I had a big argument. Without warning, she took my daughter and disappeared with her. I've hired many detectives over the years, but still haven't been able to find her. That's why I said I'm not sure if I have a family or not, and that's what brought me to Troy in the first place.

"I'm originally from New York City. When my wife and daughter had been missing a few months, I had several different detectives looking for them, without any luck. It was as if they'd disappeared off the face of the earth. Then one evening this friend of mine called me from Troy to tell me that he was sure it was my wife that he saw out pushing my daughter in a go-cart. He was trying to follow them. But when he got to the corner of the street and had to wait for traffic, he said that she recognized him and ran into the five and ten cent store and must have gone out the other entrance. By the time he parked the automobile and went looking for her, he couldn't find her. He swore up and down that he was positive it was her, so I not only had the detective come up here, but I came myself. That was the only even tiny speck of hope there was.

"I walked aimlessly around this city, showing my wife's picture and telling people she had amnesia, and that I was concerned about our daughter. But no one had seen any sign of her. Finally, I was exhausted, and without even realizing it, had walked into that place, where I had met you in the parking lot. I was deep in thought, trying to think of what to do next, wanting so desperately to find my little daughter, when I overheard a conversation between the owner and a customer. I had already noticed how he kept coughing all the time. He said, 'The doctor told me I should live in Arizona, and if I could find somebody to buy this place, I'd move tomorrow.' Now, I'm not an impulsive person, but as I looked around that place, I realized that the possibility that my daughter could be in Troy was the only lead I had, so I bought it.

"That was thirteen years ago, and I still miss her terribly, and I have been thinking of her more than ever, and wondering what happened to her. In fact, Mary, the day I met you and Molly, as I walked out of that building, I was thinking of my daughter. When I looked at you, I thought, this girl right here could be my daughter. I've heard of unusual things like that happening, when people have found relatives almost by accident. And I thought, and yes at that moment I even prayed, that this once, fate would be kind to me, and make up for the past. But no such luck."

At that moment he took out of his wallet a faded picture of an attractive light haired woman and child. The child looked just like the woman. He handed the picture to Mary, as he explained. "This is a picture of my wife and little girl, Rosemarie."

As Mary looked at the picture, it was obvious to her that she had a striking resemblance to the woman, and she could understand how it occurred to him that she could be his daughter. Mary couldn't hide feeling sorry for him as she gave him a sympathetic smile and acknowledged how beautiful his daughter was.

As he put the picture away, he continued speaking. "You see, Mary, the first time we met, I purposely told you I had no family, hoping to get your sympathy. You mentioned that you had gone to Prospect Park that afternoon, so the next Sunday, I purposely parked my automobile there on the hill, and I was watching you and Molly from a distance. Then when I saw you start down the road, I ran down the hill on the grass to my automobile and made it appear as if it were a coincidence. I purposely tried to entice you with a ride to Burden's Lake, and the following week, I more or less did the same thing, and invited you to Crystal Lake. From then on through the week, I'd find out what was going on."

Mary's mouth dropped open in surprise as she listened in amazement, remembering those meetings that she and Molly had thought were just coincidental.

"That's why I asked you about your family in a way that you wouldn't get suspicious. I knew you and Molly would be tempted by the places I suggested we go to. But after the first few weeks you girls were so refreshingly sweet that I really began to look forward to our unusual Sunday adventures." A smile came suddenly across his face to replace the frown. "You see, Mary, they call me Lucky because I'm very good at gambling, but it really isn't luck as much as it is skill. I realized years ago that a lot of people who gamble shouldn't be in the game in the first place, because they need the money so badly. When they play like that, it shows in their faces, and they make mistakes. But most times I gamble against rich men who have plenty of money to throw away. I've been gambling for years, so I've learned a few tricks of my trade. No one can tell if I have a good hand or not. My expression is always the same. The proverbial poker face. On the other hand, I've learned to read other people's faces. Most people can't hide their joy or disappointment in the hand they've been dealt. I've learned to memorize cards. I can tell every card that's been played and every card that's left. That tips the scale a little more in my favor, and even though I always have the money to back me up, and I could take chances, I rarely ever do. If my luck isn't running good, I get out of the game. So I have a reputation for being lucky as far as gambling goes, but the rest of my life has not been very lucky at all."

He looked somber as he began. "When I was a kid, I lived with my Ma and Pa in a rat and cockroach infested, rundown tenement house in New York City.

"I was only eight years old when I woke up one morning to find my Pa slumped over the bed with an empty bottle of whiskey on the floor next to him. I tried to wake him up, but it was no use. He was sleeping too heavily. I was surprised, because he never drank that early. I looked around for my Ma, but I couldn't find her anywhere. I figured she probably went to the store or to the neighbor's or something.

"My friend Johnny came to walk to school with me. I liked school because we had a really nice teacher who used to read us a lot of stories. She made learning fun. So I washed up fast and got dressed, and went to school with him.

"When I arrived at school, I found out from the taunts of some of the kids that the night before, my old lady had run off with the butcher. He left his wife and three children. The teacher made the kids stop. I could see in her eyes that she felt sorry for me. I was a sensitive little boy, and even after all these years, I can still remember how much their teasing hurt.

"I rushed home from school that day, still hoping that they were wrong and that I'd find her there. But nobody was there. I waited for what seemed to me like hours. Then I heard Pa's footsteps, but they didn't sound quite right. Then the door opened and he staggered in. He hadn't gone to work. It was obvious he had been drinking all day. I'd never up to that point ever seen him drunk. He looked so sad. His face was so white, as if all the blood had been drained from it. I can still see him now so plainly in my mind.

"I said, 'Pa, what happened? Where's Ma?' He said, 'She's gone. She's gone.' He started crying deep, wrenching sobs. 'Gone where? When will she be back?' I impatiently asked. I was crushed when he answered, 'Never. She's never going to come back.' Then in between the crying, he got mad. 'That no good son of a bitch. That tramp. I picked her up out of the gutter, and this is the way she pays me back. I should have left her there.'

"Before she left, he was a pretty ordinary man. He was kind and he'd help her, and he'd help me with my school work. After that happened, he changed. He hardly ever even spoke to me. He never really got over it. I never saw him smile again, not even once. He walked around like a corpse, just going through the motions of working, eating, drinking and sleeping.

"Before that happened, he used to stop in at the local pub sometimes for a couple of drinks. I found out some of the men at work and at the pub made jokes about what had happened and they made him feel bad. You know, Mary, sometimes people can be very cruel. After that, he started drinking at home by himself.

"Every night after work, I'd watch him go through the same ritual. He'd take out the picture of them, when they got married. He'd start drinking, and then he'd start talking to the picture and asking why, explaining that he did his best. He'd always end up in a crying jag, telling her how much he loved her.

"I really missed her terribly, and I used to cry myself to sleep and pray that she'd come back. It made me feel so bad that she never even said goodbye. What kind of a mother was she, that she could walk away from her little eight year old child? Didn't she even care what happened to me?

"After he died, I took that picture and separated them by ripping it in half. I put his picture in my pocket. Even to this day I still have it. But I took her half and with my pen knife, I cut holes in her face, wishing that she could feel the pain that she had caused us. Then I tore it up in little pieces. And I hated her all the more, especially for what she had done to him.

"But the whole experience taught me a valuable lesson about human nature and how differently people handle situations in their lives. While my Pa caved in and fell apart under the heartache and disappointment and started drinking more and more, the butcher's wife, who was a kind and caring person, used to say to him, pull yourself together. You must be strong and keep on going for the sake of the child. But her words were falling on deaf ears. She was determined to get through it. She was a strong, stocky lady who literally took over that business. She was used to helping her husband, and people were surprised when she even started butchering the meat herself. She could have resented me, but this woman would see me outside and knock on the window and call me in and feed me some good homemade soup and bread, along with her own children, and then send me home with some for Pa.

"One day I heard a neighbor lady say to her, 'You should let that little brat fend for himself. After all, it was that tramp of a mother of his that led your husband astray.' But she stood right up to her. 'In the first place,' she said, 'my husband chose to abandon his family and run off. But this poor little boy, my heart goes out to him. He's the one who's paying for their shenanigans.' She is probably the most Christian lady I've ever met.

"But Pa started drinking more and more, and even missing work now and then, and finally lost his job. Then he'd only work for drinking money. The landlord would come up and find Pa drunk and he'd say to me, 'Tell him the rent is due. If it's not paid, out you go into the street,' Here I was only a little boy, but I had to worry about the both of us. It was as if I was the father and he was the child.

"When he'd stagger in drunk, I started picking his pockets trying to get together enough for food and rent money. I'd take any job I could to make a few pennies. The first few months, I even had to steal money to make up the difference. But I only stole from people who I knew had extra money. What could I do? Why, I couldn't even count the times I went to bed hungry and worried that we would get thrown out into the street.

"Then I became a newsboy. By that time, even though I was only nine, most people thought I was ten or eleven. I was tall for my age. But even then, I had to fight for the better corner to sell papers on! I sold papers every day of the week.

"On Sundays I started selling papers across the street from a real nice church in a better section of the city. I had to get up real early and walk a long way. Sometimes, I was so cold, and my fingers were so numb that I could hardly move them. My legs felt like frozen stumps that were hard to lift up and push ahead. A lot of times my stomach was empty, and I was so hungry. It was a church that quite a few rich men and their families went to. I'd watch these people pull up in their streamlined coaches and fancy clothes. I'd think this just isn't fair. Why can't I have a little bit more so I won't have to be so cold and hungry so often? I really envied those rich little kids. They had Ma's and Pa's who loved and cared about them. They had good food and clothes, and no worries, while I'd have to stand there freezing in the winter, and dying of the heat in the summer, a lot of times hungry and tired.

"Church didn't have much meaning to me. Why, if I could have gone into the church and sold those papers, I would have. My only prayer at that time was that most of the people would come early, and buy their papers on the way in, instead of on the way out. Or that the minister wouldn't talk too long, so that I didn't have to stand there so long waiting.

"I'll always remember that there was this one really nice, kind older church lady. I can still see her now in my mind, coming across the street my first day on the corner. She smiled, and with concern in her eyes, she said, 'Oh, young man, your hands must be so cold. Did you lose your mittens or forget them?' I told her I didn't have any. She said, 'Surely your mother wouldn't let you stand there freezing your hands. Is she making you some new mittens?' I told her my Ma was dead, 'cause as far as I was concerned, she was. By that time I had made up my mind that if she didn't care about me, then I didn't care about her, either. The lady said, 'I'm so sorry.' And then she asked me if I'd be on that corner the next Sunday, and I told her yes. The next Sunday, before she went into church, she came across the street with a bag in her hand and she handed it to me and inside was a knitted scarf and mittens. That was one of the best gifts I ever got from anybody in my whole life. From then on, most times she'd come over to say hello and bring me something good to eat. She had such gentle eyes. But her husband was the opposite. He never smiled, and always looked grumpy. I never saw any children with them, so I thought they probably didn't have any.

"One day, when the carriages left, I followed, and I was amazed to see the big beautiful homes some of those people lived in. I guess right then and there I started really understanding how unfair life is. As I looked at those big beautiful homes, I couldn't help thinking of the tenement houses where two or three families were squeezed into two or three rooms, three or four to a bed. That is, if they were lucky enough to have a bed. And I thought of how cold it always was, especially when the wind blew hard and rattled the windows. My teeth would chatter from the cold and I'd be shivering and wouldn't be able to sleep, thinking that being thrown out onto the street, it would be even colder.

"I started passing the time daydreaming. One of my favorite daydreams was that this lady's husband died, and that she took me and Pa into her house to live. And that it was really warm, and there was a lot of food to eat, and I didn't have to worry anymore about the rent money! Back then, many times it was those hopeful daydreams that kept me going. Then the spring came and it wasn't so bad.

Then came the summer, and although it was really hot, I stood in the shade of the building, listening to some of the words they were saying through the open windows. I'd hear words like loving, and caring and sharing, and feed the hungry. But I guess I resented the fact that except for that nice lady and a few men that gave me good tips, that they weren't sharing anything with me. I soon began to think that not many people really cared.

"Every night before I went to bed, I'd make sure Pa was tucked in for the night. This went on for a couple of years. Then one cold wintry night, he was drunk as usual. I put a cover over him, and I went to sleep. When I woke up in the middle of the night, he was gone. I went out looking all over for him, but I couldn't find him. The next day they found him under the porch down the street, frozen to death. Apparently, being drunk, he'd crawled in there and gone to sleep, and the snow covered him over.

"I had no known relatives, and I was afraid they'd come for me, and take me to the orphanage. So I stood in the distance and I watched them bury him in a pauper's grave. I made three vows that day. One, that I would never let any woman do that to me. The second, that I would never be hungry and cold again. And third, that someday I'd return and put some flowers on his grave. I knew he was weak. But I loved him, and felt sorry for him. As far as I was concerned, she killed him. And I hated her all the more after that.

"You see, Mary, there's a physical age, but there's also a mental age, and even though I was only eleven years old, I looked at least thirteen or fourteen, and street wise, I was at least thirty. So I took the little bit of money I'd saved from selling the papers, and I hopped the first freight train going west. I only got off the trains long enough to buy enough cheap food to survive. I went all the way to California. I had read in one of the books that the teacher let me borrow, that it was always warm there. I was so tired of being cold so many times. When anyone questioned my age, I told them I was fourteen and on my way to visit my imaginary aunt and uncle in San Francisco. I lived out on the west coast for about ten years. I took on all kinds of jobs and went up and down the coast and even worked for quite a while on a boat. Then I had this overwhelming urge or desire, or whatever you want to call it, to come back to New York City for a visit. Of course this time I went back on the train in style, with nice clothes and a pocketful of money.

"I went back to the old neighborhood. I thought, I wonder if Mrs.

Landrigan, the butcher's wife, is still living. I went into the store. It hadn't changed much at all, except there was a man butchering the meat. I looked twice, thinking it could be Mr. Landrigan had come back, but it was their son Mike. I had no intention of going through that chancy dialogue, 'Remember me, I'm Dan Donovan, etc. etc.' 'Who? Where did you live?' So I thought I'll just get some cigars and not say anything.

"Mrs. Landrigan turned toward the counter to wait on me. I said I'll have a package of White Owl cigars. She took them out and handed them to me and as she glanced up, she looked again and this big surprised smile came on her face and she yelled, 'Danny Donovan!' and she rushed around the counter and gave me a big hug. 'Where have you been? I'm so glad to see you!' I said, 'I didn't think you'd remember me.' She said, 'I'd know those beautiful green eyes anywhere. I've been praying for you every day since you left. I've asked God to guide and protect you. And I'm so glad to see that He has.' She'll never know how much that meant to me. I didn't think there was a soul on the face of the earth who remembered me, or cared if I was dead or alive. And then of course she insisted that I stay to have supper with them. She was always such a nice lady. If there were only more people like her! I never in my life met anybody that was so kind, not just to me, but to everybody. And yet she really had a hard life and could have become bitter.

"Think about this, Mary. Here is a lady whose husband ran off with another woman. When I got back, I found out her youngest daughter had been killed by a runaway horse and carriage. Her son has died since from influenza. Her other daughter got married and moved to Ohio, so she doesn't get much chance to visit with her and her grandchildren. But then if that wasn't enough, since she'd become older, she's all crippled up with arthritis. But she never complains.

"I always stop in to see her when I go back to New York City. I was telling her one day how I always admired her courage and she said, 'It's faith! God has given me faith for any ten people.' She has like a special light in her eyes. I'm really happy for her. But I thought to myself, if there really is such a thing as faith, why didn't God give me any?

"You know, Mary, life amazes me, sometimes. I don't mean this in a bragging way, but more as an explanation. After all these years, I'm the one that financially takes care of Mrs. Landrigan. She's always telling me that I have a good heart!

"In fact, if it wasn't for those three kind women in my life, the teacher, the church lady, and Mrs. Landrigan, I really think I'd be an atheist, instead of an agnostic. Do you know what an agnostic is, Mary?"

"Not exactly," she answered.

He looked at her as he began to explain.

"You might say that I'm the fence sitter. On the one hand, seeing the world the way it is, I have a hard time believing in a loving God. On the other hand, with the sun, moon, stars, planets, and all the different people, and so many kinds of animals, and unexplained signs and wonders in the world, it would be very hard for me to believe it all came about by chance.

"When I first arrived in San Francisco, I went to work on a boat and I really worked hard. Before long, the captain of that ship took a liking to me. He didn't have any children and he liked to talk about astronomy. I enjoyed listening to him, because I found the subject fascinating. When we got back to San Francisco, he invited me to his beautiful house, which was built on the top of a cliff overlooking the sea. In a room on the second floor, he had a powerful telescope. When I first looked through it, I couldn't believe my eyes at how orderly everything appeared to be. The planets look like a bunch of different sized balls just hanging out in space. Each one of them seemed to be revolving around the sun on its own time schedule. I thought to myself, what is it that holds them all in place, so that they don't just fall out of the sky? Oh, I know, the manmade word for it is gravity. But what exactly is gravity? And who made it?

"Then, besides the moon, sun, stars and planets, there are such things as satellites, meteors, and comets. And when the captain explained about Halley's Comet that comes back about every seventy-five and a half years, I found it mystifying. I thought to myself, where does it go? What makes it comes back every seventy five and a half years? Then with the earth's days and nights and changing seasons, it's so obvious that the whole universe is in such detailed order.

"I'm a gambler, but I'd never take that bet. In fact, I wonder what the odds would be that everything in the universe could have evolved in such an orderly fashion, without an intelligent designer called God?

"Then there's the evidence presented in the Bible. On the one hand, I thought, why would those gospel writers have bothered to write it, enduring hardships and whippings and in some cases even losing their lives just to tell people about Jesus, if it weren't true? It wouldn't make any sense.

"But on the other hand, I thought, if Jesus was the Son of God, like he said he was, then he should have taken over and forced those people to follow him. It seems to me it would have alleviated a lot of world suffering. I've gone back and forth my whole life believing and disbelieving. I used to include my wife in that special group of Christians. I met her at a dance one night. She was an Irish Catholic girl who had been brought up in an orphanage. She was always a nice, kind, considerate person, and very easy going. We fell in love and got married and had our little daughter. Then I started believing again. Maybe there is a God who sent them into my life to make up for my miserable childhood. At that time I worked a number of different jobs, and we were really very happy. I had managed to save quite a bit of money and had the intention of going back to the west coast and starting a small business.

"Well, I got in with a group of gamblers, and I was doing really good. I thought I'd be able to make money faster through gambling and be able to leave sooner. I kept promising my wife that before long, we'd have enough saved to leave. I was only trying to save enough of a nest egg to guarantee security. There were so many times that I had gone to bed cold and hungry, that it was like an obsession to have enough money so that not only I would never be cold or hungry again, but that my wife and child wouldn't be, either. It's a terrible thing to be cold and hungry. It does something to you. That went on for a couple of years. Then one night we had a big argument. I suppose she was tired of waiting. But to me it seemed as if she was hounding me. In comparison to other men, I thought I was really good to her and our daughter. Being the man of the house, I felt as if I should be the one to make the decision, and she should be more appreciative. Besides, my luck was a little down at the time, and I guess I didn't have enough patience. I got angry and told her we'd leave when I was good and ready. I went storming out of there. And for the first and only time in my whole life, I got drunk that night.

"For quite a while I had a room down at this place on the other side of town where a certain group of us would gather together to gamble, undisturbed, most evenings and weekends. My wife knew about it. If it got too late sometimes, I'd stay over there. There was a bed in the room.

"Well, like I said, I got drunk and didn't even remember the rest of that evening. The next morning, I was awakened by a knock on the door and I groggily saw this unfamiliar attractive woman get up from the other side of the bed and go to answer it. The door was opened slightly but just enough that I could see the hurt look in my wife's eyes as she saw me in that rumpled bed. Then without saying a word, she turned and left. If I only knew that would be the very last time I would ever see her, I would have run down the hall and begged her to forgive me. That woman didn't mean anything to me. Why, I didn't even know her name.

"I knew men who cheated on their wives all the time and they never even found out. Is it fair that one mistake should ruin your whole life? She should have at least given me another chance and warned me what would happen if I did it again. It only happened once and I was drunk and didn't know what I was doing. I wasn't in control of my senses. Doesn't that count for anything?"

He stopped talking and looked at Mary. "I'm afraid I'm shocking you, Mary."

"No, nothing would shock me," she replied, with an air of confidence, that she did not feel. "My aunts were always talking about worldly things." But no one had ever talked to her in quite the same way and she sat fascinated by this autobiography being unfolded before her intensely curious mind. She was very anxious to hear more.

He continued, "I thought, 'I'll give her time to cool off while I take care of some business I had to take care of.' A few hours later, I went to tell her I was sorry, and that we'd get out of there right away and go to California. But I started feeling a sense of panic, because I couldn't find her anywhere. She had left, without leaving a trace.

"She must have known how much I loved my little girl. She was so beautiful and lovable. There was no other feeling in the world that filled me with such joy as when she'd put her little arms around my neck and say, 'I love you, Daddy.' I'd read her stories and even hear her prayers, before I'd leave for the evening. I would gladly have given up my life for her.

"All these years, no matter where I've gone or what I've done, I've felt an endless aching longing to see her again. I know it will never go away. I feel as if I've lost a part of myself. There's like a lonely emptiness inside. I admit that what I did was wrong. But what she did was worse. She was supposed to be the Christian, not me. Was that one mistake so unforgivable that she had to punish me by taking from me the sweet little girl who I loved so much? I thought Catholics were supposed to forgive and forget." He looked at Mary as if he were waiting for an answer.

Mary thought for a minute, not quite sure what to say. Then he asked her outright. "What are your thoughts about what I've said, Mary?"

Mary answered slowly, "Well, in the first place, you've made me feel very sorry for you, that you had such an unhappy childhood, and even sorrier that you can't find your daughter." Then she stopped speaking and looked at him, not quite sure she should say any more.

Almost as if he knew why she hesitated, he said, "Go ahead, Mary, say the rest of what you're thinking."

"I hesitate to say what I'm thinking because I do think you've paid a terribly high price for your mistake. But probably because I'm a Catholic woman, I can't help feeling very sorry for your wife too, because I can also see her side of it."

"What is her side of it, Mary? Maybe if you could help me to understand why she did it, I could stop hating her so, for taking from me the one thing in the whole world I loved the most."

"Well, in the first place, I never met your wife, so what I'm thinking, might not be right at all. But listening to what you've said about your wife makes me think that she must have loved you very much to be able to put up with that kind of a life for so long. Like you say, you kept promising her that you would give it all up. And I guess everybody sees things differently. Like, to you, going with that woman didn't mean anything. Well, maybe I'm just too sentimental, but to me it would be the worst thing of all if my husband went to bed with another woman. I'm afraid the bond of trust would be broken forever. I would never be able to trust him again. And maybe I'm too suspicious, but I would always wonder if it had happened before. Even though I might want to believe him when he said it never happened before, and it would never happen again. I just don't think I'd be able to. And I think you can forgive somebody, but still not feel as if you can trust them again. You can also forgive somebody, but still find it very hard to forget. Even though you may want to. Like I said, I don't know your wife at all, so I can only guess at what she might have felt. For instance, she was also human. Maybe what you did was the final straw. Like, you know it never happened before. But maybe, especially since you had your own room, she thought it did happen before, and that it probably would happen again. In fact, under the circumstances, she might very likely have assumed that woman was your mistress. Maybe, at that moment, she gave up believing that you'd ever change. Maybe she thought it was a hopeless situation, and she couldn't live that way anymore. Perhaps she didn't take your daughter away from you to hurt you, but to protect her. She, who loved her also, wanted what was best for her, and didn't want her growing up in such a questionable environment." She smiled at him as she said, "You are very nice looking, so she most likely would have thought that you would have gotten married again, and had more children to take her place. While, if she stayed in the Catholic faith, she wouldn't have been able to remarry and have more children. Maybe she was also afraid that if you found her, that you might take your daughter away from her. So she could have justified it by believing there was no other way."

"I never thought of it quite that way, Mary, but listening to you now and thinking back about the way things used to be, maybe you're right. That is a very likely possibility, even though I hate to admit it, maybe she was, in her own gentle way, pleading with me to leave, but I chose not to listen to her."

His face looked sad as he said, "I'd give anything if I could go back and relive those days over again. Why is it that we don't realize what we have until it's too late?"

Mary listened attentively as he continued explaining. "After my wife left, for a while I even used to pray that God would protect my little girl and bring her back to me. But nothing happened. Then I even tried bargaining with Him. If you bring her back to me, I'll stop gambling and I'll go to church on Sunday. Still nothing happened. So I figured if there is a God, then He's ignoring the prayers of people like me. You know, Mary, I think it's much easier for some people to believe in God than it is for others. Maybe if I was born into a good Christian home to loving parents, I'd believe, too. Some people's lives are so calm and peaceful. They work at a respectable job and have a nice comfortable home and automobile. They go on vacations and have plenty of money, so that they don't ever have to worry about doing without. Oh, I'm sure they have some problems and disappointments, but no major catastrophes. Then they go to church on Sunday and thank God for all the good things in their lives. And it certainly appears that God does take care of them. But I just can't help the questions that arise in my mind. If there is a God who knows everything, then why did He give me to a mother who would run out on me when I was only eight years old? Why didn't He give me to somebody like that nice church lady? And if this God is so kind and loving as Jesus portrayed Him to be, then why does He allow such human suffering of so many innocent people?

"You see, Mary, what that teacher did for me was to give me an instant escape from an otherwise unbearable existence, and also the hope that someday I could escape it. But the more I read, the more I begin to see the injustices, not only here, but also throughout the whole world, and just how wide that gulf really is between the haves and have-nots. From my observations it seems to me, for the most part, that rich people are just surrounded by other rich people, that they go to church with and socialize with. The plight of the poor, hungry and homeless people are the furthest thing from their minds. Like when I was young and was on the outside looking in. Those people were hearing the same thing I was, but it wasn't even penetrating their minds, because they just didn't want it to. A lot of those people were 'born with a silver spoon in their mouth.'

"I think a lot of Christians just pick and choose what they want to believe. And what it's convenient for them to hear. Some of them go to their church on Sunday and give a small token gift. I call it conscience money. But unfortunately, their consciences aren't very big. Then they figure they've done their duty for the week, and they go back to their fancy mansions. They just live in a different world.

"I see men with diamond stickpins pass by the poor, cold, hungry beggars in the street, looking through them. Not even acknowledging that they're there. Then they spend thousands and thousands of dollars to enjoy the best of everything for them and theirs. I guess I have a hard time understanding how they can call themselves Christians and justify it. Some of them are just plain hypocrites, who would sooner sit there in their high and mighty ivory towers, looking down their blue-blooded noses at the poor, downtrodden people who, in my opinion, are better than they are. It's easy for someone to say they wouldn't do this or that when they're living in the lap of luxury. But in my life I've known a lot of people who have fallen on hard times. And I've known women who have turned to prostitution just to feed their families. I couldn't help thinking that maybe if those people at the top of the totem pole really believed in the words of the Bible, like they professed to, and really wanted to save souls, why don't they just sell some of those fancy possessions and really help the people in need? As far as I'm concerned, that makes them partly guilty. It's so plain to me that some people have to suffer so much extra pain unnecessarily, just because of other people's greed.

"As I look at rich people, I can't help thinking that they have the power to alleviate so much extra, unnecessary heartache and pain, for so many of their fellow men, women and especially children. If they profess to be Christians, as far as I'm concerned, there's just no excuse for it. From what I've seen most of my life, many so-called Christians just don't give a damn. They, with their fancy words and manners, choose to ignore the heartache and degradation of the less fortunate, who in many cases are forced to live in a dog eat dog hell-hole existence." His face looked hardened and angry, like Mary had never seen it before. It was almost as if the injustices he had witnessed were at that moment passing before his eyes. "I could go on and on, Mary, but I'm afraid I'd only depress you."

Why was he telling her all this? Was it the idealism he saw within her? An idealism that he truly believed he would have practiced more often if fate had only dealt him a better hand? Or was it that he had finally found a sympathetic listener who he believed he could trust to understand, and not judge, so he would be able to unleash all the anger, frustration and resentment that he had for so many years kept bottled up so very deep within him? Or was it that he had given up hope of ever finding his daughter, and Mary's reminding him of his daughter made him feel close to her, so that he could pretend for a few minutes, that this was she, and he was explaining why he couldn't be with her before? Or maybe it was a combination of all of these things together. But now that his mental flood gates were open, he couldn't stop telling her his story, anymore than he could stop breathing.

He continued speaking, "I admit that I'm a sinner, and I'm ashamed to say that there have been times that I've been a hypocrite, too. But all in all, I think I'm better than some of the self-proclaimed Christians that I've met, with their judgementalism and double standards. As you might have already detected, Mary, I'm a little cynical. Maybe it's just because I've seen too much of the darker side of life to be able to fully believe in God. Don't get me wrong, Mary. I can understand people living in nice homes and having good food and clothes and, yes, even having a summer home. But spending thousands and thousands, and even millions, for all kinds of expensive, extravagant excesses while people, especially little children, are sick and cold and hungry, makes me angry. How do they justify it, is what I'd like to know? It bothers me, and I'm not even a Christian.

" 'Thou shalt love thy neighbor as thyself.' 'Therefore all that you wish men to do to you, even so do you also to them; for this is the Law and the Prophets.' The Golden Rule. Now I ask you, Mary, if they really loved their neighbors as much as they loved themselves, would they live in mansions of gold and marble, and have fancy paintings and silver platters and imported china? Would they wear expensive furs and fancy silks and satins and imported laces? Would they wear diamonds and pearls and gold and silver jewelry? And have at their disposal all kinds of money in the bank? While their neighbor was cold and hungry, living in squalor, with overwhelming heartaches? Do you really believe that if things were reversed, and they were the ones in need, that they wouldn't mind being on the receiving end of their disgraceful, shoddy, neighborly assistance?

"So I ask you Mary, who is more of a Christian, the person who claims to be a Christian, yet lives in the lap of luxury and doesn't put the Bible words into practice, or the person like me, who is honest enough to say he has a hard time believing, but nevertheless, just as a sense of decency, tries to follow the Golden Rule? If there is a God, then He will realize that I'm just being honest in saying I have a hard time believing. I did find some comfort in reading about St. Thomas, though. Jesus forgave his disbelief and Thomas certainly had more reason to believe than I do.

"Does it surprise you, Mary, that I can quote parts of the Bible word for word?" And not waiting for her to answer, he continued, "Well, the Christmas right before I left, that kind church lady I told you about, gave me a copy of the New Testament of the Bible. She wrote a little note with it and told me it would explain the true meaning of Christmas and why we celebrate it. I set it aside, figuring some day I'd read it. When I left, it was the only book I owned, so I read it on and off on my way to California. I thought it was very interesting. But while I admired Jesus and his apostles, it also aroused a lot of questions within me. When I got to California, there was so much to do and see that I set it aside with the few things I took that were Pa's. I was so busy that I didn't even think about it or notice it again until I was packing to come back to New York City. So I decided since I was that much older, I'd read it again on my way back and see if it would have a greater meaning to me than it had before. But I'm afraid with all the things I had already read, and the injustices I had witnessed first hand, that I was already a little too cynical of life.

"As far as I can see, in most cases it's the rich people who run this country and make the rules in favor of themselves. Some of them are worse than thieves, because they're already rich. But instead of trying to help the poor, they do the opposite, and end up getting richer from the sweat and blood of the poor. That's what I've seen time and again. To me, they're legal blood-sucking leeches." At that moment he became aware of the anger within him. His voice mellowed. "I'm very sorry, Mary. I shouldn't be taking my anger and resentment toward hypocrites out on you." He smiled as he said, "You're too good a listener. I had no intention of telling you all this."

"I've made a lot of money, but I've used most of it to help a lot of people. I don't mean to sound as if I'm bragging, but more as an explanation.

"I give a lot of money to the 'Little Sisters of the Poor' and 'The Salvation Army'. And the orphanages. To me they are the true Christians. Jesus said that God is kind and merciful, so if there is a God, maybe He'll understand and take the good that I have done into consideration.

"You're pretty quiet, Mary. What do you think about what I've been saying?"

"Well, you wouldn't want me to leave you with the impression that I agree with you when I don't, would you?"

"No, Mary, you know I wouldn't."

"Well, I think in the first place, you're a little too hard on Christians. Most of the Christians I've known have been hard working and generous people. And I could be wrong, but you sound as if you're a little mad at God. And that your belief or disbelief in God mainly depends upon what God does or doesn't do for you, personally. For instance, it sounds like if I had been your daughter, or if you find your daughter, you'll believe again. But if not, you won't believe. So you're blaming God for the things that people do, or fail to do."

He thought for a moment and then answered, "I never quite thought of it that way, Mary. But maybe you're right. And you're probably thinking, but too nice to say, that if I'd left gambling and never went with that woman, that my wife wouldn't have left me. So I'm blaming God for something that's my own fault."

Mary quickly answered. "No, I really didn't think that. In fact, what I couldn't help thinking of is some of the things I've heard my mother and aunts say.

"My Aunt Mary was very philosophical and if you asked her the question about why God would allow your mother to run out on you, she would have said that God would not interfere with her free will. But she would also have added that it was the three women who helped you that were listening to God. She used to say life isn't fair and a lot of people aren't fair, but we can't use that as an excuse. WE have to do the best we can. She was always helping everybody, and people were always telling her their troubles. My Aunt Nan would have come to the defense of rich people and told you that a lot of rich people are very generous with their time and money. Just because they don't go around talking about it doesn't mean that good deeds aren't getting done. She would also have told you that most of their money is tied up in investments, which create jobs. And that it's only natural to protect their own families first. If their friends live in beautiful homes and are all dressed up, they can't very well appear in rags. I know that's what she'd tell you because she and my Aunt Mary had this same discussion years ago."

"What else did you think, Mary?" He asked.

"Well," she laughed, "I think I've said enough."

"No, go ahead and say what you're thinking. I think you're very understanding for somebody so young. I'd like to hear everything you thought of when I was talking. Don't worry about hurting my feelings."

"Well, I certainly can understand your point of view. But when you were talking about being cold and hungry as a paperboy, it wouldn't have even dawned upon me that the paperboy was hungry. When we Catholics go to Mass on Sunday morning, in order to go to Communion, we haven't eaten or drank anything, not even water, since midnight. So you might say we're all hungry.

"I have such a wonderful mother, and I've known so many wonderful mothers that I couldn't possibly understand how a mother could leave her child. I certainly can understand how you'd love your Pa even though he drank, because my Pa's like that too, and I really love him. But when your Ma left, she might have thought that your Pa would take good care of you. It just doesn't seem like you should blame her because your Pa couldn't accept it."

"Mary, did anybody ever tell you that you'd make a good

lawyer?"

Mary answered his question with an explanation. "I guess I can just see all different points of view."

"You believe in God, don't you, Mary?"

"Yes, I definitely believe in God," she answered emphatically.

"Why?" he questioned.

Mary pondered momentarily and then said, "I believe mainly because of all the things I've learned at church and in school, and from my mother, aunts and other people. And in the many books I've had the opportunity to read. And I'm glad I believe, because I know that when I die I'm going to go to Heaven. And I'm going to see Jesus and our Blessed Mother, and all the people I love who will already be there. And knowing and believing keeps me happy and gives me much more of a meaning to life.

"My Aunt Nan read a whole set of cyclopedias and many books about the universe, science and even doctor's medical books. She said that even if she had never heard of the Bible, that with all the evidence she's come across, that her intellect would force her to believe in a Master Designer, because everything is in such order. Especially the detail of the human body, which she considers the greatest machine ever invented. She is very smart and has a fantastic memory. She said the evidence to prove the existence of God is overwhelming, and she is convinced that the people who disbelieve in God are not aware of all the evidence that proves God's existence beyond a shadow of a doubt. She used to point out that Jesus said, 'If you seek me you shall surely find me.' So if some choose not to seek Him, how can they expect to find Him or to understand? By the way, what time is it?"

He took out his timepiece. "It's three o'clock already."

Mary said, "I'm expecting a phone call around four, so I really better get going."

"I suppose now, Mary, that you know the truth, you won't be

going riding with me anymore."

"Well, no, but not for that reason. You see, I met a very nice young man a few weeks ago and he wants me to go out with him on Sunday afternoons. But I told him there was something I had to do this Sunday afternoon. That was one of the reasons I was so happy to see you yesterday. Molly's been sick and I was going to tell you that we wouldn't meet you today. But we realized that we didn't even know where to get in touch with you. In fact, we even looked in the phone book, but there were no Packards listed." She glanced over at him and smiled.

He smiled back as he asked, "Mary, do you know what kind of a automobile this is?" She shook her head, no. "It's a Packard." They both laughed.

Then Mary continued. "Then when I saw you yesterday, I thought, this is perfect. I'll tell you that we wouldn't meet you today. But after that cold shoulder of yours, well, what can I say?" She felt a little embarrassed for her lack of control as her face reddened slightly as she smiled at him.

"You know, Mary, I really wish you were my daughter. I like to think that my daughter really did grow up into a sweet young lady like you."

He started the automobile and brought her back to the Prospect Park entrance.

Before she got out, she turned to him and said, "You're very nice, and I'm really glad we met. I hope someday that you do find your daughter. And you don't have to worry, I'll never ever tell anyone what you told me, not even Molly." She leaned over and gave him a fast peck on the cheek, and then jumped out of the automobile. With a smile on her face, she waved and said, "Goodbye and good luck and thank you." She turned to the left to walk down the hill, as he smiled and waved and then turned the automobile to the right and drove off.

CHAPTER FIFTY-ONE

Although Kitty would have liked to get herself the better suit, she was glad to get the less expensive one so that she could put the money toward a new suit for Pa. She knew that Mama would be so happy the next morning, as they all dressed up to go to Sunday Mass at their new parish church, St. Patrick's. Seeing the scene in her eye brought a smile to her face. She'd do anything to please her mother. She felt sorry for the hard life she'd had.

Kitty was convinced that nothing would make her feel bad that day. This was a milestone in their lives. A dream come true that she and Mike had talked about years before. This was the day that the family was moving into their own home. She and Mike had finally saved enough money for the down payment. The only sad note of the day was that Mike and Pat were not there to share the joy with them. But Kitty always knew that Pat was happy and she believed that Mike was tough, and that he would survive the war and come home safe.

Kitty intended to wait until Mike came home so that he could help her pick out the house. But when she heard that this two-family house in this nice neighborhood, only a block away from the Catholic Church, was for sale to settle an estate, the price was so good that she knew Mike would want her to buy it.

Kitty had felt so disappointed when the bank wouldn't let her sign for the mortgage without a reputable co-signer. At that moment she had felt that right before her eyes, the dream that she and Mike had shared for so long was disintegrating.

Nan told John about it. He insisted that he would be delighted to co-sign. He considered it a privilege and the least he could do for a fighting service man and his hardworking family.

They had all worked hard that day, with their old neighbors helping them to move everything in. A few times, Kitty made her mother go sit down. She still wasn't completely well. While they were moving, they had Aunt Kate stay with the Harrisons.

Maggie walked into the room as Kitty sighed, "Oh, Mama isn't this house beautiful? Wait until Mike sees it! But remember, Mama, this is only the beginning. Don't forget, someday you're going to have your dream house, with the big front porch, and the white picket fence, and roses and flower beds. But Mama you must be so tired. It's been a long day. You should go to bed and get a good night's sleep. I talked to Pa and we'll all be going to morning Mass at St. Patrick's. Annie was so tired that she practically fell into bed."

Maggie replied, "Kitty, you and Mary have worked really hard today. You both must be exhausted. You're such good girls. I wish you'd let me do more to help."

Kitty answered, "I guess I'm too happy to be tired, Mama. I've dreamed of living up here in a house like this for so long that I'm too elated to be tired. This is one of the happiest days of my life."

Maggie kissed Kitty and Mary goodnight as she made the sign of the cross before each of them, while saying, "God bless you and sweet dreams," and then she went off to bed with a pleasant smile on her face.

Kitty looked over at Mary as she asked, "What about you, Mary? Are you tired?" Mary thought for a minute. "Well, I'll tell you Kitty, there were moments today, going up and down the stairs from the old house and then up and down these stairs carrying boxes and bags in and out that I actually thought that my legs were going to fall off. But even though I'm physically tired, mentally, I feel wonderful. I'm just so especially happy for you and Mama and Mike."

Kitty was still smiling as she walked over to the bay windows to take another look at the neighborhood. In a matter of seconds, her face fell. "Oh, no," she gasped, "he wouldn't. He just wouldn't. Oh, why does he always have to wet a new suit? He's impossible."

Mary jumped up and ran to the window as she asked, "What's the matter, Kitty?"

"Oh, no," she too gasped as she observed the scene that had gotten Kitty so upset.

There was Pa, as big as life itself, leaning against the lighted lamppost on the corner across the street from them and rather loudly preaching to the Protestant Church.

"Quick, Mary, pull down the shades," Kitty hurriedly ordered as she picked up the telephone.

"Hello, officer, I'd like to report that there's a man standing on the corner of Fifth and (at that moment she turned her head and her voice was inaudible and Mary couldn't hear the name of the other street) in front of the church, causing a commotion. He appears to be drunk. This is a nice, peaceful residential area and we're not used to such goings-on. Right away? Oh, thank you."

Mary stood dumbfounded as Kitty hung up the phone and whispered, "Hurry up and turn the lights out."

"Oh, Kitty, I feel like a traitor." Mary answered, as she turned out the light.

"Well, I don't. I consider it the lesser of two evils. He'll have the whole neighborhood out. Then he'll be bragging about being their new neighbor. Oh, the disgrace of it all! We'll be the ones holding our heads in shame. He doesn't even know the meaning of the word. What choice did I have? I'm not going to stand around anymore and have him humiliate Mama or any of us. Besides, he's so numb he'll never know the difference. He'll wake up in jail in the morning and not even remember how he got there."

Mary followed Kitty over to the window as they held the shade open slightly so that they could see out without being seen.

Within a few minutes, the paddy wagon pulled up and two police officers jumped off. "Come on Pops, let's go," one of them said as they tried unsuccessfully to push him toward the paddy wagon.

Pa struggled as he answered in a slurred voice, "You don't understand, I live right over there across the street." He pointed toward the house. "We just moved in upstairs today. Go ask and they'll tell ya."

One of the officers replied. "The lights are out, so they must be sleeping. We'll ask them tomorrow. Now come along peacefully."

But Pa was strong and so stubborn that he still resisted. One of the officers called the driver to help them. But even the three of them were still having a hard time pushing him toward the paddy wagon when Officer O'Brien came along. He had been walking his beat on the next block and hurried over to investigate the commotion.

Pa was still protesting as the four officers pulled and finally pushed him into the paddy wagon and it drove off down the street.

The next morning they were all getting ready for church when Pa came in the back door. Kitty was the only one in the kitchen at the time and she glanced up when she heard the door opening. She had already made up her mind to have a talk with Pa later in the day.

"Things are pretty bad when your own family calls the police on you," Pa said as he looked at Kitty, hoping that her answer would confirm his suspicions, but still optimistically hoping that he was wrong, and she would deny it.

His lack of concern aggravated Kitty. Her face was red and her voice angry. All the hurt and frustration that had been building up within her all these years came bursting forth. "Some people," she said loudly, staring him in the eye, "should realize that even though they're not ashamed of their behavior, although God knows they should be, that other people are. You might as well know it, Pa. There are some of us that are sick and tired of being ashamed and humiliated by your stupid, immature behavior. It was bad enough in South Troy. But I was hoping just moving up here would get you away from your drinking buddies and help you to change your ways. But I should have known better. If you choose to act in a disgraceful, disgusting, low class manner, parading up the street, waking hard-working, decent people from their sleep, with stupid, drunken gibbering, then be prepared to face the consequences. I've given up trying to change you."

Kitty paused for a moment to catch her breath and angrily continued, "This house belongs to Mike and me, Pa, and I've set up certain rules which will be enforced. I made a vow that from this day forward, Mama and the rest of us are going to get a good night's sleep. The front door will be locked and only certain people will have a key to it. So if you insist upon staying out late and drinking too much, you had better plan on sneaking up the alley and crawling quietly up the back stairs. And if you feel the need to preach, then look into the mirror, and quietly preach to yourself. I purposely made sure to purchase a four-bedroom house. From now on, Mama and I will be sharing the bedroom off the parlor, and you will be in the back bedroom off the kitchen. And if I have to, I will lock the door in-between the kitchen and the dining room." She heaved a deep sigh, and shot one last disgusting glance at him, as she walked out of the room.

CHAPTER FIFTY-TWO

A special happiness filled the room on that October evening as they all gathered at their new home for their usual Tuesday evening supper with Aunt Nan.

The move to North Troy and Kitty's promotion couldn't have come at a better time. Now that she was working at the Troy office, getting to and from work was much easier.

After supper, Maggie and Aunt Kate went into the living room and settled into their comfortable rocking chairs. Mary cleared the table and washed the dishes while Annie dried them. Kitty and Aunt Nan were still at the kitchen table discussing some of the things that were in the paper since they last saw each other.

Kitty mentioned, "Here's that ad I was telling you about from Saturday's paper," and she started reading it aloud softly so that Mary and Annie could hear what she was reading, but not Mama or Aunt Kate. "Are you thinking of gifts for Christmas – we mean those mothers who have boys in the trenches – you must send by November 1st to ensure a sure delivery: sweaters – socks – flannel shirts – gloves – razors – mirrors – wallets – billfolds – belts. Boughton Company on Broadway."

Kitty looked up from the paper as she asked, "What should we send, Aunt Nan?"

Aunt Nan answered, "I doubt if he needs mirrors, wallets,

billfolds or a belt, but I certainly think we should send some warm clothes. We can send sweaters, socks, flannel shirts and gloves just to be on the safe side. Winter in a bunker on a battle field over there is sure to be very cold. And I don't think there's anything worse than being cold. Except, of course, being cold in a war."

Mary spoke up, "I'm so glad you said that, because I'm knitting Mike a scarf, and it will be finished this week."

"That's good, Mary," Aunt Nan answered, "and I'll pick up a few good books and magazines to keep up his spirits. I'll also pick up some candy and gum and other goodies to eat. And if we all put on our 'thinking caps' I'm sure we could think of other things to send. So I'll talk to you through the week, Kitty, and I'll bring a couple of medium sized boxes next Tuesday so we can pack them. Then I'll take them with me to mail."

Kitty spoke up, "Did you also notice in Saturday's paper that advertisement about the second liberty loan? It mentioned that the government is paying four percent on either coupons or bonds in denominations of $50, $100, $500, $1000, $5000 or $10,000. Can you imagine some people having an extra $10,000 to invest in Liberty Bonds? Oh, to be so lucky."

Aunt Nan answered, "Yes, I notice that the bonds are payable in 25 years or at the option of the government any time after ten years. But Kitty, did you also notice that the bank will accommodate at no interest cost to the purchaser or profit to the bank any person desiring to buy a small bond and pay for it from weekly savings? While it may be nice for those people who have a lot of money, I think it will be the accumulation of all those small bonds that will help raise the needed money. Many people aren't even going to care about the interest. They are just going to sacrifice and do all they can to help our country and our American soldiers."

"By the way, Aunt Nan," Kitty exclaimed, "Have you read today's paper yet?"

"No, I haven't," Aunt Nan replied.

"Well, I thought of you right away because I know you're in favor of prohibition. It mentioned a constitutional amendment prohibition by statute prevails in Iowa at present," Kitty exclaimed.

Aunt Nan mentioned, "I've lost count of just how many states are for prohibition now. But it's interesting that you should think of me when you hear the word prohibition, because that word always reminds me of your Aunt Mary. She was always against prohibition and considered it to be very unfair. I can still remember her saying, 'Why should a small percentage of the people be able to dictate what the vast majority of the people can drink? Now if an individual drinks too much and causes a problem, then he or she should be punished accordingly. But there are a lot of good, decent, law-abiding people who just enjoy a glass of wine or a glass of beer or whatever, after an honest day's work. So why should they be punished for what those other people do?"

"Of course, I couldn't give her an answer. But I have always believed prohibition was for the greater good. Thinking of our Mary reminds me of how much I still miss her."

Almost in unison Kitty, Mary and Annie answered, "Me, too!"

"She was so special," Aunt Nan smilingly said.

"Another thing that I wanted to ask you about, Aunt Nan," Kitty said, "Have you heard about the Blessed Virgin Mary appearing to three young children in Fatima, Portugal?"

"Yes, I've been following that story since last May, when she first appeared to them on May 13th, Mary's birthday," Aunt Nan replied.

Mary and Annie were listening intently, and quietly came over and sat down at the table as Aunt Nan began explaining what had taken place.

"Lucy and her two cousins, Francisco and Jacinta, were tending sheep when they said a beautiful lady appeared to them. She told the children not to be frightened. Then she said, 'I come from Heaven. I want you to come here at this same hour on the thirteenth day of each month until October. Then I will tell you who I am and what I want.' She also told them to say the rosary every day. So on the 13th of June, she appeared to them again and although there were about 70 people there, only the children could see her. One of the things she told them that day was that Francisco and Jacinto would soon go to Heaven. During her appearance in July, Our Lady, in answer to Lucy's plea, promised that in October, she would work a great public miracle so that all might see and know who she was. So of course the story of the apparitions spread rapidly, and people came from near and far. So on August the 13th when the next apparition was to take place, there were fifteen thousand people in the cova. So the mayor had the children kidnapped and placed in jail. In spite of his threats to have them burnt alive in boiling oil, the children refused to reveal the secret given to them. Fearing violence from the people, the mayor released the children the next day. Then on August 19th, our lady appeared to them near the village of Vallinkos. Then more than thirty thousand people were present in September, when she appeared to them. But then last Saturday the 13th of October, by noon 70,000 people had assembled, including a number of reporters and photographers. Many came from miles away. It had rained all the night of the 12th and the morning of the 13th. People stood in the mud and prayed the rosary. Shortly after noon, our lady arrived for her final appearance. She told the children, "I am the Lady of the Rosary. I have come to warn the faithful to amend their lives, and to ask pardon for their sins.' It had stopped raining. Then Lucy said, because she saw the Lady pointing toward the sun, she also pointed toward the sun as it appeared to her at that moment, and to everyone there, to be sort of whirling in the sky, and casting off different colored rays of red, green, blue, yellow and violet. Then, after a certain amount of time, the sun appeared to be falling toward the earth. The people were very frightened as someone hollered out, 'It's the end of the world.' Some fell on their knees to pray. Then the sun appeared to return to its normal place. The people's clothes, which had been soaking wet, were now dry. Many of the sick and crippled had been cured."

Mary said excitedly, "Imagine being one of those people who saw such an amazing phenomenon."

Annie answered, "Imagine being one of those children who saw the face of Our Blessed Mother."

They all shook their heads in agreement. Then Aunt Nan interrupted, "I do not personally believe that it was just a coincidence that the Blessed Virgin Mary chose to appear to three children in Fatima.

"Fatima was the daughter of Muhammad, who lived 600 years after Jesus. It is very likely that the town was named after her.

"The Muslims have a great devotion to the Blessed Virgin Mary, because she is the Mother of Jesus, whom they consider to be a great prophet.

"The Koran mentions Mary's Immaculate Conception and Virgin Birth.

"In fact, Muhammad wrote to his daughter Fatima, 'You will be the most Blessed lady of all women in Paradise after Mary.'"

Kitty replied, "That's interesting." Then she looked at the clock and exclaimed. "Aunt Nan, you still have another half hour before Joseph picks you up. Let's play the piano and sing. Mama and Aunt Kate just love to hear the music. It's so relaxing. And I just bought a new roller the other day."

They began playing and singing. Just as one song ended, one of them would suggest another tune. Some Kitty played by hand and other tunes came forth from the piano rollers. They sang, 'It's A Long Way To Tipperary'; 'There's A Long Long Trail Awinding'; 'Pack Up Your Troubles In Your Old Kit Bag And Smile, Smile,

Smile'; 'Keep The Home Fires Burning'; 'We Were Sailing Along On Moonlight Bay'; 'Smile Awhile You Kissed Me Sad Adieu'; 'I'm Forever Blowing Bubbles'. At one point Kitty thought of two other songs, 'Mademoiselle From Armiter' and the tune that so many people were singing those days that captured the American Spirit. George M. Cohan's immortal words, 'Over There, Over There, Send The Word Send The Word Over There, That The Yanks Are Coming, The Yanks Are Coming, The Drum Drum Drumming Everywhere. So Prepare, Say A Prayer, Send The Word Send The Word Over There, We'll Be Over, We're Coming Over And We Won't Come Back 'Til It's Over Over There.'

But Kitty purposely avoided those last two songs, because they reminded everyone of the war, and she definitely didn't want her Mother and Aunt Kate to be thinking of the war.

CHAPTER FIFTY-THREE

The people of Troy, as well as people all over the country, helped to support the war effort by donating countless hours of their time. Some worked for groups like the Salvation Army, the Red Cross, church societies, the Home Defense League, the Home Garden Project and the Women's Soldiers' Welfare League. They rolled bandages, provided care packages, did many of the jobs that the servicemen had previously done. They worked in factories and some even drove trucks.

A number of nurses at the Troy Samaritan Hospital went into service with the Red Cross and served overseas. In 1917, women in New York State were finally given the right to vote.

On January 10, 1918, Jeannette Rankin introduced a Suffrage Amendment in the United States House of Representatives. The women anticipated that the vote would be very close. One Congressman was carried in on a stretcher to vote in favor of the amendment. A New York Congressman whose Suffragist wife was on her deathbed left her side to vote, "Yes." The final total was 274 in favor and 136 against – exactly one vote more than the required two-thirds. The women had finally won a small victory but knew all too well the greater task that was before them, which was to accomplish the same victory in the United States Senate.

War continued to dominate the news. South End Ferry carried

thousands from Troy to their jobs at the Watervliet Arsenal. In April, the Troy music hall hosted the nation's first Liberty Loan Event to raise World War I bonds.

By May 25th, nearly six thousand Troy women registered to vote.

The summer flew by as Mary and Jim continued to draw closer and closer, and finally even days went by when Mary didn't think of Jack at all.

In September, Johnny Evers wrote home from France, stating that baseball would be continued in France until near the holidays. He mentioned that he had visited some of the hospitals and had seen a lot of our boys and that they were cheerful. He wrote that he considered himself a patriotic American, but after seeing those fellows and talking with them, we are lucky to call ourselves Americans, "They are the salt of the earth and nothing that any of us can do is half good enough for them." He was trying to get up a team to play games in different rest camps and concentration camps.

Babe Ruth, in hitting eleven home runs helped, the Red Sox win the World Series.

By October 9, the Spanish Influenza epidemic had become such a problem that Albany health authorities gave the orders to close theaters, schools and public gatherings. By October 10th, one thousand Spanish Influenza cases were reported in Troy.

Then finally on November 11th, 1918, the front page of the Troy Times read, "Troy, New York, Monday Evening, November 11, 1918. In big bold print, The greatest war in history ends. Last hours of the mighty combat. After one thousand five hundred and sixty-seven days, the greatest war in history ended this morning at six o'clock Washington time. Announcement of the tremendous event was made at the State Department at the Capitol at 2:45 o'clock this morning. And in a few seconds was flashed throughout the continent by the Associated Press. At five o'clock Paris time the signatures of the German delegates were affixed to the document which blasted forever the dreams which embroiled the world in a struggle which has cost at the very lowest estimate 10,000,000 lives. The long-awaited dawn of peace."

Washington, November 11th: "President Wilson issued a formal proclamation at ten o'clock this morning announcing that the armistice with Germany had been signed. The proclamation follows: "My fellow countrymen – the armistice was signed this morning. Everything for which America fought has been accomplished. It will now be our fortunate duty to assist by example, by sober, friendly counsel and by material aid in the establishment of a just democracy throughout the world." Signed Woodrow Wilson.

Draft calls, stopping the movement during the next five days of 252,000 men and setting aside all November calls for over 300,000 men, was also announced.

CHAPTER FIFTY-FOUR

The war was over! And people everywhere were hugging and happily dancing in the streets. And nowhere more than in New York City, where Julie was, when she heard the exciting news.

Julie had gone to New York City with her Aunt Estelle to visit her mother and see her mother's new home. She missed her mother since she moved to New York City and had been really looking forward to spending some time with her.

When they arrived, they were surprised and delighted to find that her grandmother and Aunt Barbara would also be there for the week, knowing it would be just like old times, where the main topic of conversation would be about World-Wide Women's Suffrage.

As far back as Julie could remember, her grandmother, mother, aunts and sometimes her grandfather and her uncle, Dr. James, sat around the fireplace drinking tea, and discussing the rights of women and what was happening to the cause across the country and around the world. Always, one of the main topics was the latest cases of injustices endured by innocent people, women and children. They wrote letters, attended meetings, made phone calls, and marched whenever possible.

Julie's great-grandmother attended the Female Seminary established by Emma Williard in Troy at the same time as Elizabeth Cady Stanton in 1831. Not long after hearing about the First

Women's Rights Convention in Seneca Falls, NY, in 1848, when eight men and thirty-six women signed the Declaration of Sentiments, she too became an advocate of Women's Rights and encouraged her daughter (Julie's grandmother) to follow in her footsteps.

Many times, Julie had heard the story of how her grandparents met. His parents were Quakers, from Boston, Massachusetts, who belonged to the Anti-Slavery Society. In 1860, when he was fifteen years old, they went to New York City for the annual American meeting. Being aware that Mrs. Stanton would be speaking there, Julie's grandmother, who was twelve at the time, accompanied her parents from Philadelphia to attend the meeting. Their families met and became friends. Several years later Julie's grandparents were married and had three daughters.

Estelle, the oldest, went to Emma Williard, and while in Troy, met her husband, an attorney. Marion went to Wellesley College, about twelve miles from Boston, and met Richard, an investment broker in Boston. Their youngest sister, Barbara, graduated from Elmira College in Elmira, New York, which was the first college in the United States to grant women degrees for completing work equivalent to that offered in men's colleges. After that, she met and married a Philadelphia physician, who was also greatly in favor of Women's Rights. Having come from a family of doctors, he was well aware of the uphill struggle all women physicians had endured, and had related this history of inequality to the group.

Julie was very enlightened on this subject. An article in the Boston Journal in 1850, recorded the protest against women and blacks attending medical lectures at Harvard Medical School. In 1851, Harvard's senior class presented the medical facility with a resolution against women in the medical school.

Philadelphia was home to a large Quaker community with enlightened views about women's rights. In 1850 the Women's

Medical College of Pennsylvania opened its doors in the back room of a rented house on Arch Street. Founded by several physicians and other men and women, it was the first major Medical College for women in the world.

Dr. James was a very dedicated doctor who held the opinion that if some hadn't been so narrow-minded, so many more poor men, women and children could have been helped. He admired those women doctors and pointed out the contributions to society made by them. He believed that a woman owed it not only to herself, but to her family and community, to be able to reach her full potential.

Dr. James and Aunt Barbara had a son, Mark, who was a year younger than Julie, and a daughter, Anne, who was a year older.

For years, Julie and her mother and Matt and her aunts and cousins spent the whole month of July at her grandparents' home on Long Island. They were very happy times. Julie's father arrived most weekends, many times with little gifts for her and Matt and her cousins.

Anne was born a lady who never got her hands dirty and enjoyed wearing ruffled dresses, while Julie was a regular tomboy, hopping over fences, ripping her clothes and, in most cases, outshining the boys. She was an excellent swimmer and horsewoman and had such an extreme amount of energy that they couldn't keep up with her. The only time Julie ever sat still was to play the piano, which she loved to do.

Although Julie and Anne were very in tune to the struggle of women for their rights, they disagreed on the best way of obtaining those rights.

How well she remembered Anne telling her, "Boys don't like girls who compete with them and play games better and show them up. Let the boys win. It's good for their egos. And boys don't like girls who appear aggressive, smarter, more talented than they are. They like girls who are quiet and reserved and who ask them questions and rave about how clever they are! A girl should always make a boy talk about himself, make a big fuss over him, agree with him, and hang on to his every word. And even laugh at his jokes when they aren't funny. The best thing to do is let him win most of the games. It will put him in a good mood. Then you can coax him into seeing your point of view about women's rights. Julie, you present women as a threat to men by making them feel inferior. They'll think we're all like that. What's the difference if you win a game? It's not important. Give up winning for the sake of the cause."

Julie could still remember her answer. "Well, it makes a difference to me. I'd feel like a phony hypocrite laughing at jokes I didn't think were funny. I'm going to be honest and be myself. If I had to act like a little know-nothing dumbbell for the sake of a date, I wouldn't want to go out with that kind of a boy anyway. There's already enough phonies in the world, and I refuse to be one of them. The boys can either accept me the way I am or do without me – it's their loss."

What was she supposed to do, hide her intelligent mind and keep her mouth shut because men like Roger, who she didn't respect anyway, thought that she should? She not only wouldn't, she couldn't, and still be able to live with herself. She considered herself more than fair.

Anne was in Colorado, and Julie missed seeing her this trip. And she thought Anne would have taken a smile to herself if she ever knew how Julie had twisted her own words in order to entrap Jack.

The train was pulling into Albany and a lot of people were getting ready to depart.

It wouldn't be long before she would be back in Troy with Jack. Everyone wanted her to stay longer, but she had missed Jack so much and couldn't sleep well, wondering what he was up to. She wondered if he'd remember to pick her up and if he'd be on time.

She was always early and he was usually late. And she thought, I hope he's not in one of his sullen moods again. That's the thing that annoyed her the most about Jack. She was very open and explained her feelings and gave her opinions and ideas, and sometimes Jack communicated and they had some good conversations between them that seemed to bring them closer together. But more often, Jack was in one of his moods and no matter what she said, he just wouldn't answer her. He'd just sit there, sometimes almost looking through her, and other times staring off into space, appearing to have purposely deafened his ears to her words, hiding his innermost thoughts from her. This attitude made Julie feel closed out, and she resented him for not caring about her feelings at all. She wished she could read his mind and be able to hear with her eyes, the things he did not say. But it was a waste of time even thinking of such madness. It was almost as if he were two different people, and every so often, surfaced the one who was so sweet and caring, with a beautiful enchanting smile that melted her heart. But sadly, she realized that she hadn't seen that smile lately. What should she do? Oh, what should she do? Should she confront him? Yes, she must, if for no reason than to satisfy this gnawing within her. This constantly surfacing question that demanded an answer – even the wrong answer was better than no answer.

The train arrived on time, but Jack was nowhere in sight. Julie met and started talking with two local women she recognized, trying to control her impatience with Jack. She hoped when he did come along, he wouldn't do or say anything to embarrass her. She hoped he'd at least look or say he'd missed her and at least attempt to kiss her.

Jack finally arrived twenty minutes late, making no excuse for keeping her waiting. His apparent aloofness and unconcern embarrassed her in front of these acquaintances. He not only made no attempt to kiss her or inquire about her trip, but he looked almost as if he were sorry she was back, making her feel like an unwelcome intruder.

On the way home, while Julie was giving Jack, in no uncertain terms, a piece of her mind, a man came running up the street, shouting to people in front of the bank, "Officer O'Reilly has been shot!"

CHAPTER FIFTY-FIVE

Mary sat at Jim's uncle's wake studying the faces in the never-ending line of people. She had never under one roof seen such an assortment of characters. They intermingled and represented every nationality and religion, all colors and sizes, old and young, rich and poor. Some of them hated each other. But they were all drawn to this home, on this day, at this time, to pay their respects to a man they all loved and admired. Many, with tears in their eyes, would tell the widow or Jim of some special kindness or favor the deceased had done for them or their families. And now they had set aside their petty grievances in the common bond of mourning.

Mary would find out later that the line of mourners went all the way up the street and around the corner. It reminded her of her Aunt Mary's wake, when so many different people had come to pay their last respects and related some kindness she had done for them. Mary wondered what there was about her Aunt Mary and Officer O'Reilly that caused people to act more considerate? Was it that they had both learned to tear down the barriers of prejudice and truly see not with their eyes but with their hearts?

Officer O'Reilly had been a policeman for over twenty years. The story would be told that as usual he was on patrol when he came upon a grocery store robbery in progress. The burglar was running out of the store with the owner yelling after him, "Stop, thief!"

Officer O'Reilly pulled his gun and called out, "Stop or I'll shoot." Witnesses would testify that the robber turned around and, that when Officer O'Reilly saw how young he was, he acknowledged that fact, lowered his gun, and hesitated, giving the appearance that he was about to say something. The young man appeared to be very nervous and wild eyed as he turned the gun toward the Officer and fired. Officer O'Reilly was shot in the stomach. At first it was thought that he would recover, but he took a turn for the worse and died a week later.

Mary was sitting on the end of the third row and she recognized many people she knew. As they went by her, many would nod or say hello. Some stopped briefly to say a few words. Most would reiterate how sad they personally felt about the death of Officer O'Reilly and how sorry they felt for his widow.

Mary had just finished speaking with a neighbor when she again looked over at the waiting line. Her heart skipped a beat as she recognized Jack. She had not seen him since that night, almost a year and a half ago, when he had walked her home from the dance. A rush of bittersweet memories filled her mind. She could still remember the warmth she felt just being so close to him. The tune they danced to would never leave her memory. But the longing for him, and the waiting for the call that never came, and remembering just how hard it was to cast aside all those beautiful day dreams, still filled her with sadness she could not explain.

Mary tried not to be too obvious as she observed Julie. This was the first time she had ever seen Julie in person, and she was surprised at just how outstandingly beautiful she was. The picture in the paper did not do her justice. And the clothes she was wearing added a touch of elegance to the total picture.

Julie was wearing an absolutely stunning emerald green knee-length velvet coat over a lapis blue skirt. The coat was trimmed in matching fox fur at the collar and cuffs and had a sash belt to match the skirt. A blue satin hat with a huge ostrich feather stylishly tilted to one side and a simple gold stick pin in the shape of an angel set it off perfectly.

Mary thought, "So this is the girl who caused me so much heartache?"

Jack and Julie had gone through the line, said their prayers at the kneeling bench, and were just finishing giving their condolences to Jim, his Aunt, his mother and his sisters.

Jack introduced Julie to the people sitting right in front of Mary and then their eyes met and a broad smile came upon his face as he brought Julie over to meet her.

As soon as Julie heard the name O'Neill, she immediately asked Mary if she was related to Kitty. Julie was noticeably surprised to hear that Kitty was Mary's sister. Most people were, since they didn't look anything alike.

Jack smiled again and told Mary it was nice seeing her, as she and Julie exchanged smiles, while at the same time acknowledging their pleasure in meeting each other.

It surprised Mary to realize that even after all this time, that she could still feel her heart pounding. Even Jack's voice caused deep set feelings to come forward. She looked over at Jim, standing next to his aunt. She knew she was in love with him, there was no doubt in her mind. Then why? How could she still feel this way about Jack? She wished she could understand it.

Her eyes went back to the line of mourners. She recognized quite a few of the people. Many were from St. Mary's church. She had seen them at the Sunday Mass and other church celebrations, but she didn't know their names.

St. Mary's was a huge parish. Mary was born on Sunday, May 13th, 1900, and when the cornerstone of the new church was laid just two weeks later, the parish consisted of 1350 families, with a total membership of 7,000.

Mary again glanced over toward Jim and she was surprised to see him talking to Lucky Donovan. She hadn't seen Lucky come in and she wondered if he had come in one of the other entrances. Her eyes followed him and Jim as they went into the room off the dining room, that Officer O'Reilly used as his study. To say that her curiosity was aroused was an understatement. Her mind questioned, what could he possibly want to see Jim about? She didn't think Lucky saw her. She smiled to herself as she thought of the happy memories she had of their Sunday afternoon escapades. She hadn't seen him since that day at Prospect Park, when he told her about his life. Her sense of loyalty urged her to speak to him. But how, she thought, can she speak to him without calling attention to herself?

She thought ahead and was ready five minutes later when Jim closed the door and went back to where he was standing. She quickly put her coat on the chair so that no one would take her seat, as she walked toward Lucky. She smiled warmly as she said hello. He was very surprised to see her. He turned slightly so that no one would be able to see or hear what he said.

"I appreciate you saying hello to me, Mary, but I'm concerned about your reputation." So out loud he nodded and said, "Thank you, Miss," and moved on, giving the appearance that she had helped him in some way.

Mary could hardly wait until the wake was over to ask Jim what he and Lucky had talked about. It had even crossed her mind that he could have mentioned her, but she really didn't think so. It wouldn't have mattered anyway, because she had told Jim who the man was that she and Molly had been meeting on Sundays. She had kept her promise and never told anyone what Lucky had confided to her. But at that time Jim did not know who Lucky Donovan was.

Jim related to Mary that Lucky had introduced himself to him as a friend of his Uncle's. Jim told Mary as soon as he heard the name Lucky Donovan that he remembered what Mary had told him. He said Lucky asked if he could have a few minutes of his time in private. Jim went on to explain to Mary that Lucky emphasized how much he admired and respected his uncle. "He said my Uncle Tom was always kind and helpful and that everyone he came in contact with was not only treated equally, but always with dignity. Lucky pointed out that to my uncle, the drunken bum was just as human as someone of royalty." Mary momentarily thought of her father and how nice Officer O'Reilly had been to him. "Lucky said my Uncle Tom was the best policeman he ever knew."

Jim looked at Mary. "I understand just what he was saying, because that is just what Uncle Tom was like. He always said that he truly felt sorry for everybody. That sometimes life can be very hard. He used to say he really believed, 'But for the grace of God, there go I.'"

Mary was surprised to hear Jim say that. "That's what my Aunt Mary used to say all the time," she exclaimed.

Jim said, "You know, Mary, I almost forgot the main reason he wanted to talk to me. He took me by such surprise when he offered to pay for the whole funeral. He said he would consider it an honor and no one but he and I would ever know about it."

Mary, listening intently, asked, "What did you tell him?"

Jim answered, "I told him I really appreciated his generosity and all the kind words about my uncle, but that my uncle did have enough insurance and the family would want to fulfill that obligation. But as I shook hands with him, I told him I really appreciated his thoughtfulness."

Later, when they were alone, Jim looked a little misty-eyed as he took her hand and looked into her eyes. "Remember, Mary, how I always said I wanted to be a policeman?" Mary nodded. "I always could see myself working side by side with my Uncle Tom. I always admired him so much." His voice cracked and he had to wait a few moments to go on speaking. "Uncle Tom had told me just last week that my name was now at the top of the list." He sighed. "The Police Chief called me over, and told me he wanted me to take my uncle's place." He blinked his eyes a few times, trying hard to hold back the tears as his voice cracked and without permission, two tears rolled down his cheeks.

As Mary looked at Jim she felt a great closeness to him, and realized at that moment, more than ever before, just how much she really did love him. She hugged him as tears came into her eyes, too. "Oh, Jim, just think of how proud your uncle would be to know that you took his place." They held each other close.

CHAPTER FIFTY-SIX

Officer O'Reilly was very well-liked, and it was expected that the whole city would turn out for his wake. Julie had talked Jack into going to the wake early in the afternoon to avoid the crowd. And besides, she thought Roger would more likely go in the evening, and she wanted at all cost to avoid seeing him. She could just imagine what he was saying about her after the big argument she'd had with him. But she didn't care. She felt justified.

God knows how hard she had tried, for Jack's sake, to put up with Roger's constant derogatory comments, belittling women every chance he got. He always made a fool of his wife, bossing her around as if she was his personal slave. But his wife always seemed to good-naturedly humor him and never disagreed with him. The two most common words in her vocabulary were, "Yes, dear."

Julie had tried to talk Roger's wife into joining the cause, but it was always the same answer. "Oh, I couldn't, I just couldn't." To Julie, she was a scared little child who jumped at his boisterous commands. The big bully, Julie thought, and she felt proud of herself for cutting him down to size.

The argument between Julie and Roger had all started when they were gathered at the home of friends. People were talking together in small groups. Roger was standing over to the side of the fireplace with a few of the men, making his usual jokes about the Women's

Rights movement, ridiculing the women involved with misquotes and inaccuracies. Julie knew he was talking loudly on purpose, aiming his remarks toward her.

To men like Roger, women had but three purposes. To serve her husband's every whim, be available to him at all times, and to bear his children. Julie found it very annoying the way Roger was always asking Jack, in front of others, if he had gotten his wife in the family way yet, and what was taking him so long. In comparison, for the hundredth time, it seemed, he bragged about making his wife pregnant three times in less than three years. To Roger, somehow this was some sort of proof of his manhood. But Julie suspected, in spite of all his bragging, he had purposely gotten her pregnant this time so his name would move further down the draft line, excusing him from active duty in the war.

That evening, Julie, already angered by restrictions bigoted men like Roger placed upon women, had heard just about enough, and was ready for him. She walked over and started telling him about the mistakes he had made about the Women's Rights Movement, and what she thought of his ideas. She couldn't even remember exactly what she had said. The words had just poured out of her mouth. Roger was stunned, and obviously embarrassed. For a moment she thought he was going to strike her, but she showed no sign of fear. Instead, quite loudly, with his angry blue eyes trying unsuccessfully to stare her down, he said, "Well, in the first place, I wasn't talking to you. But I would love to tell you what you are." Then looking around the room he continued, "But I wouldn't use such language in the presence of ladies. All ladies, with, of course, the exception of one, and we all know who that one is," as he said that, he looked directly at Julie.

Julie could still remember the aftershock, as dead silence, mixed with disbelief, swept over the room. No one ever spoke up to Roger. To think that a woman would have such nerve was unheard of. On the way home, she'd sensed Jack was annoyed with her, but he uttered not one word. Nor did she.

That morning, before the wake, Sally's maid had dropped off a note addressed only to Jack. Almost by accident, Julie was made aware of it. She looked at the envelope with great curiosity, wishing that she knew its contents. She held it up to the light. She could make out the first few words, "Jack, it's important that I see you." Julie turned the envelope over, but no words were visible through the other side of the envelope, as if the writing paper had been folded over so that the rest of the message was hidden inside. Those words only heightened her curiosity. Dare she open the letter? She thought, I could steam it open and read it, and then seal it up again, and no one would ever know. But a little voice within her said, "You'll know. Look what you have become. You, who always had such high principles." She put the envelope back.

On the way to the wake, Julie had purposely tried not to talk too much, to give Jack ample time to explain the contents of Sally's letter to her, but no such explanation came forth.

Before they went into the wake, Julie warned Jack ahead of time that she had things to do and had no intention of spending the whole afternoon at the wake, twiddling her thumbs. She felt as if she were being sufficiently generous, telling him that she didn't mind at all sitting there the customary length of time, while he spoke briefly to the people he knew.

Officer O'Reilly was laid out in his uniform with a contented look on his face, as if he were sleeping. Police officers to the left and the right of the coffin acted as an honor guard. Jack and Julie proceeded to convey to the widow and family their condolences. Jack introduced her to a few people he knew, and then sat her down on a chair in the parlor while he proceeded walking toward the dining room. She glanced at her watch, it was 2:15pm.

One person after another, both men and women, stopped him one by one to speak with him, until he had gone around the corner and was out of sight. She looked at her watch, it was now 2:30pm and she was ready to leave. In fact, there were so many people coming in that she felt she should give up her seat so someone else could sit for a while. She waited, and waited, and waited and, as usual when you're bored, the time dragged by.

Julie thought of all the things she had to do for the Women's Rights Movement and all the phone calls she had to make. She was anxious to get home and get started, hoping she'd still have time to practice the piano. She believed that even though Jack tolerated her involvement in the Women's Rights Movement, that deep down he thought it wasn't very important and that she was wasting her time. She also didn't think he understood that to continue being a good pianist, she had to keep practicing. Why couldn't he understand that these were things she believe in and had to do?

Almost an hour had gone by since they had arrived at the home, and she thought, I'll bet Jack is in the back room, drinking and smoking with the other men. I wish I were sitting over further so I could see the other room. I wouldn't put it past Jack to have sat me here on purpose so I couldn't see where he went and who he's talking to.

Men's camaraderie often annoyed Julie. In her view, most times it seemed to interfere and disrupt families. Men staying out at all hours of the night drinking and carrying on, in Julie's opinion, displayed inconsiderate behavior.

Julie thought about all the times she had heard one man or another bragging about how he could hold more liquor than the other. "I can drink you under the table," one man would invariably say as he challenged the other, and pigheaded pride would surface and they'd get started. She thought, how could otherwise supposedly intelligent men think that there was anything honorable or noble about drinking more than the other men, or slurring their words, and staggering around? In her view, all it proved was who was the biggest glutton in the group. She wondered how so many supposedly normal men, under the influence of such high levels of alcohol, through anger and frustration, got into fights, or went home and took it out on their wives and scared their children half to death. If indeed they got home at all before killing themselves or somebody else on the way. There were always cases of accidents reported, some tragic.

Jack finally came back. As they walked toward the door, Julie nodded in return to the people who greeted them. Out on the street on the way to their automobile, as they passed the long line and got into the car and drove away, she was still pleasantly smiling. But the minute they turned the corner and were out of sight, she started.

"What took you so long? You were gone for well over an hour."

Jack quietly answered, "Oh, it couldn't have been that long, Julie. But you did say that you didn't mind sitting there for a while."

Julie quickly retorted. "I said I didn't mind a reasonable time, but not over an hour. I've got a lot of things to do."

"I'm sorry, Julie, I guess I lost track of time. It really did only seem like twenty minutes to me."

Julie angrily answered. "Well, it seemed like hours to me, just sitting there wasting my time. I'll bet you were out in the back room drinking. I wonder if men go to wakes because a person died, or because it's just another excuse to party? Well, what did take you so long? Who were you talking to?"

Jack tried to change the subject. "Julie, don't you even care that a good man has died and left a widow?"

Julie responded, "Yes, I do feel sorry, and I paid my respects, but my sitting there for over an hour isn't going to help the deceased or the widow." She repeated her question. "So, who were you talking to? Don't tell me Roger was there."

"Yes, Julie, he was," Jack answered almost apologetically.

"And of course you couldn't have let one day go by without speaking to Roger," Julie impatiently replied.

Jack tried to explain. "Roger motioned to me to come over just as I was ready to leave. I couldn't very well ignore him in front of a room full of people."

Julie's voice was noticeably angry as she answered Jack. "Even if he were the only one there, you would have gone over to him. Did he pat you on the head? You follow him around like a little puppy dog. Well, I'm tired of playing second fiddle to Roger and I'm also tired of the disruptive control he has over our lives. And speaking of your friends, I noticed you purposely didn't mention to me about the note Sally addressed to you, only. What does she want you to do now?"

Jack calmly answered, "There wasn't anything to mention. Here, read it yourself." He took the letter out of his pocket and handed it to Julie, while not taking his eyes off the road. Julie took the letter out of the envelope and read the words. "Jack, it's very important that I see you. Signed Sally." Julie realized then that there were no hidden words, and she was glad all the more that she hadn't given into the temptation to steam the envelope open.

Julie, still noticeably annoyed, said, "Well, between Roger and Sally, I'm just about fed up. Maybe you should have paraded a group of women in front of Roger and had him pick you out a wife, since his approval is obviously so important to you. Or better yet, you should have married Sally. Then you and Sally and Roger and Elizabeth would have made a perfect foursome. Roger would do all the talking and the rest of you would just agree. I can just see you now with four heads all bobbing up and down. How harmonious."

Jack tried to appease her. "Julie, I understand that you and Roger don't see eye-to-eye on things, but Sally has always been very nice to you and always said nice thing about you. She'd like to be your friend. She's always asking me to bring you over to visit with her.

Julie, why don't we stop there for a minute on the way home? It's right on our way."

Julie answered quite angrily, "Well, it's nice for Sally and Roger that you listen to them, because you certainly don't listen to me. I just finished telling you that I have a lot of things to do, and I'm already late in starting. You have no consideration for my time at all. You kept me waiting at the station, and now again today. Besides, I really don't have anything in common with Sally. She's another one who's afraid to get involved in women's rights. Afraid that her husband and his friends wouldn't approve. I'll admit she's not quite as bad as Elizabeth, who's so submissive to Roger that it's pathetic. But Sally doesn't have much more gumption, either. But I suppose I could learn to put up with Sally. But Roger, well, that's asking too much. He's so offensive. But apparently you don't seem to see that. You would sooner think that it was me."

They had just arrived at the house. Julie got out of the automobile, slammed the door and went upstairs to change. Jack finished parking the automobile, walked into the house, and then into the library. He grabbed a bottle of Scotch. As Jack started drinking, he also started thinking. Julie had mentioned about his being late at the station. Jack started remembering what had happened to cause him to be late.

Jack had wanted so much to be on time and not get Julie riled up that he had purposely started out early. After missing her so desperately, he longed to hold her close. He was in the car and just ready to pull out when Roger came along and parked his automobile, at an angle, blocking Jack's automobile so that he could not proceed. It didn't surprise Jack that Roger did that, because he had done it before to him and others. Jack recognized years ago that it was important to Roger to always be in control of people and situations, but Jack wouldn't dare admit it to anyone, afraid it might get back to Roger. Roger was like the leader of the group, and everybody tried to please him and not get on the wrong side of him.

Roger wasted no time in telling Jack. "You know, Jack, I might as well tell you that I was very disappointed in you when you allowed your wife to embarrass me like that in front of our friends. I feel as if you let me down, not reprimanding her when she so rudely butted into the private conversation I was having with the men. I would never have allowed Elizabeth to do that to you. And don't be surprised if you're not invited to our friends' houses. After your wife's unprovoked verbal attack on me, our friends are beginning to think that she's a fanatic. As your friend, Jack, I think I should also tell you that the men are starting to talk behind your back about the way your wife dominates you. They're beginning to laugh and crack jokes. They call her 'her highness.' I've tried to defend you. But frankly, Jack, I don't understand, either, how you can stand by and be dominated by a woman. Where's your self-respect?" Not waiting for an answer, Roger rushed on. "We've been friends for years and I'd hate to see our friendship end because of your wife's bad behavior."

Jack felt annoyed at Julie. "I'm sorry, Roger." Jack knew from experience that to say to Roger he was sorry not only helped calm him down a little, but it would appease him also, to make him believe that he agreed with him. Then Roger had gone on and on talking about trifles. Under the circumstances, Jack hated to interrupt him. Finally, Roger told him he had to go, and Jack was relieved that he didn't have to say where he was going. He didn't want to mention Julie's name and get Roger started again. He knew he'd be late and tried to think of some excuse on the way over, but nothing came to him.

Jack couldn't hide his disappointment when he saw Julie talking to the two women. He wanted so much to take her in his arms, hold her close, kiss her, and tell her how much he had missed her. But her greeting was so cold that if she ever turned away from him, he would have felt humiliated, especially in front of the men he knew standing by the wall, watching them. And he thought, was it just because he was late, or did she loathe coming back home to him? But why should she, he questioned, when he had stood on his head trying so hard to please her, even to the point of losing all his friends, and what little self-respect he had left?

Why did Julie expect so much from him? He thought of Elizabeth and Sally and all his friends' wives, and how respectful, kind, and loving they were to their husbands, always trying to please them. Why couldn't Julie be more like them? He was tired of her childish display of jealousies, and her unreasonable temperament. He always listened to her telling him about her feelings and her disappointments, well what about his? He had tried to please her and never interfered with her involvement in the Women's Rights Movement. Not even once had he ever placed unreasonable demands on her. He had been more than fair. Her demanding attitude annoyed him. It bothered him to realize that the men were laughing behind his back. And it bothered him terribly that Julie had argued with Roger in front of everyone. As he kept drinking, all the pent up anger and frustration he had bottled up and held down for so long started little by little surfacing.

While Julie was upstairs changing her clothes, she started thinking of the group that had gathered at her mother's house to talk about how to further their cause. She thought, why couldn't Jack be more like some of the husbands in the group, who actually shared in the dreams of the women for their rights by marching with them and making phone calls and helping with their moral support? But it seemed the opposite was happening with her and Jack, and that the gap was widening between what was expected of her as Jack's wife, and what she wanted for herself. Maybe their views on marriage were just too far apart.

She wanted a husband, a partner who cared and who would share his dreams and his innermost thoughts and feelings. A husband who cared not only about her body, but respected her mind, as well, who would put his wife on an equal level with himself and not expect her to be what he or his friends wanted her to be.

Maybe she shouldn't have married him. Maybe they just weren't right for each other. He was so moody and unresponsive and this was a constant annoyance. She wished she could understand what it was about Jack that still drew her to him, like a magnet. She knew it went beyond looks. It was something within him that surfaced momentarily, every so often, when things were going well between them, and she believed with all her heart that without Roger's influence, this would happen more often, and Jack would be more understanding and sympathetic, and that they could make a go of it.

Right then, Jack's words surfaced in her mind, "I understand that you and Roger don't see eye-to-eye on things." And Julie thought, He certainly couldn't think Roger was justified in what he did. And all of a sudden it seemed important to her to find out what Jack did think about the situation, and make him understand how she felt.

As Julie walked into the library, she could smell the liquor on Jack's breath and realized he had been drinking heavily. But she chose to ignore it for the present.

"Jack, I want to talk to you about something. It's about what you said about Roger and me not seeing eye-to-eye on things. You certainly couldn't think it's my fault. You certainly must realize how obnoxious Roger is, when it's so obvious." At first Jack didn't answer her, but just stared. This silent response always irked Julie. Her words hadn't even penetrated his mind. She proceeded. "I wish I had known that you were so moody and aloof and uncaring. I wish I could have seen that side of you sooner."

Finally Jack answered her angrily. "All right, Julie, do you really want to know what I think?" He looked at her through his angry squinted eyes. "I think you should have realized that that's just

Roger's way, and you should have ignored him. No harm was done."

That's all he had to say. It was bad enough that he hadn't stuck up for her. Julie was very aggravated. "I should have known that you'd take Roger's part. Well, for your information, I did ignore him the first few times. You must have been deaf and blind not to realize that he kept constantly bringing it up and glancing over toward me. And you don't think there's any harm done? Well, let me set you straight. If it wasn't for people like Roger, we'd already have our justifiable rights. People like Roger sway other people against us with their half-truths and out and out lies. If I didn't say anything, it would have left the impression that he was right. I had to say something, because too many people have worked too hard for too many years to allow somebody like Roger to peddle his prejudiced garbage. I owe it to them to expose bigots like Roger. It's a question of loyalty. But apparently you wouldn't understand that."

Jack had moved toward the liquor to take another mouthful. "That's it, drink some more and get drunk so you don't have to face reality." But the liquor fortified his feeble courage. He went over toward her, and held her wrists, just trying to explain, that if she hated Roger so much, she could have told him what she thought of him when they were alone, instead of making such a commotion in front of everyone. But Julie wasn't listening. She was trying to tell Jack that he didn't even care that his so-called best friend insulted his wife in front of everybody. Then Julie got even angrier that Jack was holding her wrists too tight. She felt frustrated and completely lost control. She quickly twisted her wrists back and forth till she got one hand free and dug her nails into his other hand, drawing blood, with the only regret that her nails were not as sharp as she'd have liked. Because of her piano playing she had to keep them trimmed. Then, with her right hand, she slapped him in the face as hard as she could as she said, "Don't ever do that to me again." She assaulted him with her words. "Why, instead of defending Roger, you should be defending me. He implied in front of a room full of people that your wife was not a lady. And you let him get away with it. What gallantry! I should never have married you. And I wouldn't have if I had known that you didn't have the backbone to stand up to the likes of Roger. How can I love a man I don't respect? And how can I respect a lily-livered jelly-fish?"

Julie didn't care about what Roger or the other people thought, because she considered them unfair. But she was just so disappointed and upset with Jack that he hadn't even tried to understand her point of view, that she wanted to hurt him. The madder she got, the louder her voice started to get. Jack already felt so low, without her embarrassing him in front of the servants, too, so he tried to calm her down. He softly said, "Julie, the servants and the neighbors will hear."

Even louder Julie said, "I don't care who hears me. But you just don't want people to realize what a louse you really are." At that moment came the full realization of his concern for everybody but her. Such anger rose up from within her that her mouth quivered, her jowls shook and her eyes seethed. She could not contain herself. She completely lost control and shouted at him, "Damn the neighbors. Damn the servants. And damn damn damn you!" How dare he tell her what to do, when it was all his fault. All of a sudden her eyes caught upon her wedding ring and she thought, this marriage is a farce and a mockery. She ripped the ring off of her finger and flung it across the room at him, hoping it would mar his handsome face.

All while Julie had been talking, Jack had been drinking, hoping to dull his senses from this latest hateful barrage. But instead, it encouraged those feelings that were now just below the surface to come forward. It made him even angrier to realize that while he's been fair to her, she doesn't even care about the embarrassment she had caused him. The ring flew at him was the final straw. His eyes were hostile as he staggered across the room to her, rage bubbling in his blood. She noticed the imprint of her hand was still outlined in white upon his face reddened with anger. She was not prepared for the torrent of words that poured from his mouth, his fiery hot eyes flashing.

"I'm tired of it, Julie. I don't give a damn anymore! Your complaints, your suspicions, your jealousies are choking me! Enough is enough! No matter what I do, it's wrong. I can't take it anymore. I've got to get out of here!"

Julie shouted, "That's it, run away! That's what you always do. Why don't you go to Sally and let her soothe your ego? She can tell you how right you are and what an unreasonable wife you have!"

Jack replied, "I'm not going there." Then he stopped and thought for a moment and said, "On second thought, maybe I will go there. Even with two kids, it's a lot more peaceful than it is around here."

"Well, don't be surprised if I also find somebody to listen to my side of things. And about the wake today, too bad it wasn't you! Then I'd be free to go on with my life!" The minute she said that, she was sorry, but she didn't think he heard her anyway as she heard the door slam. Julie's stomach was tied up in knots and she felt drained from all these unleashed emotions. Then she thought of her ring and started looking all over the carpet for it, trying to figure out where it would have landed when it bounced off Jack. She finally found it under the chair, and put it back on her finger.

Julie started thinking again, trying to second-guess Jack. Would he have gone to Sally's, or to Roger's to tell him he was right about her? Or would he have gone to the club, or dropped into a bar someplace? Perhaps, she thought, he was just driving around to cool off, or could he be going off to see some woman that she may or may not know? Sometimes she was sure he was seeing someone else, and other times she was just as sure he wasn't.

Normally, she wouldn't have thought that Jack was that kind, but after the shock she had received about her own father, who she could never have believed could be like that, she didn't completely trust any man. She came to the conclusion that Jack would come home late that night.

Julie tried to figure out what she should do. Maybe she should stay overnight at her aunt's house and cause Jack to worry a little about her and her reaction to him. She decided to at least go out for a walk to clear her mind, so she could think better. Almost without realizing it, she found herself across the street from Sally's house. Jack's automobile was nowhere in sight. She went home to read a book and wait for him.

Jack didn't come home that night, or the next night, or the next.

CHAPTER FIFTY-SEVEN

Nan Fogarty was awakened abruptly, startled at the sound that invaded the otherwise silent night. Through her tired, squinted eyes, she could see by the clock on the stand next to her bed that it was 2am Sunday morning. She could feel the chill of the night air as she left her warm bed and reached for the warm comfortable burgundy robe that Victoria had given to her last Christmas. As she stepped into her slippers and opened the door, the light from the hall cast shadows on the walls. Her slippers flipped up and down as she went in search of this unexplained sound. Gail had given her the slippers to match her robe, and although Nan only took a size 5½ slipper, she knew that these being too big for her, must be a size 6. She suspected the salesman probably told Gail there wasn't much difference between a 5½ and a 6, and Gail would have been much too shy to contradict him.

It had sounded like an automobile backfiring. Perhaps it was someone driving home from the Morgan party, she thought. Every year, the Morgans had a party the Saturday after Thanksgiving, to welcome in the Christmas season. Or perhaps the noise was caused by some stranger passing by, she thought.

Although Nan believed in modern inventions, she was annoyed that there were no restrictions placed upon automobiles or their drivers. And she thought it was ludicrous to allow just anybody to drive an automobile without any formal training. From her own personal observation, little children took better care of their toys than some men took care of their automobiles.

This was not the first time she had been taken from a warm bed in the middle of the night. John was a great believer in hospitality. Through his eyes, not to open your house and even your purse to someone in need was the greatest sin of all, and he carried this belief to such a point that Nan thought that through the years, there were those who took advantage of his good nature.

When someone's automobile broke down or they were out of gas, John would have her make coffee and Joseph help take care of the automobile while the people were invited in from the cold, to warm themselves by the fireplace, and always to make themselves at home. John had always been so good to her that she tried to accommodate him. But now, since the years had robbed her of the stamina she once enjoyed, she was beginning to really mind what she considered thoughtless people's selfish intrusions. Some of them had no consideration at all for other people's sleep needs. Many of them, on top of that, smelled of alcohol and cigars, which both nauseated her, especially in the middle of the night.

Nan had a practical, sober outlook on drinking. She didn't believe in it. She had seen too many men staggering and slurring their words. Some of them were so incoherent, they barely knew their own names. She wished they could see themselves as she and others saw them, as disgraceful, immature, and lacking in self-control. She really believed that everything would be a lot better for everyone without alcohol. Men like her brother-in-law would be better husbands and fathers. She thought of how hard it had been for Maggie, raising a family with him staggering in drunk so often, wasting money on alcohol that was needed for food for his children.

Nan thought of her own mother, widowed at thirty years old. She was only seven years old at the time, but she remembered her father as a kind, happy man who was good to his family, and she never wanted to dishonor his memory by telling anyone, even her sisters, that she had found out years later, that when he had been killed being pulled by his own team of horses, that he had been drinking. She always wondered, if he hadn't been drinking, would that have happened, or being under the influence, had he misjudged, causing his own death? How hard it had been for her own dear mother, to have to leave her children with neighbors every day, while she worked from dawn to dusk for that mean, demanding old lady. How much easier it would have been for all of them if that accident had never taken place. She didn't believe, as some people did, that a person's time was up and it was in God's plan that he or she die at that particular time. She believed instead that these people, misusing their own free will, had tempted fate and consequently lost, and had they lived longer, would have been there for the people who needed them.

Nan really wanted to join the Women's Temperance League at St. Joseph's Church, but how could she? Wouldn't it be an embarrassment for John, when he ran the local brewery? And could he easily go into another business? She had to think of Victoria's, Jack's and Gail's future. They had to have some means of support. She didn't want them to be at the mercy of the old lady. She felt torn between conflicting loyalties. She really believed that since some of these people that drank obviously didn't have the self-control they needed *not* to drink, then society should help do it for them by removing the temptation.

Nan got to the door of Jack's room, the light was sneaking in. "Jack, Jack," she called softly. Within seconds Joseph stood before her. When she saw the pain in his face, as his eyes filled with tears, a terrible lost feeling of fear crept through her body. "What is it?" she cried impatiently.

"It's Jack," he stammered, almost choking on the words. "He shot himself."

The words echoed in her mind, which rejected this thought she did not want to hear. "No, no, let me by, Jack needs me," instinctively ready to go to him, as she had done so often, when he was a child.

His hands were like steel bands upon her wrists as he held her at bay before him. "It's too late." He said softly, still trying to resign himself to this new grief he felt.

Nan's mind tried to digest this unwelcome information. "But what would Jack be doing cleaning a gun at this hour?" she asked.

Joseph looked at her through eyes resigned to the facts before him. He slowly released his hands from her wrists, but still remained cautiously ready to act again if she tried to pass, wanting at all costs to keep her from seeing the horrible sight his eyes had just been forced to behold. His voice was calm as he spoke almost in a whisper, still looking into her bewildered eyes, concern for her reflected in his own. "Nan, he shot himself on purpose. He's committed suicide."

Conflicting thoughts rushed into her mind. She couldn't think straight and all of a sudden her head started pounding in rhythm with her heart.

CHAPTER FIFTY-EIGHT

It was Saturday about midnight when Jack arrived at his former home, from the Morgan's party, staggered up the outside staircase and shakily unlocked the door to his old room, retreating once again from the stealthy eyes that made him feel so cowardly, humiliated and worthless. He grabbed a bottle of scotch and poured himself a drink.

Before he could sit down or take a breath, he had to go through the same ritual that, since he was a child, he felt compelled to go through every time he entered this room. First, he looked in the closet, then behind the chairs and dressers and finally under the bed. In between, he checked several times to make sure that he had relocked the outside door. He tried to be very quiet, having no desire to talk to anyone, for he could no longer hold back the tears. Julie had embarrassed him so much by flirting with all the men at the party. The sarcastic remarks she aimed at him made him feel so low, especially when they mixed in with the derogatory comments Bill's uncle had previously uttered in front of the men.

Jack thought of all the times since he got married that he had come back to this room to retreat from Julie's nagging accusations that had left him too dejected to face other people. How glad he was that they had left his room as it was, and that he had never finished moving all his things to his new home.

Some of the men at the party were talking about Bill's death in the war. Bill's uncle insinuated that he didn't believe Jack had flat feet, but that he or his father had paid to have his papers fixed. He had known Jack all his life. Jack thought, if he didn't believe him, how many others didn't believe him, either? Behind his back, were they calling him a slacker? Was it only his imagination that some of the men seemed cool toward him? Were they beginning to see through him, the truth that he had tried so hard to hide? From now on, would he be pointed out as a coward? Bill's uncle had talked so loud and accusingly that everybody must have heard him. His remarks had cut Jack to the core.

Roger had already told him how the men were laughing behind his back about Julie. Now with what had happened tonight, how could he possibly face anybody, knowing what they were thinking? He could feel the burning pain in the pit of his stomach and the all too familiar depression sweeping over him.

He wanted so desperately to make Bill's uncle realize that Bill's death was a great loss to him, too. He was, after all, Gail's fiancé, and had always been his very best friend. But he was already feeling so sad that he was afraid that if he tried to explain, he'd break down and cry. He just couldn't do that in front of all those people.

It was only a little over a month since Bill died, but he was still feeling sad and guilty about it. Why Bill, who was always so idealistic? From the time he was young, he always wanted to be a doctor and help people. That's the kind of a person Bill was, always thinking of others. He would have been such a good doctor, too. But when the war broke out, Bill had quit school and enlisted in the medical corps, with the intention of returning to school when the war was over. He was helping a wounded soldier off the field when he was killed.

Even though Jack knew he couldn't have gone to war because of his disability, what made him feel guilty was how glad and relieved he had been when he found out. He had spent so many sleepless nights worrying about it. He knew that he was a coward, and that if he had been sent into battle, he would have been frozen with fear. He tried so hard to put on a façade, and say how bad he felt that he was unable to go to war, and how lucky the men were who could go. He could never tell anyone the truth, or how many tears he had already shed over the loss of his best friend. He knew he would never find another friend like Bill. They had always been closer than brothers. He felt that his own life was such a waste in comparison to what Bill's life would have been. And he felt so sorry for Gail, and wished there was some way he could convey to her just how sorry he was, and how much he cared.

Jack really appreciated that even though Julie didn't seem to care about him, that when she heard the news about Bill, she had been so kind and supportive to Gail when Gail obviously needed someone to cling to. As he thought of Julie, he realized that he never had told her that Bill was his very best friend, and Julie probably assumed that Roger was.

Ted was always Roger's best friend, but when Bill and Ted and so many of their other boyhood friends had left for the war, that brought him and Roger closer. Jack always felt safer around Roger. He seemed so sure of himself. How many times he wished he could have been more like that. But one thing he didn't welcome was Roger's constant criticism of Julie and his unsolicited advice on how Jack should handle her. "You're too easy with your wife. You should have put her in her place as soon as you got married and told her that you were the boss and what you expected from her. Even in the wedding vows, the woman has to promise to love, honor and obey her husband, just like it says in the Bible." All the other men had agreed.

But all Jack ever wanted was peace and quiet. He would have gone to any length to attain it. He tried to appease Roger and Julie, but had come to the realization it was impossible. Even after the big fight he'd had with Julie, he was sorry the minute it was over. He felt so sad and dejected that he had to leave the house. Nothing had been accomplished, and he had made her angrier than ever. He purposely had stayed away, trying to give her ample time to cool off, hoping she'd forgive him, so that things could be the way they used to be.

Sally must be feeling really sad, too, he thought, Bill being her only brother. And he felt guilty that he never had gotten over to see her, especially since she'd always been so kind to him. How could Julie possibly understand that Sally was always the one person he felt comfortable talking to, and that he could always completely count on her to soothe his fears? She knew he was weak and frightened, but always accepted him in spite of it.

When they were young, Sally found him crying in his room. "Jack, what's the matter?" "Now you'll tell everybody that I'm crying and they'll all laugh at me!" "No Jack, I promise I'll never tell anybody. But don't cry, everything will be okay. I'll help you." And she always did help him. She was always so kind and considerate and always listened to him and said something to make him feel better. Sometimes she stood up for him when the kids were teasing him, and other times she helped just by being there. Jack knew that if Julie would only give Sally half a chance, that she'd like her too, instead of thinking with her suspicious mind that there was more to their friendship than there was. He remembered Julie's words, "You should have married Sally," and he thought how much simpler life would have been if he and Sally could have fallen in love with each other as Bill and Gail had.

They were all brought up closer than cousins. Mrs. Van Alstyne was Bill and Sally's grandmother and his grandmother's best friend. Both were born in London, and came to America because of their husband's positions. They each had only one daughter, who were best friends to each other. Sally, Bill, Jack, and Gail always got along so well. And they all thought Edgar was a stuck-up snob.

Since Robert, Sally's husband, worked for a company based in New York City, he had been after Sally for months to move there. But since he was away on business all week, she was afraid she'd be very lonesome without her family and friends close by. Besides, she loved Troy and thought it was a great place to raise their children, while at the same time she disliked big cities so. But Sally had confided to Jack that more and more, Robert kept telling her how tired he was commuting every weekend to Troy. He had assured her that if they moved to New York City, she could take the train to Troy with the children as often as she wanted to. Lately, he had even skipped coming home altogether a few weekends. He said it was business, but she noticed even when he did come home, he wasn't as warm as he used to be to her and the children. She was beginning to wonder if he had found someone else. Jack had gone over there more than usual, trying to reassure her. Yes, it would have been so much simpler, but he and Sally never could feel that way about each other. And he wondered, what was it that made him so obsessed with Julie? As he poured himself another drink, he started thinking of when he had first met her.

He knew there was to be a party at their house that evening. He hated parties so much, and especially the small talk at dinner, that he had purposely arrived home late. Knowing dinner would be over, he thought, would make the ordeal a little less burdensome. As he opened the door he could hear the piano music resounding throughout the house and wondered who was playing the piano. He walked quietly into the living room, trying not to disturb anyone. The chairs were all lined up facing the piano, and everyone was listening intently. He stood at the back wall, observing what he considered to be one of the most breathtakingly beautiful young women he had ever seen, with an air of confidence that radiated her whole countenance. As he stood there, listening and observing, without even a word being spoken between them, he knew he was falling in love with her. Finally she stopped playing and stood up to take a bow. He moved in a little closer while she was looking around the room thanking everyone for their applause. When her eyes met his, unfamiliar feelings deep within him rushed to the surface and moments later when he touched her, he could feel the electricity pass between them. He would like to have stayed right on that spot, looking deep into her beautiful green eyes, holding her hand, but he felt himself being pulled away, as usual, by giggling young ladies vying for his attention. For the rest of the evening, as he half listened to their ceaseless chatter, he could not take his eyes off of Julie. After that first meeting, she dominated his thoughts.

Jack felt so elated a couple of days later when he entered the house to hear that same beautiful music again. Day after day, he would rush home, just on the chance that she would be there, feeling so up when she was and so down when she wasn't. He realized that she was not like the other girls he knew, so he tried to be extra patient with her, not wanting to be too forward, even though he had all he could do to control himself from reaching out and pulling her to him.

Then one day when he finally got up the nerve to ask her out, he hoped she couldn't see the dejected look on his face when she told him she already had a date for Saturday afternoon. She was the only girl who had ever turned him down. Most of the other girls changed their schedules to accommodate him, and others were always throwing all kinds of hints, practically asking him to take them out.

The first time he went out with Julie, he was sure that he wanted to make her his wife. He could feel his heart sink when she said she would probably never marry, but go on with her career. It made him feel bad to remember that Julie never did want to get married in the first place. Now she must be sorry that she had ever met him, after realizing what a coward he really was. But he hadn't always been a coward. Maybe his grandmother was right, he thought, as he started remembering his childhood.

Jack didn't like his grandmother very much because she was always hollering at his grandfather, picking on Nan, and telling Mrs. Van Alstyne belittling things about his father. Along with his mother and Gail, they were the people he loved the most. And she was always unfavorably comparing him to Edgar, who was the highest in his class. He overheard her telling Mrs. Van Alstyne, "Now Edgar takes after me and my side of the family. You know my father and grandfather were bankers and that banking's been in our family for generations. Edgar's got the brains, and mark my words, he'll go far carrying on the tradition. But it's obvious that Jack will never get anywhere. He's lazy and apparently gets his brains from his father or his grandfather. John certainly couldn't be too smart, running a brewery, of all things.

"I hope none of my friends back home ever find out that my beautiful daughter, who could have had her pick of men on both continents, would marry so far beneath her. An Irish Catholic brewery owner has to be the very bottom of the barrel. And as for my husband, you know how weak and lazy he is. He wouldn't have gotten anywhere if it hadn't been for me goading him on. He always felt sorry for people, especially the immigrants. But I told him, 'I don't feel sorry for them. They should have thought ahead, and stayed where they were, or at least not have had so many children. They certainly can't expect us to support them all.'"

But what annoyed Jack the most was the way Edgar "pulled the wool" over his grandmother's eyes. She thought he was "a model young gentleman." But to Jack, he was a snobbish, phony liar who was always mean to him, Gail, Bill, and Sally. How could Jack ever forget that when he was seven and Edgar was ten, Edgar broke his grandmother's favorite heirloom vase. She heard the crash and was so angry when she saw the broken vase. Edgar blamed it on Jack, and even though Jack denied it, she of course believed Edgar and took a horsewhip to Jack. She kept hitting him on his backside, demanding that he "tell the truth." But when he said he didn't do it, it made her even angrier. Just then his father came in and angrily said, "What is the meaning of this?" He took the whip out of her hand and broke it across his knee. It was the only time Jack ever saw his father angry. She told him what had happened and how Jack was lying. He was noticeably irritated as he asked her if she or one of the servants had seen Jack break the vase? She said no, but Edgar had said that he saw Jack do it. John told her never to strike Jack again, that if he needed to be disciplined, that he, as his father, would take care of it. Then he asked where Gail was. Gail, who had been hiding behind the door, came running into his arms, crying because she felt so bad that Jack had been hit with the horsewhip. Jack had all he could do to hold off crying himself, but he couldn't, because more than once he'd heard that "boys don't cry." After Gail said that she didn't see who broke the vase, John looked at Edgar and asked if he broke the vase, Edgar calmly looked into his father's eyes and told him that he saw Jack break the vase. Jack was so scared that he was trembling, thinking his father, too, would believe Edgar and maybe he'd be hit some more. Instead, his father patiently looked at him. "Jack, I promise I will not hit you, but please tell me the truth. Did you break the vase?" And shakily he answered in a faint voice, "No sir, I didn't do it, honest I didn't."

John disappointingly said, "Well it's obvious that one of you is lying to me, but I will not punish two people for what only one person did wrong. God knows which one of you did it, so I'll have to put it in His hands." After that incident, Jack tried to keep out of Edgar's way.

Jack's grandmother always made a big fuss over Edgar, and every summer before his grandfather's disappearance, took him to London with her. She always made Jack feel as if she didn't like him at all, and had all she could do just tolerating his presence. But he didn't care, because his grandfather more than made up for it. While his grandmother and Edgar were gone, his grandfather, every Saturday morning, would take him on fishing trips to their favorite place on Burden Lake. His grandfather would stay over at his house the night before and sleep in the room next to his. They'd get up early, and while they were getting ready, Nan would be fixing them a delicious breakfast and packing them a good lunch to take with them. Those were some of the happiest times of his life. He loved his grandfather's gentle ways, and the peace and quiet of their special place.

Jack was a very shy, sensitive child, and the two things that happened very close in time were to shake up his emotional well-being forever. The first occurred on an average warm summer Friday evening, when he had gone to bed early, happily looking forward to the next day's fishing trip with his grandfather. He was awakened in the middle of the night by the sound on the landing outside his room. When he opened his eyes and looked over at the outside stairway door, there was a man with a scarf around his face, trying to break into his room. Jack was terrified. His heart was pounding and he was shaking all over, and as he opened his mouth to scream, only a faint, breathless, hushing sound came forth. He was so paralyzed by fear that he could not even call out for help. As he felt a weak, dizzy darkness sweeping over him, in the far off distance he could hear a voice yelling, "What are you doing up there?" The man turned and ran. In a flash Nan was in his room, and he fainted.

As he came to, Nan was feeling his head and rubbing his hand and asking, "Jack, are you all right?" As his father and mother rushed into the room, his grandfather was already at the outside door, standing on the landing yelling, "Did you catch him?" A voice replied, "No, he got away."

Jack would find out the next day that Officer O'Reilly was patrolling his beat when he noticed the suspicious man on the landing and called out to him. In the days that followed, Jack would overhear many conversations, not only about what had happened, but the different opinions on why it happened and who was responsible. There were those who thought it was just a burglar robbing the house, aware that besides the usual valuables, Victoria had some very expensive jewelry her grandmother had left her. Someone else remembered that a former employee of John's, fired because he was caught stealing, had threatened to get even. It was suggested that perhaps it was someone that was aware his grandfather was staying overnight. He was after all, in the next room. Maybe it was someone who blamed him, because the bank had foreclosed on his property.

All of these things frightened Jack, but the thing that frightened him the most was what he overheard the maid telling someone on the telephone. "They can all think what they want, but I think it was the Gypsy. It seems like an awful coincidence that the band of Gypsies left town just two days ago. You know what they say about the Gypsies, how they steal children and sell them for money. Why, it gave me the creeps the way that Gypsy couldn't take his eyes off of Jack. He's such a handsome little boy, with those gorgeous soulful eyes. You can bet they'd certainly get a pretty penny for him. There's no doubt in my mind that that Gypsy doubled back. I warned Nan that we better keep our eyes on Jack, because I wouldn't put it past that one to come back again. They've got a lot of nerve you know. I've heard that while one of them is distracting somebody, the other one can be off in a flash with their valuables. Mr. O'Connell had the locks changed, but that certainly won't stop them. They're so cunning and clever that they would probably have a skeleton key to get right through the locked doors anyway. I tell you, as long as I live, I'll never forget those sinister, evil eyes. Why he scared the living daylights out of me."

All of a sudden, Jack was frightened as he remembered the Gypsy the maid was talking about. Jack had been playing alone in the back yard. Before Nan took Gail to the store with her, she had instructed the maid to keep a good eye on him. But whenever Nan left, unbeknown to her, the maid was always making phone calls. All of a sudden Jack looked up and saw a man with penetrating dark eyes, dressed in unusual clothes, staring over the fence at him. Jack was startled and frightened.

The man said, "Don't be afraid, little boy, I won't hurt you. Do you live in this house?"

"Yes, sir," Jack answered nervously.

"This is such a nice big house with lots of rooms. Which room is yours?" he asked with a deceitful smile on his face.

Jack felt so dominated by his presence that he felt compelled to answer. "That one there at the top of the stairs," he very softly uttered.

Just then the maid looked out, and being so frightened herself by the Gypsy, told Jack he had to come in for lunch. After hearing what the maid was saying, Jack agonized over telling the Gypsy which room was his.

From that time on, Jack lived with constant fear. He was afraid of everything. He was afraid to go out and play alone, or to walk home from school alone. Passing doorways and gangways became a major task, as he expected to see at any moment, the Gypsy jump out from the shadows. He was afraid to be in his room alone, or with just Gail. Even during the day, darkness clouded his mind. But mostly he was afraid of the dark nights and afraid to go to sleep. When he heard a door opening, he jumped.

John got a gun and put it in the stand in the hallway right outside Jack's room. Jack heard him instructing Nan and Joseph what to do if the incident was ever repeated. But just the idea that such a thing could happen again, terrorized Jack. He lived with constant anxiety. Nan tried to soothe his fears. "I'll keep the door open between our rooms. Don't you worry, I'm right here. If anybody tries to get in again, they'll be the sorry one, cause I'm ready for them this time." She shook the new rolling pin that she now kept next to her bed.

But every night, Jack had a hard time getting to sleep. He'd lay awake with his eyes glued to the door and with his vivid imagination, he could see the Gypsy coming through the door, until finally, from exhaustion, he'd fall asleep. Night after night he started having bad dreams about the Gypsy, with all different variations. Sometimes he'd dream that the Gypsy got in, but Nan heard him and came out with her rolling pin and he ran away. Sometimes it was Officer O'Reilly or his grandfather or his father who saved him. Then one night he dreamed he saw the Gypsy coming toward him, and that he was still unable to scream. The Gypsy came over to his bed and put some funny smelling cloth over his face that put him to sleep. Then the Gypsy carried him out the door and took him far away. He woke up sobbing into his pillow, more frightened than ever.

Jack especially hated Tuesday evenings the most, when Nan wasn't there and he had to force himself to stay awake until she got home. Even though she had the maid stay in her room to ease his fright, the maid would fall asleep and snore. He didn't feel safe, because she was such a heavy sleeper. When Nan was late in coming home, he got himself so worked up sometimes that he couldn't sleep at all. He didn't want to tell anybody about how bad the dreams really were, because he was afraid they'd think he was a sissy, and they wouldn't like him anymore. Even remembering it now, after all these years, he could still feel his heart pounding and his breathing racing as inward feelings of fear and anxiety enveloped him. He could feel the cold sweat that always came forth every time he relived that haunting nightmare.

Then, three weeks after the attempted break-in, the second incident that occurred would push that fear down deep into the very depth of his being. Jack's grandfather left the bank on a Friday afternoon and took the train for New York City, where he was scheduled to attend a bank business meeting on Monday morning. When he failed to show up for the meeting, it became apparent that he was missing. An investigation was begun immediately, which pointed out that he had indeed checked into the hotel on Friday and after eating dinner in his room alone, it was assumed that he had retired early. The waiter would later testify that upon returning to pick up the cart, he found it outside the room with a "Do Not Disturb" sign hanging on the door knob. It was also pointed out that because of some bank mix-up, he was carrying a large sum of money, which was also missing. His picture was put in all the papers. Besides the police investigation, the family hired detectives, but to no avail. It was as if he had disappeared off the face of the earth.

The police and detectives, after investigating every possible lead, agreed that there was a very slight possibility that he could have amnesia. But the evidence more likely pointed to foul play, and was probably tied in with the break-in three weeks before. Most people accepted that theory. Others, however, believed that he had cleverly covered his tracks and run off with the bank's money.

Jack's grandfather was in the habit of eating lunch with Victoria and her family every day. He always paid special attention to Jack, encouraging him. Jack missed him terribly. At first he just kept watching the door, expecting him to walk through it any minute. Each day he felt so disappointed. Then he started worrying about what had happened to his grandfather, and if he'd ever see him again. It hurt him so when people gossiped that he ran away with the bank's money, or when he overheard the maid telling someone on the phone that she had heard that he ran off with a bank customer.

"It seemed like an awful coincidence that an attractive rich widow had left town only a few weeks before, without leaving a forwarding address."

It always haunted Jack that they could never find out what did happen to his grandfather. So many nights, he had softly cried into his pillow. "Oh, Grandpa, I miss you so. Something terrible must have happened to you. Don't they know that you would never have run out on me?" And yet sometimes he felt a feeling of hopeless abandonment at such a possibility. But most times he believed that somebody had hurt his grandfather, and he had a hard time accepting that. All of this added to the sadness he felt as his bad dreams continued at night, now interspersed with his grandfather's disappearance.

During the day, he was plagued by headaches, with a feeling of doom and foreboding looming over him like a dark cloud. Sometimes he'd feel his heart beating a mile a minute. He'd feel light-headed and dizzy, and break out into a cold sweat. He couldn't eat, and he started losing weight. The bad dreams continued and caused him sometimes to even cry out in the night. He was taken to a special doctor, who asked him a lot of questions. But ever since he was six years old, and had to have a tooth pulled, he was afraid of doctors and dentists, and shied away from grownups in general. So he only said what he thought the doctor wanted him to say. How could he explain to anyone the depth of terror he always felt? The doctor concluded that he was a very nervous little boy, but if they would help him face these fears, that he believed Jack would outgrow them.

Jack started having a hard time getting up in the morning after staying awake half the night worrying about noises, being afraid that somebody was breaking in again. Then he'd be late for school and get hollered at. He couldn't concentrate, and his school work started suffering until finally they had to keep him back in the third grade.

That made him feel even worse about himself, as he saw Bill and his other classmates go on without him. He tried so hard to please everybody and do what they wanted him to do, hoping that they would like him and perhaps that would make up in part for the way he felt about himself. He loathed himself for feeling so weak and frightened all the time. Sometimes he felt so lonely, because he didn't think anyone could understand. He tried so hard to contain the mental anguish that tormented his soul, but too many times he just wasn't able to, and fear-filled feelings overwhelmed him.

Jack started thinking of all the books he had read and how much he admired all the courageous people in them, and how he had wanted so desperately to be like them. What was the matter with him? Didn't this prove that he was a sissy? How cowardly he always felt. Would he never be free from these unnatural fears? Men were not supposed to cry.

He thought of Julie and how much he admired how confident and sure of herself she always was. How hard he had tried to keep her from discovering this deep, dark secret world of his. He was so sure that if Julie ever found out what a phony coward he really was, that she would disgustedly turn her eyes away from him and find someone else that was worthy of her. Sally had tried to encourage him to tell Julie how he felt, but how could Julie, who was so fearless, ever possibly understand what it was like to be so tormented by fear? And he loved her so much that he couldn't even think straight.

Looking back now, he realized meeting Julie was the best thing that had ever happened to him. Things had just about leveled off, and he'd been freed from the threat of the draft. His headaches had subsided and he seemed to have his anxiety and panic attacks, for the most part, under control. When he started going out with Julie, he just couldn't contain the overwhelming joy that swept over him. She was the answer to all his prayers. The weeks they courted, and the month they honeymooned were the happiest times of his whole life, and went beyond his wildest dreams. He thought, why couldn't it have stayed that way? What was it that had turned Julie against him so quickly? He thought of all the times she had made unfounded accusations and assumptions. Sometimes when he tried to explain himself to her, it just seemed to come out wrong. She was constantly interrupting him. She accused him of being moody. But when his headaches were so bad, or when somebody had said some careless thing that really hurt his feelings, he couldn't help but appear moody. Sometimes he wouldn't say anything, and that would make Julie angry, too. He tried so hard to humor her and be agreeable. But every once in a while, especially when he was in pain, the frustration he felt would build up and he'd lose his temper, and say something angry back at her. The next minute, he'd be sorry. But it was too late, the damage was done, and he'd have to leave. He just couldn't stand confrontation and pressure. It always made his headaches and anxiety even worse. As a child he had gotten in the habit of running away from it.

After Jack and Julie's big fight, he had gotten into his car and started driving south, as fast as he could, trying to get far away from her. He was so disappointed in her. She wouldn't even listen and try to see his point of view. And he kept on driving and driving. He was sick and tired of listening to Roger's and Julie's childish bickering. He was so tired of being put in the middle of it. At that moment he hated them both and didn't care if he ever saw either one of them again. They certainly didn't care about him or how he felt.

It was dark when he arrived in New York City. He got himself a hotel room, stretched out on the top of the bed, and gave in to exhaustion. After a few hours, he woke up, his turmoiled mind still angry and disappointed in Julie. Why did she always demand more than he had to give? This constant struggle of emotions had worn him down. His nerves were already so scarred.

Day after day, he walked all over New York City, for the most part in deep depression, unable to eat, unable to sleep, feeling so sad and discouraged. And all the time craving for Julie and having a hard time deciding what he should do next. Everywhere he went, everywhere he looked, he was constantly reminded of Julie. He'd see a woman that looked like her from a distance, or from the back, a woman dressed in similar clothes, or with a similar hairdo. He'd walk down the street and smell her perfume on a woman passing by. When he saw a woman wearing a gardenia, he was reminded that when they were on their honeymoon, he had bought her a fresh gardenia every evening from the peddler on the street corner. A song, the moon, the stars, the sunset, all reminded him of Julie. She was so deeply embedded in his heart and mind. It was as if she had planted herself within him and he could not seem to shake her free.

Even thinking of her now, he felt this unwelcome ingredient, desire, beat and pound in his veins, with no avenue of escape, until he thought his sizzling blood would erupt with volcanic force through his prickly flesh. The longer he was away from her, the harder it became. She obsessed his mind. He ached so just to hold her close.

She dominated his every waking thought. She had become entrenched in his very nature itself. He could still remember one of his friends one time saying, "Once you get a woman in your bloodstream, you'll never get her out. She's like a poison, and no matter how you try you can never be free. It's like an obsession." And Jack knew that the way he felt about Julie really was an obsession, and the loneliness he felt without her had become unbearable.

Julie was the only woman he had ever known intimately. There had been other girls before her that he had been attracted to and knew he could have gone with. His desire was always controlled by the realization that if the girl got pregnant, he would have had to do the honorable thing and marry her, and give the child his name. He didn't want to fall into that trap. He could not be like some of the so-called gentlemen he knew that bragged about their conquest after dumping the pregnant girl with the threat that if she didn't stop bothering him, he'd get a half dozen of his friends to say that they were with her too, and then get her arrested. And he was much too sensitive and romantic to ever go with a prostitute. A stranger in a darkened room was no temptation to him.

Jack was about fifteen when he first heard about what happened to a neighbor, a few years older than he. At first, the family said he was sick, but the word got around pretty fast that he had contracted syphilis from some prostitute. At first, it had caused him to do and say peculiar things, until finally he was committed to a state mental hospital. They didn't think there was any hope for his recovery. He remembered everyone saying, "what a wasted life." There were some who even laughed and joked about it. He had always seemed like a nice person, and Jack felt sorry for him and thought what a high price to pay for a few minutes of so called pleasure. Even if he had gotten the desire to go with a prostitute, which he never had, the thought that it could happen to him would have stopped him.

He knew Julie wanted him to move to a bigger city, but he was afraid to go someplace else and try to start over. At least working for his father, he didn't have to prove himself. His father was patient and understanding. He didn't force him to do anything. His father asked him if he would mind doing a certain thing. It was easy to make up an excuse if he didn't feel up to it. Besides, he didn't like to be in charge and have to make decisions for other people. He also realized he wouldn't be able to make any new men friends. Oh, sure, the women would flock around him, but that would only alienate the husbands all the more, and make Julie more jealous. And Julie would still be deeply involved with Women's Rights and her piano practice and not have too much time for him.

Jack thought maybe if Julie would only have a baby, then she'd be happier and more content. But Julie didn't seem to want to have any children. She was so involved in the Women's Rights Movement. Why couldn't she be different and at least meet him half way? He realized that most of Julie's unfounded accusations were caused by his good looks, and he thought if Julie only knew how much he hated being so good looking. All it ever brought him was the attention that he felt so uncomfortable with. He was by nature a true introvert and he always hated people gawking at him. No matter where he went, the spotlight was always being thrust upon him. All he really wanted was to be left alone to find the peace and quiet he so desperately needed.

Jack had also recognized years ago that some of his male friends had blamed him because their girlfriends were so enamored by him that they ignored their boyfriends when he was around. It had caused their boyfriends to demonstrate their bad feelings toward him. And look at all the unnecessary rift his good looks had caused between him and Julie. If she only knew all the anxiety he felt subjected to and the excruciating pain he suffered from the headaches that would come out of nowhere and sweep over him, so that he just wanted to hide and suffer in silence.

Jack continued remembering what had happened on his second day in New York City. He had kept walking and walking, almost in a fog, and thinking and thinking that Julie would probably never forgive him after the big fight they had. All of a sudden he was on the bridge, looking at the water. Jack always loved the water. It had a soothing effect on him. Now it looked more inviting than ever. He could hear a voice in his head saying, "Jump! Jump! Jump!" How much simpler everything would be. Now he wondered, what was it that brought him back? Why didn't he jump? He had certainly thought, more than once, of ending his life. Was it because he could still remember how good it used to be?

He knew Julie was a virgin and had nervously wondered how she would respond to his sexual advances. He was both surprised and delighted that at times, her passion even surpassed his own. She had been so loving and caring, and everything had been so perfect. Because of this, after much soul searching, he had decided, that if there was even the slightest chance that they could recapture what they'd lost, then he had to take it. He knew he couldn't go on like this. He longed so to hold her close.

Jack had decided to go back and apologize to Julie, and tell her he was sorry and that it was all his fault. Even though he didn't think it was, it was worth it to him to try to make peace with her. He would tell her he was willing to do whatever she wanted him to do. Anything was better than this.

But when he came back, what did he find? That while he had been aching and longing for her, she apparently hadn't even missed him at all. All he got in return for his apology was a cold aloofness. But isn't that his own fault, when she never really wanted to marry him in the first place? Hadn't she told him that she wanted to go on with her career and that her teacher wanted her to go on a world concert tour? If only he hadn't interrupted her career, she would have been famous and received the acclaim she deserved. She was so beautiful and so talented and intelligent. She could have had her pick of men and met someone more worthy of her.

Jack was always desperately afraid that Julie would meet someone like an artist, musician, writer, actor, or someone much more interesting that he, and that he'd lose her. Whenever he saw her talking and laughing with other men, pangs of jealousy tormented him. He felt very insecure about her love for him, but tried hard to cover up his true feelings. That was another reason he wanted to keep her in Troy, believing that in a big city, she was more likely to meet such a person.

Instead, what had he given her? He wasn't even man enough to defend his country. She must feel ashamed of him. How could he blame her? That's probably why she spends so much time practicing the piano, trying to forget this mistake she made in marrying him. Why was he fooling himself? Any love she might have once felt for him was obviously gone. He could still hear her laughing voice ringing in his ear. "You go home if you want to. I'm having too much fun," she had said sarcastically. It was hard enough when she belittled him in private, but now she was openly belittling him in public. Sometimes he felt like crawling into a hole, he was so aware of the eyes upon him.

He already felt so sad and alone without her. He remembered seeing her suitcases packed. As the scotch kept gliding down easier and easier, his thoughts started running together. Through his drunken reasoning, he assumed that her hateful behavior made it clear that tomorrow she would tell him that she was leaving him and that she never wanted to see him again. It became too painful to think about. How could he go on without her? He knew he could never find anyone to take her place.

Thoughts of never being able to touch her or hold her close were more than he could bear. He felt as if his heart was breaking. He ached so just to hold her close once more.

As he kept drinking, a feeling of hopelessness swept over him. Those beautiful alluring brown eyes were now bloodshot and filled with unceasing tears. Jack sighed, "Oh, Julie, I love you so much."

If he could have seen anything, even the tiniest speck of hope, he might have been patient. But he saw nothing but contempt. And he did not have the strength left to fight that any longer.

CHAPTER FIFTY-NINE

It was six o'clock Saturday evening as Julie sat at her vanity, getting ready for the Morgan's party. As she put on her makeup, she hoped no one would notice the deep dark circles under her puffy eyes.

Julie really didn't feel like going to this party, but she hadn't seen or heard from Jack in almost a week and felt embarrassed by his behavior that whipped her sense of pride. She was determined to go to the party, act nonchalant, and give the impression that she didn't care what he did.

Not long after Jack had left the house, her conscience started bothering her about the mean, downgrading things she had said to him. Of what good were they, she thought, meaningless words that hurt and sting. Why did she have to say them? Why couldn't she have held her tongue? But when she heard him defending selfish, bigoted Roger, of all people, she just couldn't contain her anger and frustration any longer. She knew the fight was more her fault than Jack's, and she felt aggravated at herself for allowing Roger's bigotry to get her so upset. She realized long ago that she did not have the patience that some of the other women in the group had.

Julie was a true idealist and very generous to people in need. Double standards and prejudiced people annoyed her terribly. How could she ever make Jack understand that it was men like Roger who had done so much damage to the women's cause by subjecting women to third-rate citizenship, with no voice to demonstrate their God-given mind? Expecting women to be no more than an ornament for their husband's gaze and enjoyment, like any other convenient possession. Many times since she was young, Julie had accompanied her mother and had been inspired by the stirring words written and spoken by the women who had fought so nobly for their cause. They were her heroines because they embodied everything good, fair, and noble, that she wanted to be. She remembered how sad the group had felt when Elizabeth Cady Stanton, Susan B. Anthony, and some of the other Women's Rights Advocates had died, without ever having their dream of voting fulfilled. It just wasn't fair, Julie thought. She had always been close to her grandmother, and was determined to work hard, to do all that she personally could, so that her grandmother would have the opportunity to vote, before anything happened to her.

Julie did not believe the "Founding Fathers" were fair to women at all and she could recite word for word what Abigail Adams (who had the distinction of being the wife of one president and the mother of another) had written over a hundred years before. And she could never forget the scenes she saw with her own eyes, in the spring of 1913, when she accompanied her mother to London to visit her mother's friend. They were chiseled in her mind. How angry she was when she learned that those women had been arrested and were being force fed in jail. She knew Jack was anxious to have children. She also would like two or three children some day. But not until this goal of hers became a reality. Besides, they were still young and had plenty of time.

Thinking of how much she wanted to accomplish for the women's cause made her all the angrier at Jack. He had become so deep a part of her that wondering where Jack was, controlled her thoughts. She couldn't sleep at night and consequently dragged through the days feeling weary and dejected, unable to concentrate.

The first few days and nights after Jack left, Julie worried that he might have been in an accident. She could visualize him lying in a hospital bed, and that scene filled her with remorse over the hateful things she had said to him. She felt miserable and longed for his arms around her. Then she found out his father had gone to New York City on business, and she began to believe that Jack probably went with him, as he had on many previous occasions. She thought it would be just like Jack not to even think of calling her, or letting her know where he was. He was so thoughtless. Or maybe, she thought, he was just trying to purposely punish her. She was angry at him for putting her in this belittling position. In between the worry and the anger was a desperate need she felt for him. She missed him so much and longed for him to cradle her in his arms.

Why couldn't he have had the decency to tell her where he was going, or call her to let her know how long he'd be gone, instead of just ignoring her? Why couldn't he be more thoughtful and considerate? Was that too much to ask? And while she was getting all upset, was he out having a good time? Just thinking about that made her even angrier. Was he sorry that he had married her? Or was she good camouflage for his escapades? Was it too unrealistic to expect that he could just turn his back on the women falling all over him and really be a one-woman man? She'd wake up in the middle of the night and wonder where he was and who he was with. Were there other women? Just the thought of him with another woman made her feel sick.

Did everyone know? Were people laughing behind her back? Were they saying, "She caught the prize, but she doesn't have what it takes to hold onto him"? Were they pleased that he would be available again, and that she, a stranger, would be banished from their midst? Negative thoughts continued tormenting her mind. Was it someone from out of town or someone she knew? And she'd think over and over again of some of the women they knew. Or could it be Sally, could she really trust Sally? It wouldn't be the first time that so-called friendship had blossomed into love. And she loved him too desperately to ever be able to take that chance.

Julie remembered seeing him smiling and talking to a salesgirl the last time they had gone shopping. She wondered at the time, if there was another woman, if this could be her. She thought, this is very likely how her father had gotten mixed up with that saleslady in the first place. She wondered after that, was there deceit behind his smile?

Or could Jack be with a prostitute? She had heard that there was a place on the outskirts of the city. Prostitution was a sore subject to Julie. She blamed its existence on men, in particular, and society in general.

She could still remember when she was about thirteen years old, and had gone to New York City with Matt and her parents to see the Easter Parade. She had wandered over to a side street in one of the poorer sections of town, where she saw a haggard-looking woman in dirty, ragged clothes, propositioning two men. They laughed at her as they walked away. The woman looked so desperately sad, and Julie felt so sorry for her and looked in her purse for some money to give her, but she only had fifty cents. She gave the fifty cents to the woman and told her to wait, that she'd give her more in a few minutes. Julie ran over to her father to get some more money, but by the time she ran back with it, the woman had disappeared. Julie could never forget that woman, and through the years, that scene would keep surfacing in her mind. And already forming in the back of her mind was the idea that after women got the right to vote, that her next cause would be to try to help as many of these women as she could, find a better way of life.

Julie began to wonder, was she just jumping to conclusions about Jack, as all kinds of imaginings continued passing through her suspicious mind? Hadn't Jack said that her accusations were not true? She thought about how worked up she had gotten about what Mrs. Van Alstyne had said. Then when she asked Gail about Mrs. Van Alstyne, Gail reiterated what a trouble maker she always was and how mean she had been to Jack.

She just didn't want to some day have to go through what her father had put her mother through. She would never forget that even after her father's visit at her aunt's house, how angry her mother still felt toward him. Now she could understand it even more so, for she felt as if she could very likely be "walking in her mother's footsteps." She could still hear her mother's words. "He's still under some illusion that it's okay for a man to lead a double life, that it doesn't matter, and that nobody gets hurt. You know I'm not by nature a vindictive person, Julie, but if he were to feel even a fraction of the heartache he's caused me, I can't say that I'd feel sorry for him at all. He more than had it coming to him. Although I don't believe in drinking, I could probably understand the kind of man that got drunk one night and didn't know what he was doing. But a man who, over and over again, has time to think about what he's doing, and still chooses to cheat on a good wife, well I just don't see any excuse for that kind of behavior. I have no respect for that kind of person. He knew what he was doing and showed no concern at all for me as his wife. Slapping me in the face would have been much kinder."

Julie wondered, was her father always like that? Were there always other women, as her mother suspected? Were the signs always there?

Being very close to her father, many times Julie had waited for him to come home. He was never too busy for her and listened patiently. She could always depend upon his enthusiastic encouragement. She started thinking about the time she waited outside his study when his business associate Mr. Johnson was in there.

Julie and Matt had been taught from an early age that if their father had business acquaintances in his study, he was not to be disturbed. Many times as a child, Julie had waited impatiently for what to her seemed like hours, to speak to her father.

That day she had arrived home from college early, hoping to surprise him. She was disappointed to hear Mr. Johnson's loud, boisterous voice. As she sat there she couldn't help but overhear him bragging to her father. He laughingly proceeded to go on into great detail about his latest escapades. Some of the words Julie did not understand, but she understood enough to feel her face reddening. He was telling her father about how easy and available some woman was, and about what he had persuaded her to do. She remembered thinking, this woman had been used by this selfish, deceitful, egotistical, little weasel, and she wished the woman could have overheard this conversation, so she'd smarten up.

It annoyed Julie to hear her father laughing, but she figured it must be because it was expected of him, to humor a good client. When the door opened Julie turned toward Mr. Johnson and with squinted eyes gave him the worst dirty look she could muster, without letting her father see it. She felt disappointed that her father had such a vulgar business client.

The time length Jack stayed away only made Julie madder. She felt frustrated. Why couldn't Jack just come back, argue it out and even, if necessary, tell her it was all over? At least then she could start adjusting. But this not knowing was tearing her apart. It was like a cancer eating her up inside. The longer he was gone, the more she resented him. And yet, why did she miss him so much? What was this spell that Jack had her under? Why did she need him so desperately? She could feel the ache penetrating deep within her, desire generating burning rays of longing, as this inward struggle continued.

What was it that still kept her there? Why didn't she just leave? Was it just because she still wasn't positive that Jack was with someone else, and that finding out for sure, would be the justification that would make her love for him turn to hate? Or was it because she could still remember how special and beautiful it had been?

Why didn't Jack care? Why did he cause it to fade away and all but vanish? She had given him everything she had to give, and it hurt her so much to think that in return he didn't care about her feelings at all. How could he be so cruel?

Julie had always been a very confident person. She knew that men's eyes followed her wherever she went. She always thought of herself as special, and that any man that she chose to marry wouldn't need or want any other woman. That after being with her, her husband would not be able to find joy or fulfillment in the arms of any other woman. But now her self-confidence was shaken by Jack's complete indifference to her.

By the middle of the week, Julie got to thinking that because of their arguments and her possessiveness, that Jack's love for her was gone and that he might have already found someone else.

By Wednesday evening, she had to make a decision about Thanksgiving dinner the next day. They had been invited to both Jack's parents and her aunt and uncle's houses. She figured each would think that they were having Thanksgiving at the other's home. Then, to cover herself, she gave the servants the day off, and let them assume the same thing.

Julie spent Thanksgiving Day thinking that maybe Jack had already seen a lawyer about a divorce, and that a letter or phone call might come very soon from the attorney. She debated with herself that maybe she should save face and before he got back, pack her things, and make it look as if she left him. She could, she thought, have her uncle start divorce proceedings for her, and not give Jack that satisfaction. But still, the thought of losing him was more than she could bear, while this aching longing for him couldn't be stilled.

Finally, by that Saturday morning, she had painfully convinced herself that she had lost him for good. All day long, she had a hard time fighting back the tears. She had packed her bags, made up her mind to go to the party that evening with her aunt and uncle, and leave the next day.

Her eyes wandered around her room. It had taken a lot of time and effort to get it exactly the way she wanted it, everything finally in place. But, she sadly thought, what good was a perfect bedroom without Jack to share it with her?

Julie was still deep in thought when all of a sudden she felt the uneasy presence of eyes upon her. She looked into the vanity mirror and there reflected in the doorway was Jack staring at her. She did not notice the deep, dark circles under his lusterless eyes, or the discouraged expression on his sunken cheeks, for at just the sight of him, her heart pounded wildly, as a weak feeling swept over her. She wanted to run to him, to press her warm anxious lips to his, to be wrapped so tightly in his arms that she could feel the beat of his heart, pounding against her breast. She wanted to tell him that she loved him, that she needed him, that life without him was of little value, when all of a sudden, memories of the past and of all the lonely nights in a half empty bed, flooded her mind until she felt annoyed at herself for loving him so. She looked at him, she was convinced that any moment he would tell her he had found someone else and that he wanted a divorce. So with great sarcasm, she said, "Well just look at what the cat dragged in. To what do we owe this great honor? I certainly hope that you didn't come back on my account." She was determined not to let him see the depth of her love for him. Or to let him know how much she missed him, for she still felt more dejected than she had ever felt in her life. He had stepped on her pride and wounded it beyond repair.

"Julie, I'm sorry. It was all my fault, please forgive me."

"You're sorry. Two little words that are supposed to wipe out everything from my memory. I'm expected to play the part of the dutiful little wife, who bows, overjoyed at her husband's return, erasing everything from her empty head, as if it never happened. Well, I'm sorry, too, but I can't turn my emotions on and off like a light switch, to match your moods, and I'm tired of even trying. You should have married that kind of a girl. You would have been doing us both a favor. Then I could have gone on with my musical career."

"Oh, Julie, I don't blame you for being angry at me, but I really love you. I missed you so much, and I really am so very sorry. Can't we talk things over and try again to make a go of our marriage?"

Julie's anger kept her unaware of the dejected tone of his voice. "Oh, isn't that wonderful, now you're ready to make a go of our marriage. It's just like you to expect me to change my plans because you decided to come home. Well, I don't know yet just what I'm going to do. You see, Jack, we all have choices. While you've been away, I've been thinking, too, and I'm not so sure staying here in this little town with you is one of my best choices."

"But we don't have to stay here, Julie. I'll go wherever you want to go, and do whatever you want me to do – Only please say that you'll forgive me and give me another chance. I really do love you, so please, Julie, can't you temper your justice with mercy?" Jack said pleadingly.

Julie was already having a hard time keeping down the anger that she felt toward him for what he had needlessly put her through. She turned, rays of hatred streaming from her hot, narrowed, snapping eyes. Her voice mocked. "Mercy? Mercy? You ask for mercy? Well, you gave no mercy when you've been off gallivanting all week. Did you ever even once think of me and how I felt, when I didn't even know where you were, or if indeed you were dead or alive? You don't seem to understand that I'm a human being with feelings. Now you come back, and have the gall to expect me to drop everything and just sit down and chat with you as if nothing happened. Well, I can't do that."

Very slowly and almost in a pleading whisper, Jack replied, "You mean you can't, or you won't?"

Julie's anger still kept her from hearing the despair in his voice. "Suit yourself, it just isn't very important anymore. Maybe it would be better to end this farce of a marriage than to go on living this way. Or maybe I'm just too numb to think about it anymore. But I do know right now I've got to keep getting ready for the party. And if you intend to go, you better start getting ready, too. I'm supposed to leave in a half hour and you know how I hate being late."

Jack definitely did not want to go to the party at all. It was a real effort to even think about it. But he had the feeling that Julie wanted him to go. He knew that if there was any chance of their getting back together, he had to do all he could to appease her.

"All right, Julie, I'll start getting ready," he explained.

Julie thought as she continued getting ready. How many times after one of their arguments, when he had seemed cool toward her, she would smile and talk to other men at parties and pretend she was really enjoying herself, but inside her head was aching. But, this time, she wanted him to feel in return, some of the pain that he had caused her. She was determined to try even harder that night to make him jealous, and give him a dose of his own medicine. She thought, let him stew awhile. If she accepts his behavior now, he'll do it again. She was sure that if she kept him waiting longer, he would appreciate her more. She would let him wait up for her for a change, and see how he liked it. She was determined to make him pay a high price for this latest humiliation he had caused her.

She would go to the party and show the crowd that she was in control of their marriage, and that even though he had come back, that she wasn't sure yet if she wanted to keep him or not. And that night, after the party was over, she would forgive him and they would make up and recapture what they had lost, and her patient waiting would have been worth it. Things would be different now that she had him figured out and knew how much he really loved her. All her fears and anxiety had been in vain. Now that she was in control of their relationship, she felt happy and optimistic about their future together.

Yes! She knew just how to handle him. She would give him just enough to keep him interested, but not too much that his roaming eyes would stray, and she felt a smug sense of superiority that she had finally won this war of wills.

CHAPTER SIXTY

Estelle had called her sister Sunday morning to tell her what Jack had done. Marion hurriedly threw a few things into a suitcase and took the first train to Troy to be with her daughter at this terrible, heartbreaking time in her life. Monday morning, she went out to purchase three black outfits for Julie. One each for the two-day wake and funeral. Plus a black coat, hat, and shoes. She was well aware of Julie's taste in clothes, after all the happy shopping sprees they had gone on together.

Marion tried to purchase clothes that wouldn't appear to be too frivolous for such a somber occasion, but that would not make Julie feel even sadder than she already did. She noticed but passed up the beautiful black pumps with a satin ribbon on a single strand of seed pearls that set it off perfectly, something that she knew Julie, under other circumstances, would have preferred, for something more conservative. But she couldn't pass up the stunning hat with the long black veil and single black silk rose regally placed.

Julie sat at the wake that Monday afternoon dressed in a beautiful black fine wool crepe suit with a pleated skirt and long peplum. Its beautiful buttons shined like onyx. But Julie, who had always been so meticulous about every detail of her appearance, was oblivious to what she was wearing. She didn't care at all. She was in too much mental distress to let such trifles bother her. She sat there with her hands folded in her lap. Not even trying to stop the tears that gushed forth.

Momentarily she could see herself as a young girl making a vow to have such complete self-control that she would never succumb to crying in public, considering it a weakness. But now her eyes were so red and swollen that the deep circles underneath, half framed their dismal lifelessness. She felt numbed by this tragic realization that Jack was dead.

Was this really happening to her? Could her whole life be shattered in so short a time? "Oh, God," she pleaded, "Let this be a bad dream and help me to wake up from it!"

She could barely hear the comforting voices in the air above her head, reassuring her of their understanding, sympathy and prayers, as over and over again the haunting memories kept running through her mind.

Julie had left the party with her Aunt and Uncle about one hour after Jack, feeling completely justified for her actions. She expected to find Jack at home, waiting for her.

On the way home, her uncle related what had taken place in the library when, according to him, Bill's uncle had "raked Jack over the coals" and how embarrassed Jack was.

"What did Jack answer?" Julie anxiously asked.

"Why, his face was ashen and his eyes misty, as he faintly whispered, 'I'm sorry,' and turned and left the room. I felt so sorry for him. He looked as if he was on the verge of tears."

"I said, 'You know, Tom, we're all sorry about Bill's death. He was such a wonderful young man, brave and dedicated. They don't come any better. But it's common knowledge that Jack's disability was discovered when he was only a young boy, and I'm sure he's feeling just as bad as you are. Don't you remember that Bill and Jack were best friends?' A few of the men agreed with me. Then I left the room, hoping to catch up with Jack to tell him what had taken place after he left, so he wouldn't feel so bad. But I missed Jack by only seconds. I saw him drive away."

Julie could still not forget the uneasy feeling that had swept over her. With what her uncle was saying, she was already sorry for the hateful things she had said to Jack, and she was anxious to get home to comfort him. After all, she never really wanted to hurt him deeply, just enough to teach him a lesson so it would never happen again.

She had intended that evening, after the dance, she would crawl into Jack's arms and they would reach new heights of passion as they made up for all the time they had been apart. Everything would be perfect from then on, for she would never again get so angry at him.

But when Julie arrived home, not finding Jack there, she became more anxious than ever. She had tried to read a book, but couldn't concentrate or keep her eyes off the clock. Watching precious minutes slowly fading away as, over and over again, she berated herself for not having gone home with Jack.

Now, sitting there in a sad, remorseful mood, her mind would not keep still, "If only I hadn't said such mean, hateful things. If only I had gone home with Jack. If only I tried harder to be more understanding." Jack's father had been exceptionally nice to her, but his mother hadn't even looked her way at all. Julie wondered if she blamed her for Jack's death, and hated her for it. She was not, for the most part, a talkative woman, most often holding her feelings from view. In that way, Jack reminded Julie of his mother.

Gail, especially, was taking Jack's death very hard, but Julie felt so overwhelmed by the vivid memories that tortured her mind, that she couldn't even begin to try to help Gail. She felt her own heart was breaking in two.

Out of the corner of her reddened eyes, she was not surprised as she dimly noticed Roger had purposely walked by her to give his condolences to Jack's parents and Gail, demonstrating to everyone that he completely blamed her. And for the first time, she had to agree with him.

Sally, on the other hand, had been so kind, and with tears in her eyes, bent down and kissed Julie on the cheek. With great concern in her voice, she asked if she could help in any way. But her sweetness only made Julie feel more guilty.

Julie's head was bowed down, an unending stream of tears running down her colorless cheeks, when she recognized the gold and ruby ring on the large tanned hands that patted hers, and the familiar voice, choking back the tears, "I'm so sorry, Jewel honey." Remembering when she was a little girl, how much she had idolized her father, Julie stepped once more into the safety of his arms.

"Oh, Daddy!" and they unembarrassedly cried, as they held each other close, oblivious to the eyes surrounding them. He thanking God that his lost treasure had returned.

After a few moments, Julie's mother, who had been sitting to her left, slightly behind the row of main mourners, stood up and gently touched his arm, beckoned for him to sit in her chair. Her feelings of resentment towards him were now superseded by her concern for Julie.

Matt and his wife were standing behind his father. After they both hugged and kissed Julie and exchanged some meaningless words, his mother beckoned for them to follow her into another room.

The hours dwindled away as the unending line of blurred figures passed by Monday and Tuesday. Then the funeral took place. Finally, the ordeal, from outward appearances, was over. But Julie knew that inwardly she would be haunted her whole life by the pleading eyes that she had failed to recognize. She would never be free from the thoughts that accused her, tried her, and found her guilty of Jack's death. And Julie, who detested making mistakes, would always be victimized, by the memories of the greatest mistake of her life.

CHAPTER SIXTY-ONE

They all sat around Maggie's kitchen table talking about Jack's death, wake and funeral, and about all the things that had taken place before and since. There was Maggie, Nan, Kate, Kitty and Mary.

Mary hadn't gone to the wake. After all the years of night and day dreams that she had about Jack, she just couldn't bring herself to go. She wanted to remember him the way he was that very special romantic evening when he had walked her home from the dance. She knew she wouldn't be missed, knowing half the city would be there. Besides, from what she had heard about Julie brazenly flirting with all the single men at the party, she, like most people, blamed Julie for Jack's death. Mary completely believed that if Jack had married somebody like her, who would have appreciated him, and been more understanding of him, that he would still be alive. Feeling the way she did, Mary didn't want to go to the wake and face Julie, and tell her she was sorry, when she really didn't feel very sorry for her at all. She felt sorry for Jack's parents, and she felt very sorry for Gail. But she didn't have very much pity to waste on Julie. Kitty's uncalled-for defense of Julie had fallen on deaf ears.

Nan was saying what a hard time she was having, believing that Jack took his own life, and her voice started cracking as fresh tears welled up in her eyes. And Maggie and Kate, who knew too well the sadness of life, cried with her. She sadly exclaimed, "Why I had more to do with Jack's upbringing than his parents. I always read him and Gail such beautiful, inspiring stories. Now I ponder and ask myself, was there something I failed to teach them? Did I really do my best?"

Maggie unhesitatingly answered, "God knows you certainly always did your best for everybody." All the others quickly agreed.

Nan exclaimed, "I know they say that blood is thicker than water, but Jack and Gail were always closer to me than most blood relatives. To me, they were family, just like all of you. I was in the room when they were born. The doctor delivered them, and handed them to me to take care of."

Mary could hardly wait to vindictively interject, "Well, I heard it was all Julie's fault. That she was so spoiled and used to getting her own way that she was hard to get along with. It's all over town that she flirted with all the single men at the party. I suppose now she says that she was sorry."

Nan answered, "No, Mary, she didn't say anything. It was pitiful. I never knew that one human being could contain so many tears. But I'm surprised at you, Mary, being taken in by that stupid gossip. Julie has always been very thoughtful and very respectful to me. She treated me as if I were Jack's real aunt. I know it wasn't all Julie's fault. Between them it was. Sometimes two very nice people can have temperaments that just don't blend together."

Kitty spoke up quickly, "I've been telling Mary, Julie is a very kind, generous and fair person. And, Aunt Nan, when I said goodbye to Julie, she asked me to thank you for being so kind to her. She left for Boston Saturday. She was going to try to lose herself in her music and in our cause."

Aunt Nan answered, "Jack was kind of a private, sensitive person, who didn't let most people know what he was thinking and feeling. Sometimes when I looked at him, I used to think that there was a frightened little boy inside a man's body. He always had a sadness in his eyes that I don't think most people ever noticed. I prayed that he'd meet a nice girl who would make him happy, and when he met Julie, for the first time I saw a twinkle in his eyes. He was so in love with her. But with Bill's death, he looked so sad that his eyes quickly lost that short-lived spark.

"It's ironic, when you think of it. There was Bill, who I'm sure would have given anything to come back home, marry Gail and become a doctor. And he would have been such a good doctor, and helped so many people. And there was Jack, who literally threw his life away. Sometimes it's so hard to understand, and even harder to accept.

"And speaking of Gail, she's the one we're all worried about. I never in my life saw anyone with such sad eyes. It's heartbreaking. When she heard about Jack, she was so distraught that she became hysterical. The doctor had to give her a sedative. She was already having such a hard time accepting Bill's death, and now, this on top of it is just too much of a shock to her nervous system. We're so concerned that she may be on the brink of a nervous breakdown. She's always been such a frail, delicate child, and now she's literally withering away. She and Jack were always so close, and she loved him so much. I remember so well that when they were little and I'd taken them out for a walk, Gail would be completely ignored. Everyone was so taken up by Jack's good looks, and they'd rave about his beautiful eyes. Some other child would have been jealous, but Gail was so happy, as if they were saying those things about her. But she was always so thin, and her color was never good. Since she was a little child, she was always peaked looking.

"I always thought that Jack was too good-looking for his own good. Since he was a young boy, the girls would pass by the house and peer over the fence to catch a glimpse of him. It got so bad that he stopped going out in the yard to play. Then as he started getting older, there were just so many more, with all of those college girls close by. But I knew he hated all the attention, and more than once, I had to rescue him from some talkative, giggling young ladies. Ever since he was young, Jack was very shy, quiet and withdrawn. That's why I think he and Bill were such good friends. They were exact opposites. Bill was very friendly and outgoing. Their personalities seemed to blend together.

"What really surprised me was after Bill left, Roger started coming around. When they were young, Roger was a regular bully and he picked on Jack mercilessly. If it wasn't for Bill and Sally, I'd hate to think of what might have happened. Gail told me that Bill told Roger that if he didn't stop picking on Jack he'd have to answer to him. One thing led to another until finally they got into a fistfight and that everybody was rooting for Bill. Bill won the fight, and Roger's aggressive behavior toward Jack finally ended.

"Who would have ever thought back then, when they were young, that they'd both be gone when they were barely twenty-two years old. It just doesn't seem possible. They both had so much to live for. Bill's death of course was hard to accept, but you realize that nobody could do anything about it. But Jack's death was so senseless, that it makes you feel helpless, and kind of frustrated. If we could only have seen some sign, some warning. There's always that gnawing feeling that maybe there was something we could have said or done to keep it from happening. I know we all feel that way.

"And it bothers me terribly, and I know it bothers John, too, that because he committed suicide, the Church wouldn't allow him to be buried in consecrated ground. It's just one more added grief. It makes me mad to realize how many people were buried in consecrated ground who weren't anywhere near as kind and caring as Jack was. He never hurt anyone. He certainly didn't know what he was doing. It's a good thing Victoria's minister offered their land for burial. I pray and truly believe that God, who knows everything, and who can see into our very souls, will forgive him."

Maggie asked concernedly, "Speaking of Victoria and John, how are they doing? I felt so sorry for them at the wake. Words seem too inadequate under the circumstances."

Nan answered, "Well, as you know, Victoria doesn't say much, anyway. But I can tell she's still so overwhelmed. She has been just staying in her room since the funeral. But John is like a rock. Except for reddened eyes, he hasn't shown any outward emotion. I know he has a lot of faith, but it's hard to understand how he can remain so calm. I suppose he realizes that he has to be strong for everybody else.

"In the very near future, I'm going to tell John that I'm going to join the Women's Temperance League and help to outlaw alcohol. Drinking is a curse, and the sooner we get rid of it, the better."

Kate spoke up, "Of course, if our Mary were here she'd still disagree with you. People were always asking for her help. She was always so good-natured about helping, and she was as strong as most men. But everyone knew not to bother her between 7pm and 7:30pm, unless it was an emergency. She always said, 'That's God's time.'" Because that was usually the time that she would read the Bible to me. Then most nights she would go over and get a pint of beer, and we would each have a glass, while she would continue reading the novel you had loaned us. In fact, it was Dr. O'Brien that first mentioned that a glass of beer at bedtime would be a good tonic for me."

"But you don't drink it anymore, do you?" Nan asked.

Kate replied, "No, after Mary died, I didn't want to send young Mary to pail it, and I just didn't want to bother anybody else. Besides, I felt a little healthier by then. I think Mary really did enjoy it more than I did, anyway."

Kitty spoke up, "You know, Aunt Nan, I think that you and I probably agree on almost everything, except on this particular subject. I hope under the circumstances I'm not being too insensitive, but you always encouraged us to speak up."

Nan answered, "That's fine, Kitty, we'd like to hear your thoughts on the subject."

Kitty replied, "I suppose when I think of somebody like Pa, and others like him, I should agree with you. But then I think of Aunt Mary, who was always so good to everybody, and how much she really enjoyed that one glass of beer at the end of the day. And I also think of Mr. Corbett, whose wife was telling me that in the summer, after she and her husband tucked the children into bed, heard their prayers, and told them stories, that he'd go over to the saloon, and get a pint of beer. Then they'd sit on their back porch, each have a glass of beer, and talk over their day. Where is the harm in that? And I think of Mr. Fiacco, Louise's father, who gives me a bottle of his home made wine every Christmas. He and his friends are hard working men, who enjoy one or two glasses of wine a day. I would have a hard time believing there's anything wrong with that. And speaking of Christmas, further reminds me of the one yearly bottle of whiskey that we purchase, so as to offer our company a traditional high ball during the Christmas season. And of course we always make sure we leave at least a quarter of the bottle in case anybody has a toothache throughout the year. Having a little bit of whiskey to hold in one's mouth, on a bad tooth, to deaden the nerve, has been a Godsend, when someone is in terrible pain. The whiskey is then spit out, so what harm is done? Mike pointed out that the majority of the men who hang out at the saloon only have a couple of beers the whole evening. Some just play cards or shoot darts, and mainly talk about baseball, other sports, and what's going on in Troy, and the problems in the country, and the world. And while I've seen Mike and Frankie feeling no pain, I can honestly say that I've never seen them inebriated. So what is the harm? Mike even said to me, While you are trying to get your rights, there are some women who are trying to interfere with the rights of hard working, grown up men making their own choices. So to me, Aunt Nan, it just doesn't seem fair, punishing some people by taking away something they enjoy, because some other people are irresponsible."

Kitty calmly continued, "And it seems to me that in Jack's case, the gun was more at fault than anything else. There might very likely have been other young men who were feeling just as bad as Jack, and who also had too much to drink, but they slept it off and are still alive."

Maggie mentioned with a note of sadness in her voice that she'd be afraid to have a gun in the house.

Nan explained, "We've had the gun for years, ever since that attempted break-in. Most of us forgot it was even there. Naturally, if we could have had hindsight, but who in their wildest dreams could have possibly imagined such a terrible thing happening? And while I can see your point of view, Kitty, I definitely blame the alcohol for clouding Jack's mind to the point that allowed the devil to deceive him into using the gun, making such an irrational, hopeless choice.

"The other day, I overheard Joseph ask John what to do with the gun. John said, 'Put it back where it was, the damage has been done.' A part of me just wanted to holler out, 'Go and throw it in the river, so it can't do any more harm.' But I had to hold my tongue. That decision was not mine to make.

"By the way, Kitty, I finally did finish that postscript on reincarnation. I brought it along with me in case you still wanted to read it. I decided to look over what I had written for your Aunt Mary, believe it or not, more than five years ago. I wanted to see if there was anything that I had written, that could possibly help me to understand Jack's tragic decision. But of course there wasn't. But as you read it, keep in mind that more than three quarters of it, I had written in answer to some of the things that your Aunt Mary mentioned. When you read, 'You said this or that,' I meant of course your Aunt Mary. I didn't see any reason to recopy the whole thing. And of course, I welcome your comments."

As she took the folder from her Aunt Nan, Kitty replied, "Thank you, Aunt Nan, I've always found that subject fascinating."

Nan looked over at the clock as she stood up and said, "I told John I wouldn't be gone long, in case anybody needs me." Tears came into her eyes as she said, "And please keep the family in your prayers, especially Gail."

They all nodded their heads in agreement as Kitty said, "You can be sure we will be praying extra for everybody. And Aunt Nan, if we can help in any way, let us know."

CHAPTER SIXTY-TWO

It was about five o'clock Christmas Eve, and Mary was in a happy, carefree mood as she and Jim decorated the Christmas tree. Mary loved the Christmas season, especially since they had all grown up and were able to afford a tree and decorations and be able to exchange gifts and really celebrate.

For years, she had felt saddened, not only for herself, but for her mother and the family, as they watched and heard and read about other people's very special Christmas celebrations. But now she felt very optimistic as she hummed, "Silent Night."

Annie was supposed to help her decorate the tree. But, as usual, Annie had put things off until the last minute. Mary couldn't believe that Annie had waited until the day before Christmas to even buy her gifts. And now she was in her room wrapping them. It always annoyed Mary that most times she got stuck doing not only her job, but half of Annie's, also. What good did it do for her to start early, get her work done, and then have to end up doing Annie's, too? It didn't do any good to complain, because Mary had tried everything she could think of, and nothing worked. She realized Annie was never going to change. Mary already felt sorry for the man who was going to have to try to change her. But Mary had made up her mind that she wasn't going to let anything spoil the wonderful happiness that she was feeling. She was especially appreciative that Jim was able to come early to help her. Besides, she'd much sooner have him helping her than Annie, anyway.

All while they decorated the tree, Mary and Jim had caught each other's eyes, causing instant smiles to surface. Every once in a while their hands would touch and warm feelings would surge through her body. When they were sure no one could see them, they would steal a kiss in the corner of the room. Finally, they finished the tree.

Jim's coat was draped over the chair. He reached into the inside pocket and took out a wrapped gift. "Mary, I want to give you this before everybody comes in." He smiled as he kissed her cheek. "Merry Christmas." She smiled at him as she accepted the gift, explaining that her gift to him was still in her room.

As Mary opened the package, her eyes widened in surprise as she beheld a beautiful silver watch, with a beautiful silver band, and diamonds encircling its face. She just couldn't believe that he was giving her such a beautiful watch.

"Oh, Jim, it's simply beautiful," she happily exclaimed.

"Look at the inscription, Mary," Jim said.

As she took the watch out of its beautiful velvet container, Mary looked at him and thought of how unselfishly generous he was. The inscription read, "To Mary, With all my love forever. Jim." A slip of paper had fallen out of Jim's pocket. Mary picked it up. She realized it was the sales slip for the watch. Right away she recognized the jeweler's name and realized that the watch must have been very expensive.

Jim tried to grab the paper from her hand, but she laughingly ran into the bedroom and closed the door most of the way. Jim walked quietly to the door and whispered, "Mary, if you look at the price of the watch, I'll never speak to you again." But Mary's curiosity had already been aroused, and she felt very sure of his love. With a mischievous smile on her face, she opened the door, handed him the little pink slip of paper and said, "Too late."

With a serious smile on his face, he shook his head at her.

With a bit of concern in her voice, she said, "Oh, Jim, you shouldn't have paid so much. That's much too expensive for you." It was obvious Jim was embarrassed, and realizing this, Mary went over to him and kissed him lightly on the lips. "Don't be mad at me. I do love the watch. It's the best present I ever got. And I think you're very thoughtful to give it to me." She lingered in his arms for a few moments and then they heard someone coming, and parted fast, each going in opposite directions.

Just at that moment the phone rang, and Kitty, who was on her way into the living room to see the tree, stopped to answer it. She wondered if it was Aunt Nan calling to say why she was so late.

Kitty exclaimed, "Hi, Aunt Nan. I thought it might be you." Kitty paused for a few minutes as Mary and Jim observed her face suddenly change from happy to sad. "Oh, my God, isn't that awful."

Maggie had heard her, and she hollered in from the dining room. "Is it Mike?"

Kitty hollered back, "No, Mama, it's Gail. I'll tell you in a minute." Kitty again listened intently. "Yes, Aunt Nan, of course, and if there is anything at all that we can do, please let us know."

Kitty, who normally kept her composure, looked quite shocked at the news she had just received, but quickly hid her feelings from view. Maggie had walked in from the dining room.

"What is it, Kitty?" Maggie's eyes pleaded for an answer.

Kitty went over to her mother and helped her to settle in a comfortable living room chair. "Mama, I told you that the war is over, and you don't have to worry about Mike, anymore." Her voice was filled with concern. "I want you to remember that he'll be coming home soon. Aunt Nan wanted us to know that she can't come tonight because Gail got sick." Kitty had already made up her mind that it wouldn't do Maggie any good to hear the awful truth that night. She wanted her to enjoy the holiday season as much as possible.

"Annie," Kitty called, "Get Mama and Aunt Kate a cup of tea and tell them about the beautiful Christmas things they have on display at the stores." Kitty had done this many times before, trying to divert her mother's thoughts from something sad to something happy, Annie understood and excitedly said, "Oh, yes, Mama and Aunt Kate, wait till I tell you about what we saw," as she sat down next to her mother.

At that moment, as Mary observed Annie, she couldn't help thinking that, although she considered her very spoiled, she was very good to their mother and Aunt Kate.

Kitty looked at Mary and motioned to her to go into the other room. She directed her to keep her voice down, and not say anything in reply to the shocking, sad news Aunt Nan had just told her. "I don't want Mama to find this out. I'll tell her tomorrow before Mass. But for now she needs to enjoy these few happy hours, and a good night's sleep."

"What is it, Kitty?" Mary asked with a great concern. She had also thought of Mike and hoped he hadn't been in an accident.

Almost in a whisper, Kitty went on to relate what Aunt Nan had just told her.

That afternoon, Gail had Joseph take her to the florist, where she bought a bouquet of flowers, and then to the cemetery, to lay them on Jack's grave, and while she was there, while Joseph was waiting for her in the car, he heard a loud bang and looked over to see Gail slumped on the ground. She had killed herself on Jack's grave, with the same gun that Jack had used to kill himself just weeks before.

CHAPTER SIXTY-THREE

It was Christmas Eve morning, and while many people were looking forward to celebrating the birth of Jesus, Gail was feeling very depressed, and very lonely.

As far back as Gail could remember, Bill was always there, caring for her and protecting her. She was barely twelve years old and he fifteen, when he smiled at her one day and said, "When I grow up, I'm going to marry you." And she smiled warmly back at him and said, "Alright."

They were always together. Their temperaments were so compatible that they not only never argued but hardly ever even had a slight disagreement. From an early age, they both knew what they wanted in life. He wanted to be a doctor in a clinic, and help the poor people born less fortunate than he. And all Gail ever wanted out of life was to be his wife, bear his children, and help him as much as her health would allow.

They became engaged on her eighteenth birthday, only a few weeks before he left for the army. Gail missed him so desperately that it was as if he had taken a part of her very nature with him. Now she felt so devastated by his death that with her mind full of turmoil, she could find no rest.

CHAPTER SIXTY-FOUR

The winter flew by fast. It was already the end of March when Jim called Mary to let her know that his mother's only sister was gravely ill in Philadelphia, and not expected to live. Therefore, he would be accompanying his mother and sisters to Philadelphia and would probably be gone a few days. He would call her when he returned.

She had hardly hung up the phone when it rang again. The sadness she had felt from Jim's news was still in her voice as she answered.

"Hello?"

"Is that you, Mary?"

Excitement instantly replaced the sadness. "Mike, is that you? It's so good to hear your voice again. How are you? Where are you calling from? New York City?" She had repeated the words, still not fully able to believe it. "When will you be home? We're so anxious to see you. Tomorrow? Oh, how wonderful. Do you know what time, so that we can meet your train?" She paused, listening to his reply. "Oh, yes, I understand. Sometime in the afternoon. All right, Mike, I'll tell everybody! We'll really be looking forward to seeing you tomorrow, I can hardly wait!"

The next day the door bell rang. Mary flew to the door, and flung it open. Seeing the outline of a uniformed soldier, she leaped into his arms. She did not know why, but she instinctively knew that this was not Mike.

She stepped back slightly, and as she looked into those eyes, she almost gasped as her mouth opened in disbelief. All of a sudden she felt light headed, as a weakness swept over her. Her knees buckled and her heart started pounding rapidly. She felt very confused, as mixed-up thoughts raced through her mind. How could Jack be standing here? Hadn't he died? Somebody can't come back from the dead. Or did she only dream that he had died? Or is this a dream? She was completely bewildered as she heard this strange voice saying, "Now that's what I call a real welcome."

She stepped back slightly as she looked up again. She could feel her face flush in embarrassment as she realized it wasn't Jack after all, but someone who looked enough like him to be his twin brother.

By this time Mike had paid the taxi driver, and as the cab pulled away, he came up the stairs. This time Mary was misty eyed as she hugged Mike and kissed him on the cheek. "Oh, Mike, it's so good to see you again."

"Oh, Mary, you're really a sight for sore eyes. It's so good to be home," he exclaimed, as he hugged her again. With his arm still around her shoulder, he turned to the left as he said, "Mary, this is my good friend, Steve. We've gone all through the war together. Isn't he a dead ringer for Jack O'Connell?"

Mary still felt embarrassed about her mistake, and was reluctant to look into those eyes again. She knew he had been staring at her. She felt uneasy about it and tried not to let it show in her voice. She smilingly glanced over at Steve as she put her hand forward and said, "I'm glad to meet you Steve. Welcome to Troy!"

He held onto her hand a little longer than usual, causing her to glance up at him once more. When she saw that beautiful smile, she was instinctively reminded of the evening that Jack walked her home from the dance. Those same feelings started sweeping over her.

Inside the house, Mike rushed over to kiss and hug Maggie. She started to cry. Tears of joy, she explained. "Oh, Mike, thank God that you're home safe. I knew our Blessed Mother would take care of you for me."

"Yes, Mama, thank God. I think it was all of your prayers that brought me home safe. I came very close to being killed. But when I called out for God's help, He answered my prayer. I'll tell you about it sometime."

Then Annie, Kitty, Pa (with tears in his eyes) all in turn hugged and kissed Mike. Mike introduced everybody to his friend Steve and they all agreed that he looked just like Jack. Mike explained that Steve would be staying with them for a few days. Mike excitedly exclaimed, "And you'll never guess what his last name is!" And without waiting for an answer he blurted out, "O'Connell! They've got to be related. It's just too much of a coincidence. Maybe their grandfathers or great-grandfathers were brothers. New York is not that far from Hudson."

At first, Mary thought perhaps Steve had no family. But Mike went on to explain that Steve, who was from New York City, wanted to surprise his mother. He had told her that he wouldn't be home for at least another couple of weeks. She had accompanied her husband on his business trip to Chicago and would be back the following week. Of course everyone said that they would be happy to have him stay with them.

The next day, as Mike took Steve on a tour of Troy, Albany, and the surrounding areas, he insisted that Mary come with them. "The work will always be there," he exclaimed, "and we want to look at something beautiful for a change." And Steve, with those dark searching eyes that kept caressing her, agreed.

Mary wondered if Mike had purposely planned ahead the frequent times he stopped to see somebody, leaving Steve and her in the car alone together, exclaiming he'd be right back and then apologizing that he had been held up, using one excuse or another.

Mary and Steve talked about their families and the things that they liked and disliked. They talked about Troy and Albany and he told her about his interesting life in New York City, before the war. He mentioned about his father's business and how he would soon be going to work in San Francisco, at least for a while. They talked about many of the books that they had read. But through all the small talk, Mary could not seem to stop the pull that constantly drew her to him. Every once in a while when he looked a certain way, she couldn't help but think of Jack. Even his voice reminded her of Jack.

Right from the beginning, Mary felt closer to Steve than people whom she had known all her life. During the next few days, she tried hard to fight this magnetic force that kept drawing her closer and closer to him. She tried to think of Jim and what he might be doing at that moment. She tried to avoid Steve, but their paths were constantly crossing. As the week flew by, each time they talked, this closeness seemed to deepen.

Mary never did find out if it was Kitty's or Mike's idea to go out that Saturday night to celebrate. They decided to go to the hotel, where they would be able to listen and dance to band music.

Mary lost no time in calling Molly to invite her to go with them. She hoped that Molly and Steve might be attracted to each other so that she could be freed from his penetrating eyes and the unwelcomed feelings that kept surfacing. Mary purposely had Molly sit in between her and Steve. But she could still feel his eyes upon her. Finally she could stand it no longer and she lifted her eyes to his. A blushing smile crossed her face. What is it, she pondered? What is it that drew her to him? What is this dominating force she felt? Of course, he was by anybody's standard, very handsome. But it was something that went far beyond mere looks, almost to the depth of his very being.

Mary was also glad that Kitty was to the left of her, giving her a perfect excuse for not having to talk to Steve. She had tried so hard the past few days to be just kind and friendly enough to a returning war buddy of Mike's, but not even a slight bit friendlier than was necessary. It was important that Steve not get the impression that she was romantically interested in him.

As the music started, Mike asked Kitty to dance. Kitty explained that after being on her feet all day, they were still bothering her. She suggested he ask Mary, and explained that Mary loved to dance.

Mike smiled at Mary. "How about it, Mary, will you dance with your big brother?"

"Oh, Mike, I'd really love to," she replied with a warm smile on her face.

As soon as they got onto the dance floor, Mike asked her what she thought of his friend Steve.

"He seems very nice," Mary casually answered.

"Well, I can tell that he really likes you, Mary. He hasn't taken his eyes off of you since you met. You know, Mary, Steve is a really good catch. He's not only good-looking and really a nice guy, but he's rich, too. His father invented some kind of a valuable piece of machinery, and has opened up his own business. For years now, he's been making a fortune. Steve expects to work for his father. So Mary, I can honestly vouch for this guy. He's the best."

Mary quickly replied, "But, Mike, I told you I have a boyfriend, and some day I expect to marry him."

"But, Mary," Mike asked, "What harm is there in giving Steve a chance? After all, it's not like you're engaged or anything."

Mary answered with a warm smile on her face. "Mike, you know I really care about your opinions. But I'm definitely not interested in Steve. I'm hoping that you will help me steer him toward Molly. You know what a nice girl Molly is."

Mike said, with concern in his voice, "Yes, Mary, I know you and Molly have been friends since first grade, and she is a sweet girl. But Steve has his eyes on you, and I'm certainly not going to do anything to discourage him. Please, for both your sakes, give him a chance."

The dance ended and Mike walked her back to the table. But instead of sitting down, Mary gave Molly that ladies room glance, and Molly got up as Mary invited Kitty to join them, in going to the ladies room. Kitty said she'd stay and keep the men company.

Right away, Mary asked Molly how she liked Steve, and questioned her about what she and Steve had talked about while she and Mike were dancing. Molly answered, "Well, Steve seems quite nice, but let's face it, Mary, he hasn't taken his eyes off of you to even notice I'm there. And what did we talk about? You!"

"Me?" Mary asked with a look of surprise.

Molly said, "Yes, you. I've tried making conversation with him by asking about his background, family and all of that. But every chance he gets, he changes the subject back to asking questions about you."

"What kind of questions?" Mary asked.

"Oh, just the usual," Molly replied.

All of a sudden Mary heard Jim's and her favorite song, "Let Me Call You Sweetheart."

"Oh, Molly, you know how I love that song. Let's go back to the table, and maybe I can get Mike to dance with me again." But before they reached the table, Mike stood up as he said, "Molly, I think this is our dance." And Molly gave Mary that what-can-I-do look, as she smiled and accompanied Mike out onto the dance floor. Kitty looked over and saw a friend of hers on her way to the ladies room. "Mary, there's Joan. I want to talk to her," and she was gone.

Mary tried to concentrate on the music and think of Jim. She felt guilty that she had been busy having such a good time that she hadn't thought of Jim as much as she should have. She didn't want Steve to ask her to dance. She didn't want to be so close to him. But all of a sudden, there was a touch on her arm that sent chills through her, and that special voice, "Mary, may I have this dance?" She looked over at him, and her heart skipped a beat. What could she do? She really had no choice, she thought, as out on to the dance floor she stepped into his arms.

She hoped that he was not aware of just how much her heart was pounding. Mary, who was usually quite at ease around other young men, was now reliving the uneasiness she had felt around Jack, and still could not understand it anymore now than she had back then.

CHAPTER SIXTY-FIVE

Every Sunday, Kitty and Mama and Aunt Kate always went to the 8:00AM Mass, and Mary and Annie always went to the 10:00AM Mass. Sometimes Pa went, and sometimes he didn't. But this morning, unbeknown to Mary, Annie had decided to go to the 8:00AM Mass with everybody else. Mary felt uneasy realizing that she would be in the house all alone with Steve. All week, she had tried to make sure that she would not be alone with him. She was afraid that he might be feeling the same emotions that she was, and she didn't want to give him the opportunity to express them. She was always so in control of her emotions, but Steve's presence had shaken her usual confidence. She thought, "What was this power he had over her?" It seemed that no matter how hard she had tried to avoid it, that their eyes were constantly, though silently, acknowledging this soul-attraction that was between them. She somehow knew how he felt, but still could not understand this unknown force that pulled her to him. It went beyond intelligent reasoning.

Mary had never had such a struggle between her conscience and desire. In all honesty, she longed for him to take her in his arms and kiss her, but she unceasingly prayed that he wouldn't try. She was afraid that if he did, she would be powerless, and completely lose control of her senses. Each day she had been finding it harder and harder to control these reckless thoughts, as this unexplainable hold that he had over her intensified.

As the door closed, Mary tried to act nonchalant as she smiled at Steve and offered to cook breakfast for him. He said he wasn't really hungry, but he would appreciate a cup of tea.

As Mary put the kettle on the stove, she was fully aware of Steve's eyes upon her. She was trying to think of just what to say while the water was boiling. She was already thinking ahead, and figured after she poured the tea, she would excuse herself and say she had things to do to get ready for church.

Steve spoke first. "Your family is really nice, Mary. Everybody's really made me feel very welcome. When Mike and I got to New York and I realized that my folks wouldn't be back for a week, Mike right away suggested I come home with him. But to be truthful, Mary, I was a little apprehensive. But Mike kept insisting, and I'm glad now that he did."

As she poured his tea, before she had the opportunity to say, "Please excuse me, I have some things to do," he spoke first.

"I hope you can spare a few minutes and sit and chat with me, Mary." As she glanced over at him, she could still see the loneliness in his eyes and she couldn't help but feel drawn to him. She thought, he's probably homesick, and he'll be leaving the next day. She felt obligated to comply. After all, wasn't it her duty to spend a few extra minutes with a lonely returning service man and try to help him forget about the horrors of war?

Steve looked at Mary as he said, "You know, Mary, I'm really glad for Mike's sake that he's found peace again. It's ironic the way things happen. I went to war believing in God, while Mike went to war disbelieving. And now, from our own personal war experiences. Mike believes again, while I've lost all hope of ever believing again.

"In school, when the Sisters taught us about God, they said that He created everything, that He was Almighty, and that He loved us even more than our parents did. But after the things I've seen in this war, it all seems like a contradiction. It's hard for me to believe that an all-loving God would allow such unnecessary human suffering, especially of innocent children. I don't think that I'm ever going to forget those horrendous scenes. It's as if they're burned into my memory." He looked sad, as his handsome face distorted. It was as if he was visualizing such a scene right at that moment.

As Mary saw the pain on his face, she felt sorry for him. "I'm so sorry. It must have been horrible." She was sitting next to him, and on impulse, she touched his hand just to comfort him. She instantly felt those same strong feelings sweep over her. She soon realized he must have felt it, too.

Her heart was pounding, her breathing fast and uneven as he took her hand in his and slowly stood up. Without her consent her eyes slowly rose to meet his. Her heart started pounding even harder as, ever so gently, he drew her to him. She could feel this unknown ingredient in the pit of her stomach rise upwards in answer to this invitation called desire. She stepped back slightly, trying to break this hypnotic spell. But as she looked into his eyes, she felt powerless. As her conscience argued with her raging desires, all reason momentarily left her.

As he came closer to her, she closed her eyes and leaned slightly forward in anticipation. His lips were warm as they greeted hers and she felt this warmth surge throughout her body, and something from within her was answering this pent up longing from within him. Their lips touched slowly and softly at first, then harder as his arms held her closer and tighter until she felt dizzy.

They broke apart, her face flushed as she was trying to catch her breath, believing at that moment that it would never be normal again. She turned around, too embarrassed to face him. What had she done? What must he be thinking of her? That she was easy? Would he think that she let every young man kiss her like that?

Why, he was almost a stranger to her. What about Jim? Suddenly she felt very ashamed. Even though they were not yet engaged, they were going steady, and in all fairness, she would not have wanted him kissing some other girl like that. Her shame increased as guilt possessed her.

Mary exclaimed, "Oh, Steve, I never should have allowed you to kiss me like that. I'm so ashamed of myself. Although I'm not engaged yet, I do have a steady boyfriend. Some day I expect to marry him. He's very nice, kind and considerate. Right now, I feel as if I've betrayed him."

"You mean you promised that you wouldn't go out with anyone else?"

"No, but it's sort of taken for granted. I stopped going out with other men and I know that he doesn't go out with any other girl." Mary answered.

Steve looked into her eyes as he said, "Mary, I'm sure you know that I would never want to do anything to make you feel bad. And I'm sure that anyone that you would go steady with, would be very nice. I would never make little of such a commitment. But all I know is that I love you, Mary. I knew it the minute I laid eyes on you. I didn't try to fall in love with you, it just happened. Don't ask me to explain it, for I can't. I've never felt this way about anyone before, and I'm beginning to believe that we were fated to meet. I really believe that even though you might not want to admit it, that you have strong feelings toward me, too. In all honesty, Mary, I don't believe that you would have responded to my kiss the way you did, if you were really deeply in love with someone else. You do believe I'm being sincere, don't you?" Steve asked.

Mary sighed as she looked at him in a puzzling way, not quite sure how she should reply to his declaration of love. "Yes, I do believe that you're being sincere, Steve. But I don't believe that you love me. I believe it's an attraction that's been intensified by your being homesick. And I really believe that as soon as you get back home, you'll forget all about me."

Steve said, "I know you better than you think, Mary. Even before I met you, I knew you. Mike and I, and some of the other men, had shown each other pictures of our families. Sometimes we'd talk about home, and people we knew, and some of the things that had happened in our lives. Mike shared with us some wonderful memories he has of you, Mary. He always talked about how sweet and thoughtful you were. So you see, Mary, I really do know you, and I'm sure Mike could tell you about me."

CHAPTER SIXTY-SIX

Mary and Steve were still talking as everybody returned from church. Mary still felt so guilty that she couldn't even look anyone in the eye. After having fasted since midnight, Kitty said she was famished, and the others agreed. Mary apologized for not having breakfast ready, and said she would start cooking it right away. Mike piped up and said he would really feel honored to cook breakfast for everybody.

Mary felt that Mike sensed something between her and Steve, and that he was volunteering so that she and Steve would have more time to talk. She spoke up, "No, Mike, you sit down and I'll have breakfast ready real soon. I certainly can't have you making breakfast when you haven't even been home a week yet."

Kitty spoke up quickly, as she smilingly said, "No, Mary, you go and get ready for Mass. I have the day off, and I'd consider it a privilege to cook Sunday breakfast for my heroic brother and his special friend."

Mary didn't say anything to Kitty, but she had a feeling that Kitty also sensed there was something going on between her and Steve. Kitty was always very perceptive.

It was 9:45AM when Molly came along to walk to church with Mary. On the way, Mary told her all about what had happened that morning, and how ashamed and embarrassed she felt.

When it was time for communion, she didn't go. She didn't feel worthy enough.

CHAPTER SIXTY-SEVEN

The next morning as Mary awakened, her very first thought was that Steve would be leaving that morning, and hopefully Jim would be home soon. She realized Kitty had gone to work, and Annie was getting ready for school. She hurried getting washed up and dressed.

Mary could hear Mike talking to Maggie out on the front porch. They were waiting for the taxi. The evening before, she had purposely said good-bye, and wished Steve good luck, while everybody was around, explaining that she might not be up when he left. She walked into the kitchen, and there standing before her was Steve. He was saying that he had come back to say good-bye to her once more. As she looked at him, all those feelings she had tried so hard to contain, rushed forward. She felt overwhelmed by the realization that he was walking out of her life, and that she would never, ever see him again. This thought was just too much for her to bear, and a lonely sadness swept over her. How could she let him go? She did not want to think of yesterday, or tomorrow, or what was right, or what was wrong. She just wanted to drift endlessly through time and space, holding him close, and loving him – and yet – even as she thought this, she knew she couldn't. Her Catholic conscience was deep-set within her, and her instinct would never allow her to throw 'caution to the wind.'

Steve kissed her on the cheek and as he hurriedly hugged her, whispered in her ear, "I love you, Mary. I really love you. I'll write to you."

No, don't write," she answered.

As Mary watched the taxi pull away, she tried to smile, although she was already feeling sad, knowing she would miss him terribly.

CHAPTER SIXTY-EIGHT

It was Tuesday evening and Mary was still having a hard time keeping Steve out of her thoughts. The ring of the telephone startled her. As she picked up the phone and said, "Hello," she felt so happy to hear Jim's voice.

"Oh, Mary, I really missed you terribly. Did you miss me?"

Mary answered enthusiastically, "Oh, yes, Jim, I really did miss you." For at that moment, more than any other moment since he'd left, Mary realized just how very much she had missed him. But she also realized at the same time that she had been so busy with Steve around to distract her, that she should have missed him even more than she had.

"Mary, is it too late for me to come over and see you?" he asked.

"No, Jim, come over now. I'm sure it'll be all right," she answered happily.

Mary went into her room to be alone. She sat on her bed, pondering just how she could explain to Jim what had happened with Steve, when she didn't even quite understand it herself. At that moment, she realized that Jim would probably feel bad about it. She knew she would feel heartsick if he had kissed some other girl like that. Oh, why? Why did she let it happen? She wanted to be honest and not keep any secrets from him. What could she possibly say to him to make it sound less terrible? She did not want to blame it completely on Steve.

Jim was on his way over. She didn't have much time. When she told him, would he turn from her in disgust? Would he say that her behavior was unacceptable and that he didn't want to see her again? Would he say that he didn't want to marry a girl who couldn't even control her emotions for one short week while he was away?

No, she reassured herself, Jim wouldn't do that. He would be very disappointed in her, but he loved her, and would forgive her. "Jim is back," she said to herself, almost as if the news was just now really registering on her confused mind. The thought brought a smile to her face as she went out on the porch to keep an eye out for him. When she saw him walking toward her, her heart skipped a beat, and she realized all the more just how much she really did love him.

He looked into her eyes. "Oh, Mary, I missed you so much." She pulled him into the hallway. As they kissed, she held him so tight, never wanting to let him go.

Mary had already told Kitty that Jim was coming over, and that she was going to take a little ride with him. She couldn't tell him in their hallway, or living room, or out on the porch. She'd be afraid someone would overhear. It was going to be hard enough just to confess her shame to Jim.

They drove over to the outskirts of the park, and Jim parked the car a short distance from the street light. He turned to Mary, took her into his arms, and kissed her ever so softly on the lips. She felt such warmth go through her whole body. He breathed heavily as he said, "Oh, Mary, I love you so much."

For a long time, Mary had thought that Jim was holding back from her the deep passion he felt for her, not wanting to overstep an unspoken commitment.

"Mary, I have something for you," he happily announced. He was always buying her little gifts. He handed her a beautiful little music box. "Oh, Jim, it's beautiful, but you shouldn't have."

At that moment, the gift, and his acknowledgement of just how much he loved her, made her feel guiltier than ever. What could she say? How could she possibly explain this to him? And yet she had to, right there and then, or she would never find peace of mind again.

"Jim, I have something that I have to tell you. Because I don't want to keep any secrets from you. It's very painful for me to tell you this, because I'm so ashamed of myself." With concern for her reflected in his eyes, he took her hand in his and listened. "My brother Mike brought a friend of his home, and to make a long story short, I let him kiss me on the lips."

Mary saw the change come over Jim's face. With the hurt look that he couldn't quite conceal, his face fell, as if he'd been struck. This made Mary feel even more guilty. What was he thinking? How he couldn't even trust her? He was definitely disappointed, his face acknowledged it. It made her even more sorry that it had happened at all. Perhaps she made a mistake in telling him. How could she possibly expect him to understand, when she still couldn't understand it herself?

"Oh, Jim, I'm so sorry that I've hurt you when I was only trying to be honest with you and not keep any secrets from you. I'm so sorry. I've been so unfair to you."

As Jim gained his composure and looked at her, she could see the love he had for her shining in his eyes. "Mary, I think that I'm the one who's being unfair to you."

"What do you mean?" she questioned.

With concern in his voice, Jim said, "I'm in no position to expect you not to go out with other young men, when I can't, at this time, even ask you to someday marry me. I have no right to ask you to wait. You want to be honest, Mary, and I do, too. It could very likely be a few more years before I'm in a position to make marriage plans. I have family obligations to my mother and my sisters. So,

Mary, if you want to go out with anybody else, just go, and don't feel guilty about it."

Mary snuggled up to him, as tears came into her eyes. "No, Jim, I don't want to go out with anyone else. I love you, and I'll wait for you."

CHAPTER SIXTY-NINE

After Steve left, no matter how hard Mary tried, she just could not stop him from wandering into her thoughts. When there was a knock at the door, her first thought was that Steve had felt compelled to return just to hold her close once more. She envisioned herself rushing to the door to greet him. She would look into his face, and his eyes would force her to embrace him and feel once more the passionate kiss his lips would place upon hers.

The ring of the telephone only started her mind imagining that it was Steve calling to tell her that he still loved her and missed her and that he would be back soon. From out of nowhere, thoughts of Steve would take over her mind and she would be reliving that kiss with all its ardor and breathlessness. Instantly her heart would race faster and mixed feelings of happiness, emptiness, loneliness and longing took possession of her being.

She wished that she worked outside the house so that she would be busier and not have so much time to think. It seemed that if her mind was idle but a moment, out of nowhere Steve would creep into her thoughts. But then she would return to reality and her conscience would remind her of its unfaithfulness to Jim, even though she also still thought of him many times a day.

She had been completely happy with Jim. Everything had been perfect. Most girls would give anything to be in her shoes. To have a boyfriend who was so crazy about her. She knew he would stand on his head to please her. Then why, she thought, couldn't she stop thinking of Steve so often? She knew she loved Jim. There was not any doubt in her mind that she loved him. It was as if one set of feelings were completely separate from the other.

Even sometimes when she was out with Jim, she was distracted by thoughts of Steve. Sometimes it was a certain object, a word, an army uniform, a song. One night when the band was playing that song that she and Steve had danced to, her mind started wandering.

After a few moments, Jim looked at her as he took her hands in his. "Mary, what are you thinking of? You seem to be miles away."

She sighed as she looked at him and realized that she couldn't tell him. It would only hurt him. She smiled softly as she looked into his eyes, so gentle and kind. "I really like that song a lot." She thought how lucky I am to have you. On impulse she leaned forward and kissed his warm lips.

As she studied Jim's face, she thought, how kind and thoughtful you are. It is not fair to you that you have to share my love with another. I don't want to love him, too. Why can't I help the way I feel? And she also came to realize that even if she were with Steve, she would be missing Jim with the same intensity.

Once in a while, mixed in with her daydreams of Steve, she would be reminded of the evening when Jack had walked her home and how much she had wanted him to kiss her, and the emptiness she had felt when he hadn't. And she wondered if what she felt for Steve had anything to do with the love that she had felt for Jack for so long.

Even though she had told Steve not to write, she couldn't help feeling disappointed that he hadn't. She felt that he could have at least taken a few minutes to acknowledge that he had a good time and that he was glad that he met her. Reiterating this thankfulness to Mike and asking him to thank everyone for him, just didn't seem to

Mary to be personal enough.

Over the course of time, she began to question Steve's motives. Was she just a substitute for his loneliness? Would he have felt the same if it had been some other girl? Or was it only because it had been a romantic time, like living a dream, because everyone was so happy that the war was over and the men had come back home?

As she looked at the clock, she wondered what Steve was doing at that moment. Did he ever think of her at all? Or was he too busy to be bothered? Maybe in the long run it meant nothing to him. In comparison, was it to him no more than a romantic moment, one of many to be added to his already full and soon forgotten escapades? He probably got back home and started going out with the many girls he must know. For after all, he was quite good-looking, and the fact that he was financially well-off would certainly have made him even more attractive to other young ladies.

She wondered if he looked back and realized that she just momentarily filled the lonely void in his life, and now some other pretty girl had caught his eye. Or was it just that men were different by nature and just didn't take things as seriously as women did?

More than once, she had heard Mike say that the reason he didn't keep going out with a certain woman anymore was because he felt as if she was becoming too serious, while he just wasn't ready to settle down yet. "Once you get hooked, you're hooked forever," he always laughingly joked.

Day after day, as Mary wrestled with her thoughts, she still felt warmed by the memories. But by the third week, she missed him so much that she wished she'd never met him. The aching longing she felt for him was too high a price to pay for a few warm beautiful moments. By this time her pent-up emotions had intensified to such a degree that the pain of missing him far outweighed the joy of knowing him. Oh, Steve, why did you have to walk into my life, to charm me with your handsome smile and beguile me with those tempting eyes? What good was it that we met? What good could come from such a meeting, when I'm left aching for your nearness? Longing just to touch you and be close to you, just one more time. And yet ashamed of my thoughts and feelings of disloyalty to Jim. Wouldn't I have been better off never meeting you? Oh, why can't I erase you from my mind?

She thought, what was wrong with her senses? How could she possibly love two men at the same time? It wasn't normal. She sighed as she shook her head. "Normal? What is normal? It certainly can't be normal to keep trying so hard to forget somebody and stop thinking of them anymore and yet not be able to control your own mind." She felt exasperated. Why couldn't she break this hypnotic spell that bound her to him? There wasn't anything that she had ever read that had prepared her for this strange dilemma. Was she destined to never, ever forget him? Would she always stumble through life, always thinking of him, day after endless day? "No," she thought to herself. It took a long time, but she did finally get Jack out of her system. She felt confident that she would, no matter how long it took, free herself from Steve's control.

Aunt Mary had said that you can't think of two different things at the same time, so she would try harder to divert her mind to Jim or other things.

I will get over this, she thought, as a new wave of determination swept over her. She reminded herself, if I could get over loving Jack, I can get over loving Steve. After all, Jim is here to help me.

CHAPTER SEVENTY

Over ten months had gone by since Mary had last seen Steve. As she and Jim grew closer together, her thoughts of Steve grew little by little, less and less. It was February, Friday the 13th, and while some people considered it a bad luck day, Aunt Mary used to say that's just superstition. If you believe in God, every day can be looked upon as another opportunity to do good deeds.

Mary went out to get the mail and she stared at the letter addressed to her. She did not recognize the writing. As she checked the return address, she was surprised to see that it was from California. She instinctively thought of Steve. As she raised her eyes to the name of the sender, she felt a mixture of joy and apprehension as she realized that the letter was indeed from Steve.

She wanted to open it right away and read what he had to say. Her curiosity was at its peak. But it was time to make Maggie and Aunt Kate's lunch, and make them comfortable for their afternoon naps. As Mary put the letter in her apron pocket, she thought it would be better to wait until she could sit down in the living room all alone, in the peace and quiet of the afternoon, and give Steve's letter her undivided attention.

About a half hour later as she sat comfortably in the rocking chair, she opened the letter and read:

"Dear Mary,

As I begin this letter, I am finding it very difficult to choose the right words that could possibly convey to you the depth of my true feelings. When we parted, you asked me not to write. I have until now respected your wishes. But I find that I can no longer be still.

You believed in the beginning, Mary, that it was only an attraction that I felt for you. But I know that I fell in love with you the moment you ran into my arms, when such a warm and wonderful feeling swept over me. I never believed in love at first sight, but now I know from personal experience that it does happen. Since I saw you last, I have been in the presence of many young ladies, some truly beautiful, but they have all fallen far short in comparison to you.

I have truly tried so hard to forget you. I have tried to lose myself in my work, but to no avail. You've been in my thoughts morning, noon and night. No matter how hard I've tried, I have not been able to free you from my mind. When I think of you countless times each day, I feel such a great warmth from so many happy memories that are still so vivid in my mind. My love for you has become even deeper than I could ever have imagined.

Even though I've been physically home for months now, my heart is still there with you. Time has only added to this longing I feel to be close to you, not for just one day, but every day of the rest of our lives.

Mary, I want you to marry me. I am thoroughly convinced that we were fated to meet. Perhaps this God of yours is calling me back through you. I'm sure that you know that I would do all in my power to make you happy. In fact, you can have everything you ever dreamed of. Money is no obstacle. My family, like yours, is very special. I know that you would feel right at home here. As you know, Mary, I have two brothers and I know my mother would look upon you as the daughter that she never had.

Mary, I hope you realize that I wouldn't minimize in any way the commitment that you made to Jim, but I'm saying these things for his sake as well as ours.

I guess above all, Mary, I'm hoping that even after all this time, that you also still have warm feelings toward me. If you can honestly tell me that you never think of me, then I could at least feel content in wishing you the best of everything that you so truly deserve. I know forgetting you is beyond my human capacity.

Although I will be anxiously waiting for your answer, I want you to take all the time you need in thinking everything over very carefully before making a final decision.

Mike is planning on making a trip out here in the near future. I hope that you will come with him.

So please, Mary, try to remember that "special" week we spent together and the closeness we felt. Then read my letter over and over again, until you can really begin to understand the depth of my love for you. I'll always love you.

With All My Love,
Steve

She finished the letter and burst out crying, "Oh, Steve, I can't help loving you!"

CHAPTER SEVENTY-ONE

Mary pondered about what to do about the letter. She decided not to tell Mama, Kitty, or Mike, yet. She did not want to disturb Mama and she knew that Kitty and Mike would give her all kinds of unsolicited advice. They were both quite opinionated.

Jim had to work that evening. She and Molly had planned to get together and go shopping. They would walk and talk and look around. Then as usual, stop for ice cream.

From the time they were young, Mary and Molly always found a lot of things to talk about. They had confided in each other all their hopeful dreams and deepest secrets, including Mary's attraction to Steve, and the problem she had trying to forget him. Mary considered Molly a perfect friend whose opinion she really sought after, and highly respected.

Molly always seemed to really care. She was a really good listener. She had the type of personality that would give you her opinion if you asked for it, but not try to talk you into her way of thinking, like Kitty and Mike. YES, she would tell Molly, and then Jim, before telling Kitty and Mike.

As they sat at a corner table in Manory's, Mary told Molly what had happened. She showed Molly the letter and asked her opinion. Mary pointed out to Molly that she probably knew her better than anyone else knew her.

Mary watched Molly as she read Steve's letter. Mary had reread the letter a number of times and almost knew it by heart. She sat silently and waited patiently for Molly to finish reading the letter.

"It's a beautiful letter," Molly said, as she handed it back to Mary.

Mary looked at Molly with questioning eyes. "Oh, Molly, what am I going to do? I love them both."

Molly answered with concern in her voice. "I wish I could think of something to say to help you, Mary, but I can't even imagine what it would be like to be in love with two men at the same time."

Mary thought for a moment and answered slowly. "The only way that I can explain it to you, Molly, is that it's like two separate entities. One completely separated from the other. Like, for instance, you love your mother and you love your father, and one love does not interfere with the other. Or, like, a mother has a child that she loves, as much as she can possibly love her child. Then she has another child. She doesn't love the first child any less, now that she has two children. One child in no way has lessened her love for the other child. And I suppose that is the only way that I can possibly explain this. I do know for sure that I love Jim, and I love Steve. But I just don't know what I'm going to do about it."

Molly said, "Pray over it, Mary. Pray that you will make the right decision. I'll pray for you, too!"

Molly hesitated. "I don't know if this is the right time to tell you, Mary, but I have made the most important decision in my life. I have decided to become a nun."

"What!" Mary was flabbergasted, as she tried to digest Molly's very surprising news. "I don't understand. I know you have always been religiously inclined, but I never for one moment ever thought that you were even considering becoming a nun. Why didn't you tell me? I thought that we didn't keep secrets from each other?"

Molly answered with a contented smile on her face. "I didn't say anything because I still wasn't sure. The idea has come in and out of my mind since we were in third grade, but never as strongly as it has recently. But I was still having a hard time being completely sure. Saturday morning I was over at church praying in front of the statue of Jesus, and I said, almost pleadingly, 'Lord, if you want me to become a nun, then take this tiny bit of doubt from my mind. At that very moment, Sister Mary Bernard came out of the Sacristy. And I knew, definitely, beyond any doubt, that I wanted to become a nun, and serve the Lord, by helping children, like she has always done. I looked up at the statue of Jesus and I smiled as if to say, 'Thank you, Jesus!' Immediately, that Bible quote came into my mind, 'You have not chosen me, but I have chosen you.'"

CHAPTER SEVENTY-TWO

As Mary proceeded to get ready for her date with Jim that Saturday evening, her mind was clouded by indecision. She hadn't slept well the night before, feeling torn between her love for Jim and her love for Steve. No matter how hard she tried, she just could not seem to set these thoughts aside.

It was Valentine's Day and Jim had invited her out to dinner and then to the picture show to celebrate. She had made up her mind that the first opportunity that presented itself, that she had to make Jim aware of Steve's proposal. But she still wasn't sure if she should actually show him Steve's letter or just tell him about it. She really wanted to spare his feelings as much as possible. Or, she wondered, should she try harder to make up her mind and perhaps she wouldn't have to tell him at all. No, she thought, she owed it to him to at least prepare him, just in case.

Mary was ready early, so she decided to get some fresh air and wait out on the front porch. Maybe it would help clear her mind. Jim was always punctual, so she knew he would be along soon. She kissed Maggie and Aunt Kate goodnight, and told Kitty she was leaving.

"Have a good time," they all called out.

When Mary saw Jim's automobile coming down the street, she ran down to the curb. He got out of the automobile and smilingly touched her arm. They tried to be on guard, because Mrs. Foley was always peeking out the window through the side of the drapes, and Mary didn't want to give her any ammunition for her wagging tongue.

As Jim opened the passenger side door for her and helped her into the automobile, he seemed quite happy. "Mary, I was hoping that you'd be ready early so that we could drive up to the park and talk for a few minutes before we go to dinner."

As he parked on the hill overlooking the city, he took her into his arms and kissed her and held her close. Then he handed her a large envelope and a big heart-shaped box of candy. She smiled at him as she said, "You're always so thoughtful."

He seemed impatient as he said, "Mary, open the envelope."

It was the most beautiful Valentine card that she had ever seen and as she read the beautiful, romantic words, she felt warmed by the realization of just how much she really loved him.

At that moment, thoughts of Steve were farther away than they had ever been before. She was not prepared for the next words on the card. In Jim's handwriting were the words, "Mary, will you marry me? With all my love forever, Jim."

Mary was filled with conflicting emotions. So many times she had envisioned this scene, when the man she loved would propose. For years she thought it would be Jack, and without hesitation she would be saying yes to everything she had ever wanted in life. But Jack and Julie's marriage had hastily ended that dream forever. For months now she had believed that someday Jim would propose to her, but because of his family obligations, she had no idea whatsoever that it would be this soon. She always thought it would be a perfect time. But now with Steve's letter hanging over her head, she felt somewhat melancholy. At that moment, she wished Steve's letter had never arrived. Maybe it's better sometimes not to have a choice, she thought.

She did not want Jim to see the bewildered look on her face. She laid her head upon his shoulder as he was explaining that since one of his sisters had finished school last year and was working and his other sister would be finishing school this year, and the fact that his mother was working part-time as a saleslady, that now he could ask her to marry him.

Jim was excitedly exclaiming, "But I want you to pick out the ring, Mary. After all, you're the one who's going to wear it, and I want you to get the ring that you really like. I have saved a down payment, and I can pay the rest in weekly installments." He was so happy, his voice was bubbling as he continued. "In another month I'll be able to start saving more money every week toward our wedding and the things we need."

Mary couldn't help but be reminded of the importance of money in people's plans. As she felt the warmth of his cheek next to hers, she couldn't help wishing that he had been in a position to ask her to marry him before she had ever met Steve. She believed that if Steve had come into their home and she was already wearing an engagement ring, he probably would not have acknowledged his feelings for her at all.

Jim was so happy. She just couldn't tell him now about Steve's letter. She couldn't rob him of this very special evening, even though she wished that she could free her own mind. She hoped that the picture show would be good so that she could at least escape her thoughts for a short while. Her mind was made up. They would go to dinner now, even though she had lost her appetite, and then to the picture show. She wouldn't say anything to Jim until she had more time to think it through.

CHAPTER SEVENTY-THREE

"When Irish Eyes Are Smiling, sure 'tis like a morn in spring.
In the lilt of Irish laughter, you can hear the angels sing.
When Irish hearts are happy, all the world seems bright and gay,
And When Irish Eyes Are Smiling, sure, they'd steal your heart away."

"Have you ever heard the story of how Ireland got its name
I'll tell you so you'll understand from whence old Ireland came.
It's no wonder that we're proud of that dear land across the sea.
For here's the way my dear old mother told the tale to me.
Sure a little bit of Heaven fell from out the sky one day.
And it nestled on the ocean in a spot so far away.
And when the Angels found it sure it looked so sweet and fair.
They said, suppose we leave it, for it looks so peaceful there.
So they sprinkled it with stardust just to make the Shamrocks glow.
It's the only place you'll find them, no matter where you go.
And they dotted it with silver to make its lakes so grand.
And when they had it finished, sure they called it Ireland."

"My wild Irish rose, the sweetest flower that grows.
You may search every where, but none can compare

To my wild Irish rose.
My wild Irish rose, the dearest flower that grows.
And some day for my sake, she may let me take
the bloom from my wild Irish rose."

It was March 17th, St. Patrick's Day. Even though two feet of snow had fallen that day on Troy, it did not dampen the spirits of those Irish hearts, and the hearts of their friends, who gathered at the O'Neill home to sing and to play traditional Irish music.

Mary had made a larger than usual big pot of Irish stew for supper and everyone was invited to partake of it.

Mike had just finished eating and in between his singing he was getting ready to go with his friends to the state armory for a big wrestling match.

One song after another was played and sung that evening. Some of the tunes Kitty had the sheet music for and played them on the piano. Others were on rollers, the music coming forth as Annie pumped the piano pedals. Then of course there were Irish tunes that someone would start singing and some of the group would just join in on.

Among Maggie and Aunt Kate's favorites, "Did Your Mother Come from Ireland?" Their mother did indeed come from Ireland. Their other favorite was "Danny Boy." Maggie would always reminisce about her little Danny Boy. She would add that she found comfort in knowing that they had a little angel in Heaven.

All in all, it was a very happy evening that flew by rather quickly.

Two days later, March 19th, would be looked back upon by some as an opportunity denied, that could very possibly have changed the course of history.

In World War I, millions had been killed or wounded. Homes, farms and factories had been destroyed. Famine threatened many regions.

At the Paris Peace Conference, President Wilson urged, "Peace Without Victory."

President Wilson's dream was to create an "International League of Nations" to guarantee peace for the future. With the League in place, he felt sure that any mistakes made in Paris could be corrected in time.

For his efforts to bring a just end to the war, President Wilson would receive the Nobel Peace Prize in 1919.

Millions of people home and abroad looked to the League of Nations to ensure the peace.

Wilson predicted that without the League of Nations, there would be a worse world war.

More than forty nations joined the League. They agreed to negotiate disputes rather than resort to war. Members of the League promised to take common action, economic or even military, against any aggressor state.

Although Wilson believed that the United States' participation in the League was necessary for its success, the United States Senate refused to ratify the treaty.

CHAPTER SEVENTY-FOUR

So many times over so many days, no matter how hard Mary tried, she still could not make up her mind between Jim and Steve. Many times her head ached from the weight of indecision. The mental anguish she felt was unbearable.

She could not evaluate what was the right decision and what course she should choose. All she really understood was what she felt. They were very real to her, and she couldn't deny it. Sometimes she longed to have Steve near and hold him close, just once more.

When she had told Jim about Steve's proposal, he was very surprised. Since Steve left, she had never mentioned him to Jim again, so naturally he assumed that Mary never thought of Steve at all.

Kitty, who always said that nothing ever really surprised her, was not as surprised at Steve's proposal as she was that Mary would even consider a proposal from a man that she knew for less than a week. Kitty had a lot to say when she first heard about it, and over the weeks that followed, she added her almost daily ideas on the subject. It was very obvious that Kitty considered Jim a much better choice. "And in making your decision, Mary," Kitty exclaimed, "You shouldn't consider the money at all. It just wouldn't be fair."

Mike overheard her and felt compelled to answer. "Why shouldn't she consider the money? It is a big part of the choice that involves her whole future lifestyle. Since you're in love with them both, Mary, then you should definitely marry the one with the money. I'd say that even if Steve wasn't one of my best friends."

Kitty right away had to defend the other position. "How would you like it if you were in Jim's place and a girl you loved chose someone over you, just because he was rich?"

Mike answered quite emphatically. "Well of course I wouldn't like it, but I'd certainly understand. And I wouldn't blame her for wanting more out of life. In fact if I really loved her, I'd tell her to marry the other fella because that would be what was best for her."

"Oh, yes, I'll bet you would," Kitty retorted.

When Annie overheard Mike, she added, "I think you should marry Steve and move to California."

Mary surprisingly answered, "Annie, I thought you liked Jim."

"Well, I really do. But if you love them both, then I agree with Mike that you marry the one with the money. Just think, then I'd be able to go visit you. And I'd probably also meet a rich man to marry. Maybe one of Steve's brothers, or one of his friends. Why, I could probably even have my own horse. You know how much I love horseback riding."

Upon hearing that, Maggie scolded Annie. "Annie, I'm ashamed of you thinking of yourself. Mary has a very important decision to make that will influence her whole life."

Annie replied, "Yeah, Mama, but it could influence all of our lives, too!"

Maggie continued, "I have to agree with Kitty, Mary. In making up your mind, you shouldn't be influenced by the money at all. It's just not fair. And Heaven knows, like your Aunt Mary used to always say, money isn't everything. There's a lot of unhappy rich people. God knows it never made the O'Connells happy. I've often thought and prayed for them all. Poor Jack and Gail, and poor John and Victoria, left to mourn for them."

Mike exclaimed, "Of course I feel sorry for them, too, Mama. But I think there's probably a lot more unhappy poor people than unhappy rich people."

Maggie answered, as she looked over at Mary. "Steve seemed like a very nice young man, but I don't think you could ever get anybody nicer than Jim. He really loves you so much. You can see it in just the way he looks at you." Then Maggie looked a little sad. "California is so far away, we'll probably never see you if you move way out there. Oh, dear, I'm thinking out loud and I don't want to influence your decision in any way."

Mike quickly added, "But that's not true, Mama. Steve's family has money, and he said she could come back as often as she wanted to. So don't let that trouble you. Besides, I plan on going out there for a visit in the very near future. I believe Mary should come with me before she makes up her mind. And anyway, when you have money, you can go where you want to, whenever you want to, and stay for as long as you want to. And having money isn't always being selfish. When you have money, look at all the people you can help."

Mike continued explaining. "Steve's been after me to go out to California to work. I could get a job in his father's business and make a lot more money myself. Maybe I'd consider relocating the family out there. The weather is warm and beautiful. It would be good for Mama's and Aunt Kate's health. They wouldn't have to worry about falling on ice. Why, out there, they could go to church every day. And if I was making three or four times the amount of money and didn't have to bother with winter coal or clothes and things, we could get that house with the white picket fence. The flowers would bloom all year." He looked over at Annie as he said, "I could probably even buy you a horse."

Annie, who had been listening intently to the conversation, enthusiastically answered, "Oh, great!"

Kitty quickly answered. "Well, I have a good job at the telephone company and I'm not about to relocate."

Mike quickly retorted, "The telephone company is out there, too, you know."

Kitty exclaimed, "I'm telling you now, no way am I going to relocate! And Mama and Aunt Kate would miss Troy. So you go if you want to, but don't count us in your plans. Besides, I don't see why she should have to go out there in the first place. He should be willing to come here. It takes quite a few days to go out there, and then quite a few days coming back. Even if you only stay a week, that's quite a bit of time you'd be gone."

Mike chose to ignore Kitty's suggestion. "Just think, Mary, they're rich! You'll be able to travel all over the world, just like the other rich people. And you will be able to give your children not only a beautiful home, but the best of everything. You can go anywhere your heart desires, instead of working hard and dying in Troy without ever getting any further than Albany. This really is opportunity knocking at your door, Mary! But only you can open the door and let it in."

Mike continued, "I'll always remember the inside of the O'Connell house. I saw it one day when I was delivering coal for Mr. Stewart. We'd had a lot of snow and weren't able to put the coal in the coal bin the usual way, so they had us bring it through the house. Aunt Nan was there directing us. I remember thinking to myself, someday I'd like to live in a house like this. I can still see it in my mind. I may never have a house like that. But you, Mary, you can have a home even more beautiful than that. So don't be a fool. Go for it!"

As Mike was talking, Mary too could see that house in her mind, and remember so vividly the first day she saw Jack, and first started feeling drawn to him.

Mike exclaimed, "Besides, Mary, you owe it to your future

children. With Steve, you'd never have to watch them doing without. Suppose Mama had that choice. Don't you wish that she would have chosen the man with the money?"

"That's ridiculous," Kitty rushed to point out, "Maybe she'll never have any children."

Mike answered emphatically, "It's more likely she will. Then someday she may be sorry that she didn't look ahead."

Kitty lost no time in answering. "Besides, if she was to think of her future children, maybe she should stay in Troy. Remember the 1906 earthquake in California when so many people got killed? Maybe they'll have another one."

Mike was quick to point out, "Well, I'd be willing to bet you that more people have died out here from pneumonia and tuberculosis than died out there in all the earthquakes they've ever had!" He looked at Mary as he said, "Marriage is forever, Mary. You should at least go to visit Steve so that you can really understand just what you'll be giving up if you choose Jim. I think that you feel sorry for Jim. But you can't throw away a beautiful future because you feel sorry for somebody who doesn't have the financial opportunities that the other person has."

Mike pointed out. "I think that Steve is right, and that you were fated to meet. Look at what happened to me when I almost got killed. The bombs were bursting all around me. I knelt on the ground and covered my head. A voice within me called out, God help me, my family needs me! When the noise finally stopped, I looked and realized that everything around me had been hit. But I had been spared. When I called over to my buddies they couldn't believe that I was still alive. I believe that in God's plan for me, I was fated to live. And I believe that you're fated to marry Steve. Besides, I just can't believe that if you really loved Jim, you could have fallen in love with Steve in the first place. It's my personal opinion that you love Steve, but you feel a loyalty to Jim after going with him for so long."

Then Mike turned to Kitty. "Kitty, are you sure that you're not in some way thinking of yourself in wanting to keep Mary here?"

Kitty answered with a slight bit of annoyance in her voice. "You should know that I wouldn't do that. I want what's best for her. And I think Jim is the best choice."

Kitty at that point decided to let Mike give all his opinions on why he thought Mary should marry Steve, and she would listen. Then some other time when he was not around, she would talk to Mary and make sure that she realized that there were many other things to consider that were much more important than money.

Not too long after that, Kitty found the perfect time, when she and Mary were alone.

"Mary, I'd like to talk to you about some of the things Mike said about Steve and Jim that I definitely don't agree with."

Mary was still feeling so confused that she welcomed any insight that anyone could give her.

Kitty explained, "I personally think that you're in love with Jim, but somehow attracted to Steve at the same time. I think that your feelings for Steve are all mixed in with what you felt for Jack all those years. It's just an attraction that you've misinterpreted as love. Perhaps you've taken some beautiful moments and magnified them out of proportion. I don't think it's real, or that Steve's the person that you think he is. It was a romantic time! Steve in uniform, added to the illusion, and you were swept by emotion. But I don't think that you're thinking logically."

"Don't you think that I loved Jack, either?" Mary questioned.

Kitty answered with concern in her voice. "It really doesn't matter what I thought of your love for Jack, but since you asked, I think that there are many kinds of love, and that your love for Jack was a romantic, childlike, immature love."

Mary was surprised at what Kitty said, and replied. "You mean that in other words, you don't think that I've been in love with Jack or Steve?"

Kitty exclaimed, "I don't think you really knew Jack well enough to really love him. I suspect, Mary, that to your romantic mind, Jack was the rich handsome prince on the beautiful white horse that you expected to rescue you from this dreary, humdrum life. Just like in a fairy tale, you thought that you would live happily ever after.

"But let's get realistic," Kitty warned, "You really don't even know Steve. You certainly can't know somebody in one week. Just like everybody has faults, but you haven't seen any of Steve's. I just don't want to see you get hurt and lose everything in the process."

"But Kitty," Mary replied, "Mike knows Steve well, and he said, he's the best."

"That may be true as far as good friends go," Kitty answered, "But that doesn't mean he'd be a good husband. There's a big difference. There are all kinds of marriages, Mary. And you have to ask yourself what kind of a marriage you want. Do you want a shared marriage where you have a part say in the decisions that are made? Or do you want a marriage where your husband makes all the decisions. And even tells you what you can and what you cannot do? Like Mike himself, for instance. He's a wonderful son and a wonderful brother, always there when you need his help, but I'd hate to be married to somebody like him. He'll definitely be the boss in his family. To men like Mike, that's just normal and honorable. He thinks he's so open minded, but he doesn't even see any reason for women to vote. He's so conservative. The only way men like Mike would understand is if they were women, or treated like women, for even one day. We can be sure that Mike will marry a quiet girl, who, if she has any opposing ideas to his, she won't say anything. She'll believe that he knows best. Like Mrs. Reilly. 'Yes, dear, whatever you say.'"

"Well, I like Mrs. Reilly," Mary was quick to point out. "She's nice to everybody. Maybe she just doesn't think it's important enough to argue over."

Kitty quickly replied, "Well, that's just what's wrong with a lot of people. If it doesn't disturb them, personally, they won't take any time or trouble to make life better for anybody else. The injustices in the world really make me terribly aggravated, but what makes me even madder is how complacent some people are. Now, if that's the kind of a marriage a woman wants, then that's her choice. Some women love a man who is in complete charge, but personally, Mary, I don't think you'd be happy in such a marriage. You just don't have that kind of a temperament. In fact, in certain ways you remind me a little of Julie."

Mary was very surprised to hear Kitty say that. "What do you mean?" She questioned.

Kitty explained, "Well, Julie is a very independent woman. And while you aren't quite as independent as Julie, you're certainly far from the clinging vine type, or the selfless Christian martyr like Mama. I can't see you blindly following your husband's bidding. If you are to be happy in marriage, you would have to have your say in making decisions. I think you would have that with Jim, but I think it's debatable with Steve. Let's face it, Mary, the whole situation is like something out of a romantic novel, and you are a romantic young lady. So I think the main thing is that you better get your thinking straight, because life can be very hard if you marry the wrong person just because of romantic illusions. The sooner you break free from such illusions and face reality, the better off you'll be."

Kitty continued, "Besides, Mary, I suspect that there's another very important difference between Jim and Steve. I think that Steve is more likely to hang out with men at the saloon or in his case, a men's club, whereas Jim will be more of a family man like Mr. Corbett. I used to think poor Mama and lucky Mrs. Corbett. While

Pa wasted his time and money at the saloon and came home staggering in a drunken stupor, Mr. Corbett took his children to the park, or sat on the porch with his wife. What a difference! But let's say for the point of argument that you did love Jack, and you do have feelings toward Steve, the bottom line is you still can't have both Jim and Steve."

Mary thought, how could she expect Kitty, who always boasted that she had no intention of ever getting married, to possibly understand that it wasn't by choice that she thought of Steve, but that at will he just intruded into her thoughts? And this thought prompted her to ask, "But, Kitty, weren't you ever in love or even attracted to a man?"

Kitty pondered for a moment. Then a smile came to her face and she answered, "Oh, there were a couple of men that I suppose I felt attracted to. But fortunately, most of the men I've met are married, and most of the single ones, I've always considered pretty immature. One time I remember a very nice, kind, single young man in the men's clothing store. I went there with Pa's measurements to pick out a suit for him. I did feel drawn to this young man, not because he was nice looking, but because I sensed a strong, quiet quality about him. As he talked, it became obvious that he was interested in me. So right away I discouraged him so that he wouldn't ask me out. So you might say that when I first felt my heart flutter, I ran from the scene.

"You see, Mary, I believe that many people make a big mistake thinking it will only be once that they will go out with a person they are attracted to. Then they get trapped in a snare that many times ruins their whole life. Remember that time I sent you to pick up Pa's suit when it was ready?"

Mary exclaimed, "Of course, that nice-looking man that asked me questions about you and told me to say hello to you for him."

Kitty quietly answered, "Yes, Mary, that man."

Mary questioned, "You mean you just never went back there? You never saw him again? Didn't you want to?"

Kitty answered, "Yes, Mary, I did want to. That's why I didn't allow myself to go back. I have no intention of ever changing my mind, so there's no sense in giving in to an attraction or wasting a man's time by drawing him on."

Mary asked, "But weren't you curious to see what might have happened?"

Kitty replied, "Curious to a point. But, I made my curiosity take a back seat to my intelligence. I know what I want out of life. I am determined that I'm not going to be sidetracked by any man, no matter how rich or good-looking, or by anything else he has to offer. I feel as if I helped raise all of you, and while I think I'll make a wonderful aunt to your children, I don't think I've got it in me to raise children of my own. Besides, I'd actually be afraid of getting stung like Mama. That's why, when Julie invited me to parties, I wouldn't go. I've always avoided being tempted. My motto is: Be organized, put first things first, keep busy, and do the best you can with what you have. And above all, don't waste time day dreaming, about what might have been. As I follow this way of life, I feel a great sense of accomplishment. I just know that I wouldn't be happy living any other way. I'm fully aware that if I ever tried living Mama's hard life, I would have ended up in an asylum. That's why I don't have much sympathy for the people who throw caution to the wind, make senseless choices, and then wonder why it didn't work out."

Mary listened intently as Kitty continued to express her views. "In my observation of people, it seems to me that when two people meet and supposedly fall in love, that they are looking through rose-colored glasses. Each one of them brings to their marriage certain expectations. In many cases, each expects the other to make their wildest dreams come true. The more unrealistic those dreams are, the more disappointed the person will be. It's like they've set themselves up for a big let down. That's why I'm trying to get you to face reality, and not be hurt by it. You know that whoever you choose to marry, that I'll always wish the best for you."

Mary responded, "I know you will, Kitty. But you seem to be painting a picture that if I were smart, I'd marry Jim, because I wouldn't be happy with Steve."

Kitty was quick to point out, "What I mainly try to do, Mary, is to make sure that you don't go into marriage wearing those rose-colored glasses, and that so-called love blinds your senses out of proportion. Life can be very hard sometimes. And before you go traipsing across the country, Mary, I also think that you should consider Jim's feelings in this."

Mary answered emphatically, "Kitty, Jim wants me to go. He's told me he wants me to be sure."

Kitty replied, "Of course he wants you to be happy. But he's only encouraging you to go because he feels as if he has to. I certainly wouldn't say that he wants you to go. It's just that under the circumstances, he probably feels that it's necessary. But what you're not considering is, how is it going to look? It's not fair of you to subject Jim to all the talk that's bound to start about you gallivanting off to California to become acquainted with another handsome young man. Why, I think that's downright embarrassing to Jim. And I think I ought to warn you, Mary, that as soon as you go, I'll bet there are quite a few other girls that will try to help Jim get over his loneliness for you. Any young lady would consider him a good catch. He's just as nice as he is nice looking."

Kitty's words got Mary thinking. She had taken Jim's love for granted. She knew how deeply he loved her. And before Steve's visit, she would have all but laughed at Kitty's suggestion. But now, realizing how fast things can happen, she didn't completely feel that same old confidence. She thought, suppose while she was gone, Jim also met another girl that he was deeply attracted to? If it happened to her, couldn't it also happen to him?

"But, Kitty," Mary asked, "What if God did want me to help Steve regain his faith?"

Kitty retorted, "Mary, that's ridiculous. You're certainly not responsible for his disbelief. He's got you feeling sorry for him. You should put that idea right out of your head. That's his problem, not yours. In fact, if anything, that should be more of a reason not to marry him. What kind of a marriage would it be when he doesn't even believe in God? How will you explain that to your children?"

Mary exclaimed, "But people do change! Look at Mike. And at least his family is Catholic, so the children would be raised Catholic. And I wouldn't be a bit surprised that through love, he would believe again."

Kitty replied, "That sounds like wishful thinking to me. But, Mary, I've got to get going. I just realized what time it is. So the bottom line is that only you can make the decision."

After Kitty left, Mary got to thinking about some of the things she had said. She wondered if Kitty was right about her feelings for Steve being all mixed up and intermingled with all the feelings she had for Jack since she was a child. Or was it that when Jack married Julie, it ended once and for all the daydreams she had of him and snuffed out any possibility that she could ever be his wife. She had to look upon it as if he had died to her, because even if Jack and Julie had ever divorced, she would not have been able to marry Jack in the Catholic Church, and she knew deep down that she couldn't turn from what she realized was an important part of her. And was thinking of Steve the exact opposite? Had he opened up to her the wonderful possibility that all those childhood daydreams could come true? She questioned if it really was an attraction or love? At what moment do you fall in love with someone, she wondered? And if it was an attraction at the beginning, then was it love now, or merely a deeper attraction? And if you can't get someone out of your mind, no matter how hard you try, and yet at the same time want them near, with such an aching longing, is that love? Or was it just a fascination, like Kitty had suggested? If this was true, how could she tell the difference? Or was Mike right when he said that he believed she admired Jim for his nice qualities, but that she was in love with Steve? As he had pointed out that if she really loved Jim, she would not have been so deeply attracted to Steve in the first place.

Mary continued thinking. Everything had been so easy and simple before. She really wished that he had never come to their door. But it was too late, he had come. He had kissed her and aroused in her a passion which had been buried far beneath the layers of her character. And try as she may, she could not erase the overwhelming feelings she still felt, just thinking of him.

In comparison, Jim was so gentle with her, sometimes treating her as if she were a breakable china doll. But sometimes, when he kissed her just a little more amorously and held her just a little longer than usual, she could feel his heart beat and hear his heavier breathing in her ears. Then he'd break away. She felt as if he were holding back the passion within him, not wanting to frighten her. Thinking of Jim and the way he kissed her and held her tightly in his arms, and feeling the warmth of his cheek next to hers, always made her feel so special and secure. At such times she felt so sure of his love for her, and her love for him, that Steve's love didn't seem quite as important.

Mary thought, how could she help it if that same compelling force that makes the average woman want to be close to that one and only, that she felt for two? And that each was separated and unconnected to the other? It was almost as if she had twin minds and hearts. One completely loved Jim and the other completely loved Steve. She knew that no matter what choice she made, she would always feel close to the other one.

Sometimes she felt as if she were two different people. The one loved Jim and wanted to stay in Troy and be content in raising a family. The other wanted to go to California, marry Steve, and live the life of a lady, traveling extensively, having servants, and a Governess for their children. It just seemed that sometimes one idea was more important than the other, and then vice-versa.

Sometimes she felt as if she were on a path that split in two, giving her a choice of which path to choose, left or right, and wishing so desperately that she could see where each path would take her. She felt as if her heart was being pulled in two, and either way it would never be the same again. And she was fully aware that the choice she made would not only affect her life, but the lives of her future children and yes, even her grandchildren.

One day when Mike and Kitty were at work, and Mary and Annie were at the sink just finishing the dishes, Maggie came into the kitchen and said, "I want to talk to you, Mary. And I think it would also do Annie some good to hear what I have to say. I've been concerned about your important decision, and I want to make sure that money doesn't influence your decision in any way.

"I realize that you have not seen the best of marriages in this house, but I do want you to know that it wasn't always like that. When I first met your Pa, the first thing I noticed was how tall he was! Being six feet tall was much taller than most men. And the second thing I noticed was how handsome he was. But, the main reason I married him was because he was so good and kind. And had a great sense of humor! He didn't drink much back in those days, and after we got married, we had a lot of wonderful years together. But, as the time went on, and problems kept surfacing, I guess while I turned more and more to the Lord in prayer, for consolation, he started drinking more, trying to block out the problems. I've always considered it like a sickness that just makes things worse. But I want you to know that even after all this time, knowing what I know, if I had to do it over again, I still would have married him. Oh, sure, I've had my share of problems in life, but everybody does. But the joys I've known have far outweighed the sadness. The happiest day of my life was the day I became a mother. There were just no words that can adequately describe what it is like to be a mother. I believe it is God's greatest gift! There just isn't any other earthly joy that can be compared to the joy and happiness of being a mother. Looking at your beautiful newborn baby, and holding it close, and instinctively realizing that it is a part of you. I thank God every day for my children."

Mary answered, "I'm glad for your sake that there were good times, Mama. And I'm glad you still feel that way about Pa, because I love Pa, and I'm glad you married him, too! And I'll really try hard not to let money influence me in any way."

Trying to decide, Mary tried to visualize what it would be like to be married to Steve. There was an elegant party going on, and she could see herself descending the staircase in a beautiful strapless blue satin gown, with a princess waistline. Atop her perfectly curled hair was a three-tier diamond tiara. She was also wearing a diamond necklace, bracelet and earrings. And of course, a huge diamond engagement ring was upon her finger. Steve was waiting for her at the bottom of the stairway, his eyes transfixed upon her. His mother was standing by his side, with smiling approval on her face. All eyes were upon her as she gracefully descended the staircase, a confident smile of joy upon her face. She was very, very happy. She had everything that she ever dreamed of. Steve put his hand out to her. Just thinking of his touch sent a chill throughout her body as her heart started pounding. His face was radiant and his eyes more beautiful than ever as he proudly introduced her to the guests. She felt confident that she could comfortably fit into that kind of a lifestyle. After all, she already knew the social graces, and Aunt Nan could answer any small questions she might have.

Other times, she saw herself in the living room of a modest house, dressed in a blue printed house dress. She was singing a lullaby, rocking a little baby dressed in pink, with a small two year-old boy seated at her side. She looked up, and Jim, in his policeman's uniform, was coming in the door. She smiled in answer to the look of love that was always in his eyes. A warmth swept over her as he came and knelt beside her, giving her a warm kiss. While the little boy started climbing on his lap, Mary and Jim looked happily at the children and then smiled again at each other. She felt perfect contentment, and overwhelming joy and happiness. As Mary thought this, she was reminded of what Sister had said one day. "When a young lady chooses a husband, she should consider choosing a man who would be a good father to their children."

Sometimes she saw herself traveling in London, Paris, Rome and visiting the castles in Ireland and Spain. She saw herself on a yacht cruising down the Hudson with servants helping to take care of the children.

Other times she saw herself standing at a kitchen stove cooking supper with children playing around her, or running through the house. And on and on her day dreams went, with Steve or Jim in the center of them. When they ended, she felt more confused than ever.

All of a sudden Mary's own words came back into her mind. "But Kitty, Jim wants me to go." She and Jim had talked at length about the situation after he had gotten over the initial shock. One day when Jim picked Mary up, they went for a ride to the outskirts of Troy to talk more in depth. Looking at Jim, she was always warmed by the memories of happy times that they had shared. Thinking of their hopes and dreams always brought a beautiful contented smile to her face. Of course, she was well aware that she still loved him, with a love that was whole and secure and uninterrupted from the love she felt for Steve.

Each love was somehow separated from the other. Beautiful and meaningful in its own way. And again that realization swept over her that it could not be this way. All longings can not always be satisfied. Sometimes choices have to be made. She realized that one of them was going to be hurt by her decision. The last thing she wanted was to hurt Jim or Steve. As she looked at Jim, she thought, why doesn't he help her make up her mind by speaking against Steve, even though he never met him? Jim is here now, so he should have the advantage. Why doesn't he just sweep her into his arms and convince her with words and actions that she would be better off marrying him? But her thoughts were interrupted by his words.

Jim, with an element of love in his voice, began to explain, "You know, Mary, my mother always said that good marriages are made in Heaven. My Mother and Father had a beautiful marriage. The best I've ever seen. Each one of them always put the other one ahead of themself. There was never, as far back as I can remember, even one hateful word spoken between them. I have wonderful memories of my father. When he died, he and my mom had just recently celebrated their fifteenth wedding anniversary. I still remember a neighbor saying to my Mother, 'It's a shame you had so few years together.' And I'll always remember my Mother's eyes were aglow as she said, 'I would sooner have been married to my husband for those fifteen wonderful years than to be married to anyone else for fifty years. He was the best. And I'll be warmed by the beautiful memories we shared. Although I know I'm going to miss him terribly, because we were so close, I'm going to go on for our children's sake and I know that he'll be right there with me, in spirit.'

"You see, Mary, I think that we could have that kind of a marriage. And I truly believe that if our marriage is meant to be, then not Steve or anyone else can ever come between us, not now or ever. And if it isn't meant to be, then it's better that we find out now. So Mary, I'm not going to try to persuade you, because some time in the future there may be hard times, and I don't want you to think of this moment and regret it. It has to be your decision. But Mary, while you're making up your mind, I want you to know that I love you from the depth of my soul, with a love that is as strong as it is possible for a man to love a woman. I would gladly give up my life for you." And there it was again, that special look in his eyes.

"But, as much as I want you to be my wife, even more than that, I want you to be happy. Because I couldn't be happy unless you were happy. Steve sounds like a nice person, Mary, and I agree with him that you must think everything over very carefully. I'll never be able to give you the material things that he can give you. Right now I can only offer you my love, my heart, and a dream. But I also believe there are some things that are much more important than material things. I want you to know, Mary, that if you choose Steve, I would understand."

Mary tearfully exclaimed, "Oh, Jim," as she hugged him. "I wish I didn't feel like this, as if I'm being torn between you both. I'm so sorry! Oh, why do things like this have to happen, anyway?"

CHAPTER SEVENTY-FIVE

April, May, June, July, had all flown by quite uneventfully for Mary, who was still trying to make up her mind between Jim and Steve, and if she should go to California with Mike.

Woman's Suffrage legislation had already been enacted in New Zealand, Australia, Finland, Norway, Denmark, the Soviet Union, Canada, Germany, Luxembourg, Poland, Austria, Czechoslovakia, and the Netherlands.

During World War I, the British Suffragettes favorably influenced public opinion with recruiting drives and notable contributions to the war effort.

In 1918, Parliament enfranchised all women householders, householder's wives, and women university graduates over thirty years of age.

In the United States, it was a cautious, optimistic but anxious time for the cause.

Thirty-Five states had already ratified the Woman's Suffrage Amendment. They needed Tennessee.

It was hot that summer in Nashville, Tennessee, as the pro- and anti-suffrage people from all over the country assembled, and set up at the Hermitage Hotel, a block from the Statehouse.

Mrs. Carrie Catts worked behind the scenes, leaving public lobbying to the Tennessee women.

Alice Paul directed strategy from Washington.

The anti-suffrage women, calling themselves The National Association for the Rejection of the Susan B. Anthony Amendment, tried to persuade legislators to vote against it.

As the summer wore on, votes in favor of the amendment seemed to be slipping away. On the night of August 17th, it was feared that the amendment, to be voted on the next day, could very likely lose by one vote.

As the work-weary workers separated that evening, Mrs. Carrie Catts told them that, "All we can do now is pray."

The next morning, the Tennessee statehouse was packed, and the overflow crowd stood for hours in the heat.

After twice voting against the amendment in procedural ballots that ended in ties, the youngest member, twenty-four year-old Harry Burn, with a letter from his mother in his pocket, switched his vote, following her advice, "Hurrah and vote for suffrage."

It was now August 26th, and that morning the 19th Amendment to the Unites States Constitution had been quietly signed into law by Secretary of State Bainbridge Colby, granting women the right to vote.

Kitty and her friends had gathered once more at the O'Neill home to continue their weeklong celebration, singing and playing happy songs on the piano and toasting with Sarsaparilla not only each other, but the Suffragettes who, by their hard work and determination, had helped the dream to become a reality. They also toasted all the men who had helped the cause.

On the 18th, when they had first learned the good news, they had toasted first Elizabeth Cady Stanton, Lucretia Mott, Susan B. Anthony, and a list of the others that had already passed away. Some they had known of on the state and national level, and some they knew personally from Troy and the surrounding areas.

They had felt a sense of sadness that they didn't live long enough to celebrate with them, when one of the women happily said, "Why, I'll bet they're all up in Heaven applauding," and they all laughed in agreement.

Mary could hear the music and their melodious voices from her room, and really felt sincerely happy for them all as she pondered what choice she should make, realizing that her time was running out.

When Mike returned from the war, he had gone back to work for John at the brewery.

The Prohibition Movement in the United States had gained much support. The message, save the women and children from the evils of drink and drunken husbands and wife beaters, spread across the country.

Many optimistically believed that Prohibition would uplift the working class, and with an absence of drunkenness, the human character would be improved and the family made whole.

The National Prohibition Act, commonly known as the Volkstead Act, was passed by Congress and submitted to President Wilson, who vetoed it in October, 1919. He was overruled by Congress. Prohibition went into effect as the 18th Amendment on January 16, 1920.

The United States Supreme Court in June, in a unanimous decision, sustained the validity of the 18th Amendment.

From the very beginning, thousands and thousands of otherwise law-abiding citizens chose to ignore the law that they considered was forced upon them by a small group of misguided legislators.

John, realizing that Prohibition would only be a matter of time, had bought a furniture store in 1919 and closed the brewery. Mike continued working for him.

Steve had kept in touch with Mike and still encouraged him to make the trip out to California, hopefully escorting Mary. He tried to persuade Mike to allow him to pay their expenses, but Mike, being very independent, said he would want to pay for the trip himself.

Over the course of time, Mike had decided that he would definitely make a trip to California with or without Mary. He wanted to see first-hand what his opportunities were. He had analyzed that if he were able to make a lot more money out there, as Steve kept insisting he definitely could, then he would perhaps live there a few years, and send money back home. Or, even try to convince the family that moving to California was in their best interest.

Mike had explained the situation to John, and John had already given him permission to take any part of, or even all of the month of September off. Mike was planning to leave early the following Friday, the third of September. Mary had just seven full days left to make the most important decision of her life.

Even though Mary found it hard to make up her mind, she always was thankful that she was lucky enough to have such a choice. She couldn't help thinking of her Aunt Mary. Now she could see her in her mind as a beautiful young woman who had lost the love of her life. And that realization also reminded her of Gail and her Bill.

And vividly a familiar scene came into Mary's mind once more, of Jack and Gail in the hallway, so many years before, when she had first fallen in love with Jack, and she felt saddened by their tragic deaths.

Mary was still trying to decide what she should do when her eyes caught upon the small statue of the Blessed Virgin Mary that had belonged to her Aunt Mary. As she looked at the statue, she was reminded of all the times she had seen her Aunt Mary kiss the statue and kiss the feet of Jesus on the Crucifix. She had said, "I believe in miracles, and I like to think that Jesus and his beautiful mother can feel those kisses in Heaven."

Looking back, Mary realized that her Aunt Mary must have known that some of her daydreams were unrealistic, but she never discouraged her. Instead she had cautioned her. "Mary, there isn't anything wrong with wishing that you have more than you do, for as long as you can keep from wishing your life away. Some people focus so much on what they don't have that they lose sight of what they do have. Always try to look on the bright side of life. Thank God for everything, no matter how small, and you'll be happier. And never take anybody or anything for granted. We never know when someone we love will be taken away from us, like my darling Robert was taken from me.

"And some day when you have extra time, use it to write down your favorite Bible quotes, hymns, books, poems, and picture shows, and place those lists into your Happy Memory Box. And if things aren't going good someday and you're feeling down, go back to your Happy Memory Box and relive those happy days and thank God again for each and every treasured moment. And always keep reminding yourself that 'Better Days are Ahead', and they will be, most likely in this life, but if not, definitely in Heaven."

Mary couldn't help remembering what a wonderful thirteenth birthday celebration she'd had. Her Aunt Mary was her usual happy self, with her beautiful blue eyes aglow, appreciating the fact that she had finally been able to ride on a train and go to Mass at the Cathedral in Albany.

Mary would always remember how big and beautiful the church was, with the extremely beautiful stained glass windows, whose pictures vividly told Bible stories and uplifted people's spirits. And the stations of the cross that her Aunt Nan pointed out had won first prize at the Paris Exposition of 1897, were unique. Then the dinner and the picture show, and then back home on the train. It had been a perfect day! Who could possibly have imagined that her Aunt Mary would die three weeks later?

Mary couldn't help wishing that her Aunt Mary was there with her at that moment, so she could talk her choices over with her. It seemed that no matter how bad things were, talking it over with her Aunt Mary always made it seem so much better. And she heard her own voice questioning out loud, "I wonder what you would have told me?" And then, she answered her own question. "I do know what you would have told me." For all of a sudden, Mary was remembering.

It had been a warm fall day, and she had come home from school for lunch to find her mother very upset, because Annie was running a high fever. Their own doctor was out of town and her Mother had made up her mind to put Annie in the go-cart, bundle her up, and take her to the O'Connell family's doctor. It was Aunt Nan's doctor, too, and she had said he was very nice. She didn't want to leave Mary home alone so she made her a sandwich to eat on the way. After the doctor had examined Annie, he reassured Maggie he would give her a prescription for some medicine that would clear up the problem. He looked over at Mary as he said, "I notice that this little girl has a turn in one eye. I believe it could be straightened out if she started wearing glasses. If she were my daughter, I would take her to Albany, to an Optometrist friend of mine. The glasses they sell in the five and ten would not do her any good."

So he wrote the name and address on a slip of paper, and gave it to her mother. As he was handing her mother the prescription for Annie's medicine, her mother looked at the only money she had, the fifty cent piece she had taken out of her pocket, to pay the doctor for the visit. He saw the perplexed look in her eyes, and guessed that was all the money she had. His eyes were kind and his voice was soft as he said, "Mrs. O'Neill, you use that money for the prescription. You don't owe me anything. The medicine should make her all better within a few days. But if she still has any trouble, call me and I'll come to your house to see her."

When Maggie got home and mentioned what the doctor had advised about Mary needing glasses, everyone seemed to have a different opinion. Pa said he had a cousin whose eye was like that, but he lost touch with him years before. Someone else mentioned it was from weak eyes, and if she ate a lot of carrots, her eyes would straighten out without wearing glasses. Kitty thought that Mary should follow the doctor's advice, and offered to take her to Albany to the doctor's. Kitty said that she would pay for the glasses on time.

Mary pointed out to Kitty that some of the boys would tease her and call her four eyes. She said she would die of embarrassment if Jack ever saw her.

Kitty said, "Mary, don't let things like that annoy you. If you ignore them and pretend it doesn't bother you, they'll stop. It's more important that you do what's best for you, and in time the doctor believes your eye will straighten out."

Mary took a smile to herself as she remembered that Kitty was mostly right.

She did ignore the words "four eyes" directed at her, and it wasn't long before it stopped. But there was one boy who persisted, and made her feel aggravated. One day he was behind her, and called it out again. "Four eyes!" Enough is enough, she thought as she turned around fast and punched him in the nose, giving him a nose bleed. But, that was the end of the name calling.

Maggie said she would let Mary make the decision about the glasses, since she was the one who had to wear them. Mary pondered for days and just couldn't make up her mind what to do. She decided to go over and talk about it with her Aunt Mary.

Aunt Mary had gone shopping and would probably be home on the next trolley, her neighbor Anne Leonard told Mary. Anne had just come from looking in on Aunt Kate, who she said was sleeping.

The day had started out fairly warm and Mary hadn't worn a sweater. She felt quite cold as she huddled in the doorway waiting for her Aunt Mary. She felt as if the time was going by so slowly. Finally she saw the trolley coming up the street and stopping at the corner. A few people got off and then her heart was joyful as she spotted her Aunt Mary. She ran up to her, momentarily forgetting about the cold. "Oh, Aunt Mary, I have a terrible problem."

Her Aunt Mary brought her into the kitchen and wrapped her sweater around her. Then she gave her some milk and cookies. She closed the door to Aunt Kate's bedroom and talked low so that they would not disturb her. Then Aunt Mary listened very attentively as she always did. After Mary finished telling her, Aunt Mary pointed out that one choice is usually always better than the other, and when she had a choice to make, she would always get a sheet of paper and a pencil. Then she would say a prayer, and draw a line down the middle of the paper. On one side she would list all the things in favor of that decision, and on the other side, all the things against that decision. Doing this, she pointed out, helps you to see the problem more clearly. But, she cautioned, "Once you've made up your mind, Mary, never look back in sorrow. What's done is done, and you can't change the past. Why, I'll bet there isn't a man or a woman living who, if they could, wouldn't like to change something in their life. And even if you know you've made a mistake, try to make the best of it. Learn from your mistakes. Let each mistake you make be a link in a chain of understanding."

Mary could see in her mind her Aunt Mary's smiling face, and she always felt warmed by the happy memories. And she realized it was the reflection of love that she had always seen in those kind, gentle blue eyes. And she smiled as she thought, "How lucky I was that I had you in my life."

Mary opened the drawer, and took out a sheet of paper and a pencil. As she sat on the edge of the bed, she took one more look at the Statue of the Blessed Virgin Mary, pressed her hands together, closed her eyes and prayed.

Alice Corbett Fiacco

Remember, O most gracious Virgin Mary,
that never was it known that
anyone who fled to thy protection,
implored thy help,
or sought they intercession,
was left unaided.
Inspired by this confidence,
I fly unto thee,
O virgin of virgins, my mother,
to thee I come;
before thee I stand,
sinful and sorrowful.
Oh Mother of the Word Incarnate,
despise not my petitions,
but, in thy mercy,
hear and answer me. Amen.
Mary, Queen of Peace,
pray for us."

~ The End ~

ABOUT THE AUTHOR

Alice Corbett Fiacco was born in 1930 to Mary Duffy Corbett and Watervliet Fire Chief James J. Corbett. She was the third of five children who included an older sister and brother, Margie and Jim, and would go on to include two younger sisters, Mary and Rita.

In Watervliet, New York – just across the Hudson River from Troy – she grew up during the Great Depression and World War II within a two-block area of every nationality (Polish people next door and across the street) and different religions including Ukrainian Greek Catholic, and a very nice friendly black man. In the Irish-American Catholic family she grew up in, she learned early on the importance of family, faith, love, and self-determination.

In 1952, she married Leo J. Fiacco, and nine months and one week later, their first son was born. He was named James (Jim) in honor of her father, who had died seventeen months earlier. In quick succession came Ronald (Ron), Lee, William (Bill), and a few years later, twins Christopher and Kenneth (Chris and Ken) and, five years later, the last of their seven sons, Michael.

The decades of her life spent as wife of an insurance salesman, mother to seven boys, homemaker, Scouting and School and Church Volunteer, sometime outside-the-home employee, and, ultimately, Grandmother of eleven and Great-Grandmother of seven (to date) have provided the joy and meaning she has found in her life.

Forty years have passed since the idea surfaced in her mind and moved from note-taking at the kitchen table as her mother (who died in 1975) regaled family and friends with stories about life in Troy in the early 1900's, to years of researching the period at the Troy Public Library, to writing an epic historical romance novel, whose title is the author's assessment of how each one of us perceives life: "Thru The Eyes Of The Beholder."

Made in the USA
Middletown, DE
14 September 2021